WHITE

Frontispiece: Gin Indian Diamond

WHITE

A NOVEL

BENJAMIN ZUCKER

OVERLOOK DUCKWORTH
NEW YORK • WOODSTOCK • LONDON

First published in the United States in 2007 by
The Overlook Press, Peter Mayer Publishers, Inc.
Woodstock & New York

NEW YORK:
141 Wooster Street
New York, NY 10012

WOODSTOCK:
One Overlook Drive
Woodstock, NY 12498
www.overlookpress.com
[for individual orders, bulk and special sales, contact our Woodstock office]

Cataloging-in-Publication Data is available from the Library of Congress

Book design and type formatting by Bernard Schleifer

Manufactured in China
ISBN 978-1-58567-976-8 hc
ISBN 978-1-59020-051-3 pb
1 3 5 7 9 8 6 4 2

I dedicate *White* to:

HIRAM (HARRY) BINGHAM IV
whose courage and idealism aided me and my family
to begin our lives again in America.

David Jaffe
whose encouragement and warmth enabled me always to continue.

and to JOHN FLATTAU
whose wit and wisdom has made it all possible.

*B*lue, *Green* and *White*, like Julio Cortázar's *Hopscotch*, *"consist of many books, but two books above all."*

White, like life, may be approached and understood in various ways. I would suggest reading the central text of Chapter One first, then returning to the first page and reading the commentaries together with each page's central text. After reading Chapter One thusly, the reader should read the central text of Chapter Two and then return to the beginning of the chapter to read the commentaries along with each page of Chapter Two. And then by Joyce's slow *"commodious vicus of recirculation,"* finish the remainder of the book, chapter by chapter.

The commentaries may be read starting from the upper left hand corner of the page, clockwise around the page until one arrives, or in Joycean parlance: *"rearrives,"* at the upper left hand corner. Each commentator takes a tag line from the central text and muses on it. The pictures are a further commentary on the text. And yet the central text and the commentary itself may be seen as a commentary on the pictures.

The order in which to read is ultimately your choice. To the extent that all of us accept commentary on our lives, welcome it or don't listen to it; to the extent we feel the central text of our lives is of interest to others or not; to the extent to which we feel our lives move forward chronologically or that although Gatsby's green light *"recedes before us we beat on, boats against the current, borne back ceaselessly into the past"*—so, too, can one read this novel forward or backward, circularly or in a linear way.

A second method for reading *White* is to regard the novels *Blue, Green,* and *White* as an entire, interwoven novel. Place *Blue, Green,* and *White* on your desk (or spread them out on your beach blanket). And begin

> *Blue* Ch 3/*White* Ch 10/*White* Ch 1/*Green* Ch 6/*Green* Ch 2
> *Blue* Ch 6/*Green* Ch 7/*Blue* Ch 1/*White* 2/*White* Ch 6
> *White* Ch 3/*White* Ch 4/*White* Ch 5/*Blue* Ch 4/*Blue* Ch 7
> *Blue* Ch 8/*White* Ch 8/*Green* Ch 3/*Blue* Ch 2/*Green* Ch 4
> *Green* Ch 5/*Green* Ch 1/*White* Ch 7/*Green* Ch 8/*Blue* Ch 5
> *White* Ch 9/*Green* Ch 9/*Blue* Ch 9/*Green* Ch 10/*Blue* Ch 10

As with *Hopscotch*, it is to be noted the first nine chapters of *Blue, Green,* and *White*, a Jacob's ladder, are set in the present. The tenth chapter in each novel is set in the future and can, of course, be read (or written) by the reader while ascending to Heaven.

■ VAN GOGH: Light—Three are painting here. The old man who is young, Tal. He is me in Arles. "*I am convinced that I shall set my individuality free simply by staying on here.*" Tal is thinking like me. His Greenwich Village, my Arles. Tal is painting the young woman with his hands, who is painting Tal with her eyes: "*Painted portraits have a life of their own that springs from the very soul of the portrait.*" She knows this. And the young woman is breathing life into the old man while her eyes gaze at his soul, her canvas.

The third painter. Is it not me in poor Nuenen in Holland with Father and Mother? I wrote to Theo: "*They are as reluctant to let me into the house as they would be to let in a big shaggy dog.*" Fisher and I outside, peering through the window. Young Fisher is painting Dosha and Tal. His love can see what Tal and even she cannot see: the halo of light surrounding Dosha. He and I "*want to paint men and women with that something of the eternal which the halo used to symbolize and which we seek to convey by the actual radiance and vibration of our coloring.*"

■ CHIEF JOSEPH (Hinmatitooyahlatkekt) Nez Percé: White—"*My friends, I have been asked to show you my heart. I am glad to have a chance to do so. I want the white people to understand my people. Some of you think an Indian is like a wild animal. This is a great mistake … I will tell you in my way how the Indian sees things … it does not require many words to speak the truth. What I have to say will come from my heart, and I will speak with a straight tongue.*"

■ JACQUES DE PAIVA, Sephardic gem merchant in Madras: White light streamed across Tal's shoulders—Tal is frozen. Not in the present but in his past. Our past. He is from across the river, as my Hieronyma would laughingly tell me, "Not an ocean but a river. Crossable after a number of days. Who counts years? Rather it is the direction of our voyage that counts." Tal is frozen. Pure Sephardi. He is in the Americas. His feet are in Antwerp. But his heart is in Portugal. And his soul in the Holy Land. I can tell it by the white light crossing his shoulder. Whiter than any stone I ever saw in Golconda, in the rough examined by Abendana in Golconda or cut and polished by Salvador Rodriguez's brother Joseph Salvador in Amsterdam.

Diamonds can be white, whiter than your skin, paler than moonlight, but the pure light, cascading over your shoulder, resting on Hieronyma as we lie together across the "river" in Hindustan, that white light streaming over Abraham Abendana Tal's shoulder, resting on this young woman, that light, its purity, will freeze his sight in his memory forever.

C H A P T E R   I

WHITE light streamed across Abraham Tal's shoulders, illuminating the nape of his neck above the collar of his immaculately white shirt, a half size too large to make him appear thinner. The tricks the man had, anything to catch Dosha's attention, thought Fisher as he gazed through the window at Dosha in a ground floor apartment in Greenwich Village.

Tal's body seemed frozen: a self-portrait framed by the sparkling window, diurnally cleaned by Tal himself, thought Fisher cooly.

Dosha looked frozen too. Staring. Or was she modeling for Tal? Vermeer-like, Tal seemed to Fisher. Just like the postcard of Johannes Vermeer, broad around the middle, painting himself painting that Flanders angel.

But not more beautiful than Dosha. Had Tal given Dosha the postcard she had propped up on her side of the night table?

■ VIRGINIA WOOLF: Illuminations—Life is not, as in older novels, "*a series of gig-lamps systematically arranged; but a luminous halo, a semi-transparent envelope surrounding us from the beginning of consciousness to the end.*"

■ LUCIA JOYCE, JOYCE'S DAUGHTER: He—"*What is he doing under the ground, that idiot? When will he decide to come out? He's watching us all the time.*"

■ CRAZY HORSE: Man—"*We did not ask you white men to come here. We do not want your civilization. We would live as our fathers did and their fathers before them.*"

● RACHEL BELLER, TAL'S GIRLFRIEND: Dosha looks frozen or was she modeling for Tal?—Is Dosha staring at my Tal? For he always will be mine. Whether wed or unwed. Bedded or not. He, ever at my bidding. Forbidden to everyone else. I walked in the park across from his house on Van Eycklei in Antwerp every Sunday morning. Only to come back so he could have lunch with his precious father and mother and of course his brother who must have been gazing at us through his bedroom window on the fourth floor of their house—more palace than house, it appeared to me.

Abraham moving his hands as he walked his hands gesturing more as though they held a painter's brush than a writer's pen.

"What are you doing, my love?" I asked him. "Writing a novel about us?"

"No, no, Rachel," he insisted. "I'm painting a masterpiece."

"A portrait of me?"

"Of course," he stammered. "Without you as my model, how can I hope for a masterpiece?"

"Is it almost finished?"

"Almost," Abraham said so softly I could barely hear him. And certainly not his brother or, G-d forbid, his father or mother just across the park, waiting for him to come home.

And what of me? Tal's unfinished masterpiece? I am immobile. For I have vowed to wait for my Tal. Though he tarry.

■ VERMEER: White light streamed—White light streamed across my shoulder. And who should know better than I? I could see the light and paint. I could feel the light on my shoulders. The weight of it, pressing down onto me, each year heavier.

Praise G-d for my dop stick steadying my hand. For I was trembling before Maraika Duarte, though sometimes she called herself Maraika Abolais. I could see the light on her cheek. I could feel the white light on her forehead melting and draining down her eyelids, onto the bridge of her nose. I could feel the light encircling her neck, riveting down her body, filling the blueness of her frame to the brim. But could I paint a canvas and freeze the white light? Never. All I could do is scratch at the canvas and incise it with the outlines of Maraika's body. I could paint the glory of her blue and green crown. But her wondrous body, I could see and feel and touch and my hand and heart and mind would never forget but I could not create nor re-create Maraika on my canvas. Neither in my youth nor in old age. Neither in life nor in death

◆ Simha Padawer, Dosha's grandfather: Light—Why do we find the names "Urim" and "Tumim" in scripture for "Light and Truth." Urim means "light up their words," and Tumin means "fulfill their words."

My granddaughter is facing Tal: I like him. I like his name—the dew of blessings. She has come for a blessing from Tal. Tal and Fisher are peering at my granddaughter.

They are in one room together. But they are separated from each other by a glass window. My granddaughter is facing them: a queen.

The young man has quoted his teacher and written it upon Tal's walls. It is not Tal's shop but a Yeshivah and there is no teacher, but thank G-d the students teach each other.

"Hear O Israel. Hashem is our G-d. Hashem the One and Only. Teach these words thoroughly to your children and speak of them while you sit in your home, while you walk on the way, when you retire and when you rise.

Fisher is on the way. Tal has no children. My granddaughter is studying with the both of them, thank G-d. "The One and Only."

■ William Faulkner: Watched—Locked. Locked in a book. A book locked in a drawer.

"Do you know," he asked, "what Cyrano said once?"

"No, what?" Patricia asked. But he only looked down upon her with his cavernous, uncomfortable eyes. "What did he say?" she repeated. And then "Was he in love with her?"

I think so . . . yes, he was in love with her. She couldn't leave him, either. Couldn't go away from him at all . . . he had her locked up. In a book.

"In a book," she repeated. Then she comprehended. "Oh . . . that's what you've done, isn't it? With the marble girl without any arms and legs you made? Hadn't you rather have a live one? Say, you haven't got any sweetheart or anything, have you?"

"No," he answered. "How did you know?"

Tal has no sweetheart. This young Dosha knows it. And Tal knows she knows it and Tal and Fisher are transfixed. Watching Dosha. But she is just the same, searching for a book. It may be locked in his drawer. Or it may be upstairs in his apartment. Or in hers. Or even in her boyfriend's mind. Or in both of theirs. But she will find it—for she is a painter whose canvas is a *"man who is always writing for a woman."* It goes round and round. And round again.

Fisher watched Dosha and Tal in Tal's "Advice Shop" on Hudson and Perry Street, as if they were gems seen through a microscope. He felt he could clamp Tal on the shoulder and examine him closely, as he spun him around in a 360-degree revolution, head first, then arms, then legs and then, once again, spinning him on his axis.

Fisher wondered what Tal was saying to Dosha. His eyes fell on the lines of Blake that he had given to Dosha four months before.

G-d Appears, and G-d is Light
To Those poor Souls who dwell in night;
But does a Human Form Display
To those who dwell in realms of Day.

Four months before, in Spring, Dosha had been sitting outside the White Horse Tavern and had waved him over to join her. "Darling, dear old Tal has a springtime job for us. Decorate his advice shop. I have the contract." She pushed a frayed 8 x 10 white envelope toward Fisher."

■ Leonard Woolf in 1965: Watching—*"It's more like Virginia in its way than anything else of her."* This painting of Virginia by her sister Vanessa, only a painterly sister's eye can see it. Only a sister's hand could paint it. Virginia is becoming. Anything and everything. I can see it in her face and in her face my reflection. This young Dosha, is she not like Virginia? Because she is becoming. Anything and everything. Virginia and Dosha, immobile. Staring or modeling for her sister, for Tal, for me, forever. Watching, musing and writing about her sister, Tal, me, forever.

■ George Orwell in a letter to F.J. Warburg: Spring—*"I asked the doctor recently whether she thought I would survive & she wouldn't go further than saying she didn't know. If the 'prognosis' after the photo [X-ray] is bad, I shall get a second opinion. . . . They can't do anything, as I am not a case for operation, but I would like an expert opinion on how long I am likely to stay alive. I do hope people won't now start chasing me to make me go to Switzerland, which is supposed to have magical qualities. I don't believe it makes any difference where you are, & a journey would be the death of me. The one chance of surviving, I imagine, is to keep quiet."*

Tal must keep quiet. Silent. Frozen. Life is too much for him. Certainly this Dosha is. He must choose between silent seeing and a deathbed. Jobs assigned to those in their final spring times. Instructional talk. But he will attempt both. Do not we all?

■ Virginia Woolf: Street—Fisher, the lover, is looking at Dosha from across the street. He is examining Tal closely, peering at him, searching through his rival's mind, for a lover's teacher is always a rival, but Fisher is young and can stand on one side of the street and touch and feel on the other side. So too with me—even from Bond Street to Gordon Square. But after youth, later *"I lost friends, some by death . . . others through sheer inability to cross the street."*

■ Laurence Sterne: Spinning him on his axis—The young man has Tal in the palm of his hand. He is clamping Tal onto the base of a microscope. Spinning him on his axis. Fisher has the wisdom of Uncle Toby—for do not the young always reign in the kingdom of love? *"I'll not hurt thee,"* says my Uncle Toby, rising from his chair, and going across the room with the fly in his hand. *"I'll not hurt a hair on thy head: Go,"* says he, lifting up the sash, and opening his hand as he spoke, to let it escape;—go poor devil, get thee gone, why should I hurt thee?—This world surely is wide enough to hold both thee and me."

But will Tal fly away once Fisher opens the sash of the window?

Vanessa Bell, *Virginia Woolf*.

◆ ISAAC TAL, ABRAHAM'S FATHER: Jerusalem—He is here. My son. In his office. The Grand Rabbi. The teacher. The student. The patron. He is hiring. He is commissioning. Words of Art. He is publishing. A single volume. A complete set of a sacred text. Or is it business? Big business? Advertising. Publicity. Interior Decoration. Color, all important. He is keeping to the letter of our law. "I shall place Jerusalem above my chiefest joy."

Yes, he is abiding by the spirit of our law. Why not Safed, with the woman of mystery, and the young maggid. Fisher, standing across the street entranced by the vision of my son and a woman young enough to be his bride.

If not Safed, why not Tiberius? Abraham is fixing the canon of the Masoretic text.

Who knows? Certainly not I. And not Tuviah, Abraham's brother. Not even my blessed wife, Rachel. Though she thinks she understands Abraham, certainly she was never able to make him clear to me.

■ TECUMSEH: Contract—Imagine. Three children of the same Spirit. Tal. Dosha. Fisher. All of the same tribe. All living on the same land. Tal, the elder, can he not trust them to keep their words? But if the children of the same Great White Father can and do not and will not trust each other without a contract, what was I to think? General Brock? A man. A white man but still a man.

We spoke from the rise of the sun until the setting. I spoke of all of that had made the hearts of my people heavy. Of the Whites seeking to drive us from the land of the Great Lakes. Until we can sleep in peace on the banks of the Ohio, until our own chiefs are chosen by ourselves, we will war.

Brock listened. His feet did not move when we spoke. He did not circle about me. He looked into my eyes. And when I finished, he said "Look at my hand, Tecumseh." He took out a white paper and wrote on it, speaking as he wrote.

"Among the Indians whom I met at Amherstberg, and who had arrived from distant parts of the country, I found some extraordinary characters. He who attracted most of my attention was a Shawnee chief Tecumseh, brother to the prophet . . . A more sagacious or more gallant warrior does not, I believe, exist. He has . . . prevailed on all his Nation and many other tribes to follow his example. They appear determined to continue the war until they obtain Ohio for a boundary."

Brock stopped writing and looked up at me and spoke to me eye to eye, face to face, head to my head. "I am writing these words to Lord Liverpool, my chief, my prime minister. We shall write a contract with you. It will give you the Ohio. Forever."

"I do not want a contract," I said. "I want your words, General Brock." "No, Tecumseh," he said, gently. "You need a contract. No man is forever."

I placed my hand on his shoulder and said, "General Brock, you are a good man. No man born of woman is forever and no contract born of man is forever."

Brock whispered something I could not hear and walked away with his eyes on the ground. Amazing, these Whites. Even among themselves, they need a white paper.

"Tal is old but he's not dear," Fisher remarked as he scanned the contract written in large capital letters.

CONTRACT:
• PAINT: Color: Blue
• SHADE: Pure: No gray in it.
• ADVERTISING SLOGANS
• QUOTES FROM LITERATURE
• TOPICS: Jerusalem:
    • Special Requirement: Words Of Wisdom
• COST TO BE AGREED UPON.
    _____ Tal
    _____ Dosha
    _____ Fisher

"Oh, Darling, Tal is old, but he's an old dear also."

"And what am I?"

"Why you're my old man," Dosha laughed. She put her hand on Fisher's, letting it rest there. "Let's go upstairs," said Fisher.

Dosha continued as if she hadn't heard him. "What do you think? Shall we help Tal?"

■ ELIHU YALE: Tal is old but he's not a dear . . . Cost To Be Agreed _____ Tal _____ Dosha _____ Fisher—They are a pair, Fisher and his dove. Tal is old but he's not dear. When the Hebrew de Paiva showed at Fort St. George in 1685 with his bride Hieronyma, it marked the end of my sleep. Forever.

Will this Tal be different? Is he not a Portuguese just like de Paiva, and Salvador Rodrigues, and all the Duartes—Princes of Antwerp, they all were, to hear Hieronyma tell it to me.

Are they not all of a piece? Including Abendana, and even the Chardins, and G-d be my judge, even I, all of a piece we are.

Tal is old but he's not a dear. He would seek to bind young Dosha. And Fisher. Did I not bind young Hieronyma. And the cost, at such a price, Lord, G-d, how I tremble, for the cost is yet to be agreed.

■ SHITAO (1642–1707): old man—Why does Dosha call Tal old and why does she call him "an old dear." Why does her boyfriend call Tal "old" but not "dear." Why, and most important of all, does she call her Fisher her "old man."

Dosha is an artist. She can see. Could I not see where I traveled: in Anhui, in Nanking, wandering across all of Yangchow. And why to travel? To see how others see and see how others see what they think others saw.

My cousin, Bada Shanren—others called him mad—for he didn't speak, but he was not mad, more clear-minded than all the rest. Things are not stable. Nor the same. Nor without end.

Dosha is a painter. She can see that Tal's thoughts are in the sky where he lives. With the books of his ancestors. Priests and emperors of the spirit.

Tal is a patron. He has commissioned her. To her, he is dear. And old. But she can see her lover, Fisher. Do not his ancestors speak to him? Surely he is old also.

"I reply with a hearty laugh that I do not know whether I am of a school, or the school of me; I paint in my own style."

Tal, what is he to Fisher? Or Fisher to him? Or Chu Ta to me or I to Chu Ta? One school. In which manner do I paint? In which manner do I teach? Or Tal? Or Dosha? Or Fisher?

■ BADA SHANREN (1625–1705): old . . . dear . . . man—What am I?

He enters my room, with the audacity that only a man whose ancestor was a Ming emperor can have. And I, whose ancestor was also a Ming emperor was silent. He had written to me for a year. Messages on the whitest of paper. Gifts. A scroll: a branch from a plum tree blossoming in winter. Liu Shiru. And wine. Always wine with each note. I did not reply. What should I reply to his question? When would be a favorable time to visit? Autumn. Winter. Summer. I had hung my flag outside my door: a single ideograph: YA: DUMB.

He entered at dusk as I knew he would with a brace of bottles. He walked about my room, looking at my scrolls. Now one, now another, and laughed and drank and mumbled, "You . . . are old. Dear . . . old."

I heard the words "old man" again and again and again. I heard the question, "What am I?" said with such intensity that even I trembled. I was standing before my ancestor, the Emperor of all Emperors. I could not speak. But I dripped my brush before Tao-Chi and lay on the floor beside the brace of bottles he brought me. I sketched two birds swaying on a rock for that was what I was. And Tao-Chi and Tal and Dosha too. What we all shall ever be. I opened my eyes not but a short time after daybreak. He was gone. Tao-Chi, flown away. He had taken my answer scrolls with him, leaving me with three unfinished bottles and his question, still flying above my head in my room.

◆ SARAH PADAWER, DOSHA'S GRANDMOTHER: Can you help me?—Simply put. This young man is asking my granddaughter, Jerusha, to marry him. A helping hand they call it in America. Or asking the father for her hand, they call it if you're rich in America. And in Slonim—what was the question—always unasked because it was as simple as why the Good Lord put your eyes in front of your head and not behind. As my mother, Gittel, would say, so you should look to the future not be stuck on the past, what's behind you. Not like Tal. If you're a *meshugeneh*, fine, walk backward your whole life. The question was so simple. The man asked his parents who asked the *Shadkhan*: "Can the woman help the man," and of course the girl was asking her parents who asked the *Shadkhan*: "Can the young man help the woman." Small things. A hand on his head in the middle of the night when he was sleeping. A *Hallah* with raisins the way he liked it. And small things for him to help her—a look of astonishment that her beauty was the same in his eyes even after years and years. Help is the core. *Pashtut mi Pashtuta*. The simplest of the simple, my father would say. But this is America. My son is not here for the young man to ask his permission for my granddaughter's hand. And Jerusha is not Jerusha, she is Dosha, but the question, Can you help me?, is the same through all of time and in all the world. For does not love mean that we are all in the same Eden?

"This advice shop sounds nutty. It's probably a scheme to meet women."

"Well then, why do you care? You're always accusing him of dreaming of me."

Fisher lowered his head. "Moonlighting is the American way. I hope Time Inc won't sue me for serving two masters. Normally I'm supposed to hoard my great ideas for His Eminence, Henry Luce."

"Your secret is safe with me," said Dosha, lifting her finger and pressing her lips against it with a slowness that drew blood from Fisher's face. His skin whitened, he couldn't breathe. How often she did that to him!

"Can you help me? Which is the wrong way to Charles Street?" Fisher had asked Dosha when he first saw her two years before leaning against the building on Hudson Street.

■ RABBI MEIR: Can you help me?—Why does the young man not ask simply: "Which way to Charles Street?" He comes from a line of fourteen generations of Talmud scholars who know that each word should be counted. From a mother who thought and then gently turned each phrase in her hand before she uttered it. Because he knows that he has become lost. He has become another. *Aher*. My master. Did not Elisha ben Abuya, who was the most learned sage in my academy, become another? *"He found a harlot and solicited her. She said, 'Are you not Elisha ben Abuya?' But when he transgressed the Sabbath by plucking a radish and giving it to her, she said: 'He has become another, 'aher' person.'"*

But did I not journey to Elisha's house each morning before the sun rose to discuss Torah with him? And when he came to visit me once in the school in Tiberius, did I not go out to greet Elisha?

"Thou turnest man to contrition," I whispered to my master Elisha on his deathbed, for even at the moment of death, G-d will accept repentance.

At that moment, my master wept. *"I believe my teacher died repenting."* When I found my master's grave burning, I spread my cloak over it and said, *"If G-d will not save you, I will."*

And if Elisha can be saved from punishment in the next world, surely young Fisher can be helped, even saved, no matter how lost he may be.

■ JULIUS MEYER, DOSHA'S GREAT GRANDFATHER'S BROTHER: Can you help me?—The young man is asking the question every young man asks in every country on every continent, a question asked in Blomberg, Germany, where I was born—in both German and in song.

In Omaha too, even though my eldest brother Max, more a father to me, he claimed when I came to Omaha at the age of 17: "I can help you and I will help you. And Moritz and Adolph will help you. We'll find a *Yiddishe Kallah* for you and she will help." "I'll help myself," I said grandly. There was no music in Omaha. Certainly not like the music I had heard in the conservatory in Blomberg. I was alone in Germany, 15, and walked into Herr Schmidt's school. "I'll clean the floors, wash the windows, cook your meals, if only you'll let me sit in the corner of your classroom." I guess I looked like a sausage to him. He said "Meyer, you'll go to America just like your older brothers as soon as they send you passage." From what Max tells me, there's no music across the ocean, only money. Though when Schmidt refused, I simply stood outside the conservatory peering in through the windows, day after day until in the midst of a blizzard Herr Schmidt invited me in and announced: "Herr Meyer will be with us as an observer/student until his passage money is sent." No fool, Capelmeister Schmidt. Max, hearing music was my passion, said "Fine. We'll sell musical instruments in Omaha." Moritz said, "There's no orchestra. You'll start one, Julius." And I left Blomberg. But outside of Omaha there was music. Pawnee chants. More lyrical than any lieder. With

■ VAN GOGH: Can you help me?—Of course he is asking a woman, "Can you help me?" I asked Eugénie Loyer. Did I care a whit that she was already engaged.

And in Etten, I asked Kee Vos: "Can you help me?" Did I care that she was my cousin? And of course Mother and Father were enraged.

"Which is a better mate," I asked them slyly. "One who is spoken for, one who is blood, or one who is a prostitute." Father would not answer. Mother wept. Even Theo's eyes widened and his hands tightened into a fist when I spoke to him first of Sien Hoornik—mother, expectant, prostitute and my heart's dream.

And if it is not to be a woman. Then *un bon coup*, a drink and a smoke.

Or Gauguin.

Or Gachet.

But always and ever the question: Can you help me?

rhythm played differently each time. "You'll lose your head, mark my words," said Max, "roaming around in Omaha country with the Ponca and then you won't be able to smoke any of our cigars." They could see the future. I almost got scalped, had Two Moons, the daughter of the Ponca Chief (Afraid Of His Horses), not helped me, as she called it, though saving me was more like it. But she would not settle in Omaha. The Meyer boys would not let me live beyond their shadows. They did sell instruments and they did found an orchestra that I headed but Two Moon's music escaped me. What was life without my heart's song?

■ VAN GOGH: Reading . . . leaning against a wall—A Madonna, reading, propped up against a wall. A breviary in her hands. Praying and staring. Her body itself a cathedral she is praying in.

She, staring at him. A canvas before her eyes. And staring so hard that even he can see his reflection. *I much prefer painting people's eyes to cathedrals. For deep in a human eye, there's something that a cathedral does not have—however impressive and solemn it may be. I am more interested in the human soul, be it the soul of a poor devil or that of a harlot than in structures.*

They are each painting the other in black and red, in red and black.

■ SITTING BULL, Oglala Sioux (1841–1876): "Can I help you?—Can I help you, Sitting Bull," the Omaha trader, Mr. Julius Meyer, asked me. He must not have been more than half my age, though the Wasitchus age much quicker than we do, more like crows they are. I said nothing but he persisted. "Can I help you, Sitting Bull? Or can you help me? Or will you help me? Or who am I to you?" For with the Whites you must repeat everything they say—for they do not mean what they say. And if you repeat their words to them then perhaps they hear them for the first time. And they listen, like startled deer and you can tell in their eyes if they meant what they said. But still, it is like rain on tree bark—over quickly. Changing if not in an hour, then in a day. But never for many moons and certainly not for years. "I can help you. I will help you. You are Sitting Bull."

Already at that time, men thought me a Hunkapapa, but I was not. And who is Sitting Bull to you, Mr. Meyer, for to a man—they all wished to be called Mr.—like a chief, though they were not all chiefs.

But the man looked at me straight in the eye. "You are Oglala. Sitting Bull. You are the victor on the Bozeman trail. And I am Box-ka-re-sha-hash-ta-ka—not Mr. Meyer—the one who Chief Standing Bear calls the Curly-headed-White-Chief who speaks with one tongue."

Mr. Meyer looked at me without taking his eyes away from mine. "I will advise you how to talk to the Great White Father. I will take you to the picture maker and make a picture of you. You can take copies to all your lodge." And he did. Red Cloud had to be photographed standing prominently. Spotted Tail was wise enough to be below Red Cloud. Swift Bear wished to sit in the middle. They all wore the white man's clothes. I alone had my Oglala dress. Nor for the world would I change. Mr. Meyer was truly Box-ka-re-sha-hash-ta-ka. He spoke with one tongue but he told me simply. In the city of Washington, none would speak with one tongue. If more white men than Mr. Meyer were in the picture then all Indians must sit below them. I should not have gone farther East than Omaha.

"Can I help you? I thought you said no one could help you," Dosha said, looking straight at him. She saw him the way she knew he would someday look.

How had she known that he had just been in a coffee shop half a block away. And *tumler* that he was, when asked by the grandmotherly Italian proprietor, "Can I help you?" he had replied, "No one can help me." A trifle really, half a joke, a have-a-nice-day rejoinder. But how did Dosha know that he'd said those lines?

She had been reading *The Red And The Black* while leaning against a Hudson and Perry Street wall.

That had been the start. Lucky he was that he hadn't stopped and asked her name or whether she liked pistachios or what was the capital of Madagascar. That would have been too ordinary.

■ GAUGUIN: Can I help you?—Dosha knows the question is the answer. The young man Fisher has asked her, "Can you help me?" For he is praying that Dosha will ask him to ask her, "Can I help you?" Is it not the woman who asks a gentleman with her eyes and then he being a gentleman, proffers help. My grandmother Flora's eyes resting on her uncle's eyes. The last viceroy of Peru, Don Pio Tristan de Moscosa, too grand to offer my grandmother a sum to live, too cruel to offer so little as to die. *The Perigrinations of a Pariah*, 1854, my grandmother's account of her request, turned into art, the book burned in the streets of Lima, her gentleman uncle's response.

Mother too, asking with her eyes Don Pio's heirs for help and yet again being offered half of very little or all of nothing. The young man, Fisher, is looking at the young woman with artist's eyes. She will return his glance and plea for help. Fisher is asking for nothing and expecting everything. My own young artist's eyes forever frozen looking at all who look at my portrait. Receiving nothing from a woman and expecting everything.

■ ABD AL-QADIR AL-JAZIRI (1558): Coffee—*At the beginning of this [the sixteenth] century, the news reached us in Egypt that a drink called 'qahwa' had spread in the Yemen and was used by Sufi shayks and others to help them stay awake during their devotional exercises, which they perform according to their well-known way ('ala tariqatihim al-mashura). Its appearance and spread there had been due to the efforts of the learned shaykh, Imam, mufti, and Sufi Jamal al-Din Abu 'Abd Allah Muhammad ibd Sa'id, known as al-Dhabhani. He remembered having qahwa in Ethiopia and drank it after falling ill again in Aden. He found that among its properties was that it drove away fatigue and lethargy, and brought to the body a certain sprightliness and vigor. In consequence, when he became a Sufi, he and other Sufis in Aden began to use the beverage made from it, then the whole people—both the learned and the common—followed [his example] drinking it, seeking help in study and other vocations and crafts, so that it continued to spread.*

Fisher, now spry and now vigorous after his coffee, has come upon another of the people of the Book. Still he needs help, and she is no Sufi, but she will lead him to a master. Ask and it shall be shown. On the very place. For the building she is leaning on, will not the Master himself teach them there?

■ ISAAC LURIA: Still looking at her—Dosha is there. And not there. Tal is in the room with her and he is not in the room. For he is with his Rachel. And Dosha is with Fisher.

Tal's room is a synagogue. Fisher is about to begin a prayer:

"Before an individual begins to pray in the synagogue … he must take upon himself the precept 'thou shalt love thy neighbor as thyself.'"

The young man should concentrate on loving all people as he loves himself, after which his prayer will ascend, bound up with all the prayers of Israel.

My teacher, Moses Cordovero—may his memory be an everlasting blessing—taught me that the Day of Atonement in its entirety includes confessing those sins which one had not personally committed.

The young man is looking at Dosha and she is gazing at Tal. They must respond: *"We have sinned. Rather than I have sinned. This is because the people of Israel constitute a single body of which every Jew is an organic part. This is the mastery of the unity of souls."*

■ MARCEL PROUST: Looking—The young man is looking at Mademoiselle Dosha as through a telescope. Tal has invited Mademoiselle to tea. But truly it is the young man who is hosting this literary party. It is he who is looking at his guests from across the boulevard.

Le Figaro 26 May 1897:

"Yesterday, a literary dinner party of the most elegant kind, was given at the home of M. Marcel Proust, who was inviting his many friends for the first time. The guests included: M. Anatole France, Comte Louis de Turenne, Comte Robert de Montesquieu-Fezensac de La Gandara, Jean Béraud, G. de Borda, Reynaldo Hahn, etc.

The Marquis de Castellane, who had been unable to send his apologies, made a brief appearance, but left immediately after dinner to call on his cousin, the Prince de Sagan.

M. Marcel Proust's father, the celebrated doctor, had absented himself, leaving his son to perform the honors of a dinner which sparkled with true Parisian wit."

And I, Marcel, was I not the truly absent one, yet ever present behind the telescope of my mind? Is not this dinner hosted by young Fisher, of the most elegant kind, free from the clatter of dishes, with Tal and Mademoiselle Dosha, dining on Blake's verses themselves?

And here he was, two years later, still looking at her: engaged, enthralled, riveted.

Fisher's eyes moved to the wall directly facing Hudson Street.

"England! Awake. Awake. Awake.
Jerusalem thy sister calls!
Why wilt thou sleep the sleep of death
And close her from thy ancient walls?"

Dosha had kept at Fisher. "We agreed to help Tal. I've found the paints. Mixed them. I'll do the painting myself.

"Dear Tal seems to think there's no difference between a canvas and a rent-controlled apartment wall. I've gotten William Gottlieb Realty's permission, but we must act quickly. A rent-controlled landlord's prerogative."

"He can always change his mind," Tal had cautioned Dosha. "What quotations does Fisher suggest for my advice palace?"

■ ALBERT CAMUS: Here he was still looking at her—At the Maison française, in New York, in 1946 after the War, after the Maquis, Eugene Sheffer invited me to speak directly to undergraduates. Answer questions from Columbia students themselves. "Sit on the floor," I told the 50 students that came in and before they could ask a question I volunteered a question myself. For I was an exile in New York. *"I loved New York, with that powerful love that at times leaves you full of uncertainty and abhorrence: there are times when one needs an exile."*

Why is it that in various European capitals *"men would stare at women on the street but it doesn't seem to happen in New York?"* I asked the students. There was silence. Not a word. They had come to see me: described as *"our Kafka without dreams."*

This was their question I was asking! Professor Otis Fellows broke in with *"Monsieur Camus, in this country we believe that there is a time and a place for everything."*

It was my turn to be silent. And then my turn to laugh. And then they all laughed.

Young Fisher is on the street gazing at cloistered Dosha. And because she is not on the street, he is still looking at her, engagé, enthralled. He is held riveted. Two years have passed. And more will pass. I had to come to New York to understand this.

■ PERCIVAL LOWELL: Looking—Young Fisher, an astronomer, is looking at Dosha every evening, moonlit or not, and each and every day as through a telescope. Years will not pale his enthusiasm, nor dim her beauty in his eyes.

Nor Mars nor Venus mine. For fifteen years, I courted the planets, sketched them, sang to them. Schiaparelli had seen some of Mars' beauty, canals he called them but only I could know my virgin Venus well enough to see her as she truly was and far from desolate, visitors and guests built and rebuilt structures and spiked roadways all across her. But does Fisher see Dosha as she is through his telescope? Or has he to *"reduce her glare and steady her image narrowed the aperture of his 24 inch telescope to only three inches or less."* As I had mine. He, I, Vermeer, Tal, all men—humans viewing our own *"shadows of our blood vessels and other structures in our own retinas."*

Dosha, and every other woman, too, distort their vision in their microscopes, touching really, for through our passion we continue to search night after night, day after day, as long as love and life last.

Julius Meyer, callling card.

11

◆ ISAAC TAL, ABRAHAM TAL'S FATHER: His own quotation—What would my son Abraham have written on the wall? His own quotation from Ezekiel, the only Biblical passage he would always quote sanctimoniously to his brother Tuviah. "*Teshuvah, repentance, makes atonement for all transgressions; even if a man has transgressed all the days of his life, if he does Teshuvah at the end, nothing of his wickedness is remembered unto him, as it is said in Ezekiel 33 verse 12.* Abraham would always move his right hand before Tuviah's face though writing the verse before his eyes. "*And as for the wickedness of the wicked, he shall not stumble thereby in the day that he turneth from his wickedness.*"

Then Abraham would pause and look Tuviah in the eye, inches from his face, and continue: "*Do not say that one does repentance only for transgressions that involve an act such as theft or robbery . . . one must search out his evil thoughts and turn from anger, from jealousy, from pursuit of money or honor. These inequities are more serious than those which involve an act, for when one is addicted to them it is difficult for him to leave off doing them. As it is said in Isaiah,*" and Tuviah would laugh and say directly to Abraham's face: "*Chapter fifty-five verse seven: Let the wicked forsake his way, and the man of iniquity his thoughts.*"

What a pair my two sons: together they would have made one good Rabbi. But Abraham wishes only a secular quotation. And on this fragile foundation to guide Dosha and Fisher to the marriage canopy, to bring them both to fast, to atone, and as on Yom Kippur, through their repentance to have not only all their deeds but even Abraham's and even all those of mankind forgiven.

"Let Tal choose his own quotations from his own vast library of pseudographia, Arcana, Kabbala, Hermeneutics and even the Scriptures themselves," Fisher had parried, but Tal had held firm. The quotations had to be secular, literary, not religious. Something to draw Americans into the shop. A British bit would be best.

Fisher wrote quotes from Blake on four index cards. He gave them to Dosha, who passed them onto Tal. That was the drill. Dosha: secular matters. Fisher, matters of the spirit. Strict separation of church and state.

"And when and what will we get paid for the greatest decorating job in New York since Stanford White's design of the Morgan Library?" he asked Dosha in the middle of the night.

"Oh, Tal will decide. Let's go back to sleep. I've got to be at the museum at eight with Abigail."

■ MIKHAIL TAL: Fisher parried but Tal held firm —"*I hardly ever used this opening and it was a surprise for Fischer. Positions of this type were very rare in his games, and an analysis of the game revealed that the American champion felt far less confident than usual in unfamiliar positions. In all fairness, I must admit that having decided to play the French Defense while still at home, I spent 10 minutes at the board hesitating.*"

Abraham Tal has prepared well for young Fisher. He will insist Fisher develop his opening.

■ GAUGUIN: Fisher wrote . . . Dosha passed them to Tal—Fisher writes and Dosha paints and together they dance around and around, passing their works to Tal. Singing together, three children holding each other's hands, circling so quickly that none will stumble as long as they hold each other tight. When I told Vincent that "*when sailors muster the effort to move a great weight they sing together to sustain each other and bolster each other's spirit*" he sighed and said, "*This is what artists lack.*"

■ TIGRAN PETROSYAN: Let Tal choose his own— "*A great deal has been written in our country about Fischer, but as a rule, the writers have concentrated mainly on his eccentricities . . . The young grandmaster has confidence in his powers. He does not doubt he will succeed—when he is just beginning a tournament and when his position on the board arouses grave apprehension. It is well known that an excess of self-confidence has proven the undoing of many talented chess players. But it is equally well known that without faith in oneself there can be no rapid advancement or genuine tournament success.*"

This Fisher is wily too. He claims Tal should choose his own opening flourishes. But he knows that Tal will not. Fisher has enough self-confidence to seize the advantage if Tal refuses to choose his own movements. Tal will hesitate, and Fisher will triumph.

He'll triumph with Abigail too. For is not Fisher jealous of her friendship with Dosha? So he has fixed her up with his friend Hamilton. Every night for a month, they've seen each other. Leaving Fisher alone with Dosha. Too simple an end-game, really. A King, a Queen, alone on the board. Like Morphy. Brilliant. American. Almost crazy.

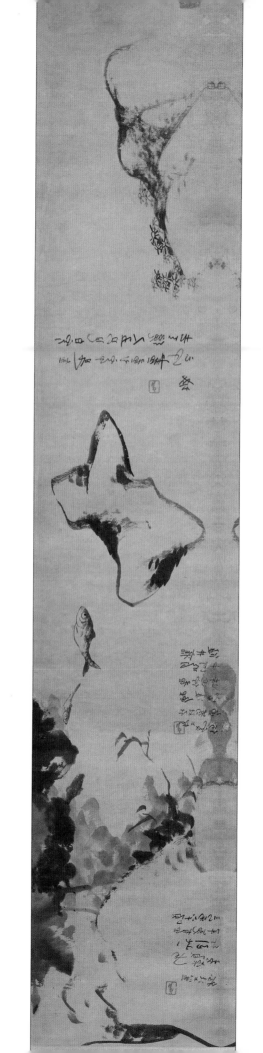

■ BADA SHANREN: Fisher's mind watched—Fisher's mind watched. What does it see? It sees two fish swimming away from each other. The old man back into his past days in his Native land. And the young woman swimming through the waters toward him.

And do I write of Fisher's vision?

"In the old days there was a river
Above which the bright moon used to shine.
Mr. Huang had two golden carp
Which have gone, becoming dragons."

And what of the young woman's eyes? What does she see? She sees her lover. She is swimming toward, through him, and with him into immortality.

And what do I write of her?

"Under the thirty-six thousand acres [of lotus]
Day and night fish are swimming
Coming here to the shadow of a Yellow cliff
All creatures become immortal."

And the old man, is he not like my cousin Shitao? Both see with the same eyes.

"A foot and a half from Heaven only white
*   clouds are moving.*
Are there yellow flowers there?
Behind the clouds is the city
Of gold."

■ GAUGUIN: Listen to me . . . who is coming to whom for advice?—"Listen to me," Vincent would shout as I sketched next to him in the yellow house. More an apartment than a house. More a studio than a home. Each square of space covered with paint drippings, stalactites of dirt, books perched uncertainly on each wooden stalagmite plank.

And through the caverns of it all, Van Gogh slashing at his canvas, quoting from Zola, preaching from the Gospels, who is coming to whom for advice, I would think. Asking me of every village I slept in: Martinique, Brittany. Vincent speaking of the Borinage, London, Antwerp. Map upon map, stuck upon each other, pages fused together like an old romance book of travel. *"Disciples of a new religion."* Living, talking, thinking, all together. All in a soup spiced with Millet and novels of redemption. Mad Vincent chanting: *"Everyday I take the remedy that the incomparable Dickens prescribes against suicide. It consists of a glass of wine, a piece of bread with cheese, with a pipe of tobacco."*

All still present in the air. Vincent and I breathe together. Yesterday's stale smoke, last weeks' wine, cheese ripened years ago in Vincent's mad Dutch mind.

Every wall covered with his canvases, painted last week, to be painted in the next weeks, all bubbling madly, as Vincent stirred us both in a cauldron of paint and ink and paper.

All this coursed through Fisher's mind as he watched Dosha through the window, standing stock-still across the street in Tal's Den of Advice.

Tal rested his left hand on Dosha's right. "For only one dollar, Dosha, I can give you advice that will change your life. For two dollars I can give you advice that will change it back again."

"For three dollars, you will let go of my hand, you dear, sweet, ever-changing old man hidden in a poet," said Dosha with all the tenderness she felt for Tal.

Dosha looked up, eyeing her boyfriend across the street, but would not give Fisher the satisfaction of removing her hand from Tal's.

Fisher suddenly moved left, using his right hand as an imaginary fulcrum and spun on his heels counter-clockwise, disappearing eastward down Perry Street

■ DELMORE SCHWARTZ: Poet—On Mem Drive right next to the ever rejoycing Sir Harry Levin, he parsing Molly Bloom as though he and she were Gaelic sweethearts. And I teaching poesy at Harvard without citizenship papers—"My but you've learned English so quickly, Mr. Schwartz," his look said but no one, no one called me anything ever but Delmore.

"Next door there lived a poet,
*   His name was Mr. Black*
He sent his verse to the editors,
And the editors sent it back."

"Wine brings all things closer— vivider
I see the Harvard houses, neo-Georgian,
Just like Petersburg, as Harry [Levin] said/. . .
*   the cure is wine/*
Wine is inspiration, exaltation
Magic, Pegasus, and peerless peaks"

And drink we did. Levin and I. Very sweet. Memorial Drive until the death of "our poor dead king." 1941. Joyce almost at 60. I at 28. Both finished. Poetic justice.

■ SEMIR ZEKI: Poet—Why does Fisher look at Tal and Dosha and not try to hear them? *"We see in order to be able to acquire knowledge about this world. Vision is not, of course, the only sense through which we can acquire that knowledge. Other senses do just the same thing. Vision just happens to be the most efficient mechanism for acquiring knowledge and it extends our capacity to do so almost infinitely. Moreover, there are certain kinds of knowledge, such as the expression of a face, of the colour of a surface, that can only be acquired through it."*

Fisher is young enough to be revolutionary enough to prefer seeing Tal to hearing him. He is old enough to to be wise enough to insist on watching and listening to Dosha.

■ VINCENT VAN GOGH writing to Theo van Gogh: Old—To Theo: London 1874:

"I am glad you have read [L'Amour by] Michelet and that you understand him so well. Such a book teaches us that there is much more to love than people generally suppose.
To me that book has been both a revelation and a gospel at the same time: 'No woman is old.' (That does not mean that there are no old women, but that a woman is not old as long as she loves and is loved.)…that a woman is quite a different being from a man, and a being that we do not yet know—at least, only quite superficially, as you said—yes, I am sure of it. And that man and wife can be one, that is to say, one whole and not two halves, yes I believe that too."

Fisher is a writer, and Tal can read what Fisher has not yet written. And Tal already sees that Fisher's Dosha will never become old as long as she loves Fisher and is loved by him.

Their home will be like the little Loyer's House on Hackford Road. Together, ever young. Living on the top landing.

מסורת הש"ס שבעת ימים קודם יוה"כ מפרישין כהן גדול . שכל עבודת יוה"כ
אינה כשירה אלא בו כדיליף בסוגיי' בפרק בתרא [דף
יג:] דכתיב גבי יום"כ וכפר הכהן אשר ימשח אותו ובגמרא [דף פ:]

ו.) מפרש למה מפרישין : ללשכת פרהדרין . כך טעם ובגמרא
מפרש למה נקראת כן . ומתקנין
לו . ומזמנין לם אחר כהן גדול תחתיו אם יארע בו פסול כדי
או שאר טומאה המעכבין מלבוא
למקדש : ובעד ביתו . גבי יום"כ
כתיב בלאחרי מות : אם כן . דמישת
למימרא : אין לדבר סוף . שמא גם
זו תמות : גמ' שריפת הפרה .
פרה אדומה : שעל פני הבירה .
לקמיה מפרש מאי בירה : צפונה
מזרחה . במקלוע מזרחית צפונית
של כל מעשיה . תורה אור

שבעת ימים קודם יוה"כ . יש מקומות שטעות הסמכין צריכים כמו עין משפט
בכאן ובבבא קמא (ד' ג.) . ולבבע' אבות נזיקין ובפרק נר מצוה
קמא דל"ה ו' . ד' לאשי שנים וליכא לוכי דמני מייכא
לבסוף לפני מגיסן של עכו"ם . ו' יום בר"פ קמא דעבודת אלילים
(ד' ג.) ובפ"ק דקידושין (ד' ג.)
הואשם נקפים בב' דכים ושאלן
ודולגין בהלכות (סנג*) לפני [ל"ל הסמב]
(סנג*) שלשים יום (פסחים ד' ו.): [ל"ל הסמב]

שבעת

"ימים קודם יום הכפורים מפרישין כהן גדול
מביתו ללשכת פרהדרין ומתקנין לו כהן אחר
תחתיו שמא יארע בו פסול *ר' יהודה אומר אף
אשה אחרת מתקנין לו שמא תמות אשתו שנא'
וכפר בעדו ובעד ביתו זו אשתו אמרו לו
אם כן אין לדבר סוף : **גמ'** תנן התם "שבעת
ימים קודם שריפת הפרה היו מפרישין כהן שורף
את הפרה מביתו ללשכה שעל פני הבירה צפונ'
מזרחה ולשכת בית האבן היתה נקראת ולמה
נקרא שמה לשכת בית האבן שכל מעשיה בכלי
גללים בכלי אבנים ובכלי אדמה מאי טעמא
כיון דטבול יום כשר בפרה "דתנן 'מטמאין היו
הכהן השורף את הפרה ומטבילין אותו להוציא
מלבן של צדוקין שהיו אומרים במעורבי השמש
היתה נעשית תקינו לה רבנן כלי גללים כלי
אבנים וכלי אדמה דלא ליקבלו טומאה כי היכי
דלא ליזלזלו בה מאי שנא צפונה מזרחה כיון
דחטאת היא וחטאת טעונה צפונה וכתיב בה
אל נכח פני אהל מועד דלידהי לה רבנן לשכה
צפונה מזרחה כי היכי דלידהי לה היכירא *מאי
בירה אמר רבה בר בר חנה א"ר יוחנן מקום היה
בהר הבית ובירה שמו ור"ל אמר כל המקדש
כולו קרוי בירה שנאמר "הבירה אשר הכינותי
מנא הנ"מ *א"ר יוחנן אמר קרא °כאשר עשה
ביום הזה צוה ה' לעשות לכפר עליכם אלו מעשה
אלו מעשה פרה לכפר אלו מעש' יום הכפורים
בשלמא כולי' קרא בפרה לא מתוקם לכפר כתיב
ופרה לאו בת כפרה היא אלא אימא כוליה קרא
ביום הכפורים כתיב ומתיב וכתיב °צוה ה' לעשות
°הבא צוה ה' לעשות ומתיב וכתב התם °זאת חקת
התורה אשר צוה ה' לאמר מה להלן פרה אף
כאן פרה ומה כאן פרישה אף להלן פרישה
ואימא

משמע לסמם מתניתין דהמס
דלמיתה דמד חיישינן לתרי לא
חיישינן וקמה מתכי' דהכל קביל
ליה דהי נמוי ממיד כמו כיחוס נמי'
לתובלא יי"ל דם"ק הכל כמו דמיחה'
למיתה דמד לזמן מרובה כמו בהסיא
דפרק ד' אפין (ג"ז שם) דלמא
אדמייבם סד מיית אידך ק"ו למיתה
דזמן מועט אע"פ כי סכל לא הוי לן
למיחם משום מעלה דכפרה
חיישינן לזמן מועע אפי' כיחוס אפי'
לתרכי ותלת אי כמי דסם מסמא
סיא משום זינולא מלוה
יבאין וליכא איסלוקא כולי סאי אבל
בזה כיחום אפי' לתרכי ותלת חלי'
זה משום דכפרה לכל ישראל תלי'
לזמן מועט וא"כ אין לדבר סוף
סלכן ליכא למעבד תקנתא לסאי
מששא וכי פריך בגמ' (דף יג.)
מאי שנא לגבי נומאה דטכיס נפי'
מומיה כדאמר בגמ' לקמן
כהן אחר תחתיו וסכא חיישינן
לתרכי ותלת הוה מני לשנויי כי
סאי גוונא מפסא משום מעלה
סיא ולא הוה נריך לספרים אחר
כי משמואל יטלאו מרבם בעלמא
רצוין לעבודה אלא מעלה בעלמא
סלכך סני במד אלא כללו תכי :

להוציא מלבן של צדוקין . לאו
בעוומאה דאורייית' מנעו
ליה דלא סוי מזלזל בם כולי סאי
אלדכב' אמרי' בפרק אין דוכסין (דף
ים.) כהדי אוכלי' קדם מדכם למעות
אלא כדתסן בפ"ק דמכ' סרם סמכו
ידיהם על ראשו ואומרים לו אישי
כהן גדול כד נעול אמת דמומא
סנעוגין לו מעביכין ליה כנומא
כעומאם דרבנן דמחייין סכסכים מסיני
כעניכן לנכיב דידי' דבנדיסס
מדרכ למעלם כדסריסים :

שבל מעשיה בכלי אבנים וכו' .
דוקה בללו ז' ימים של
שריפת ספרה אבל בשעת קידום
הסכן בפ"ב דמכ' פרה בכל הכלים
מקדשים ואפי' בכלי גללים וכו'

ויקרא
יו
ויקרא
ט

במדבר
 יט

ל.) מפרש למה מפרישין : ללשכת
מל כמס נקראת כן . ומתקנין
לו . ומזמנין לם אחר כהן
גדול תחתיו אם יארע בו פסול קרי
או שאר טומאה המעכבין מלבוא
למקדם : ובעד ביתו . גבי יוס"כ
כתיב בלאחרי מות : אם כן . דהי
למימרא : אין לדבר סוף . שמא גם
זו תמות : גמ' שריפת הפרה .
פרה אדומה : שעל פני הבירה .
לקמיה מפרש מאי בירה : צפונה
מזרחה . במקלוע מזרחית צפונית
של כל מעשיה . תורה אור

עשיית כלי . לפני עבודת יום אמד:
דלהוי הבירא . לעשות מטמפוכם שם
כדי להטביל עליו עבודת פרה
סקרים מטנאת וטעונה מזרח ויסס
לג לסיום זריז במעשים וסדר
עבודתם . הבירה אשר הכינותי . י"ס
אשר זימנתי לם מקום גורן אכונה
[ביום) גם לבנותם בם ודוד קאמר לים לשלי
ל' בס ל' קאל בדברי הימים : מנא הנ"מ
דעני פרישם ליום"כ ולפסם : כאשר
עשה . במילואים שלום אותם
לפסוק מעים ז' ימים סכמ' (ויקרא
ח) ופתח אוהל מועד תשבו יומם
ולילה וגו' ובשמיני עבדו סכ' (סס
ט) ויהי ביום השמיני קרא וגו'
וכתיב קרב אל המזבח וגו' כאשר
עשה וגו' לעשות לכפר עליכם דלפני
עשייה . קיום מלואים : ואימא

■ BOBBY FISCHER: How can I get him to marry me?—Dosha is precise. She knows what she wants. A great strategist. Like my mother, the Queen, although everyone called her Regina. Mother could see it all from the start, knowing what she wanted. Which in those days after World War II was simply knowing what she didn't want: Dad. Call him Gerard. Call him Gerhardt. Call him anything. He's gone. Disappeared. Vanished. Rumor says the suburbs of Chicago. Or Santiago. Perhaps back to Germany. Mother's strategy got what she wanted. Get him out. And me, in the center of the game. In our one-room Arizona house in the shadow of the Sierra Estrella Mountains. I had the edge, the favored position. In 560 Lincoln Place, when we moved to Brooklyn, I was the Crown Heights Prince. The king, thank G-d, was missing in action.

"How can I get Dreamboat to marry me?" Dosha is asking Tal.

Tal is a brilliant tactician. She has come to the right coach. But he is tired. Weary. Not too old, however; Tal is a gambler, and gamblers always have hope. But he is not at the top of his form. For Tal is hoping he will be the champion for Dosha's hand. For her head, her eyes. All of her. Foolish really, for he is playing with his prewar love, Rachel Beller, going over his moves in Antwerp with her again and again, replaying each game and hoping for a rematch. Death means nothing in chess. Do I not play Capablanca endgames each night in my head? Tal is off guard. He repeats Dosha's trust in words. Not the same as . . . he mumbles. Of course she knows that. All of Dosha's moves to this point have revealed her strategy: She lives with Dreamboat, dines with him, dreams of him. She wants Tal to be the tactician. She speaks to Tal's mind. Not to his heart. Tal is a professional. What is it that Dreamboat wants more than anything, he thinks. Not Dosha. He has her already. To be a novelist. That's where her beau's endgame tends. Dosha must convince Dreamboat that if he marries her, he will become a great novelist. Tal may be crazy, but he's not stupid. He is starting off with a tale for Dosha. Abandoned by father. I too, by King Gerhardt. But gypsy? Only Tal could gambit that one. For Tal knows that Dreamboat will not believe the tale. But in the disbelieving he will . . . . *"When I was eleven, I just got good."* I can't follow where it will lead, this move of Tal's but it's not just good, it's brilliant.

"Listen, Tal," said Dosha, moving close to him. "Give me the two dollar advice. Make it about Dreamboat. How can I get him to marry me?"

"Dreamboat?" rasped Tal.

"Raphael Fisher, the angel behind you across the street." Tal whirled around but saw no one.

"How to get Fisher to marry you? Not the same as asking him to marry you. Not the same as staying married," said Tal mechanically, as though reading from an ancient text.

"Listen, dear Tal. I can't expect miracles for two dollars."

Tal began: "This is what you must do. Tell your tale of a gypsy childhood . . ."

"Tal, you're shameless," interrupted Dosha. "You've asked me endless times about my mother's great great uncle Julius Meyer who spoke Omaha and took his Ponca friends to Paris in 1889. You've told me my mother's character was formed by Meyer and mine by my father's father who studied in a Yeshiva in Slonim—so now to be a gypsy?"

"Abandoned by your father," continued Tal without pausing, "who has just now returned. Take off the locket around your neck with a flourish and fling . . ."

"Tal, you gave me that locket," interrupted Dosha, shocked.

"The locket's not important. The tale is important. Even the tale itself is nothing. The teller is everything. Once you tell your tale, Fisher will want you to listen to his."

"Fisher's a novelist, not a storyteller. And I'm a painter, Tal."

"Not so fast. He's watching you paint so that he can start to write. It's all the same: the canvas, the paper, the story."

■ EMILY POST: How can I get him to marry me?—Not the same as asking him to marry you. This young woman seated in a room with her paterfamilias, perforce Mr. Tal, as her mentor is properly asking him a question. Her beau, young Master Fisher, is across the street. *"In cities twenty-five years ago, a young girl had beaux who came to see her one at a time; they in formal clothes and manners, she in her 'company best' to 'receive' them sat stiffly in the 'front parlor' and made polite formal conversation. Invariably, they addressed each other as Miss Smith and Mr. Jones, and they 'talked off the top' with about the same lack of reservation as the ambassador of one country may be supposed to talk to him of another. A young man was said to be 'devoted' to this young girl or that, but as a matter of fact, each was acting a role, he of an admirer and she of a siren, and each was actually an utter stranger to the other."*

The scene here is perfect. All Mr. Tal need do is immediately request that the young girl, Miss Padawer, ask her beau, at present conveniently across the street, to enter and discuss the proposal directly with Mr. Tal: *"Usually, however, when the young man enters the study or office of the father [in this case in loco parentis] the latter has a perfectly good idea of what he has come to say and having allowed his attentions, is probably willing to accept his daughter's choice; and the former after announcing that the daughter has accepted him, goes into details as to his financial standing and prospects. If the finances are not sufficiently stable, the father may tell him to wait for a certain length of time before considering himself engaged, or if they are satisfactory to him, he makes no objection to an immediate announcement. In either case, the man probably hurries to tell the young woman what her father has said, and if he has been frequently at the house, very likely they both tell her mother and her immediate family, or more likely still, she has told her mother first of all."* But Mr. Tal, whilst acting as father, is not summoning the young man at all. Mother is not to be found. True, Father's existence is deemed unknown. A knotty problem indeed. Far from being made easier by Mr. Tal.

■ Hershel Tschortkower, Anshel Moses Rothchild's rabbi: Money-back guarantee—He was special, Anshel Moses was. My shul klopfer. Every morning walking by each of the homes in Tschortkow, knocking on their doors: "Arise! Arise to serve the Maker." Anshel never missed a day. He was never too sick. For even when he was sick, he seemed stronger to me than Reb Feivish who could lift his horse-drawn wagon out of the mud by himself. Anshel Moses was never too sick to rise in the morning, knock gently at my window and proceed to knock on each and every synagogue goer's door. I once followed him, curious which path he used and later said, "Anshel, I know which path you take in the morning." He smiled without answering. I sketched out the path starting at my house and wandering down by the river past Reb Aron's, crossing the bridge and finally back along the winding path just past where the Gutweins lived finishing at the Tschortkower shul. "Well, now I know how you never miss anyone and it's all downhill even though I would have thought it would take longer for you than going uphill first to Reb. Aron's." But all Anshel did was smile in reply. He never spoke much. He counted his words like the coins in the tzedakkah box, one by one, never saying a word he didn't mean. One day Anshel tapped on my window—and in truth I hadn't been able to sleep all night and was still in my clothes from two hours before when I tried to read from Messilat Yesharim which I read each year before Yom Kippur—so I followed him again. This time Anshel started at my house but reversed himself and passed Berglas' house before Stolz's and walked sharply downhill before crossing the river, a way that left me breathless by the time Anshel reached the synagogue. I don't know why it held importance to me but I followed him in the two years that Anshel was my shammas, from when he was 16 until he was 18, 36 times. Never did he take the same path and each path seemed quicker than the other. Never did anyone precede Anshel to the Tschortkower shul. Each time, through the window, I would watch Anshel as he entered the synagogue, kiss the red velvet paroches in front of the holy ark, remove the wooden tzedakkah box and place it on the bima, where the worshippers could give tzedakkah and then put on their tefillin and wait patiently for ten to arrive to pray. Now it was my custom to learn Talmud after each morning's prayer session with Anshel. "Every other Friday even before I opened my talmud I would first deposit the tzeddakah collected during those two weeks in a blue cloth bag, which was hidden behind one of the many bookshelves in my study." Anshel was a sponge. He listened and watched me study. He prompted questions in my study, even without asking a question. It was almost as though we understood each other without talking. He was straight and honest. People in our town thought him naïve but to Anshel there was only one way, the truthful way. It was that simple. He was the son I never had. He was the Blessed One's gift to me. When Anshel was matched to be wed to Schönche Lechnick from Snaiten, it was my most grateful moment and my most difficult. Anshel was to be wed just before Pessach. The marvelous klezmer Reb Yossele played throughout the wedding night. In the morning, the wedding was over and I walked about the town, knocking on each door myself for now I was both father and son. Passover was coming and each year I looked for hometz myself, checking with my own eyes, standing on a ladder, even checking behind each shelf of books and each bookcase. What a shock. To suddenly realize the small blue bag, filled with tzeddakah had vanished. More than five hundred gulden, I thought. Gone!

"Listen to me, Dosha. Fling it out the window, twine yourself around your lover like a ribbon around a birthday present, and Fisher will weep. Throw a glass or break a dish; after making love with him completely differently, your life will be totally recast—no Radcliffe, no Zaideh, a blank canvas. All for him."

"But it's crazy," said Dosha. "My grandmother would turn in her grave. My father died just two months after I started to work as a butterfly girl at the Museum of Natural History, the month I moved to Hudson Street. I've told you this countless times, Tal."

"Who is coming to whom for advice? Fisher is a writer. He will write his tale on you, with a pen of light on pale white paper. You have asked one question but you are thinking of another. I have moved from minor to algorithmic major. If this won't keep Fisher yours forever, I'll return your two dollars."

"Tal, you're shrewder than you look and I love you, but I'd like my money-back guarantee in writing."

And with that, she left the shop, closing the door behind her, glancing to her left at a Blake poem suggested by Fisher.

> He who binds to himself a joy
> Doth the winged life destroy;
> But he who kisses the joy as it flies
> Lives in Eternity's sunrise.

Those Blake lines were calligraphed by Dosha on a wall of Van Gogh blue studded with words of starry white.

All the money collected for the past two weeks, but more, much more, for the Maot Chittin, the money given to tzedakkah before Passover was the biggest collection of the year, even greater than Yom Kippur. How could Anshel take it? Did I not say to Anshel before the wedding: "You know, sometimes it is not good to ask one's father-in-law for anything. At least not in the beginning. Anshel, do not hesitate. You know you are more than a son. What is mine, is yours. Just ask." But Anshel had not explained. He simply smiled. I could not breathe at the Sedarim. On the third day of Chol Hamoed I rode my horse and carriage to Snaiten. I prayed to G-d: May Anshel repent and start anew.

Anshel was overjoyed to see me enter his house. He served me tea and nuts. But I couldn't wait to talk: "Anshel, I hope you believe me when I tell you that if it had been my five hundred gulden, I wouldn't have minded. I'm sure you intend to return the money bag. And I know you had a good reason for taking it. Nonetheless, it was money for the tzeddakah, money for people who might starve without it. Therefore no one has the right to borrow from these sacred funds." I don't know what I expected to happen, but Anshel immediately rose and went to the corner of his kitchen. Without saying a word, he emptied a box of coins totaling two hundred gulden. What could I say? At least part was paid. I burst out crying and Anshel too, white as a ghost, was crying. Truth to tell, not a week went by after that without my receiving either from his hand or from a messenger in a "sealed bag" coins so that a week before the next Rosh Hashanah all the debt had been cleared. But still I couldn't sleep. For Anshel hadn't asked my forgiveness and Yom Kippur was approaching. The day before Rosh Hashanah the village policeman came to my house. "Rabbi, you must come to police headquarters. Are you missing money from your house?" I said, thinking of Anshel: "No." "Does this bag belong to you?" asked the policeman. He spilled the bag with many coins still in it. "But the money has been returned!" I shouted. "Are you completely crazy?" the policeman exclaimed. "The peasant woman who cleans your house found this bag in your house. She kept it but soon spent so much of the money that she was noticed and I myself questioned her and she has confessed. I don't understand you, Rabbi. Why should you want to protect someone who has robbed you? Anyway, take the bag of money. It's yours." I didn't understand any of it. I rushed to Anshel's house and asked him: "Forgive me! Pardon me! Why did you say nothing? I have never been able to follow you, Anshel. Or how you think. I am an old man. A rabbi. A sinner. Please talk." "Reb. Hershel, 'when you came here on Chol Hammoed I saw how pained you were over the loss of the tzeddakah. It hurt me so much to see your sorrowful expression . . . I felt I had to do something. I realized you wouldn't let me give you any money' so better I should say nothing to your charge of theft and simply give you all my wedding gift money back. We don't yet have children and G-d gave me parnosseh that I could pay the remaining three hundred gulden." I placed the blue bag in Anshel's hand and I wrapped my fingers around his. "Take these coins still in the blue bag and go to Frankfurt. In a bigger city you will have greater opportunity to succeed in business and to help others. Go and may G-d bless you and your children for all generations." Anshel settled in the Frankfurt ghetto under the sign of the red shield and prospered greatly. He called his first son Mayer Anshel, his second Kalman and the third Moses Anshel. May G-d bless him and his children to succeed and help others in all generations.

● EZEKIEL BELLER, RACHEL BELLER'S FATHER: The first question one asks—Is the first question one asks, the only question?

"Abraham, Abraham."

Does *Hashem* mean these words as a question? Is Abraham answering by saying, "Here I am."

For does it not say "Abraham, Abraham." And not, "And the Lord asked." Abraham may have heard a question that G-d did not ask, but that Abraham heard. And is that what is asked of us by G-d, wherever we are.

Or are we answering a question that G-d has not asked? Or are we waiting for G-d to ask us, ever the bashful bride, Israel.

And what of me? In my tears when my wife Malkah died. Chills for a month. Fever. My Rachel holding my hand so tightly, by Malka's bedside. My Malka. A mother in Israel. Lost. Rachel, an orphan at two. For the best part of me died at that time.

I weeping tears filling every crevice in my body from the moment of Malka's passing. Rachel repeating over and over, "Mama, where are you? Where are you?

And I repeating Malka's name over and over. And not being able to ask: "Where are you?" Who among us can ask the Holy One's question? His first question. The only question.

■ AHER: Paper—This young man is me when I was a young man. *"Learning in youth is like writing with ink on clean paper but learning in old age is like writing with ink on blotted paper."*

This young man has a vision. His vision is clear. He is writing with ink, fresh, dark, on the whitest of paper. And I. I, on my deathbed weeping. My past years before me. My tears blotting the paper of my life. Rabbi Meir sees the question through my tears, in my eyes; Can you help me? And he quotes the psalms. *"Thou turnest man to contrition."* Even on blotted paper, even as one's eyes are closing forever, one can learn, one can learn.

C H A P T E R 2

WHITER than snow, Fisher thought as he stroked Dosha's skin. Her eyes opened wide as his eye scanned her body. She's looking at me just the way she did when I asked her directions to Perry Street.

Is the first question one asks the only question? It's never answered between two people. Lovers. Friends. And because it's never answered, it is repeated over and over and yet over again. G-d, I'm starting to sound like Tal, thought Fisher. Dosha wanted to give Tal a key to "our apartment" so that when we occasionally house-sat Abigail's new three room apartment on Perry Street on the weekends, Tal could look in as a favor to us.

"No way. Never. Tal would read every scrap of paper I've written on," Fisher had protested.

■ DELMORE SCHWARTZ: Directions to—Actually, Fisher said: "The wrong way to Charles Street." What Dosha heard is another matter. What Fisher will write in his novels to come, yet another. The year 1967. Dosha and Fisher in a daydream: *"The novel will exist as long as the daydream."*

■ VIRGINIA WOOLF: Apartment—*"A woman must have money and a room of her own if she is to write fiction."* What shall we say of Abigail? A would-be painter. Pots of money, but not of paint, she is dreaming of a canvas to paint on but has placed her bed in front of it. Odysseus' tree trunk. Unmovable, shakeable but unmovable. Abigail has *"a room of her own"* but is wise enough to invite Dosha as a house guest. Dosha, her Muse.

Fisher too, has Dosha as his Muse. *"On or about Dec. 10, 1910, the world changed."* Some things immutable. Dosha has neither money nor an apartment or a room of her own. But through her, Fisher has already begun his novel —not on paper but just above the surface of his unearthly white unlined quire of writing paper resting on his desk. A man does not need money or a room of his own if he is to write fiction. Now, as in my time, 1910 or half a century later. Just an amusing Muse.

What doth a woman painter require? Certainly not money—arsenic it is, if mixed with lead white. Fry explained it to me all, but I did not understand it until his show in 1911 at the Grafton Gallery. It explained all. Seeing is never believing, it is understanding. Gauguin and Van Gogh.

Two painters, men or women, do not need money or a room of their own. Far better an Arles studio, white light to share together. Fisher has been launched. Dosha and Abigail too, if they wish and will it.

■ MARCEL PROUST: Asked—Monsieur Fisher is asking Mademoiselle Dosha, "Can you help me?" He is not asking her for such a question cannot be answered, but he is thinking he is asking her. She realizes his question for he is asking with his eyes, never looking away from hers.

Just as I asked Celeste with my eyes, "Can you help me find the way to …" The Princess Soutzo. The Ritz.

"To leave my bed once or twice a week and dine out." To remain in bed. To write. To dream. To find *"the essential part of me, that is, my book."*

My eyes moved toward the dark oak cabinet given to me by Madame Nathé, and Celeste Odilon gazed at me and understood that I was but not yet two—unable to speak beyond a "non" or a nod of my head. She caressed the key in the lock before she turned it, and all the pages of a budding grove were there.

Should I change addresses permanently? She understood that she was able to help *"the essential part of me, that is, my book"* find its way to Gallimard, typeset and corrected, book by book, separately, as though awakened a thousand times each night, from the dream of my life.

■ MIKHAIL TAL: Drivel—Tal understood Fischer. Just as I understood Fischer in Curaçao in '62. Fischer wouldn't eat with anyone. *Chess Life* had proclaimed his playing in Stockholm "*the finest performance by an American in the history of chess.*" He was a teenager chronologically but dreaming of the chess championship of the world. Of course when Tigran Petrosian won, Fischer claimed all the Russians had "ganged up" on him except for me. Only Fischer, bless his soul, visited me in the hospital when I was devastated by my kidney but for that I would have been champion. But I digress.

Of course Fisher knows this is drivel. A gypsy Father and a family grave in Ceneda. But Dosha is telling him this in the middle of the night. Her face pressed to his. She is rearranging the moves of her life, with breathtaking ease. He can see her altering her past and her future. She is his Muse. If he remains with her he will be able to do what he dreams of doing, writing the novel of his dreams, and of Dosha's dreams, and even of Tal's dreams. Novels that freely alter time. Where the past can be changed. Where everyone's story intersects on a three-levelled chess board. Each move influencing and influenced by other players—many long dead, some not yet born nor yet loved. Novels of the hands of Dosha, her painting of the voice of Tal, but still and always Fisher's own novels.

Tal is a brilliant tactician. He has Dosha making all the wrong moves knowing that Fisher, in his youth, will pounce upon her errors and make the correct ones himself. For of course, the young maiden wishes her beau to win her hand. Forever.

■ PROUST: How does Dosha know of Ceneda? *Les jeux sont faits.* Tal has instructed Mademoiselle Dosha. Princesse, really. To tell her story, her secret tale, to her Swann.

And what of Fisher for are not all ardent lovers Swann?

"*Besides her very admissions—when she made any—of faults which she supposed him to have discovered, served Swann as a starting point for new doubt rather than putting an end to the old. For her admissions never exactly coincided with his doubts. In vain might Odette expurgate her confession of all its essentials, there would remain in the accessories something which Swann had never yet imagined, which crushed him anew, and would enable him to alter the terms of the problem of his jealousy. And these admissions he could never forget. His soul 'carried them along, cast them aside, then cradled them again in its bosom, like corpses in a river. And they poisoned it.'*"

A dangerous game, fabulating a past—far, far better "to pronounce the names Balbec, Venice, Florence within whose syllables had gradually accumulated the longing inspired in me by the places for which they stood . . ."

"Darling," Dosha said. "Tal doesn't need a key. He's a *passe partout*, as Henri Peyre would say." He's already here.

What's all the drivel about having a gypsy father and a family grave in Ceneda? Didn't she tell me that her father had died more than a year before we met? And that she didn't want to talk about him until she was ready. How does Dosha know of Ceneda, wondered Fisher.

The hands are the hands of Dosha, but the voice is the voice of Tal.

He's the mole that's entered Dosha's thoughts, Fisher thought as his hand ran along the curve of Dosha's breast, down to her rib cage. He flipped her with a dexterity that surprised him.

■ BOB DYLAN: The hands are the hands of Dosha but the voice is the voice of Tal—Dosha's hands are blessing his voice. "*May G-d bless and keep you always. May your wishes all come true.*"

And Dosha's hands are lifting Fisher and twirling him around her. He is flying. His feet will never touch the ground—neither in New York or parts West.

May your heart always be joyful
May your song always be sung
May you stay forever young
Forever young, forever young.

And what of Fisher's song—sung over and over, voice heard, overheard, quoted and misquoted. We're all the same. Every voice, each pair of hands. "*You're a Big Girl now.*" "*Well, I read that this was supposed to be about my wife. I wish somebody would ask me first before they go ahead and print stuff like that. I mean it couldn't be about anybody else but my wife, right? . . . I'm a mystery only to those who haven't felt the same things I have.*"

Another's hands upon ours, lifting us onto the first rung, leaping gaily above us, we ascending in windy pursuit, our voices, above and below chanting in miraculous chorus.

May you build a ladder to the stars,
And climb on every rung
May you stay forever young.

■ SWIFT BEAR, Brulé Sioux Chief—She didn't want to talk about him. The daughter does not wish to speak of her father. For he's no more with her. Perhaps he is with her but it is some trick I do not understand. For although Standing Elk and I were the most friendly of friendlies to the white man, still we did not understand them.

After the spring of 1865 we were forced to flee the fort, but by October we signed a peace and informed Colonel Henry E. Maynadier that Oglalas, mostly hostiles, were coming in. The winter was the coldest of all my life. My daughter died. "*She asked me to bury her beside Old Smoke on the high ground just west of the fort. Colonel Maynadier gave his agreement. We were not given enough to live but we could choose where to die. I did not wish to talk of me. But the Whites gave us no choice. The friendlies were turned into hostiles by soldiers in the fort. The hostiles were hunted and then lied to, and then brought into the fort yet again. Only to be slowly killed by the winter or quickly by the Whites.*"

■ Delmore Schwartz: The White Horse—Scott would say: "When drunk, I make them pay and pay and pay."

Fisher has it all. The woman. The novels. A future. Middle twenties. Together in the White Horse. I as alone in the White Horse as I was "*Alone, in a hotel, almost penniless in the 44th year of my age—my second wife having taken flight after eight years of troubled and quarrel-wracked marriage.*"

I, alone, in the White Horse surrounded by "*an attentive supply of girls*" two steins of beer in front of me, reciting *Finnegans Wake* from memory, a closed book—always—my vaudville trick, singing for my supper. Elizabeth Pollet is flying overheard, watching me hawk-like as I make all in the White Horse pay and pay and pay.

Actually, it was a bit the reverse. My wife Elizabeth watched me pay and pay and pay.

Had I been Fisher—or his age or with his Dosha—my eyes would not have wandered once, certainly not at the White Horse.

■ Sitting Bull the Hunkpapa: Crumpled—Dosha, as much a pretty bird as a woman. Lying on Fisher's bed. What he does for her, she will do for him.

When I was fifteen, a singing bird, a meadowlark with a yellow breast with black crescent-moon shaped markings on its throat, lay on its back, wounded and crumpled beneath a tree. I rescued it. Just two moons later, Brother Meadowlark came to me while I lay under a tree, asleep at night under a full moon.

"Lie still, lie still," it sang to me its softest song. I awoke and saw at twice my length a grizzly bear. I lay perfectly still until the bear wandered away. I made up a song for the meadowlark, for the meadowlark speaks Lakota.

Pretty bird you have seen me
And took pity on me
Amongst the tribes to live, you wish
For me
Ye birds from henceforth,
Always my relation
Shall be.

Dosha will return to Fisher, again, under the fullness of the moon.

She rolled over, anticipating his desire. She's different from the rest, thought Fisher. Not like Skidmore Sue, with her impossibly long hair, always waiting for him to smile before she laughed, clueless if he were joking or serious. And Dosha, trying not to smile before he cracked a joke, always before. How could he ever surprise her? That was the big question.

Fisher started to massage Dosha's back as she lay on her side, with the bokhara crumpled halfway onto the floor. Tonguing her every rib as he pressed into her bones. I don't have him yet, thought Dosha. Fisher still doesn't believe me.

Her eyes were wet, stuck, face down on her pillow. "Back rubs lead to front rubs," she had told him when he tried to massage her back on their second date at the White Horse. They'd sat outside until three in the morning.

■ Isaac Luria: White—"*Place these words of mine upon your heart and upon your soul. Bind them for a sign upon your arm and let them be tefillin between your eyes.*"

The eyes. Ah, the eyes. For do not the eyes search everywhere, especially when closed. And see everything or nothing. Each year, on the Day of Atonement, I would don my clothing of white and begin to pray, "We have sinned" rather than "I have sinned." Even those sins I did not commit, even for them I prayed, "We have sinned."

I would look at Hayim Vital dressed too in white. Hayim Vital would gaze at me. His eyes did not wander once from the white tallit I wore. I too was transfixed at the white he wore. We chanted together, each of us, "*We have sinned.*"

All thirty-six in our Safed congregation sang together, "*We have sinned.*" And the world gazed at Safed and sang in echo: We have sinned. And the world was pardoned.

And white—My Sabbath clothes all white for that is the color I shall wear—follow my death in the world to come.

■ Melville: The White Horse—"*Or white marbles. Or white pearls. Or elephants. Or the white bear of the pole or white shark of the tropics. Or the milk-white fog or white friar. Or a white bride or even a white rum.*"

All the same—that which we search for on this earth or the high seas: "*The colorless, all-color of atheism from which we shrink.*" Fisher's eye will not wander. He will be transfixed once he has gazed at the white—be it horse or whale.

■ Maharaja of Patiala: And what will you have?—"And what will you have?" I said to Louis Boucheron.

"Will you have diamonds?" And I myself—not any of my twelve pink turbaned Sikh bodyguards who had brought in six treasure chests of my jewels from the Punjab—dug my hands into the first casket.

"What will you have, diamonds?" And I balanced on my palm a series of pear shapes gathered by my grandfather in the previous century when Patiala was far poorer. "Will you have diamonds, white?"

"Will you have diamonds of color?" I unwrapped my silk pouch containing my three favorite colored diamonds—my blue square shape, my 84 carat pink and my Maharani's deep green cushion cut. "Will you have these, Monsieur Louis?"

For that is what Baron Fouquier told me to call him. That is what his school chums call him. You must think of yourself, Patiala, as a boy of fifteen when showing him your treasures. He knew the English, and the French well, Le Baron.

"And what will you have?" I said to Monsieur Louis. "Will it be pearls or emeralds?"

My treasures were silken wrapped and I opened them with a slow motion, caressing the gems' surface through the cloth, much as I would my Maharani or any of the twenty wives—dancing girls both the French and English called them. "What will you have?"

Suddenly I saw the color drain from Boucheron's face as I caught him staring at my Maharani, standing frozen next to me. Her fringe of diamonds and emeralds lay on her shoulders, visible under the white silk sari that covered the jewels and the jewel of her body.

I understood what Monsieur Louis Boucheron would have if he could have anything. I stretched my head toward his ear and said like one fifteen year old to another with a wink at his pallid face, "Ah, Monsieur Louis, that is the one thing you cannot have."

Boucheron mumbled to me, more deranged than I had ever seen a court jeweler, "I will have whatever your Highness will favor me with."

I snapped my fingers and said, "Patiala will decide within a week."

I winked at my Maharani and we slowly walked to meet the other Louis, Louis Cartier, who by the time we arrived knew full well what we intended to have from La Maison Cartier, from Paris, from the West, indeed from all the world.

"And what will you have?" the waiter had asked Fisher, looking at Dosha all the while.

"Not the check. And not another beverage but here, my good man, extend your hand."

The waiter did, and Fisher put a two dollar bill on the waiter's open palm and the waiter disappeared a half hour, only to ask each half hour how they were and what they wanted.

Fisher must have brought a stack of two dollar bills from one of the coin dealers near Tal's office, thought Dosha.

Charming really. And clever, cheaper than drink and more effective than food, for had they eaten and drunk, they would have had to go home. Talking hour after hour—quite different from all of those Cambridge dates at 44 Brattle where Le Dauphin couldn't wait to make his move, and was not a patch on Fisher.

■ Louis Cartier: What will you have?—It didn't matter what Patiala said. Or his jeweler. Or what he promised. Or his Maharani for that matter.

For to me, to my brother Pierre, to his viceroy in India, he was India. And to me, to Cartier, he was the World.

"And what will you have?" I asked him as he entered. "Your jewels set in radiant platinum by the house of Boucheron or La Maison Cartier?"

"Patiala has given you our word, Monsieur Louis. Monsieur Louis will prepare my ancestral gems—as our face to the world."

"Yes, but which Monsieur Louis? You spent three hours and twenty minutes with Louis Boucheron this morning," I said crisply.

Patiala gazed down at the time piece La Maison Cartier had sold his Majesty at the Durbar. "Three hours and twenty-two minutes if your gift watch is to be trusted, but let us not speak of trifles. There is only one Monsieur Louis in the world, and that is who Patiala will deal with."

I looked at Patiala in the eye and said, "Patiala has owed sums to us for ten years for sales we have made to your Majesty."

"Ah. Ten years. Ten years," said Patiala looking at his Maharani whose eyes had not blinked during our entire conversation.

"What do you say, my Princess, shall we settle today?

"We will give Cartier the 141 carat emerald. Shah Jahan's gem carved from his own hand. And we will pay you one tenth of the bills and estimates to set all our gems into à la mode Parisian platinum that you have sent us in the Punjab."

I insisted, "Two tenths and your wishes will be respected, Patiala. You are aware, your Majesty, the Taj Mahal emerald was not sold at the Exposition in '25 . . ."

Suddenly, the prince made a motion to his Sikh warriors—twelve in number they were—and with a great clanging, they closed the chests and started toward the door.

Patiala and his lady stood before me and did not move. The Maharani smiled at me with teeth that far exceeded the whiteness of the diamonds shining under her transparent off-white sari. Her neck glistening like the minarets of the moonlit Taj. The emerald drops visible under her silken sari's sheen moved slightly and I saw her body quiver.

I could hear the echo of the closing of Patiala's jewel chests, the end of my royal dreams for La Maison Cartier. Within me a voice, sounding more like my father's, "Ten percent it will be. My Maharani, I am sorry to have troubled you with these matters."

The Maharani bowed low and in a soft voice said, "We are grateful to you. You, Monsieur Louis, are a true friend of Patiala."

Responding to her Maharaja's eyes, they both marched out of our office like Prussians. At the transom, Patiala turned to me and shouted, jovially waving a ruby encrusted watch at me. "But this is a gift mind you, strike it from your school boy sums. I will not have it otherwise." And both disappeared, and the twelve Sikhs, beturbaned with silken headgear, bearing the six jeweled caskets disappeared.

I walked into the showroom and quite beside myself shouted to no one in particular, "Tomorrow we begin." Then I mumbled to myself, "Thank G-d Pierre is not here," and wiped a tear from my eyes and said, "If only, if only Father were here."

■ SAMUEL LANGHORNE CLEMENS (MARK TWAIN): Le Dauphin—Of course, le Dauphin is moving his eyes from Nina's body to the other young damsel. For aren't they both seeking a charming prince? He knows that Americans wish it both ways: forbidden heavenly delights on Earth and celestial pleasures ever after. If the Dauphin should choose their pleasures for them, surely the great author of us all cannot hold them accountable.

But these are lasses being educated in Boston. In '69 I wrote my sister Pamela:

"*Tomorrow night I appear for the first time before a Boston audience—4,000 critics.*"

Tonight le Dauphin has met his match. He knows that he must make them open the bidding. If either foreswears him forever, his is bliss. For "*To promise to not do a thing is the surest way in the world to go and do that very thing.*"

The Boston lasses, Nina and young Dosha, though I much prefer the Yankee name Jerusha, know this too. And they neither ask nor answer. Laughter always wins the day in the end.

■ PIERRE CARTIER: American ladeez always choose for themselves—Indeed they do choose. American ladies always choose for themselves. And not only Evalyn Walsh McLean—first the Star of the East in '08. Then the blue Hope Diamond with its 300 year stream of curses thrown in gratis by me. Then she chose not to choose the 32 grain pear and the hexagonal emerald hanging above the Star of the East.

"You'll deal with it, Pierre, won't you be a dear or how else can I choose the Hope?"

Of course I know Madame Evalyn that you shall choose which gem. Which setting. Which dress and which ball. But which faithful husband and which doting child and which quiet grave's end? That, even an American lady cannot choose. Other than my wife, of course.

■ EVA STOTESBURY'S (a Philadelphia heiress) costume secretary: An American lady always chooses—An American lady always chooses for herself. And it was far far from a simple task for Eva Stotesbury of Philadelphia: "*A full-time personal fashion designer and costume secretary whose talents included sketching her employer in her projected attire for an evening down to the last clip and finger ring so that she might see how she was going to look without the trouble of dressing and could amend the whole arrangement without inconvenience . . . Nor was Mrs. Stotesbury willing to play second fiddle to Palm Beach hostesses who went to elaborate lengths to rotate their jewels and avoid appearing on successive occasions with the same combination of necklaces, tiaras and bracelets. In a dressing room specially assigned for the purpose adjacent to her private apartments, her entire fabulous collection of ornaments was arranged, as in the window of a jewelry store, on the necks and wrists of mannequins with heavily annotated memoranda as to the date and occasions where they had last been worn.*"

Le Dauphin, a law student from Lyons studying at Harvard Law School. Constantly moving his eyes from Abigail's body to Dosha's. "Can I help you ladeez," he would croon. "And how do you suggest you help us, Pierre?" Abigail would tease.

"Oh but you must choose le façon, as we say, American ladeez always choose for themselves, or perhaps both of you wish Le Dauphin would reply." Abigail and Dosha would laugh hysterically. It was all so predictable. An open book. It was different with Fisher.

His head on Dosha's back, listening to her heartbeat. What can he hear on the wrong side of my body, thought Dosha. Still, Fisher's trying. Never stops. Never will.

■ CHARLES DUDLEY WARNER (Samuel Clemens' friend): Le Dauphin—He wrote me:

Dear Chanly,

"*The committee of the public library of Concord, Mass., have given us a rattling tip-top puff which will go into every paper in the country. They have expelled Huck from their library as 'trash suitable only for slums.' That will sell 25,000 copies for us sure.*"

And what of it all: Huck, Jim, Tom Sawyer, Aunt Polly, Le Dauphin, Bilgewater. Every Nabob from Cairo to New Orleans, will never give him Sir Walter Scott's peace: The same Sir Walter "sets the world in love with dreams and phantoms, with decayed and swinish forms of religion; with decayed and degraded systems of government . . . most of the world has now outlived a good part of these harms . . .; but in our south they flourish pretty forcefully still."

But as he writes of Le Dauphin, Twain dreams of board games, memory builders, pamphlets teaching Susy, Clara, and Jean the history of England, the history of the world, and all to finally built his own impregnable castle surrounded by millions, safe forever.

Fortunately for Sir Walter, he did not dream of patents. Is Samuel so different from le Dauphin? It has always been so: it takes one to know one.

■ MARK TWAIN: Le Dauphin—This one is much taken with these two damsels.

"'*Bilgewater, kin I trust you?*' *says the old man, still sort of sobbing.*

'*To the bitter death,*' *he took the old man by the hand and squeezed it, and says* '*The secret of your being: speak!*'

'*Bilgewater, I am the late Dauphin!*'

You bet me and Jim stared this time. Then the Duke says:

'*You are what?*'

'*Yes, my friend, it is too true. Your eyes is lookin' at this very moment on the pore disappeared Dauphin, Looy the seventeen son of Looy the sixteen and Marry Antoinette.*'"

And by jove, isn't Nina my Jim and Dosha my Huck?

And isn't the Dauphin with them all in "*Boston where they ask; how much does he know?*" They are going to New York but they are not there yet. "*In New York, how much is he worth?*" In Philadelphia, where Miss Nina is from, "*they ask who were her parents.*"

Le Dauphin's moment is here: Now or never.

■ KAFKA: Book—"*I was walking through Prague one day with the son of a colleague. He stopped outside a bookstore and looked in the window. He bent his head right and left, trying to read the titles of lined-up books, I laughed and said: 'So, you too are a lunatic about books, with a head that wags from too much reading?' My friend's son assented: 'I don't think I could exist without books. To me, they're the whole world.' What could I say but, 'That's a mistake. A book cannot take the place of the world. That is impossible. In life, everything has its own meaning and its own purpose for which there cannot be any permanent substitute. A man can't, for instance, master his own experience through the medium of another personality. That is how the world is in relation to books. One tries to imprison life in a book, like a song bird in a cage, but it's no good.*"

■ LOUISA MAY ALCOTT to the Library Committee of Concord, Mass.: stop—"*If Mr. Clemens cannot think of something better to tell our pure-minded lads and lasses, with the moral weight of well-loved books behind every word, he had best stop writing them.*"

◆ SIMHA PADAWER, GRANDFATHER OF DOSHA: Backward and forward—And whose hand finished the Torah? My hand saith G-d. Backward and forward. So it is written in the Talmud:

"Joshua wrote the book that bears his name and the last eight verses of the Pentateuch. This statement is in agreement with the Baraita, which says that eight verses in the Torah were written by Joshua, as it has been taught: It is written, 'So Moses the servant of the Lord died there.' Now is it possible that Moses was alive and wrote the words, 'Moses died there?

The truth is, however, that up to this point Moses wrote, from this point on, Joshua wrote. This is the opinion of Rabbi Judah, or, according to the others, of Rabbi Nehemiah."

■ RABBI SIMEON: Hand—I said to Mar: *"Can we imagine the Sefer Torah being short of one word? …No, what we must say is that up to this point the Holy One, blessed be He, dictated and Moses repeated and his hand wrote, and from this point G-d dictated and Moses wrote with tears."*

■ AZRIEL OF GERONA: Self—Fisher is going to tell Dosha of her inner self. Her true center. Essence.

She is stretching her hands away from her body, backward and forward. Her hands, palms down and outstretched.

He is the son of a daughter of a Cohen. Tuviah Gutman Gutwirth's grandson. Unable to grant the Cohanic blessing and yet he is blessed by whom? By the knowledge he has blessed her to bless him. They are as close as two sides of one leaf. Each thinks but of the other. Thought is like a mirror. *"One looking at it sees his image inside and thinks that there are two images, but the two are really one."*

Dosha's palm earthward pointed. Fisher's toward heaven; raised, both parts of one's hand.

■ MARK TWAIN in *Huckleberry Finn:* Women …. man—*"Don't go about women in that old calico. You do a girl tolerable poor, but you might fool men, maybe…throw stiff armed from the shoulder, like there was a pivot there to turn on—like a girl; not from the wrist and elbow, with your arm out to one side, like a boy. And mind you, when a girl tries to catch anything in her lap she throws her knees apart: she doesn't clap them together."*

Dosha's caught Fisher, fast and sure, but he doesn't know it.

Clear as the fingernails on my hand. As I turn them toward me, backward and forward, Dosha mused.

"I'm going to tell you about your inner self. Look at your fingernails," Fisher said. "And make it quick." Dosha stretched her hand out. Fisher smiled and said, "A true female you are. A man would have bent his hand and lowered his fingernails halfway across his palms. Women always look at their fingernails palms down and fingers outstretched."

"And you need this proof to understand I am a woman? When you look at my hands, what do you imagine them doing? You seem to be daydreaming."

"Oh," replied Fisher. "You're painting. There's a fleck of white under your thumbnail. I imagine you in front of your canvas, moving your brush, moving and looking."

"And you, what are you doing?"

"I'm watching. Watching and writing."

"Muse to Muse," said Dosha. "Do we ever take off time from our work?"

"Even artists can unionize, Dosha."

"To return to your examination, what size statistical survey have you employed in your sample study?"

■ CHARLES FOLEY, naturalist: Female—Fisher, a male, is watching Dosha, a female. More in common she has with a female elephant—African or Indian, newly born, unmarried, mother or matriarch. Fisher a scientist, observing Dosha from afar, although across a White Horse Tavern table. He can see her in all her feminine phases.

"Very few people are fortunate enough to witness an elephant being born in the wild…only twice have I seen an elephant give birth…I had come upon a group of 60 elephants tightly bunched on the road. By their behavior, I could tell they were excited. Several were trumpeting, chasing imaginary objects… the focus of attention appeared to be a cluster of females in the middle of the commotion. Through the hubbub I recognized the matriarch and a young female in her '20s. As I watched the young female spread her rear legs, and a little gray bundle plopped down into a large puddle of water. Just seeing that event was remarkable … immediately pandemonium! Some trumpeted! And screamed, chasing each other around and around the bushes. Others ran in circles, ears spread out, urinating, defecating, and emitting long, loud guttural rumbles. They showed genuine excitement, and they were putting on a true celebration of birth. Into the chaos entered several large bulls, pushing their way to the center of the group to inspect the infant, sniffing it gently with their trunks…In the confusion mother got separated from baby, which I could see through all the legs splashing in the puddle. Then the matriarch took charge. Pushing her way toward the infant, head-butting the other elephants, and jabbing them with her tusks, she made a clearing around the baby that allowed the mother to close in. Together the matriarch and the mother pulled the little one to its feet with their trunks. It was a female, a tiny replica of an adult elephant."

Dosha the newly born; Dosha the young, the mother or the matriarch, always and ever female. Fisher knows this, is fascinated, cannot take his eyes off her and Dosha knows Fisher knows this, and loves him.

Detail from *The Battle of Samugarh.*.

■ REMBRANDT: Oh, I just made it up—Saskia's relatives had sued me claiming that I, and our children, and my nighttime friends, and our daytime guests and even my sweet Saskia *"had squandered her parent's legacy by ostentatious display, vanity and braggadocio."*

And the royal We replied that We *"were quite well off and were favored with a super-abundance of earthly possessions for which We can never express sufficient gratitude to the good Lord."*

In January 1639, we purchased with a loan of 13,000 gilders a palace on princely Jodenbreestraat not far from the house of my doctor—Ephriam Bonus—nor far from Duarte Rodrigues, chock-a-block by the family of de Pina's mother.

My mother was still alive. When she came to my house, I leapt from my etching stone, greeted her in my arms. Mother weak, almost dead, whispered: "My, my, and is that a Jewish cap you are wearing, my son. Have you become a Levantine?"

What did my mother know of the gentleman artist I had become? Closed lips to the world, lest sadness overwhelm me. "No mother, not a Levantine, though they understand grief better than I. The costume, I made it up. And my life from here, that too I will make up myself."

My mother's tiny eyes surveyed my studio filled with ermine wraps, felt hats, halberds, scepters, crowns of cut Prague glass piled on the floor and simply said: "The Lord will decide. Do not bring more death upon yourself." I felt Saskia's hand tremble in mine as she too eyed my mother. Within a year, our third born child perished, and Mother perished, and my fine embroidered felt cap fell from my head, and sadness nearly drowned me, but I held firm to my stone sill. While all about me sank.

Fisher blushed. More feeling than any Cambridge man, she thought.

"Oh, I just made it up. You're my first and sole interview."

Abigail had told Dosha at work that afternoon: "Fisher's going to make a move on you. I'll bet a ten dollar bill against a quarter."

■ DANIEL CHARDIN: blush—My Lord Governor and partner, Elihu Yale, would tell us in our own parlour that the money would be there.

He would arrange it with the widow Hynmers. Though she was married to Yale, she trembled at her first husband, Joseph's, memory. Had not all of us believed she had sinned with Elihu well before her husband, Joseph's death.

I threw my arms about Elihu's shoulders and said of course widow Hynmers would consent to Elihu's wishes, as she has always.

I slyly teased him but Elihu was not one to blush over a woman, any woman, wed or unwed, Catholic, Huguenot or Portuguese Jewess, in Hindustan, in Siam, in China or in England, nowhere on earth, and perhaps not in Heaven.

He shrugged his shoulders and repeated "We have come this far, Daniel, G-d will not permit us to stumble."

And one way or the other, with Tavernier or without Tavernier, with Hymners or without, with our blessed Lord or Heaven forbid with another, Yale would win out. A fine partner, Yale, but quite a dreadful foe.

■ ELIHU YALE: Fisher blushed—What does a young man do but blush? And what should I have done when Catherine Hynmers, the wife of the Second, the assistant to the Govenor of Ft. St. George, himself, walked by me with her four sons. Joseph Hynmers looked me full in the face. Ten years in India had made his wife brazen. What to do but blush. I left the Fort House and climbed into her bed and fortune, Catherine singing to me songs she no doubt serenaded the Second himself with, though now her second husband, what should I do but blush in the dark?

Each night before I went to her bed, for it had been hers first and second, and I, her second husband, would never be first. I would study the Baron of Aubonne's drawings, *Six Voyages to the East*. Gemstones blue and white. Pried from Golconda merchants' hands, and after awakening in the morning, leaving Catherine's bed, I would walk to my secret Hueguenot partner's house, book in hand.

I would open the page in Tavernier's book with diamonds as large as robin's eggs and press Daniel Chardin: "We must buy stones as these."

Chardin would coax me and say: "And how will we pay for them?" I would lower my eyes and say "I will speak to my lady Catherine."

Chardin said, "If you will provide the honey, I will provide the bee that will sting each merchant's humid hand in the Golconda mines—the master merchant himself.

With a flourish, Daniel would wrest Tavernier's book from my fingers and point at the merchant's picture. "My brother will write him and draw him post haste from his Aubonne retirement."

I was like a young jubilant bridegroom, blushing from head to toe.

◆ Simha Padawer: Should Dosha have told Fisher that it was her grandfather's fingernails that she remembered—My granddaughter Jerusha would stand before me on the eve of Yom Kippur. She was but six. I would rest my hands on her head.

It was my chance. I was not a Cohen but all Israel are Cohanim on that evening. I would intone softly in my broken English:

"On Rosh ha-Shanah it is written and on Yom Kippur it is sealed:

How many will pass away and how
Many will be created;
Who will live and who will die,
Who in due time and
Who not in due time;
Who by water and who by fire;
Who by sword and who by beast;
Who by tremor and who by plague…
But repentance, prayer, and righteous giving can avert the ill decree."

And my hand would shake and I would do this each Yom Kippur from when Jerusha was five, in my broken English, not broken in America but broken by the War.

For I could see before my eyes the swollen waters at the Balione Bridge, sweeping over the bridge's opening—Shlomo Chaim was shot and swept off the bridge.

I could feel the tremor and the plague. All of it: Slonim, Bereza, Stolin, the forests. And I could feel my wife Sareles' eyes on me, thinking, my G-d, Simha, Jerusha is only a girl.

Always as I came to the words "repentance," "prayer" and "righteous" giving, my miracle, each year renewed, would take my shaking hands off her forehead, and put her tiny palms on my fingernails and look at me with her wide eyes.

I would lower my eyes to my feet, for I knew that Jerusha was blessing me. Dosha will tell Fisher of my fingernails that she remembers, but not now, and not here, but at the very instant of the right moment and in the holiest of all holy places. Her two tiny hands, two witnesses of all trials I have suffered and all the blessings my children's children shall receive. G-d be praised.

Should Dosha have told Fisher that it was her grandfather's fingernails that she remembered, stretched out, palms down. And then inward and then outward again each week at the Havdallah service, signaling the end of the Sabbath.

Or was it her grandmother Sarah's fingernails over the braided candles for Havdallah, and her grandmother holding Dosha's hand in hers, squeezing it, as though to hold the memory forever. But memory is preserved in the eyes, not in the hands.

Should Dosha have told Fisher so soon—too soon, certainly not on a second date.

◆ Sarah Padawer: Her grandfather's fingernails—Simha's hands would shake so, and he would weep without stopping each Yom Kippur eve. He would go to Jerusha's bedroom and lay his hands on her forehead and bless her.

And that *unmensch*, Reuven's so called "wife" said from the doorway: "Oh mambo jumbo time, gramps, this is America. If we don't leave now for temple, we don't get a seat up front." But Simha would continue: *"Who by water and who by fire."*

And my Jerusha, how she loved us, would not move as Simha whispered through his tears: *"Teshuvah, Tefillah and Tzedakka"* will avert the evil decree.

And finally Reuven would come to the door and say: "Father, we really must go." Jerusha would put her hands on Simha's and say, "Grandpa, I will walk you to synagogue." Hand in hand they would go off, her hands covering her grandfather's fingernails.

Her goodness covering all the floods and the fires raging in his head throughout the year.

Once a year, each year, each would bless the other.

■ Jean-Baptiste Tavernier (1605–1689): Remembered—They pressed me, young Chardin, Daniel, and Sir John, his elder brother, far the more capable of the two. Together they were stronger than I. Sir John, like me: Knighted. Honored. Strung with medals. Fellow Huguenots, to be trusted, though if gold makes men mad, pearls and diamonds will turn a saint into the Devil himself.

"Come to Golconda," they sang. "Do you remember Hindustan." And could I, or would I, or should I have forgotten Hindustan?

I would look at Baffin's map, seated at my desk in Aubonne, hard by Geneva, as I wrote my *Six Voyages to the East*. I remember more clearly that rascal Doe's map than Baffin. Remember? I had not forgotten one facet on any Moghul stone my fingers had touched.

I did not dream of idleness. Did I care to live as young Daniel Chardin did in Fort St. George, a prince? Or as their partner the Englishman Yale did? Or as Salvador Rodrigues, a Jew late of Amsterdam, a Portuguese in Goa and a Hindu in Golconda and the Devil in wherever, Lord forbid, we may end up. Remember? Does one remember France when one is banished to England. Can anyone who saw Shah Jahan on his peacock's throne ever forget?

But in Aubonne, day after day, writing my memories, walking at dawn to the lake, what cared I for my barony? My own brother's son, yapping at my heels: "Do you remember Hindustan?" What should I tell my nephew? I am eighty? I am tired?

No fool like an old Baron. I sold it all—my lands, my barony, for an equipage that must be so splended that Sir John Chardin, Daniel Chardin, Yale and his Portuguese, the Nawab and even the Emperor himself should be startled as I raced back toward the Golconda youth of my dreams. Gems that kept my eyes from closing each night. And race I did, for at eighty I had but little time to remember.

■ Moses Benjamin, 18th century Baghdad Kabbalist: First date? . . . Can you help me?—What does it mean, first date? It means the time before which no time existed, no day moved forward. What does Fisher ask of Dosha? The same that Abraham wishes him to ask of her. The same that Tal wishes for himself from his Rachel, to begin the road of repentance through paths of prayer and charity that wind through Holy Jerusalem and end in everlasting joy.

"Everyone must prepare themselves thirty days before with Teshuvah, prayer and charity for the day when they will appear in judgment before G-d on Rosh HaShanah. Those who interpret the Torah metaphorically say the Hebrew initials of Ani Le-dodi Ve-dodi Li, I am my beloved and my beloved is mine (Canticles 6:3) when read consecutively read the month of Elul. "If Israel will long to turn in a complete Teshuvah, repentance, to the Father who is in heaven, then G-d's longing will go out to them and the Almighty will accept them in Repentance."

Before one starts to repent there is no movement, no time. Will Dosha and Fisher reach Jerusalem? Tal did not nor did my wife and children who perished in an epidemic—may G-d approach them both as they, Dosha and Fisher, approach G-d—and may they all be sanctified under a Jerusalem wedding canopy.

■ Imre Emes, the Gerer Rebbe: Tal created—Tal is the teacher. He knows Europe from before the War. He has dreamt of the life that was. By night and by day. None of us can forget what was. Now Tal is with his student. Creating. Advising her how to rebuild the House of Israel. He is reading from an ancient text, reading to himself because Dosha cannot read the holy text. But who knows what will come from the union of Dosha and Fisher. After the War, I wrote to my Hasidim in America. *"I appeal to you all now at such a time as Israel has never known since becoming a nation, the nation of G-d. In order to overcome all the troubles that have befallen us, we must be strong. We must place our faith in G-d, that he will now deal mercifully with us, showing us His loving kindness and His salvation. For this does the wisest of all men, Solomon, teach. 'In the days of prosperity be joyful and in the days of adversity reflect (Koheles 7:14).' That is to say, that from one's happy times one should draw strength for hard times, G-d forbid. So too when difficult times come, we should reveal the good days of the past, when G-d wrought salvation and showed us his long kindness. That is what is meant by the phrase: 'In the day of adversity, reflect.' In the day of adversity one should look back at the good days that have passed, and that will yet return. These days of evil have now passed over us; we must hope that from now on good days are awaiting us."*

Tal would have Dosha tell a tale of childhood. Happy before the War. The unspeakable evil during the War. Wandering like gypsies, which of us did not feel abandoned by our Father, G-d forbid.

But in the remembrance of joy, even during the greatest of adversity to come, Dosha and Fisher, and countless others, all Israel, shall we not all, please G-d, live in Peace and dance in Joy in a Holy Jerusalem?

When he later asked her when their "first date" had been, Dosha had answered him with the promptness of Abraham—"Oh when you asked me, 'Can you help me.'"

Should Dosha tell him more of her Tal-created gypsy father? And of Ceneda? And the plate, and the glass and ceiling?

If I look into Fisher's eyes, I'll laugh myself silly, she thinks. He doesn't believe a word of it.

Though these tears that I've shed are real, how can it be I've never acted in a play? Not even in the third grade. Oh no, Mother wouldn't allow it.

■ Laurence Sterne: Tal created—To Tal, no one is more beautiful than Dosha. Is he seeing her? His posture frozen. Before she enters his shop, after he leaves. His Dosha, my Eliza.

"I leaned the whole day with my head upon my hand; sitting most dejectedly at the table with my Eliza's picture before me—sympathizing and soothing me."

"Indeed, indeed Eliza! My life will be little better than a dream, till we approach nearer to each other—I live scarse conscious of my existence—or as if I wanted a vital part; & I could not live above a few hours."

Is Eliza Reverend Sterne created? A flower of my mind? Dosha too, is she an emerald-flower headed amaranth carved and created by Reverend Tal, too pure created for these northern climes.

■ Van Gogh: her Tal-created father . . . if I look into . . . eyes, I will laugh myself silly—The old man Tal has created a gypsy father for the young woman Dosha. He has told her a tale but when she tells it to her beau she will come to believe it too even if her young beau doesn't.

For old Tal is wise and is preparing her for her travels. Travel is in her blood. Gypsy no less. Though I would think being an Israelite was travel enough.

"I always feel I am a traveler, going somewhere and to some destination. If I tell myself that the somewhere and the destination do not exist, that seems to me very reasonable and likely enough. When the brothel bouncer kicks anyone out, he has a similar logic, argues well too, and is always right, I know. So at the end of my career, if I shall prove to be wrong. So be it. Then I shall find not only the arts but everything else were only dreams that one was nothing at all oneself . . . then the doctors will tell us that not only Moses, Mahomet, Christ, Luther, Bunyan and others were mad, but Franz Hals, Rembrandt, Delacoix too, and also all the dear narrow-minded old women like our mother. Ah, that's a serious matter, one might ask these doctors: Who then are the sane people? Are they the brothel bouncers who are always right?"

If Dosha looks young Fisher in the eye, he will not believe her and she will not believe herself. But she looks into her own eyes. Her own eyes give him his own white canvas to see its mirror image. His own eyes, looking. Each will then believe the other. Silly how simple, how deep it all is. Always.

■ LAURENCE STERNE: Father always absent—Father always absent even though he was always there. For where was . . . Mother. My dear Wife, Elizabeth. Waiting for me *"to preach, to show the extent of our wit, to parade . . . with accounts of learning, tinseled over with glitter and convey less light and less warmth. For my own part . . . I had rather direct five words point blank to the heart."*

I was ever there. For were not my characters speaking to me aloud and plain as the coat nail on the wall:

"Amen," shouted Trim in my ear loud enough for Elizabeth to hear, and certainly for Lydia with her young ears.

"'The Inquisition is the vilest—I have a poor brother who has been fourteen years a captive in—I never heard one word of it before,' said my uncle Toby hastily in a voice so loud my dear daughter bounded down the stairs.

'O sir,' cried Trim to my entire household. 'My brother Tom went over a servant to Lisbon and then married a Jew's widow, who kept a small shop, and sold sausages, which somehow or other was the cause of his being taken in the middle of the night out of his bed, where he was lying with his wife and G-d help him . . . and tears trickled down Trim's cheeks. A dead silence in the room ensued for some minutes."

Dear, sweet Elizabeth and sweetest Lydia and Corporal Trim and Uncle Toby and ever Dr. Slop silent, and I wept and wept, always there.

■ JAMES JOYCE: Father always absent even though he was always there—In my *Portrait of the Artist:*

"Mr. Tate read out a sentence from Stephen's weekly theme: here. It's about the Creator and the soul. Rrm . . . trm . . . ah! Without a possibility of ever approaching never. That's heresy Joyce."

I already knew: When I was a boy of nine, Father might as well have been a gypsy. Always absent even though he was always there.

"Ireland is the old sow that eats her farrow."

Father and son. Twiddledee and dumb. Father always absent. *"'Poor Parnell!' my father cried loudly. 'My dead King!'"* From Dublin to Cork, my gypsy father, pleading for Parnell. And when I die, will He be there? Not so tidy as it was for little Jim:

The cottage was a thatched one,
Its outside old and mean.
But everything within that cot
Was wondrous neat and clean.

And dying Jim's parents praying for him:

"In heaven once more to meet their own poor little Jim. Wait for Father. Better to wait with my Barnacle, who waits for her absent Father and feel her breasts all perfumed yes."

"Greater love than this, he said, no man hath that a man lay down his wife for a friend. Go thou and do likewise."

Too bourgeois. No daughter of mine. Etc. Etc. And Father might as well have been a gypsy. Always absent even though he was there.

Where was Mom? Out. Marching, stapling fliers, telephoning from the Club's headquarters. Population. Hunger. Guatemala. You name it, she'd be there.

"Your mother will be in later," Dad would say. "But call me Father."

"How patriarchal," Mom would say to Dosha. "Call me Suzanna, *moste vertuous and G-dlye.* Aren't we great friends?"

■ ELIZABETH STERNE, Laurence Sterne's wife: No daughter of mine. Etc. Etc. Father always absent even though he was always there— *My husband (and I use the many) were always absent, for Laurence was not of a single part, but of many parts, his lips would move and the words from our Uncle Toby would roll off his tongue. Alarming it was for Lyd and for me.*

How should our daughter wed a gentleman and a purse at the instant? "No daughter of mine," Laurence would thunder, "will settle for less than our dream." But surely Laurence meant Col. Trim's and his brother Toby's dream. Not our dream.

And Lyd *"fizzled."* At being in Paris. *"I wish Lyd may ever remain a child of nature. . . . I hate children of art."*

What to do with Lyd. For was she not truly a child of art and I a wife of art?

Even in our chateau in Avignon, a continent away from old Bond Street where Laurence dwelled he wrote Panchaud our banker.

"My daughter has an advantageous offer just now at Marseilles, he has 20,000 livres a year and much at his ease. So I suppose Mademoiselle with Madame ma femme will negotiate the affair."

Copy to me, of course. Laurence, always absent even though he was always there.

■ NORA JOYCE: Always absent—In July 1911, I returned in triumph to Ireland. "Italian speaking child Geogie Porgie image of Jim," said John Joyce himself. We all sent postcards to Him who was absent. In Trieste less than a dozen Austrian crowns in our royal account.

Jim always absent even though he was always there writing me back *"Having left me five days without a word of news, you scribble your signature with a number of others on a postcard. Not one word of the places in Dublin where I met you and which have so many memories for us both!*

I can neither sleep nor think. I have still the pain in my side. Last night I was afraid to lie down. I thought I would die in sleep. What are Dublin and Galway compared with our memories? Jim."

That's Jim for you. When I am in Dublin, he cannot sleep nor think but of me and when I am with him, he dreams of Dublin.

■ Max Brod: Long lost friends—"*I returned to Prague in June 1964 to see my long lost friends Eduard Goldstücker and Arnost Kolman in Frantisek Langer's home.*

Kolman was an elegant mathematician, and a Marxist philosopher to boot. In Frantisek's home he could not resist to remark that there were the four types of Czech Jews: Goldstücker, who tried to revive the study of German literature into Czech. Langer, a playwright and novelist who tried to have Jews assimilate into the Czech language and culture, myself, who argued that Czech Jews should form their own nation, Zion, and emigrate to the Holy Land, and finally Kolman himself, who argued as a Bolshevik that only communism held the proper answer for Czech Jews."

I waited and said, "Yet there were two more paths. That of Alfred Fuchs, who converted to Catholicism only to perish in Dachau, and finally, finally, Jiri Langer who went to the East to the court of the Belzer Rebbe, to become a Hassid.

I once asked Jiri, why to the East? And he replied, "The greatest Rabbi of us all, the Maharal, went to the East to Polish Posen. Was he not sent there by mad Rudolph? For Rudolph believed that the Hoch Rabbi Loew could create a golem and the Maharal knew he couldn't so he went to the East toward Chelm, where Elijah of Chelm—blessed be his name that used the ineffable name—had truly created a golem. Only after three years did Jiri permit himself to return. Jiri, like us all, searched to create a golem, one that could protect us all, but, alas, it was not to be found in Prague.

"Are you saying that Jiri then is to be the Chief Rabbi of Prague!" shouted Kolman with Bolshevik fervor.

"Oh no," I protested with my wry Prague sensibility not lost in the forty years wandering in the wilderness of Tel Aviv. "Oh no, our Chief Rabbi remains Franz Kafka, the greatest German stylist, a passionate lover of Milena's Czech charms, a champion of the people—accident prevention methods, workers' insurance—forever entranced by Dora Dyamant's longing for Zion."

Franz Kafka—containing all of us within himself—like his namesake grandfather Amschel, he himself Elijah of Chelm, each day writing his own name with his own blood, on a piece of paper inserted in his own mouth. Poor, magnificent Franz, our chief golem and Chief Rabbi—forever.

"And what will you have?" the waiter had asked Fisher, looking at Dosha all the while.

"Not the check. And not another beverage but here, my good man, extend your hand."

The waiter did, and Fisher put a two dollar bill on the waiter's open palm and the waiter disappeared a half hour, only to ask each half hour how they were and what they wanted.

Fisher must have brought a stack of two dollar bills from one of the coin dealers near Tal's office, thought Dosha.

Charming really. And clever, cheaper than drink and more effective than food, for had they eaten and drunk, they would have had to go home. Talking hour after hour—quite different from all of those Cambridge dates at 44 Brattle where Le Dauphin couldn't wait to make his move, and was not a patch on Fisher.

■ Franz Kafka: Grandfather—"*In Hebrew I am called Amschel like my mother's maternal grandfather, whom my mother remembers as a very devout and learned man with a long white beard. She was six years old when he died and remembers that she had to hold the toes of the corpse and to ask to be forgiven for anything she might have done to offend him. She also remembers her grandfather's many books, which filled the walls of his room. Every day he bathed in the river and even in the winter he would cut a hole in the ice. My mother's mother died early of typhoid. From that day onward her grandmother became melancholy, refused to eat, spoke to no one. Then, a year after her daughter's death, she went for a walk and did not return.*"

■ Maharal of Prague, Judah Loew ben Bezalel Der Hoche Rabbi Lowe: Long lost friends—On the third day of Adar, 5352, by their reckoning 16 February 1592, Emperor Rudolph II called me to the Palace.

At the time I entered the Palace there came into my mind two sentences:

His Majesty was standing in front of a drawing. Behind the royal head appeared apples, pears and other fruits I did not know the name of. Meshullam Maisel had spoken to me of the drawings—do not look for a moment at the walls—for you may G-d forbid begin to shiver or even worse, begin to laugh. Their world is not our world, at least not until the Messiah shall arrive. And if he or the "gabbai", as Meshullam called him, the valet of the Emperor, is by his side, do not say anything—not a word—until the Emperor has dismissed him with a wave of the royal hand. Does one speak if a snake lies coiled before one's leg? Never. Wait, Reb Loew, until the gabbai is sent back to his cage.

But I was prepared and I was not prepared for the scene: the Emperor frozen in front of his self portrait and by his side, frozen, but poised to bite, his valet—teeth glistening with a half smile.

"What do you wish to say to the Emperor?" the Emperor's valet asked.

"Blessed be the name of the Creator who shares his glory with kings," I said.

And I thought, One makes a blessing upon seeing a king. But some will argue that the Emperor of the Hapsburg is not king of Bohemia nor even a man, such is the diverseness of reality each human intelligence understands. "Each one receives one aspect of reality in accordance with his lot."

With a wave of his hand, the Emperor dismissed his valet, who seemed to crawl out more like a dog than a human and suddenly disappeared behind a framed picture that had hidden a tiny door in the corner of the palace.

Rudolph said: "Good. Your words are fine. Spoken like putti. Let us take a stroll."

We walked about his palace, each room crowded with paintings, vessels of gold, caskets of jewels. I could hear footsteps on the other side of the wall.

I do not know if the footsteps were of his "adviser" valet van Langenfels, baptised as a youth, or of Langenfels' predeccessor, for they all looked and dressed alike but there was an echo to our steps, angelic or demonic, I do not know.

We walked and walked. And walked yet more. Did I speak? If I could not speak of what I spoke of to my wife or to my son-in-law, how should I speak to Gans or even to Meshullam Maisels?

Ich hut spatzirer I went walking with the king, walking, walking. I kept repeating to Maisels as he pressed me for more details. But when Meshullam could not fish from my mouth more details, he said with a faraway look in his eyes. Hut iz der zeit for spatziven nach Posen. Now is the time to take a walk to Posen. I did and only when Maisels bade me return did I, after several years, to die peacefully in my beloved Prague.

■ SALVADOR RODRIGUES: Boys will be…—"You're a fine one to call me a boy, and not a man, Hieronyma. Let's both return on the Abigail to London. I'll tell my tale of my Hindu wives at Golconda. And of all the diamond rough I've purchased near the Godvari river at Kollur, all of the stones, hidden, swallowed, secreted, bartered, lost to thieves, a diary of sweat, dream and lost hopes. I'll tell my tale and let the Bet Din in Shearit Israel hear both our tales in Portuguese, or Ladino or even in your master Elihu Yale's, lord of Madras, perfect English and as G-d is my witness, either you will be called a wayward girl and I a naughty boy or both of us a man and a woman, more to be pardoned and pitied than mocked. But do I care what Manuel Levy Duarte or sanctimonious Abraham Salvador say in our temple in London or in belle Amsterdam? I do not. For if Duarte had come here, to this hot land of Goshen, he would have taken ten wives to every one I have been gifted with. If his wife had come here, as you have, with him and her husband had perished, as your husband did, and G-d is my witness, a purer Jew than Jacques de Paiva never breathed. Jacques lovingly cut the diamond roses himself from the rough diamonds that came from Golconda. He matched them with rubies and pearls he bought from Antonio Rodrigues Marques—He must have owed him a fortune for them. He gave you these gems set cunningly in the finest pendant earrings any Queen could dream of.

Jacques brought a Sefer Torah to Hindustan. He illuminated our darkness here with his lovely silver chanukah lamp. He purchased a burial plot for our nation at *Peddenaipetam*.

And then he died. If that same Rachel Duarte had journeyed here and been widowed she would have born ten children to Master Yale to your one. Have our elders sent for you or me, for that matter, to Amsterdam, to London, to Barbados or to Recifé? They have forgotten us!"

By then I found that I was screaming at Hieronyma. Suddenly I stopped shouting and looked at dear Hieronyma. She seemed so tiny.

I heard her whisper: "What if I had died? My blessed Jacob, would he have taken another into my bed?"

We both wept in each other's arms. So far were we from home, from love, from everything.

Men will be…whatever. But boys will always be boys. And what does Tal want of me? Always talking about his Rachel, and his mother Rachel and of my Rachel in years to come, always in years to come.

And of his Ring of Blue and of our Ring of Blue. Why did I listen to Tal? I should have followed Abigail's advice: "Never plan, but keep your eyes open. Just like the dear Dauphin, all men, always cajoling. They are the princes of love aren't they, those French frogs."

Dosha had burst into laughter.

But the more obscure, the better the tale, Tal had insisted.

■ SHITAO: Men—Men will be men. And will be seen as men. And painted as men. "I am always myself and must naturally be present in whatever I do. The beards and the eyebrows of the ancients will not grow on my face, and the lungs and bowels of the ancients cannot be put into my body. I give vent to my own lungs and bowels, and I present my own whiskers and brows. If at some time my paintings happen to bear resemblance to those of some other man, it is he who copies me. I do not try to copy him."

■ ELIHU YALE: Men will be…—When Thomas Pitt, or Diamond Pitt as he came to be known, came to my house on the north side in July 1698—not hours after his ship Martha put into Fort St. George, Madras, he stumbled about the hall of my mansion and said, "I have not come to the heat of Hindustan to bake here. Let's go immediately to the coolness of your garden villa, Elihu."

Pitt was "a fellow of haughty huffing, daring temper." And if I did not move to be his host, he would have let himself into my home with the greatest of dispatch.

So we went. In the middle of the night. And we spoke until dawn. "*A thousand a year*," Pitt kept repeating. "*And you can become a member of Parliament. Here, my dear friend Elihu, you will never be more than a boy. Elihu, this damned heat will stifle your growth.*" Ten thousand pounds and your daughter can claim any lord in Christendom, and on and on.

"And why have you returned then, Thomas?" I asked him. "To get yet more thousands—diamonds—noble caratage to invigorate your heirs and house forever."

Pitt looked at the two bedrooms off the garden where we sat drinking toddy for want of beer. He slyly smiled at the two bedrooms, one with green shutters which Elizabeth Nicks would stay in and one with blue shutters which was the Portuguese Hieronyma's and he looked at me bemused and said, " Elihu, my lad, is this what keeps you from going back to Mother England, you besotted boy, my lord boys will be boys and men will be men."

I said to Diamond Pitt simply, "I do not fear becoming a man in England. I tremble to become an old man."

■ KAFKA: Tale—Tal is talking about writing a book, each day, of Dosha's future. For no old man can write of himself. Dosha is not reading any of this book for which young woman has the time to read a memoir of her life while she is still furiously living it?

I could always write and ever read the tale of my own life but was I not old while young? "*Altogether I think we ought to read only books that bite and sting us. If the book we are reading doesn't shake us awake like a blow on the skull, why bother reading it in the first place? So that it can make us happy, as you put it? Good G-d, we'd be just as happy if we had no books at all; books that make us happy we could, in a pinch, also write ourselves. What we need are books that hit us like a most painful misfortune, like the death of someone we loved, more than we love ourselves, that make us feel as though we had been banished to the woods, far from any human presence, like a suicide. A book must be an axe for the frozen sea within us.*"

■ CONSTANTIJN HUYGENS THE YOUNGER (1628–1697): Painting—"Not a patch on his father," my father would say. "Gaspar Duarte, jeweler in ordinary to Charles I and a fine musician. Not even a patch on his grandfather Diego Duarte."

What did Duarte do as I paced, nay raced, to catch up with him as he sped down the halls of his much too grand house—more palace—and weren't they all the same, those Portuguese? Ten floors of paintings and a cellar full of jewels or stark empty for you never went down there, only they and their sons and their daughters.

Fine they were old Gaspar's daughters, Catarina, Francisca and Isabel. My father would always smile when he mentioned Gaspar's house, "Oh yes, Gaspar and his treasures, his art and his daughters." Then Father would pronounce their names slowly and pause after each, recalling Isabel, picturing Francisca, painting Catarina in his mind. "As close to marrying a prince as these two fingers are," said Father, holding up his index and middle fingers and waving them slowly before my eyes.

What did I want of Duarte but that he should accompany me to visit Vermeer of Delft. When I compared Vermeer to whichever picture we passed, a Raphael or a Titian, Duarte's eyes didn't wander once from gazing at his treasures on the wall.

He was a strange fish Duarte, silent, ice cold. Never to marry, unless he could divorce himself from his father's—old Gaspar's—painting and grandfather Diego Duarte's jewels.

"Vermeer is one of us!" I shouted to Duarte. He was already in the velvet room, as my father would call it, staring at his Holbeins. "He is one of us," I repeated even louder. Duarte turned ashen and said, "What do you mean one of us?"

"You," I said, putting my hand on Duarte's shoulder. "He loves music. Light. Women," I said with a twinkling smile. "Old and young."

But Duarte did not smile nor move, nor even breathe. "What do you mean," he repeated with an odd weariness.

And I said, not removing my hand from his shoulder, "Duarte, Vermeer, the master of Delft, of Holland, and in my opinion, all painters. He is a Catholic like all of us."

Duarte looked down at his feet, and I could see his left hand start to quiver. "Then I guess it is time for us to go to Delft," he said in a child's voice.

But still it took me more than a year to arrange the visit.

Dosha felt Fisher's head on her back. He listened to her body so hard that he could hear her blood coursing through her.

His eyes hadn't wandered once at the White Horse. She knew she could count on him. Who knows how or why it should be thus. But it was. She'd stake more than ten dollars. She'd stake everything.

When Fisher told her he had gone to Yale, and paused to see her reaction, she had countered: "What's your favorite painting in the Art Gallery?" He said, "The Night Café. All my life I've been in a haze and I can't find my way out." Dosha brushed her hair back with her right hand keeping him in her sight, and said evenly: "Take my hand and I'll lead you to the exit. You can't see it. It's directly behind you." It was Fisher's chance to talk. "How do you know?" Dosha responded: "I'm a painter." With the most marvelous of smiles, Fisher rested his hand on hers and said, "Whither thou goest, I go. Forever."

More than she can trust even herself, she can trust his passion 'til the end of time, he will stay with her if she wants him to. From dusk's gloaming to daybreak's white.

■ DIEGO DUARTE II (1616–1691): Painting—Constantijn Huygens the younger had prepared me well. "Vermeer is one of us, Duarte. A lover of music. Of light. Of the glint in a woman's eye. His paintings are fit for princes' palaces. He is one of us. You must meet him. I will take you to him." Each time Constantijn paused, and he paused twice as long as his father to show he was Constantijn Huygens the younger and the wiser, I thought of my father Gaspar Duarte and my mother Rachel Salom. He told me clearly: "To princes we are jewelers, to jewelers we are princes of art."

For a picture is the honey that draws the prince. And the queen, shall she not follow? Huygens' eyes did not wander from my walls as he paced by my walls, walking by my Rubens, Van Dyck, and my Pieter Brueghel the Elder.

"Vermeer is one of us. One of us—you must meet him."

What shall I tell the younger? What my father Gaspar would have told his father Huygens the Elder: Nothing. For if I began to speak of Vermeer, I would finish by ending my life. "Think everything. Say nothing," my father Gaspar would whisper to me, ever and always. I walked about the corridors—each lined with pictures—I let Huygens the younger breathe the air and drink the water: the Rubens and Van Eycks in my indoor garden.

I said nothing.

■ JOHN CHARDIN: Yale—Men will be men and boys will be boys. Everywhere and anywhere. When we Huguenots were banished by the revocation of the Edict of Nantes, 1685, our rights revoked, our freedom seized, our boys held onto their mother's skirts and our men plotted revenge as they floated, flotsam and jetsam over the Seven Seas to the west and as far east as the Indies. The Armenian nation that I settled in Madras—did the boys not cling to their mother's skirts, dreaming of their far away birth place? Did not the Portuguese Jewish men speak of Lisboa and Jerusalem in their sleep? I spoke enough Persian to speak of the Muhammaden and the Hindu too. All the same, I kept telling Elihu Yale, "they all love their mothers and dream of their native land." Even Elihu, with his cold merchant's heart, longs for his Wales. Elihu would misquote me to all, to Mrs. Nicks, to Madame de Paiva, to my brother Daniel. Boys and men praise the Lord, all desire diamonds.

◆ SARAH PADAWER, DOSHA'S GRANDMOTHER: Earnest—Even as a child, our granddaughter Jerusha, whom I called Sha-Sha, she was so earnest, and my son Reuben called Dosha for his wife said "If you call her Dorothea Jerusha, I will leave you" and she did anyway or he left her first or they both left, it didn't matter what he called our little Jerusha Sha-Sha. Reuben couldn't call her Jerusha and he couldn't call her Dorothea. So there you have it—in America everyone calls each by a different name but she doesn't change; our granddaughter, she presses her friend with a question not with an answer. Just as when I would wrap my arms about her and ask how she was with all the screaming in her house. Her mother never stopped shouting and Reuben never talking, which was worse. Sha-Sha would look into my eyes, and press her lips on my cheeks and whisper, "Bubbeh, tell me another tale of when you lived in Slonim with the snow higher than your house."

■ STEPHEN C. CLARK, heir to Singer sewing machine fortune: Hopper—A dealer came to my office with a painting wrapped up in a white beach towel. "I've got a portrait study of you by the American painter Hopper."

"I've never sat for a Hopper," I said sharply and gestured for the dealer to leave my office. "Oh but you did. It was the spring before you entered college. You were waiting for your acceptance letter and your father brought it to you in your cottage on the Cape." And with that, the dealer unfurled the beach towel off of the canvas. I stared long and hard at the painting. Waves of color crossed my eyes. It was eerily still, yet full of movement.

"I don't get the portrait story."

"Surely, you do," the dealer parried. "Father brought you the letter. The door to the beach was open. You were white as a sheet before opening the letter. If Boola Boola turned you down, you might as well jump into the ocean. But hurrah, you made it. Joining the class of '03. Well son, you're in. Now you're an Old Blue. Just jump into the water and sink or swim."

I couldn't stop laughing. That canny fox of a dealer, right on the mark about how I felt. Shouting, I asked him the price and said, "OK, but throw in the towel." I handed him a check for just 90% of what he said, leaving him to think I was a bit deaf. He took it and disappeared. I left that painting in my office, resting next to the window, on the same towel for ten years.

I never ceased to see something new in it each time I looked at it. Quite beautiful it was. And one day I decided: My portrait belongs at Yale. And I went with it in its "towel" carrying case. They hung it the very day I brought it—gingerly handing me back the towel. "Mr. Clark, this is yours as a souvenir." That young woman curator who had my wife's eyes said to me.

Funny thing, I took the towel back to my office and left it by the window. In my mind's eye, I could perfectly visualize my portrait still nestling on the towel, although it had decamped to Yale.

CHAPTER 3

"WHITE is what I see," Nina Abigail Coggeshall said to Dosha.

"What else?"

"Green. Blue. A rhomboid of blue, a parallelogram of green. But white through all."

"What am I supposed to see, Hopper?" asked Nina earnestly, tossing her blonde hair, which flowed down her shoulders onto her right side. She tilted her hand and looked sideways at the painting.

How could Nina always instantly understand her paintings, thought Dosha. The two of them laughing. It couldn't have been at Radcliffe playing "The Mad Woman of Chaillot." Lord knows Dosha just had to see every performance of Nina's although then she was always Abby, as in the Abbey theater.

"Nina, stop *tumling* for a moment. You'll hurt yourself. These floors have splinters."

Nina froze. "Oh stop the presses. It's a Magritte. Or a 'Boy Dolly.'" Her name for Salvador Dali. "Yes, that's it. A lampshade without an electric source. No light bulb. Heaven forbid. For aren't we all Sue Chow or Sooooo Chow as you pronounce it darling Dosha in Ming Ming."

◆ SIMHA PADAWER, DOSHA'S GRANDFATHER: What else?—My granddaughter is the Rebbetzin and her friend Nina is her Hasid. My granddaughter has painted a picture. Her friend is asking her what it means.

But Jerusha, my grandchild, is a true guide. She encourages, does not contradict or G-d forbid, argue but says gently "What else?" pressing her friend to find the answer within herself.

"Rabbi Azriel Hurwitz, hearing the Lubliner say he was not a 'Rebbe' asked him:

'If you are not a Rebbe, why do you teach thousands to follow in your footsteps?'

'What else can I do?' replied the Lubliner, 'They refuse to leave unless I give them instruction.'

'Then tell them you are not Rebbe and they will leave you,' said Rabbi Hurwitz.

The Lubliner promised to do so. Later, he met Rabbi Hurwitz and told him that the more he humbled himself, the more followers clung to him.'"

My granddaughter has the gift. Those who speak with her follow her. Not only her intended, Fisher. She does not hold herself as a guide, but all who come across her path stay close to her. My Sarale and I, did we not become her Hasidim? Did she not bring us back to life after the War and her parents too? And not only in her life time. But afterward, too. A guide to children's children's children. Others too, a miracle she is.

■ SITTING BULL, THE OGLALA: White is what I see— "When the transcontinental telegraph line went through along the Overland Trail in 1861, Oscar Collister came to operate the station at Deer Creek, up above Fort Laramie." Then I was called Drum Packer but to my enemies I was still Sitting Bull. White is what I saw, everywhere. In Deer Creek, in Fort Laramie, Napoleon's campaigns in a book I borrowed from the post library at the fort. White is what I heard on the tap tap machine that Collister taught me how to use. "Imagine the consternation if they knew at the other end it was a fighting Sioux sending them a message." He roared with laughter as I sent out my daily report. White is what I would read—black and white—when I'd order my newspaper with a lead bullet scratching my signature, a haunched bull with a man's head. White was everywhere. Soon, too soon, the Pawnee I fought, every last not white thing would simply vanish.

■ SITTING BULL, THE BAD, THE HUNKPAPA (1831–1890): White is what I see—White is what I don't see. Why should I look at them? "My Father died in battle and was left by the Whites on a scaffold up on Cedar Creek, off the Cannonball River." They are horse eaters, the Whites, fleeing before my eyes—the Powder River expedition—to punish our people. I do not need the white man's gift of tabacco. I do not need to see the Great White Father's teepee in Washington. I do not need to see him in the fort. Or anywhere. I do not choose to see him. Should the White Man's hand force my eyes open, the Great Spirit will carry me into a sleep that will outlast each and every White Man's life. When the Hunkpapa awaken, only I, the Hunkpapa and the buffalo will see each other.

47

Edward Hopper, *Rooms by the Sea.*

■ ABRAHAM b. Mordechai (Or Ha-hammah) the Zohar: Roll—"I am dark but comely. O ye daughters of Jerusalem. This means that when she [the moon] is very lovesick for her beloved, she shrinks to nothing until only a dot is left of her."

Is not the moon rolling toward Dosha? Around and around her, the moon is singing to Dosha as she becomes smaller and yet smaller.

A moon of yesteryear. Dosha speaks to her of her beloved who is coming.

And he is.

"Once, when R. Isaac and R. Judah were on a journey, they came to a place called Kfar Sachnin, where Rab Hamnuna the Elder used to live. They put up at the house of his wife. She had a young son who was still at school, and when he came from school and saw the strangers, his mother said to him: 'Go up to these distinguished gentlemen that you may obtain a blessing from them.' He began to approach but suddenly turned back, saying to his mother: 'I do not want to go hear them because they have not recited the shema this day.'"

That Yanuka is the right one for her. For both of them. For all of us. And these women, are they not the moon itself?

■ SPOTTED TAIL: Talk—White is what I saw. But Red Cloud did not see white. He only saw himself. He had burnt their fort. Like dogs, the whites had fled Ft. Kearney. Taunting them as they fled, Red Cloud danced and drank in the smoke of Ft. Kearney as it burned. But what of the other forts?

Where were the buffalo? Could Red Cloud bring them back too? And the ammunition the hostiles got. For how many winters will they last? Red Cloud does not hate whites. Rather he loves himself. Sitting Bull, the Hunkpapa, hates himself, for he realizes that he cannot hate the whites forever. Red Cloud is a blind man who cannot see himself, and certainly not the whites. Of course, Red Cloud would want to come to Washington to see and talk to the Great White Father. All he could see was white. And I, I too had to go. The whites were soft, but they were not stupid. Did I care if the whites thought Red Cloud the leader of all the Sioux? For did I care what the whites thought? Only what they did concerned me. But Red Cloud, he needed more than a carriage, he needed even more than the horses the white man gave me to ride about Washington. His hunger no white man would even dream to feed.

By now Nina had rolled onto the loft floor toward the painting, talking as she rolled. Her blonde hair over her face, her long legs, one half-cocked behind her torso, the other in front of her, Harry Lloyd climbing a clock and Nina repeating over and over again: "Ming, Ming, Ming, Ming." Between giggles: "Sing, sing, sing, sing Ming."

"Stop it!' shouted Dosha, still shaking with laughter. "I must be crazy to be rooming with you."

Nina jumped to her feet, and with one acrobatic motion dove onto the bed directly behind her.

"You're not my roommate anymore, you're my ex-roomie. You're my college roommate. You're my prep school wheezing rheumate. But you are not in any way, shape, color, nuance, my current roommate. Unless you want to drop Mr. Right, Rafaello Fisher, and come live with me as in days of Shepard Street Briggs Hall yesteryear."

"I thought you liked Fisher?"

"Oh I do, but I don't have my Mr. Right just yet, so I thought we could talk together and wait for our lads to gallop into our movie at the very same instant."

■ HAYYIM VITAL: Mr. Right—Fisher has come to Dosha and she is the right one for him. She shall be the grace to complete the pleasure of their feasts together.

They shall sing together.

But Dosha, is she not also the Yanuka for her companion Nina? As it is written and R. Isaac and R. Judah "were dumbfounded, and could say nothing. R. Judah asked the boy what was the name of his father. The boy was silent for a moment, then went to his mother and kissed her saying, 'Mother, those wise men have asked me the name of my father, shall I tell them?'"

Fisher has asked Dosha her father's name and his dwelling place.

"And the yanuka's mother said: 'Have you tested them?'" Fisher is being tested. Only through being tested will he become, himself and not another or, G-d forbid, one unformed.

In this young woman's generation, stars can be seen but faintly over her city, the moon itself, but a pale withered version of Safed's crescent, like our learning before our master Isaac Luria arrived, but Dosha will whisper into Fisher's ear. "The Yanuka's mother then whispered and the yanukah returned to R. Isaac and R. Judah and said, 'You asked about my father. He has departed this world, but wherever holy saints travel on the road, he follows them in the form of a peddler."

They are all, the two women, Fisher and the other lad, all galloping on the very same road.

■ RED CLOUD: Gallop—When I see it, I ride. On the 21 December 1866 I wiped out Fetterman and captured Fort Kearney. "The Bozeman forts were dismantled. A new treaty was signed." I, and not Spotted Tail, defeated the White Nation. I forced the soldiers to leave Powder River. I did not rush in to beg for axes, knives and blankets from the White Men, even when the lodges of the Bad Faces led by Little Hank, the uncle of Crazy Horse, came in. Only when the troops galloped away from Fort Phil Kearney and we set fire to it, would I come in to sign the treaty. Feed them or fight them, the friends of the Indians had proclaimed. I fought and I was the victor. Now I would order the Whites. Either feed us or we will fight you again. Whatever Spotted Tail felt or said, it was I whom the Whites saw. And feared. Not him.

Bada Shanren, *Flower, Buddha's Hand Citron, Hibiscus and Lotus Pod.*

■ GROUCHO MARX: Elephant—"*I shot an elephant in my pajamas. How an elephant got in my pajamas, I just can't imagine.*"

■ JOHN GODFREY SAXE (1877–1953), Elephant—

It was six men in Industan
to learning much inclined
who went to see the elephant
(though all of them were blind)
that each by observation
might satisfy his mind.

The first approached the elephant
and happening to fall
against his broad and sturdy,
at once began to bawl:
'G-d bless me!' But the elephant
is very like a wall…

The sixth no sooner had begun
about the beast to grope,
than, seizing on the swinging tail
that fell within his scope,
'I see," quoth he, 'the elephant
is very like a rope.'

And so these men of Industan
disputed loud and long
each in his own opinion
exceeding stiff and strong,
though each was partly in the right
and all were in the wrong!

■ DAVID LLOYD GEORGE: Women—I drove with Bonar in the south of France.
  Me: What beautiful scenery!
  Bonar: I don't like scenery.
  Me: What pretty women.
  Bonar: Not interested in women.
  Me: What do you like, Bonar?
  Bonar: I really like a good game of bridge.

"We are two schoolmarms, darning our socks and doing our sweatered art in our humble but honest home."

Nina began to pace up and down the loft. Fluffing the pillows on her bed directly in the center of the room, pirouetting across the parquetted floor, oak, she insisted, just as the Philadelphia Coggeshall women have always had in their sitting rooms for three centuries past. She reached Dosha's bed, a simple white-sheeted coverlet, hospital cornered, tight as a drum, drawn sheet covering it. No pillow.

As far as Nina could remember, Dosha had made the bed up three years before and had never, ever, even so much as sat on it—much less slept over or on it since December 22, 1965, the day she had moved in with Fisher.

Nina had found the apartment in the *Village Voice*: "Do you want to be a Rembrandt? Eight huge windows. Washington Street. Cooking gas stove in corner. Absolutely no white elephant. Walkup. $185 a month. Future fame guaranteed. Modest fee. Call William Gottlieb: 475-1400."

Why not: "Do you want to be a Cassatt?" But as her father Phillip Coggeshall IV would remark, Rome wasn't built in a day.

■ JERRY FODOR, Professor of Philosophy, Rutgers University: Elephant—"Given the conventions of English, there are two ways of reading the set-up sentence: roughly either as

[1] I (in my pajamas) (shot (an elephant))

or as

[2] (I) (shot (an elephant in my pajamas)."

■ MU XIN: White-sheeted—What does she need, Dosha, more than a bed? Does she need that? Certainly not a simple white-sheeted coverlet. For sure, she does not require a pillow.

In my "*people's prison*" in Shanghai for eighteen months, starving, I wrote and wrote and wrote: 650,00 characters. Paper that was provided by my jailers for "*self-criticism*."

I folded and refolded and folded yet again, all my precious papers and hid them in the cotton padding of my prison jacket.

"*I feel that those tragic experiences are extremely hard for human nature to bear. Human nature does not need to bear them …In a gravely adverse situation, you are obliged to hold your own life in your mouth—like a tigress holding her young in her mouth—and be the first to advance—not retreat—to prove yourself worthy of your moral responsibility. Thus life, when linking life, grows vigorously, ad infinitum.*"

Or no beds. Yet always a space to create. No matter what Dosha and Nina must do in the daytime.

For in Shanghai "*by day I was a slave*"; by night, when I created, "*I was a prince.*"

Dara Shikoh riding the imperial elephant.

■ LEONARD WOOLF (Virginia Woolf's husband): Office—His office: Apartments for lease. Houses for let. Floor plans. Sketches he's done himself to explain to his Jamaican carpenter the window sashes he wants to build on Charles Street. "How do I know you can make a window," I said to Ingram. "I'll make one and bring it back this afternoon," he said. And Ingram did, and can make anything. Simple if you think you can do it or can find someone who can. My office, Hambantota, Ceylon, 1909. I, a judge. Taxman. Magistrate. Not a problem. My father was a barrister. Died when I was eleven. I inherited his knowledge. Policeman. Planner. Keeper of the peace. What I learned in Jaffna, "British Conversation."

Vet, ah there's the rub, ask him what does the bullock need. And do it, or look over his shoulder, and direct his hand, Brekekekex Koax Koax. Talk to him as the Apostles.

It was my office. One hundred thousand people of Ceylon. Only the numbers at Gottlieb's office differ. *Plus ça change.*

■ GRACE GOODYEAR COGGESHALL, NINA ABIGAIL COGGESHALL'S GRANDMOTHER: Nina— A piece of work, my granddaughter is. I remember her saying:

"And don't forget, Dosha dearest, in the theatre I'm Abigail, theatrical name it is, and in New York, of course, Abigail too, but in our own adventures I'm Nina when I'm plain Jane and Abigail when I'm Zelda Fitzgerald. It goes without saying I'm Abigail to Prince William Gottlieb."

My granddaughter is lecturing her school chum. Since I was a girl of three, I was lectured: "Never forget, wherever you are, whoever you're with, you're a Coggeshall—Philadelphia born, no less."

My granddaughter, changing her names at will, tacking her sail to the prevailing winds. She'll not marry another Coggeshall cousin as I did. Still, I find her immensely charming. More of me in her than her mother.

Nina had sauntered over to Prince William's office and Mr. Gottlieb had shown her the apartment. She took it immediately and asked Prince William if she could share the apartment with her Cliffie roommate.

"Who is she?" asked Gottlieb. Dosha had, thank G-d, been at her mother's. She came down within a half hour.

Dosha had loved it even more than Nina. "And what about the fee?" Nina asked. Gottlieb, who certainly knew his mind, looked straight at Dosha, "Forget the fee and are you, Dosha, free for dinner?"

Bless Dosha's heart, she did go to dinner and brought back a signed lease within two hours. Of course, Prince William was interested in Dosha and not in Nina, A.B.C. really. Dosha wasn't interested in Gottlieb. She could see Fisher coming even a year away.

Nina stopped directly in front of Dosha's canvas and said, "So, what do you see? White, blue or green, or all of the above? Or is it the Hopper Professor Welch took us to see at the Yale Art Gallery in '61?"

■ MARY CASSATT: Office—I wrote to Louisine: *"How well I remember, nearly forty years ago, seeing for the first time Degas' pastels in the window of a picture dealer on the Boulevard Haussmann. I used to go and flatten my nose against that window and absorb all I could of his art. It changed my life. I saw art then as I wanted to see it."*

Nina, no different than I, nor Dosha different from Louisine. We all peer into men's offices. And what do we see, our noses pressed against the glass, or their glasses, but, they peering, unblinkingly back at us. *Ça ne change pas. Jamais.*

■ JOHN LEHMANN: Office—*"After a honeymoon period of a few weeks when Leonard would instruct them, the managers, in their manifold obligations with fatherly patience and humor, he would become increasingly impatient, intolerant of little mistakes, and testy—indeed often hysterically angry—when things were not going quite to his liking; and when he was testy he could be extremely rude. The result was that each attempt to lift the burden on to a young man's shoulders ended in more time wasted, mainly in altercation, and nerves frayed all round."*

Gottlieb's office, child's play compared with Leonard's. For Leonard is with Virginia throughout the night, and in the day time his mind is minding Virginia. Gottlieb, well, the odd evening with the odd lady, to get even, with who knows whom, a part-time Casanova and a part-time property dealer. Touching how deeply both care for their charges, more like a mother, they both are, than lovers.

■ VIRGINIA WOOLF: Office—I'd bind books in neat stacks of blue, or orange, or white. Lovely really. Castles on the beach. Rearranging Vanessa's covers. All the type set by me, after deciding which manuscript should be our royal edict for the season. A chess queen I was, bringing to life the babe, swaddling it, binding it in cord and posting it merrily on its way. More king than queen I was in our realm of the office.

Leonard, like all court treasurers, of course thought himself king. When Lehmann left, how Leonard carried on, with his *"desire to dominate."* How small, how very, very tiny. *"The inane pointlessness of all this existence; the old treadmill feeling of going on and on for no reason…terror at night of things generally wrong in the universe."* Of course I must think of Leonard's *"goodness and firmness; and the immense responsibility that rests on him"* but the office, our office, my office that could have been a giant, a Ming Emperor and Empress instead became a mere way station, a backwater Turkish posting.

◆ Simha Padawer, Dosha's grandfather: Friends—What are true friends? Those who each month prepare each other for the month. The month of the great day. Which, please G-d, will come for Dosha. Dosha is wandering in a forest. Her friend Nina, her other friends, Tal and Fisher too.

Said our master, Hayyim of Sanz: "*A man had been wandering about in a forest for several days, not knowing which was the right way out. Suddenly he saw another man approaching him. His heart was filled with joy. 'Now I shall certainly find out which is the right way,' he thought to himself. When they neared each other, he asked the man, 'Brother, tell me which is the right way. I have been wandering about in the forest for several days.'*

Said the other to him, 'Brother, I do not know the way out either. For I too have been wandering about here for many, many days. But this I can tell you, my friends, do not take the way I have been taking for that will lead you astray. And now, let us look for a new way out together.' Our master the Sanzer added: 'So it is with us. One thing I can tell you. The way we have been following thus far, we ought to follow no farther, for that way leads one astray. But now let us look for a new way.'"

They are all guides for each other, each only knows part of the road. Tal and his lost Rachel, his pupil Fisher, Nina and my blessed granddaughter Jerusha.

■ Shitao: Friends—Dosha and Nina are friends. Not because they are in the same room. Nor even in the same city. "*In 1696 a collector asked Bada Shanren to write out Tao Qian's 'Essay on the Peach Blossom Spring' and then send the calligraphy to be illustrated by me.*" I was in Yangzhou. With my heart I wrote: "*Bada Shanren's calligraphy and painting are the best in the entire country. My friend sent this scroll to me in Yangzhou and asked me to add a painting...Bada Shanren and I are one thousand li apart, but we are two of a kind.*"

Nina and Dosha are two of a kind. And will be, whether they live in the same dwelling in the same city or even across the seas from each. Even though each may not speak to the other for years still will they converse with heart's warmth.

From memory, Dosha quoted the Chinese poet Li Liu Feng:

"*My greatest pleasure was sitting in my study or in a boat on a clear day by the window at a clean desk, listening to my friend, Ch'eng Chia Sui, chanting my poems while watching him paint.*"

"Ah, the nine friends of painting. Do-sha. Or shall I say, reverse your name. Sha Mi. That's what you christened us with in Art 604. Laura Meers was Wang-Chien. The extraordinary Kibler was Wang Shih Min. Nobody was dull Chang Hsueh-Tseng. And any of us, or all, of course, could change our 'patri-mony-destiny,' you called it. We could become Tung Chi-Ch'ang. You got an A+ and Pierson wanted to publish your paper."

"And he did, under his own name."

"And by the way, Dosha, each month I am now treated to a new wisdom scribbled white on white on my side of the wall of our atelier."

Nina stood in front of Dosha's new graffito. The great 17th century Ming Individualist painter Shih-T'ao had written on a scroll painting that he gave to a friend:

■ Julius Meyer, Dosha's great grandfather's brother: Friends—Nine friends. Chinese painters. Did I not deal in "*Indian, Chinese and Japanese curiosities?*" I too had nine friends.

First, Standing Bear, who among the Pawnee saved my life when hostiles robbed me of my pack containing the month's collecting of wampum pouches, tomahawks, moccasins and more than five hundred beads. I told my niece Lena Rehfeld that "*in my life Standing Bear should never want for anything and after I pass through the mist, you're in charge to see Standing Bear is still spoken for.*"

Second would be Sitting Bull, the Good Sitting Bull, the Oglala. A man who could cross his hands and listen. Look at you. Never lied. Trusted whites because he trusted me, though lord knows I warned him about Washington and especially about the Great White Father.

Third would be Red Cloud who led the Indians to victory but surely not against the whites, but against those who lied and stole from him. I knew he knew that white men are ghosts.

Fourth, Spotted Tail, a Brulé. Uncle of Crazy Horse. Teacher of the Bad Sitting Bull, if truth be told.

Fifth would be Max, almost a father and a mother to me. Sixth would be Moritz, who rode with me to the outskirts of Omaha and always, G-d only knows how, would be waiting for me in my *Indian Wigwam* at my store on Farnam Street with a smile and a: "What have they given you now, Box-Ka-Re-Sha-Hash-Ta-Ka as a birthday gift, Curly Headed White Chief Who Speaks With One Tongue?"

Seventh, Adolph who taught me the insurance trade and took me in after I said I'd never return from Paris. I know who my other two friends are. One is the author of us all, G-d of the skies and the water, who created all of it and asked me to eat eggs and Standing Bear to eat dog, and it's all the same as all friends shall soon, oh so soon, see.

And last, the one who vanished, who saved me. Two Moons, whose name I could not speak of, certainly not to Max who could not be father and certainly not Rabbi to me. Nor to Moritz or Adolf. Nor any of the Pawnee or Oglala, even in their own tongue. Yes, Two Moons, who would not live with me in Omaha just as I could not stay with her on the plains. Perhaps G-d himself will finally arrange for myself and Two Moons to live bundled together. Braided. Forever.

■ HILLEL SEIDMAN in his Warsaw Ghetto Diary: Friends—"*Now I am in Schultz's factory; I have come at the time when people are both hammering in nails and reciting Hoshanot prayers.*

Here are gathered, thanks to one of the directors, Mr. Avraham Hendel, the elite of the Orthodox community: Hasidic Masters, Rabbis, scholars, religious community organizers, well-known Hasidim. Sitting beside the anvil for shoe repairing…is the Koziglover Rav, Yehuda Aryeh Frimer, once Dean of Yeshivat Hakhmei Lublin. He is sitting here, but his spirit is sailing in other worlds. He continues his studies from memory, without interruption, his lips moving constantly. From time to time, he addresses a word to the Piaseczner Rebbe, Rabbi Kalonymos Shapira, the author of Hovat ha-talmidim, who is sitting opposite him, and a subdued discussion on a Torah topic ensues. Talmudic and rabbinic quotations fly back and forth; soon there appear on the anvil, or, to be precise, on the minds and lips of these brilliant scholars—the words of Maimonides and Ravad, the author of the Tur, Rama, earlier and later authorities. The atmosphere of the factory is filled with the opinion of eminent scholars, so who cares about…the overseer, the hunger, suffering, persecution and fear of death? They are really sailing in the upper worlds; they're not sitting in a factory on Nowolipie 46, but rather in the Hall of the Sanhedrin."

Friends. Eternally.

■ SHAO CHANGHENG, the biographer of Bada Shanren: Kinds of madness—Shitao will call himself mad, Nello Nanni will regard Nina as mad, she will think Tal mad. Gauguin will call Van Gogh mad and Van Gogh will call the world mad. "There are many who know Bada Shanren, but none who truly knows Bada Shanren…what is he supposed to do? By acting suddenly mad, or suddenly mute, he can conceal himself and be the cynic he is. Some say he is a madman, others say a master. These people are so shallow for thinking they know Bada Shanren. Alas!" Shitao, Nina, Tal, Van Gogh, and even my master Bada all mad, yet but half as mad as their shallow friends and critics.

"*In olden times Hu-T'ou Ku K'ai'chih had three incomparable attainments. Now I have three kinds of madness: I am mad, my words are mad, my painting is mad. How can one achieve true madness? Now I shall present this piece of madness to my venerable elder Mr. Sung. Then I shall have achieved true madness.*" Shitao ended with: 'This is only to provoke a laugh' and signed it.

"The next day, Shitao added another verse:

In a moment, smoke and clouds can return to their previous form:
The whole sky is full of red
trees spreading fire all over heaven.
I invite you to get drunk with my black brush strokes;
to lie and watch the frosted forest where the falling leaves spin."

"Dosha," Nina interrupted. "Nello Nanni, late of Venezia, whom I dazzled at the Figaro, has invited me and friends for supper at the Limelight. Do you and Fisher want to join?"

"You and I have a breakfast at the Museum of Natural History tomorrow and Fisher's got to be in early at *Time*."

■ SHAH JAHAN: Now I have three kinds of madness: I am mad, my words are mad, my painting is mad—Now my lotus, Mumtaz, is dead. Now that as the sun rises and her glorious beauty no longer opens, I have three kinds of madness.

I am mad with a desire that will never be filled until I shall be with Mumtaz in Paradise. Not for me a thousand *peris*, just one sole flower. My words have commanded that a jeweler's sheet of marble, set with gems, an everlasting peacock throne, for my Queen to rest on awaiting to join me in Paradise, shall be erected on the banks of the Jumna, the waters flowing from the Himalayas to the holy Hindustani River of the Ganges.

My painting is mad, for I am told that twenty-thousand laborers working twenty years will be needed to complete it. Of course, it is my will, it shall be done. A speedy job, twenty thousand times twenty to capture but a portion of her glistening skin, the reflection of the sun on her tapered neck.

I shall stand each night in the moonlight garden, the Mahtab Bagh, and watch with my eyes as her flesh becomes marble, glistening in moonlight, as it ever did, as I gazed at her sleeping by moonlight. That is what she is doing: not dozing, she is sleeping, silent, soon to awaken.

No court painter shall paint or sketch my painting of her on pain of death. Only I may paint her with my eyes, a one-haired brush over and over, twenty-thousand times each night, for twenty years on end.

■ MICHELANGELO: I am mad, my words are mad, my painting is mad. I am mad. My words are mad.

Now I know how fraught with
error was that fantasy
that made Art my idol and my king
che l'arte mi fece idol' e monarca
My painting is mad.
No brush, no chisel can quiet
the soul
Once it turns to the divine love
Of Him.

How can I achieve true madness? By finishing, completing, ending. How can I avoid true madness? By finishing, completing, ending. How can I avoid true madness? By leaving my chisel on the floor, by circling my hands about Tommaso de' Cavalieri, again and again, by praying for death.

Deh quando fia, Signor, quell che s'aspetta
*   per chi ti crede?*
When will that day dawn, Lord,
For which he waits who
Trusts in Thee.

◆ EMIL FISHER: I have one question—My son Raphael, after finishing his three novels *Blue*, *Green* and *White*, was invited by an English professor at Yale to discuss his writing. To me it was wonderful to be invited to the university. Instead, what does my son do after the teacher isn't in the classroom when the class is supposed to start? My son begins to read: "*Said Fisher as he tried to stand one of his ballpoint pens directly into the center of Tal's jerry built, twelve pen, three level, tic tac toe structure…*" My son actually, very slowly, put ten pens in a child's game on the desk in front of him. And then he continued reading from *Green*. "*Fisher jammed the pen into the center of the three-level structure and then into a crevice in the table. The pen swayed back and forth, a barometric needle recording the Hudson Street weather, fulcrum to Fisher and Tal and even Dosha, not present but always present, along with invited and uninvited guests.*"

At that point the professor rushes in. He looks younger than my son, apologizing and looking at the ball point pen structure which was swinging slowly back and forth. "I'm so sorry Raphael. I was caught in traffic. I was all set to introduce you but you've already started, I see."

"No problem," said my son to my astonishment. "I'll introduce myself. I was born at the same time as Raphael Fisher and in fact on the French Riviera, but he left after only one day. Oddly, I attended the same parochial school but he attended very few classes because he allegedly was a bit sick but truth to tell I suspect he enjoyed being home with Mom. I too was in his class at Yale but he rarely attended, staying up all night with Gates Gill talking philosophy. As to Harvard Law School, and the splendid white suits he wore to parade his knowledge gleaned a week before each exam from Messrs. Reilly, Flattau and his cousin, John Grosz, I will remain silent. Afterward I remained in close contact with Mr. Fisher, even accompanying him to India and to the London gem markets, but truth to tell, he didn't speak much, writing and talking in his head. Mostly the usual, 'Let's have a drink after work.' But I certainly am happy to be here today to hear him talk but as I notice he's reading, which I suppose is more like his thinking and writing than anything else."

At that point, my son jammed the last ball point pen in the hole in the desk and totally stopped talking. To his credit, the professor politely laughed and three students applauded and one with his hand raised shouted, "I have one question, Fisher: Are you saying to us that the three-level tic tac toe board is symbolic of your trilogy which in turn is a deconstructionist representation of Jerusalem, Safed and Tiberius?"

"How about coming with mad Tal? He seems like a night owl. Perhaps he even went to school with Nello," giggled Nina.

"And speaking of Tal, what's with the monthly graffito? Since Tal commissioned you to do his advice shop, you've been treating me with painter's fortune cookies every four weeks. What gives?"

"Oh, I think his advice is working on Fisher with me so I thought…" Dosha lowered her eyes.

"That's sweet, Dosha. But I have one question. Why after showing Fisher this studio just once, with the beds, the canvasses, the spartan cabinet, judicious and decorous furniture, have you never brought him by again?"

Practically each time she entered their apartment, Dosha thought of Fisher, seated in front of her paintings. "What are you doing?" she'd once asked him.

"Looking and writing," he'd say.

"Where's your pen?" she'd asked and he answered slowly. "First I look."

Dosha looked at Nina: "It's late. I'm late. I'll tell you tomorrow at the Departmental breakfast. But in a word…" Dosha walked toward the door. She shouted on her way down the staircase, "Here, Dreamboat wouldn't be my celestial Knight of White!"

■ VIRGINIA WOOLF: Judicious and decorous—"*On Sunday, April 14, 1918, Miss Weaver came to tea bringing with her a large brown paper parcel containing the Joyce Ulysses manuscript.*" Weaver. Still. Whispering.

"*I did my best to make her reveal herself in spite of her appearance, all that the editress of the Egoist ought to be, but she remained unalterably modest, judicious and decorous. Her neat mauve suite fitted both soul and body; her grey gloves laid straight by her plate symbolized domestic rectitude; her table manners were those of a well-bred hen. We could get no talk to go. Possibly the poor woman was impeded by her sense that what she had in the brown paper parcel was quite out of keeping with her own contents. But then how did she ever come into contact with Joyce and the rest? Why does their filth seek exit from her mouth? Heaven knows. She is incompetent from the business point of view and was uncertain what arrangements to make…and so she went.*"

■ SAMUEL BECKETT: Lowered her eyes—Harriet Weaver would lower her eyes when she saw me, Mr. Beckett she called me and, needless to say, Mr. Joyce. *I'm told when she was in her final sickness, she would not have her physician Dr. Richardson examine her before she had the photographs of Eliot, Pound and Joyce that lined her bedroom turned to the wall, lest they gaze at her—but when Sylvia Beach told me of her passing, I said, "I shall think of her when I think of goodness."*

■ HARRIET SHAW WEAVER, Joyce's publisher: Cabinet—Should I not be bashful, carrying his ms. to her? Her incessant chattering, nattering, flattering tone circling about Mr. Eliot, Mr. Pound and Mr. Joyce like a butterfly, while waving to her husband Mr. Woolf that he take the ms. and place it into the top drawer of the cabinet in the sitting room.

She wasn't fit to light a candle at Mr. Joyce's altar. And then in 1953, I read her diary entry: "*1941…Wednesday, January 15th. Then Joyce is dead: Joyce about a fortnight younger than I am. I remember Miss Weaver, in wool gloves, bringing Ulysses in typescript to our tea table at Hogarth House…would we devote our lives to printing it? The indecent pages looked so incongruous: she was spinsterly, buttoned up…*"

The nerve of it all. Who more dead now, Mr. Joyce or she? "*And what is wrong with woolen gloves?*"

■ LEONARD WOOLF: Cabinet—"*We put this remarkable piece of dynamite, the ms. into the top drawer of a cabinet in the sitting room…Miss Weaver was a very mild, blue-eyed advanced spinster.*"

Everyone started shouting and using language I didn't understand and frankly, I guess, I didn't get the whole thing. Not Yale. Not Harvard Law School. Or a white suit. But thank G-d there he was: a writer and writing about jewelry just like I said he could do when I asked him to come into my business.

ter, Rabbi Nachman of Breslov, told three stories. The first for those who sat before his chair
and listened.

*"Once there was a king. He had six sons and
one daughter. The daughter was very precious to
him. He was very fond of her and used to play
with her. One day when they were together, he
was annoyed at her, and the words flew from his
lips. 'May the Evil One take you!'"*

Now all who were there before my master's
storytelling chair listened. For all who were not
there, I wrote these tales down. Now it came
to pass that my master passed away. "Better a
dead Rabbi who is alive than a live Rabbi who
is dead," he had taught us. So we ourselves told
these tales for ourselves and for those who
were not there. A second storytelling:

*"That night she went to her room and in the
morning no one knew where she was. Her father
the King was very distressed and he sought her
everywhere. On seeing that the King was in great
sorrow, the King's chamberlain asked to be given
a servant, a horse and money for expenses, and
he went to look for her. He searched for a very
long time until he found her."*

And what of the third story? This was the
third part of the first story, the main story, the
only story. The story for all the world is but one
story our master has taught us. *"The way things
begin is the way they end."*

What is the holy Torah but a story with the
words *"In the beginning?"*

Now the third story was told and exists in
the wood of the chair our master sat in. Did
not our master foretell the coming times: "At
the end of days, the summers will be cold and
the winters warm; men will dress as women,
and women as men; crooks will be Rabbis and
Rabbis crooks."

Rabbi Nahman's chair itself speaks to us all,
within the din of Jerusalem in the Holy Land
itself.

*"The Chamberlin journeyed through deserts,
fields and forests. Once when he was traveling in
the desert he saw a side path. He decided that
since he had been in the desert for such a long
time and had not found her, he should try that
path, and perhaps he would reach a town or village. He went for a long time and in the end he
saw a castle and many soldiers standing guard
all around it. The castle was beautiful finely laid
out, with well-trained guards. He was afraid that
the guards would not let him in. But he decided,
'I shall take the risk.'"*

Praised be G-d, the start of the story itself,
the In The Beginning itself, whispers to us to
whisper back to the story itself: *"I shall take the
risk."*

Shah Jahan as an old man.

CHAPTER 4

WHITE HAIR parted ever so
slightly off the middle of his
forehead, eyes set deep in his head
and staring at Dosha, not moving a
centimeter, Hastings Stokes III had
called the June "breakfast confab"
for precisely 8 o'clock—the ever-
regular first Monday of the month
meetings. "That will give us 120
minutes to decide: butterflies or
birds," Hastings had said, adding,
"If it's too early or too inconvenient,
then how about my place the night
before?

How lovely his bow tie looks,
thought Dosha, nervously fingering
her sketches of Cairns birdwings, a
Koh-I-Noor butterfly and a silvery
white mother-of-pearl Morpho.

The outline of Hasting Stokes'
bow tie started to shimmer and
expand before Dosha's eyes and fill
the entire frame of Hastings' face.
Only his eyes peered out from
behind the long, slender antennae
of the Koh-i-Nur butterfly that had
suddenly sprouted from his bow
tie, obscuring his face.

His prematurely white hair was
not completely under control. A
baffled cottony voice asked Dosha
something:

"Where is she to be found? Where
is she?"

■ Chuang Tse, 4th–3rd century B.C: Butterfly—

*I do not know
whether I was a man
dreaming I was a butterfly,
or whether I am now a butterfly
dreaming I am a man.*

■ Li Po: Where is she to be found? Where is
she?—He is searching for her. But his hands are
quivering. Dosha's eyes do not see it.

All last evening and through all of the moonlit night Stokes has dreamt of her. He has
poured two cups of wine in his home, one for
her and one for himself.

Where is she? She didn't come home last
evening, not in his night time dreams. He drank
his own wine cup, and then hers too.

"Wine makes its own manners."

All night long he has been drinking. T'ao
Ch'ien's idleness. He can see all now, wu-wei as
spontaneity.

But where is she to be found? Where is she?

*It's September now.
Butterflies appear in the West Garden.
They fly in pairs,
And it hurts. I sit heart-stricken
At the bloom of youth in my old face
Before you start back from out beyond
All those gorges, send a letter home.
I'm not saying I'd go far to meet you,
no farther than Ch'ang-fend sands.*

But where is she to be found? Where is she?

■ Shah Jahan: White—*"Six months after the
melancholy event of the death of my empress
Mumtaz Mahal, I entrusted my son the Prince
Shah Shuja, to bring the corpse to the capital,
Agra. Throughout the whole journey from
Burhanpur to Akbarabad, the last resting place of
the deceased, food and money were distributed
among the poor and the needy. Immediately on
the arrival of the corpse at Akbarabad it was
interred on the 16th Jumada II 1041 A.H. (9th
January 1632 CE) in the paradise-like tract of
lands situated south of the city facing the Jumna
River, which was the property of Raja Man Singh.
For this piece of land, I gave a lofty edifice to him.
On this spot a temporary grave with a dome was
constructed in haste so that the corpse of the
chaste lady might remain concealed from the
public eye. Then on this blessed spot the foundation of the sky-like lofty mausoleum was laid,
which later on was built wholly of white marble
with an adjoining garden."*

ימי חייך: וראה בנים לבניך שלום על ישראל

בסימנא טבא ובמזלא מעליא

בחמישי בשבת שלשה עשר יום לחדש תשרי שנת חמשת אלפים ושש מאות
ועשתי עשרה לבריאת עולם למנין שאנו מנין פה מנטובה מתא דיתבא על
נהר מינצו ויזל מי לאגו ומי בארת בא הבחור היקר כמר מצליח מנחם בן
המנוח כמר נתן יהודה הזק זל ואמר להכבודה מרת טובה דמתקרית בונה
בת המשכיל המנוח כמר שמואל אליעזר חיים בסאנו זל הוי לאנתו כדת
משה וישראל ואנא אפלח ואוקיר ואזון ואפרנס יתיכי כהלכת גוברין
יהודאין דפלחין ומוקרין וזנין ומפרנסין ית נשיהון בקושטא ויהיבנא
ליכי מהר בתוליכי כסף זוזי מאתן דחזו ליכי ומזוניכי וכסותיכי וספוקיכי
ומיזל לותיכי כארח כל ארעא וצביאת מרת טובה מבת בתולתא דא
והות ליה לאנתו והנדוניא דהנעלת ליה מבי נשא והתוספת דהוסיף לה
מדיליה ומפומה כמר מצליח מנחם יצו הנל חתן דנן עם המאתן זוזי
דחזו לה הכל כאשר לכל נתבאר בשטרות שנעשו ביניהם וצבי כמר
מצליח מנחם יצו הנל חתן דנן וכך אמר אהריות וחומר כתובתא נדוניתא
ותוספתא דא קבילית יצלי ירתאי בתראי להתפרעא מכל שפר
ארג נכסין וקנינין דאית לי תחות כל שמיא דקנאי ודאקני מטלטלי אגב
מקרקעי דכלהון יהון אחראין ויערבאין למפרע מנהון כתובתא נדוניתא
ותוספתא דא עד גמירא ואפילו מגלימא דעל כתפאי בחיי ובמותא מן
יומא דנן ולעלם ואחריות וחומר כתובתא נדוניתא ותוספתא דא קבל
עליו כמר מצליח מנחם יצו הנל חתן דנן כאחריות וחומר כל שטרי כתובות
נדוניאות ותוספתית דנהיגי בישראל דלא כאסמכתא ודלא כטופסי דשטרי
וקנינא אנן סהדי דחתימי לתתא מיד כמר מצליח מנחם יצו הנל חתן רני לוכות
מרת טובה מבת בתולתא דא יצל כל מאי דכתיב ומפרש לעיל במנא דכשר
למקנא ביה ויעם ועל ד רבה ד דשפר דיעהנ הכל שריר וקים

■ VLADAMIR NABOKOV: Understand—The young Dosha is surveying Hastings, her eyes a net, about to fix him.

"Wide open on its pin (though fast asleep).
And safe from creeping relatives and rust,
in the secluded stronghold where we keep
type specimens it will transcend its dust."

Her discovery, so efficient, a new taxon, among a million and a half known species, already known, perhaps two hundred million yet to be named, described, pinned and labeled.

One per American.

How original: she is seeking to understand and name him, and he, fluttering about, lusting to be pinned by another. All in our very own museum. My own, my Uncle Konstantin Nabokov, and the honeyed Dosha and Hastings stoking for Nina. All to be expected, quite normal.

What do you want to do most in the next two years? I was asked.

I answered:

"Hunt butterflies, especially certain whites, in the mountains of Iran and the Middle Atlas. Quietly take up tennis again. Have three new suits made in London. Revisit landscapes and libraries in America. Find a darker and harder pencil."

All of us, quite normal.

■ THE KOTZKER REBBE: You—If Hastings will talk to Nina she will come.

"If I am I because you are you, and you are you because I am I, then you are not you and I am not I. But, if I am I because I am I, and you are you because you are you, then I am I and you are you and we can talk."

If Hastings will not hide himself from Nina, he will see that she is already in the room.

"Oh," said Dosha. "In India or in Pakistan, in Malaysia and the Philippines."

"What? Whatever has gotten into you?" Hastings jumped to his feet.

"Miss Padawer, are you on drugs? Have you gone insane? Where is Nina Coggeshall? What's all this drivel about India, Pakistan, Burma? Nina, or Nye-Nah as she calls herself if there's any eligible bed-worthy human about, Nye-Nah was here on Friday."

"Oh she'll be here, Hastings. Why not start with me?"

"Start with you? Start with you? Where? Here?" said Hastings Stokes pacing across the room with a not-bad-at-all Groucho Marx imitation. "Where do we start?" Stokes got on the floor and stood on his head.

Dosha slapped her legs together and broke into laughter. "Hastings, get back on your feet. I understand. Really, you know my situation. I'm taken."

■ MARCEL PROUST: Understand—Dosha understands Hastings. But Hastings will not understand Dosha. Her young beau Raphael Fisher may understand Dosha. But only through the *carte postale* of a Johannes Vermeer that Tal has given Dosha, and she has placed this key to her soul, an icon of her spirit, beside their bed. Vermeer, *"artiste toujours inconnu* (an artist who is forever unknown)." For if Fisher learns but one letter of Tal's teachings it will be that once Fisher accepts that in his love, even after his death, still will he only begin to hazard a guess in how to truly know her—then, at that instant, he will have begun to fathom Dosha's depths.

But Hastings will never begin to remotely guess who Dosha is or is becoming.

■ BOB DYLAN: Where is Nina Coggeshall?—Nina Coggeshall, with her "mercury mouth," is not to be found. Nina or Nye-Nah is just the fudge Hastings dreams of in daytime. For at night he does not sleep. Even if he bed weds her where will it end?

With your sheet-metal memory of
Cannery Row
And your magazine-husband
Who one day just had to go,
And your gentleness now,
Which you just can't
Help but show,
Who among them do you think
Would employ you?

Hastings needs Nye-Nah more than she needs him. But all Debs need each other. Sometime. Somewhere.

Aw, come on now,
You must know about my debutante…
Your debutante just knows what you need
But I know what you want.
Oh, Mama, can this really
Be the end?

But Dosha doesn't need her sad-eyed lady. Nor Nye-Nah Nina, Nah she doesn't need Dosha. So Nina Coggeshall will yet arrive. To the sound of "my Arabian drums," though Hastings won't hear it—with the sea roaring at Nina's feet.

Sad-eyed lady
…my Arabian drums,
Should I leave them by your gate
Or, sad-eyed lady, should I wait?

Ketubbah (Jewish Marriage Contract) Mantua, 19th century

■ DIEGO DUARTE II: In this day and age—"In this day and age," Constantijn Junior told me, as a father to a son, "one hand laves the other." "Duarte, I'll have a Ruckers Virginal for a friend, Johannes Vermeer and Vermeer will part with a painting of his. But mind the price, Duarte, Delft is not Antwerp, and I'll not pay Father's prices.

As though he need tell me: Constantijn Junior, he was no more my father than his father was kin to me.

But I knew of the man of Delft more than Huygens knew of him. I remember my father quoting Grandmother Leonor who always framed her Ladino sayings in the mouth of her father Isaac Rodrigues, "Let the horse lead you where you wish to go or else you will be the horse, and he the rider."

So I said nothing but, "My lord, if it is to be Delft, it is to be. You will fix the price of the Rukkers. And should you wish me to acquire a painting in Delft, I will do so, as I have done in all things. With you just as with your blessed father dear Constantijn Senior."

■ BALCHAND: Constantijn Huygens: Looking down—Dosha looks down at the table in the museum's rather dark room, better to see the gentleman: Hastings Stokes III. Her camera obscura. The one I bought off Drebbel in London. The camera "*certainly produces admirable effects in reflection—painting in a dark room. It is not possible to describe to you the beauty of it in words: all painting is dead by comparison, for here is life itself, or something more noble, if only there were words for it.*"

Dosha, my Stella, all wise men or women know that to stare is to be blind, and to look down is to see all.

These are things reflected to you,
Secrets told within our fortress,
Mirrors of the world without:
As the camera obscura
Topsy-turvy through its lenses
Draws the sunlit world inside.
Topsy-turvy, Stella mark this:
Not the real thing, but reflection,
Just as lies may work upon
Truth that's tender and newborn,
Transparent as the noonday sun.

"Ah," said Hastings, back in his chair. "Taken by storm. Taken by surprise —mistaken? Taken aback by my offer?"

"Ah, dear, sweet Hastings, we are not for each other."

"Why not?" smiled Hastings Stokes III. "I'm Yale. I'm eligible. I've got an extraordinary roof garden just two blocks from where you live. With whom are you…"

"With whom?"

"With Nina, NYE-NAH?" suggested Stokes.

"Oh my G-d, reject a man and immediately one's accused of rejecting all men." There was music in Dosha's voice as she continued to shuffle butterfly sketches.

"No," she said, looking down at the table. "Nina and I share a loft on Washington Street. And I'm not anti-Elihu Yale because I share an apartment with…" Before she could utter Dreamboat's name, Hastings was off on a tear.

"It's not the age factor, not in this day and this age, is it? Or why each time I pass your castle do I see you and creepy 'Professor Tal' as he calls himself."

■ VERMEER: Immediately—They burst into my room though I had fastened the peg without so much as a knock. When my wife Catharina's mother, Maria, smelled money, Hell itself could not bar the way. And Catholic treasure at that.

"Duarte of Antwerp," Huygens shouted as he good naturedly pulled a gentleman behind him into the room.

Maraika, startled, immediately edged her way, like a fawn, around the gentleman who bowed but not toward me but directly before Maraika. Though their eyes did not meet, I knew they saw each other.

Huygens, not one to waste a second, shouted, "The end of the painting day. Johannes, dismiss your Muse and let us talk of art. This Duarte provided you with the Antwerp Rukkers you had off me. Show him your handiwork, Johannes, he is the greatest collector in Antwerp and he is one of us."

Maraika had already left the room, and once again Duarte bowed, this time both toward the portrait of Maraika and myself, back turned, and toward the other painting of the music teacher.

To his credit, Duarte rose slowly and said nothing. But looked at Constantijn and spoke into his ear.

Then and there I remembered with shuttering clarity the bow, the flourish. I had seen it as a child in my blessed grandmother's house. Duarte was one of us.

Our eyes met, and Duarte, still not speaking, swept my eyes gently with his toward Huygens. Duarte raised his two fingers and pointed at the paintings and as quickly as he had entered, left my studio, leaving me alone with Huygens.

It could not have been more than a quarter hour. "Duarte has asked me to purchase on his behalf these two paintings." And on and on Constantijn went. Of course I could sense that Duarte was standing a hair's breath beyond the door, slightly ajar, a joke really, if not so much like my past.

And on Constantijn dribbled. "But he provided you with the virginal. And he can help you with your sales Johannes and is able to pay you in diamonds. In pearls." And on and on. But finally, he was no fool, Huygens, like his father cunning to the core, "Fine" he said. "Johannes, a mule is ever a mule. Do not part with your precious paintings. He will commission a painting from you."

I nodded, like Duarte, for I had not said a word, and in an instant Duarte appeared again, and once again bowed. I knew I would see him again. Without Huygens. And we would speak of the unspeakable.

■ JOSEPH B. SOLOVEITCHICK (the Rav): Asleep—The young woman, Nina, was asleep. "*Sleep is an absolute passive state, in which a person is pure object. The insistent demand of the Shofar, the ram's horn, according to Rambam is the imperative to awaken one's self.*"

The young woman is fully awake. She "*can protect herself and control her environment, but she was powerless when sleeping…*"

The young woman has become a subject in her own right—not an object. "*The ultimate subject in the most absolute sense is Hashem [the name]. G-d's omnipotence is expressed in a number of ways: the creator of worlds, the Ein Sof, without end. Hashem continually renews His creation [Mehadesh betuvo bekhol yom tamid ma'aseh bereshit, makes new creations in His goodness each and every day] such that our very world depends on His constant involvement as Creator. Men and women all are created in G-d's image and should walk in G-d's ways. Imitate G-d. Strive to become a subject, not an object.*

"*A person as subject is blessed with free will. Sin occurs when man becomes an object when a person is transformed from a creator to a victim.*"

Adam, responding to G-d without taking responsibility for eating from the Tree of Knowledge. "*The woman who you gave to be with me, she gave it to me…*" (Genesis 3:12).

Eve too: "*The snake tricked me and I ate.*"

"*The shofar on Rosh Hashanah and Yom Kippur must serve as the alarm which warns a person that because of sin he is pulled ever downward, staring into an abyss. He must heed the cry of the shofar.*"

Nina is fully awake. She is in full energy. Rising, she creates with G-d's miraculous and breathtakingly beautiful ingredients of nature— all manners of feathers—objects to open and delight the eyes and minds of children. We are all children of the Holy One.

■ MISSISSIPPI JOHN HURT: Butterfly—In 1963, Tom Hoskins showed up at my door with a map of Avalon and a little crumpled piece of white paper, exclaiming "We've been looking for you for years." My first reaction was, "I thought he must be an FBI man. I said, 'you've got the wrong man! I ain't done nothing mean.'"

*Bought my gal a great big
diamond ring
Bought my gal a great big
diamond ring
come right back to me
and caught her shak-in that thing.*

I sang plenty and my voice was a song bird and my eyes were a butterfly but I ain't done nothing mean.

"'Isn't my Miss Padawer a wonder doctor?' Professor Tal always shouts out of his Advice Shop at me as I pass your apartment house.

"I hope to G-d you're not rejecting me for Dreamy, Creepy." Stokes looked at his watch. "Do you know what time it is, Dosha?"

"No. I don't wear a watch, Hastings."

"Not to belabor the point, but apparently neither does Nina. It's 9:05. It's 9 oh my G-d five. You were three minutes late. Bravo. And Nina is asleep. Or is she tied up at an airport trying to jet in from India?" Hastings was pacing about the room. Sweating, furiously fingering his bow tie.

"For the last month," he said slowly, using the chalk to indicate punctuation as he hit the blackboard. "Nina, you and I have had eight meetings. Monday, Friday, Monday, Friday, Monday, Friday. And Monday, Friday. As you are well aware, we've decided on a theme. Butterflies and birds or birds and butterflies."

■ JULIO CORTÁZAR, author of *Hopscotch*: The blackboard—What is he doing, this Hastings? Pacing, sweating, fingering…Is he writing as he starts to speak directly at the blackboard. Or is he speaking to the blackboard which like a divine writing instrument of the future will simply record his voice, leaving him only to erase over and over as he amends his errors trying to search his mind for the perfect phrase, a coherent thought.

In my later years, I have admitted that I am "*writing worse all the time.*" My good friend the charitable Vargas Llosa covered for me: Julio Cortázar "*meant that in order to express ideas in his stories and novels he was increasingly obliged to search out forms of expression further and further from classic forms, to defy the flow of language and try to impose upon it rhythms, patterns, vocabularies and distortions in such a way that his prose might more convincingly represent the characters or occurrences he invented.*"

But what if as I get older, what if we all (if I may include Mr. Hastings-Stokes whom I quite like) are simply erasing erasing erasing faster than our hands can write, standing and poking a piece of chalk against the slate.

Did I not write in my child's game, *Hopscotch*: "*Morelliana: If the volume or the tone of the work can lead one to believe that the author is attempting a sum, hasten to point out to him that he is face to face with the opposite attempt, that of an implacable subtraction.*"

■ R. AHRE DOKSHITZER: Dream—I came to the Tzemah Tzedeq and asked him how could I "*grow in Hassidut.*"

He replied, "*study each discourse well and meditate on it sixty times. What a person thinks of during the day, he dreams at night. When does a person grow? When one sleeps. Study as I tell you and you will dream Hasidism and thus grow into it.*"

When I became an old man, my daughter once came to wake me to go to services. I resented the intrusion but my young daughter exclaimed, "Today must you do it. Tomorrow is the time of reward."

In this country of Professor Stokes, people reject other people. Tal cannot be his Rabbi.

But in this country the old seek the young as Rabbis. They study from them, they tell them their dreams and G-d be praised the old learn from the young.

Mississippi John Hurt at the Newport Folk Festival, Summer 1964.

67

■ CYNTHIA MOSS, American Naturalist: Feel and shape—The feel and the shape will decide all. Even the shape itself."*Every elephant is unique, due to its pattern of holes, tears, scars and veins.*" Not so different from the slightly more blessed Dosha and Hasting Stokes, my elephants, though elephants only live for approximately sixty-five years, each is different, recognizable. Dosha should carefully examine Hastings' ears, not his eyes, and mark the differences. As I've done with generations of Amboselli elephants.

I can't wait until Nina makes her Elephantine entrance. "*After years of watching elephants, I still feel a tremendous thrill at witnessing a greeting ceremony. Somehow it epitomizes what makes elephants so special and interesting. I have no doubt even in my most scientifically rigorous moments that the elephants are experiencing joy when they find each other again. It may not be similar to human joy or even comparable, but it plays a very important part in their whole social structure.*"

We are all waiting for Nina to appear: Dosha for a steadfast friend, Hastings for a matriarchal lover and I for a demure debutante—all avatars of a young Amboselli elephant stepping out of white Kilimanjaro's shadows.

■ SITTING BULL, the Good, the Oglala: It was my idea—When I first went to the post library at Fort Laramie, I waiting outside the room and Lieut. Caspar Collins went in and borrowed the book about Napoleon.

Collins had asked me which book I wanted to read. "The book about the greatest white warrior," I answered. "That would be Napoleon's," answered Collins and he brought it. Did I want to be like Napoleon, he asked me. First I did not answer for if one says nothing, the white man thinks you think what he thinks. Red Cloud taught me that. Oscar Callister, who taught me how to use the telegraph, asked me many questions. He was a lonely man and only wanted to talk. Not really to hear any answers. Collins was different. After he got me the book the third time, he again asked, "Do you want to be like the white chief Napoleon." Finally, I said "I want to be a great chief. I will never be a white." But the book saddened my heart. Napoleon called for troops from each white tribe. From Ireland, from France, from Italy. He attacked tribes many winters march away. Now the white man had the telegraph line. No smoke signals necessary. The Crow fought against us. The Pawnee too. We were divided. Never could we defeat the whites. But even Napoleon was defeated at the end. Living on a faraway island fort surrounded by his enemies. That would be my end too. If I was lucky.

"I get it," interrupted Dosha. "Believe me, I get it. Hastings. Cut the 'we've.' It was my idea."

Hastings was staring at the blackboard, erasing a section of the enormous sperm whale recently found entangled in a submarine cable off Madagascar and soon to be displayed in Hayden Hall. In the previous day's session, the whale had been sketched, argued over and "kicked upstairs" to Traub's mammal department.

"For one month, 'we've' known Nina-Ninah, yourself and I, the chief acting deputy director—that this Monday morning we were to decide the shape, the feel and the colors of the birds and butterfly show."

"Well, then, let's stop waiting and get on with it," whispered Dosha. She knew the whispering would catch his attention. He was either gaping, gawking or shouting. Must have been a Boola Boola football acquired syndrome, she thought.

"White's the color, Hastings. And as to the feel and the shape, why don't we decide without Nina? Although I can't for the life of me understand what is meant by 'feel' or 'shape.'"

■ NIGEL NICOLSON: Butterfly—"*In her childhood, Virginia Woolf was a keen hunter of butterflies and moths. With her brothers and sister, she would smear tree trunks with treacle to attract and capture the insects and then pin them like corpses to cork boards, their wings outspread. It was an interest that persisted into her adult life, and when she discovered that I too was a bug hunter, she insisted that we go hunting together in the fields around Long Barn, our house in Kent, two miles from Knole, my mother's birthplace. I was nine years old.*"

Hastings is nine. Dosha is nine. And I am nine. We are all nine, waiting at Mother's to spread treacle on each other, on a tree trunk, praying for a butterfly to alight upon our bodies, gently, forever.

■ VIRGINIA WOOLF: Waiting—Charming, all three present. Young Dosha, eyeing old Hastings who is peering at Nina, more present than either but whose absence renders them both alive.

They are waiting for Nina in the American Museum of Natural History, my Long Barn, waiting with pins and cork boards, they are breathless.

And Nina, she is waiting for them to give up the chase, despair, cast their gaze downward and then she will fly in with an insouciance that belies her age—with her own cork board, and her epee pins—like Leonard waiting for me to wait for him.

"*Here I am waiting for L. to come back from London & at this hour, having been wounded last year when he was late, I always feel the old wound twingering. He has been seeing Nancy Cunard, so I expect a fair gossip. Vita was here for Sunday, gliding down the village in her large new blue Austin car, which she manages consummately…Vita…is like an over-ripe grape in features, moustached, pouting, will be a little heavy; meanwhile she strides on fine legs, in a well-cut skirt, & though embarrassing at breakfast, has a manly good sense & simplicity about her which both L. & I find satisfactory. Oh yes, I like her; could tack her on to my equipage for all time; & I suppose if life allowed, this might be a friendship of a sort…*"

◆ SIMHA PADAWER: Nature hut—What are they doing, my granddaughter, this man Mr. Stokes and her friend not yet here. What is a "nature hut?" Of course: In Slonim we learned: If one made a *Sukkah* under a tree, it is as though one had constructed it inside the house. If one *Sukkah* were above another *Sukkah*, the upper one is valid and the lower one is invalid. Rabbi Judah says, "If there be no occupants in the upper one, the lower one is valid."

Outside the museum building, in the Central Park, they are not permitted by the government to build their "nature hut." Inside the building, they are talking about building. And above them are other floors. Only if they build in the building's central courtyard, open to the sky, will the children who will be brought by the teachers, feel the presence of G-d…without G-d, will the children understand what a butterfly, a bird or a man really is?

■ ANNIE OAKLEY: Carnival—*"In Saint Paul, Minnesota, on the night of March 19th the chief, Sitting Bull, was in attendance in box B at the Olympic theater where I was performing with the Arlington and Fields Carnival. When I came onstage and snuffed out a candle with a rifle shot the chief came to life."* Hastings too is coming to life right here. He's right on the edge of his seat for Dosha. He'll be up and running for Nina sure as they call me little sure shot.

The chief was *"as much taken by my shooting stunts as anyone ever has been…He raved about me and would not be comforted. His messengers kept coming down to my hotel to inquire if I would come and see him. I had other things to do, and could not spare the time."*

That's the main thing. Once a man, any man, a plain man, a doctor, a President of France, even the chief himself knows you have other things to do and can't spare the time then they'll do anything to get your attention. Nina knows that better than anyone.

"When the chief, Sitting Bull, sent 65 dollars to my room that got my full attention…it amused me." And I agreed *"to meet the chief the next morning. I returned the money accompanied by a signed photograph of myself. The chief was so pleased with me, he insisted on adopting me, and I was then and there christened Watanya Cecila or Little Sure Shot."*

Dosha's warming Hastings up. She's got him looking directly at her. Nina's coming right in through stage center left. She and Dosha are one great act.

"You would if I showed you, Dosha."

Dosha jogged to the door and opened it onto the long institutional corridor just opposite the room marked "Board Room." She stared defiantly at Hastings.

"You just don't get it. Nina isn't here to help build our exhibition nature hut because three-quarters of your comments are innuendo and fantasy. You expect either or both of us to circle about in your office, masticate your lunch, feed it to you from our lips, carry you to your home nest, be your mother, your sister and your daughter before you're asleep and as you're slumbering. Well you'll fill in the etc. etc. etc. ad paradisium."

Stokes could see it all now. Forty minutes to go and he'd be across the hall in the director's room without a plan. "Chit," the managing director of the Morgan Bank, would be asking him, "Well Mr. Stokes, what carnival have you rounded up for us in elephant country?" Mr. Stokes, by G-d he'd known my name well enough at St. Paul and certainly at Yale when I got him into Keys, thought Stokes. This all was getting quite out of hand.

■ JUDAH HALEVI: Azariah Rossi, 1511–1578: Nina isn't here to help build our exhibition nature hut—Perhaps Dosha's friend Nina is studying. And why not? Did I not study? And read and think and pray, day and night, for 60 years until the earthquake in Ferrara sent us, all of us, Jew and non-Jew, believers and doubters—all into the fields outside the city.

I returned and wrote *Enlightenment to the Eyes*. G-d touched me and one can only write or teach truly if so touched.

They have many choices: Dosha and her friends.

"If one builds a sukkah on top of a wagon or on the deck of a ship, it is valid…If at the top of a tree or on the back of it is valid, but they may not go up into it on a festival day. If two sides of the sukkah were formed by a tree and one by hand or if two by hand and one by a tree it is valid but they may not go up into it on a festival day. If three by hand and one by tree, it is valid and they may go up into it on a festival day. This is the general principle in every case, where, if the tree were removed, it could stand up by itself, it is valid and they may go up into it on a festival day."

Where the three will work together on the construction of this hut of nature, there will it be suitable for visitors of any age.

■ HIRAM BINGHAM IV: Yale—What was it about Elihu Yale that riveted Father so? My brother Alfred who saw the world through the lens of money—those very few who had a Tiffany fortune and those very many who didn't—always assumed it was that the fascination was due to the happenstance that Elihu, like Father, had married money, the widow Hymners and then was smitten by Hieronyma de Paiva, the mysterious Portuguese lady merchant. I always thought of her as Japanese from my time in the consulate in Tokyo.

Of course the Tiffany fortune, mother's fortune, she never reminded father of it and he was a good steward of it. The very same self-generating, ever-increasing fortune that bought for Professor Bingham, my father, our 35-room, endless corridored house on Prospect Street in New Haven, that launched the Yale Peruvian Expedition to Machu Picchu, that paid for the campaign for Senator Bingham from Connecticut. All Tiffany diamond money, and all Yale. Father advised Mother to sign over to him the Tiffany shares, all 336 of them; after all, he argued the Senate was about to pass legislation to make such gifts impossible. "Now or never Alfreda." As did Mrs. Hymners for Elihu. His concern was not himself, but Alfreda's and his descendants.

Well of course his 7 sons, all would go to Yale, all would receive Tiffany diamond money for tuition and $2,000 per year for five years after they left Yale. All would wed, Father was so certain, with Tiffany diamond stock certificates to start their own families. It wasn't that Father was fascinated by Elihu Yale. Rather I told Alfred and all my brothers: Woodbridge, Charles, Jonathan, Brewster, Mitchell, he was Yale. And all his sons, loyal sons of Yale.

ANTWERPIA IN BRABANTIA

■ Diego Duarte II: You went to our library and didn't come out all night— They came to my palace off the Meir together, more like sisters than mother and daughter. My ever dear cousin, Constantia Duarte and her daughter Rachel Duarte. Though in Amsterdam they are Deborah Abolais and Rachel Levy.

They were lovely in Amsterdam and equally lovely in Antwerp. I welcomed them myself in the long hall off the staircase, where I had Maria set out sardines and Port on a long oaken table. "Welcome, my dear cousin Rachel, to our library," I murmured.

Rachel blushed. She was but fifteen yet said firmly: "My cousin Diego, this is not a library. It is a picture gallery." I could see her mother Constantia put her hand on her daughter's as though to restrain her. I interrupted Rachel with a force that surprised me "Here in Antwerp, as in motherly Portugal, we are allowed no books, only pictures."

"Diego, we are not here for philosophy," Constantia interrupted sharply. "We are here to discuss life. What will you do for your cousin, my daughter?"

"More than you did for me, Deborah,"

"Diego," said Constantia. "That was years ago and my mother, my blessed Rachel Salom, would not hear of a match between you and me. I do not think we should talk of this in front of my daughter Rachel. She is 15. And in earshot of your servants."

"Deborah," I whispered. "I have dismissed Maria and her husband for the evening. What we say in any event you will say to your Rachel after you return to Amsterdam."

I turned to Rachel and said simply: "Whom do you wish to marry?" Rachel looked at me with a calm, beatific expression. With the same look I had seen on her mother's face a lifetime before. Her mother put her hand again on Rachel's and said: "We are not in Portugal, Don Diego Duarte II. We are not in Antwerp. Your cousin and my daughter Rachel Levy Duarte will live in Amsterdam. She will marry, G-d willing, in Amsterdam. She will die in Amsterdam.

"She fancies our cousin Jacob de Paiva who you sent to us to be trained as a cleaver. A fine figure of a man. Quick. With eyes like his mother's. Dark. Unreadable. A traveler. But Amsterdam is what Manuel my husband and my brother-in-law Jacob Athias wish for. They are weary, we are all weary, they wish to rest in the port of Amsterdam."

"Why can't de Paiva wed and stay in Amerstam with Rachel?" I asked calmly. My cousin Deborah took my hand and lifted it to her right ear. An Antwerp rose-cut diamond rested on her earlobe with a pearl dangling below. My eyes fixed on her ear. "Just as this ear will never see the other, so too will de Paiva, raised in Antwerp, dreaming of Hindustan riches, never see an old age in Amsterdam."

I could have told them, both then and there: the Abolais women in our family take the Duarte name too. And the Duarte women decide in all

"A moment, Miss Padawer. I regret the innuendo and fantasy. Please accept my apology." Stokes rose to his feet and bowed. "But what were my other quarter of comments?"

Dosha hesitated at the door, smiled perfunctorily, and went back to her chair.

"Actually, your other quarter is quite lovely. You're a quick study. Everything I've ever given you to read, you've read and commented on. You know more about Cramer's Blue Morpho butterfly than anyone outside my department. When I mentioned the Koh-I-Noor, you went to our library and didn't come out all night, reading every scrap of paper on the Koh-I-Noor Nymphalidae and your curiosity brought you to the Punjab, backward to Victoria the Queen, all way to Babur.

"You're striking-looking with your premature mother-of-pearl Morpho hair but you're not my type. What irks me is that were I to fall—and note I use the subjunctive—I'm not sure you'd really respond. You're a skipper. Yes, that's what you are, a Regent Skipper.

■ Proust: Butterfly—Bergotte "fixed his gaze like a child upon a yellow butterfly that it wants to catch, on the precious little patch of wall."

The young woman Dosha believes Stokes believes the exhibition to be for children to study and become enchanted by a butterfly flying about.

The man is far, far different. He believes the exhibition to exist solely for him to see, to remember as an old man, just before his death—to contemplate upon and prepare for his end.

"That's how I ought to have written," he said. "My last books are too dry."

Stokes, last books, all unwritten, and because they will be unwritten, Stokes can already read them, even in the midst of his life, with the eyes of his childhood

■ Van Gogh: A moment—I have written to Gauguin "that as I too might be allowed to stress my own personality in a portrait, I had done so in trying to convey in my portrait not only myself but an impressionist in general...a disciple of the art of the future."

Stokes is asking for but a moment. An instant not very much really. For in this brief time so much, so very much can be done. If she will be with him and truly listen.

I wrote Gauguin in the simplest, most direct way:

"What days these are, not for what happens in them, but I feel so strongly that both you and I do not belong to the decadent school and not to those who are done for—it will never come to that...this art that we are working in, we feel it has a long future before it."

The woman, Dosha, should not hesitate at the door. She should close it tightly. Latch it against the world.

No more is needed than the two of them. Not even her friend. Their own yellow house—Gauguin's and mine—a heart's cave away from the winds of the world. Just a moment's time to dream together—and then to create, even apart, for the rest of their days.

things. "My sweet cousin, spend the night here, speak with your dear daughter and tell me of your decision in the morning." I heard them pacing in my picture gallery all night. In the morning, I saw Deborah and said: "You went to our library and didn't come out all night? What is the decision for Rachel: Jacob de Paiva or Abraham Jessurun Rodrigues?" Deborah smiled the smile that I dreamed of each night as I lay down, and saw each morning when I awoke. "My dear cousin Diego, I must trust the decision to Immanuel who entrusts all decisions to the Lord of us all." Without an instant of delay, Constantia returned to her daughter's guest quarters and left by the private tunnel exit on the other side of the Meir.

Anonymous, *Antwerp in the Province of Brabant.*

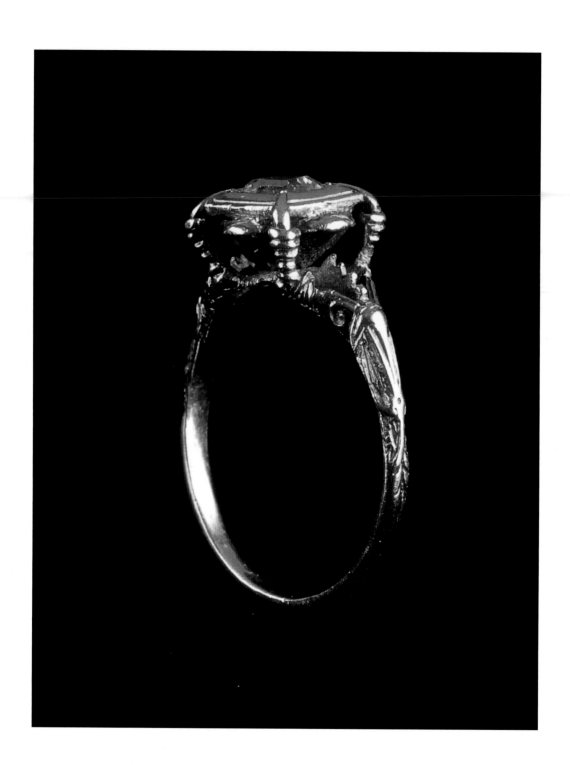

■ ISAAC LURIA: Run—I spoke to Vital: "Look, this verse chases after you and looks out behind your wall like a hind of the field skipping after you and cleaving to you."

Vital did not meet my eyes. For we both could see the verse, which runs before us, behind us, about us—always…"*In the beginning of the word of the king…*"

What should Vital say to me or I to him? Without a word, Vital circled about me and we stood back to back. He could see the verse chasing after me and I could see the hind skipping after him.

Could I not see what followed Cordovero and did not Samuel Vital write what his father Hayyim saw skipping after me.

Do not children skipping after their mothers see what their mothers do not see? Do not their mothers see what the children do not yet see?

"Never say that you have arrived; for, everywhere, you will be a traveler in transit."

■ FRANZ KAFKA: Children—June 13, 1923. Only thirty-six steps from me, I have counted them over and over, from my balcony, at Hans Gluckhauf, is the Jewish People's home. *"Through the trees I can see the children playing. Cheerful, healthy, spirited children. Eastern European Jews whom Western European Jews are rescuing from the dangers of Berlin. Half the days and nights the house, the woods and the beach are filled with singing. I am not happy when I'm among them but on the threshold of happiness. Today I shall celebrate Friday evening with them, for the first time in my life, I think."*

Who shall be my Sabbath bride if not Dora? But can I be her groom? She will ask her father's permission and he will ask the Gerer Rebbe's permission if she ran from Herschel, her father's house when she was sixteen to Breslov and if she fled from the Rebbe's Beis Yaakov school in Cracow six months later. Is not the answer given before the question is asked.

But for me I feel what it could be in my bones. What I felt in Prague. *"There is no one here who wholly understands me. To have someone possessed of such understanding, a wife perhaps, would mean to have a foothold on every side, to have G-d."*

"But, most important, you care passionately about this museum. About the children who come here wide-eyed, running through the halls. The mothers who return day after day. You don't want a life in finance. You want to work here until you die. And I suspect be buried in a diorama if you could. You love this place." Dosha looked down at her sketches to avoid Hastings' eyes.

"Thank you, Miss Padawer, for your frankness and many thanks for not making me an inquisitive monkey moth. We've only got fifteen minutes before the Trustees turn me into a pumpkin. What's the plan?"

"Use mine," said Dosha, holding up her three sketches. "The ceiling to be white. The whitest of whites. I'll paint orange sulphur overhead, luscious green Cairns birdwing, Adonis blue Baskers all over. We'll have butterflies frolicking through the hall."

"And high near the ceiling a bird diorama with the models made in 1906 that have been in storage since. No other museum can boast those."

"What does Nina think?" asked Hastings with surprising tenderness.

■ GAUGUIN: You don't want a life in finance—Even Gustave knew the phrase, "You don't want a life in finance." Who did? You want a father who spent his life in finance. Or better yet, a grandfather who spent a life in finance. And have the money descend like *manna* straight from heaven.

Cheerful he was. Gustave Arosa. Not a care in the world. None that he showed. Money just flew down on his head, just like it did for his father in Peru. Laugh he did when he talked of his father's fortune, based on bird drippings, guano, endless, costless, pure profit, enough to last for two generations. Gustave himself and the next. But did that mean my mother, my "Aline" he called, her or me?

Holding my hand in his right hand, big, fleshy, never a day's work, only Señor Arosa's fingers, a bit calloused from counting money. Year after year, Peru to Paris, while he marched me in front of his pictures, as he called them. Talking all the while, more to himself than to me in his private three-floor gallery in his Paris mansion on rue Jacob.

"That's one by Camille." (Corot was a dinner guest.) "Just outside of Aix. Must be worth at least five hundred." "There's Delacroix, strong colors." And on and on. But his Aline, my mother, was dead, I was told, in India. 1867. There was to be no second and certainly no third generation of Arosa Guano diners. Mother's will was to the point.: *"My son Eugène Henri Paul should get on with his career, since he has made himself so disliked by all my friends that he will one day find himself alone."*

Brilliant mother. Dead mother. Did I want a life in finance? *Non.* Even after Arosa landed me a stock exchange agent's job. Even after Arosa introduced me to Mette Gad, even after five children followed shortly.

Brilliant mother. Dead mother. Whispering to me softly from the grave. "One day I will find myself alone." So disliked by all her friends: *Arosa et compagnie*: Mette Gad. Her family, even our five children.

No life in finance for me. Sunday painting. I will turn every day into Sunday.

And pay with everything.

And find myself exiled, stranded, sinking and totally alone.

Table-cut diamond ring..

■ JULIO CORTÁZAR: Desire—All together now, they are: Dosha, Chit, Nina and Stokes. A kibbutz of desire. Children really. Waiting for Auntie to put them all to bed. Or to let them stay up past their bedtimes. But little supervision really. A child's dream. An adolescent fantasy. As powerful in the heat of Israel as in the chill of Paris.

"It wasn't as cold along the Seine as in the streets, so Oliveira raised the collar of his lumber jacket and went over to look at the water. Since he was not the jumping-off type, he looked for a bridge to get under and do some thinking about that business of the kibbutz, for some time now the idea of the kibbutz had been working on him, a kibbutz of desire… Strange that all of a sudden an expression should come up like that, one that has no meaning, a kibbutz of desire, until the third time around it begins to take on some meaning little by little and suddenly the expression doesn't seem so absurd anymore… the kibbutz of desire is not absurd at all, it's a way of summing up closed in tight this wandering around from promenade to promenade. Kibbutzim colony, settlement, taking root, the chosen place in which to raise the final tent, where you can walk out into the night and have your face washed by time, and join up with the world, with the Great Madness, with the Grand Stupidity, lay yourself bare to the crystallization of desire, of the meeting."

Stokes has summoned Nina, Dosha too. Nina is here—soon to lay herself bare—with Chit, and Auntie Susannah, the matron, our kibbutz of desire is complete.

"Obviously she's not too concerned, or she'd be here," snapped Dosha.

"To quote you, dear Dosha, you just don't get it either," said Stokes. "Nina is Chittenden Coggeshall's cousin. That's why she got the job after a two minute interview and you got your position without an interview. She's the family flapper but also the family star. Chit's the family banker. He desires to go back to Aunt Susannah and tell Auntie to come to the Nina Abigail show.

"That's what this is all about, Dosha. We've got to be able to figure out what show Nina wants."

"What Nina wants!" shouted Nina. "Nina gets what Nina wants." She burst into the room, reaching down into her huge knapsack and scattering peacock plumes, duck satinettes, turkey pointers, Lady Amherst pheasant tail feathers, Venere feathers high in the air.

■ EMILY POST: Reaching down—*"Under formal circumstances a lady is supposed to bow to a gentleman first; but people who know each other well bow spontaneously without observing this etiquette."*

Nina Coggeshall is Philadelphian born and bred. But it should be remembered that her mother's people are Broadbanks from Savannah.

"The reputation of Southern women for having the gift of fascination is perhaps due not to prettiness of feature more than to the brilliancy or sweetness of their ready smiles… How many have noticed that Southern women always bow with the grace of a flower bending in the breeze and a smile like sudden sunshine? The unlovely woman bows as though her head were on a hinge and her smile sucked through a lemon."

While reaching down into her knapsack, young Miss Coggeshall is bowing to Mr. Hastings Stokes who with his fine breeding I hope will respond in style. As for her school friend Miss Padawer, I pray she may accept her friend's friend William Hamilton. A suitable and fine pair Miss Coggeshall and the elegant Mr. Hamilton would make.

■ BUFFALO BILL: She burst—If I could I'd sign up Nina right now, as she bursts in, for Buffalo Bill's Wild West Show.

From the Upper West Side I'd travel it to London, Paris, anywhere.

I can see the peacocks, ducks, turkeys and pheasants circling through the air above her. Why should she perform for an audience of two when she could tour with me?

She'd be bigger than Annie Oakley. She's got Annie's pout. The *New York Sun* reported *"When Annie doesn't hit a ball, she pouts… she evidently thinks a great deal of her pout, because she turns to the audience to show it off."*

Nina's got *"Annie's blue eyes, white and perfect teeth and a low sweet voice full of melody."*

Annie was *"ambidextrous and could fire hand guns from either hand or from both hands at the same time."*

The *Springfield Republican* newspaper said *"Annie handles a shotgun with an easy familiarity that causes the men to marvel and the women to assume airs of contented superiority."*

That's Nina for you. Men will marvel. And women will delight in their superiority.

How can I book her?

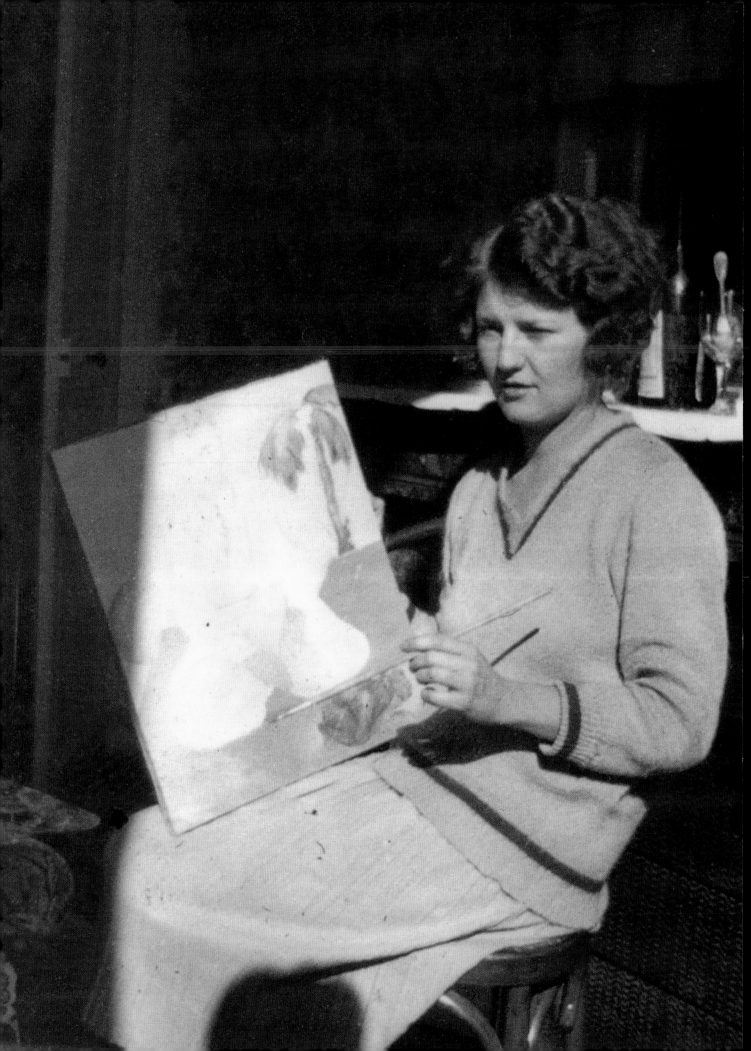

■ JIRI LANGER: I want—I have just received by express mail, a strange letter from Kafka. But because everything in life is strange, nothing is strange:

Dear Jiri, in the same home, the Berlin Jewish People's Home, the same home that I urged Felice Bauer, my former fiancée, to work in as a volunteer with children, I have now met Dora Diamant. I had written Felice over and over on the palimpsest of my body that the Home offered her *"the only path, or threshold to it, that would lead to spiritual liberation." Not only that but "the helpers will attain that goal earlier than those who are being helped."*

I was fearful to wed Felice for she could not climb the threshold to the Berlin Jewish People's Home. Now D. would carry me in her young arms, across the threshold, if only her father, a Hassid of Abraham Mordechai Alter, the Rebbe of Ger would permit it. Of course, the answer of the Rebbe was "No." Jiri, *"a man is only fully aware of himself when he's either in love or in danger of death."*

I am both. It is strange. But when we too were in Marienbad together you presented me to the Rabbi of Belz—Could you ask him for a review of my case. A "yes" from him would change my life. This is everything I want. My life. Either D.'s father would consent to the Belzer Rebbe or Dora would flee from him yet a third time—to Palestine as my bride. Act quickly, Jiri. All depends on you.

■ SITTING BULL, THE BAD, THE HUNKPAPA: A feather to be given to each child—If they give a feather to each and every child, these *wasichus* will forever be children.

One must earn a feather.

At fourteen years of age, I caught up with good-voiced Elk, my uncle. I had painted my gray stallion the red of the setting sun. I was covered from my head to feet with yellow paint. Did I have a feather? No. Was I given a feather? No.

I screamed the war cry, startling the Lakota with me, and charged at the stunned band of our enemy, the Crow. These Crows fled. All but one who notched his bow aiming directly at me. But I came with the speed of a child and the cunning of an elder, thrusting the Crow into the ground. *"I, Slow, have conquered him!"* I bellowed.

That night we held a dance until morning. I received many horses and a feather. I received my father's name: Sitting Bull. Each battle I fixed another feather.

My blue shield, fluttering with eagle feathers, always before me like a vision. These feathered children, they will dance until morning, but they will ever be children.

Zelda Fitzgerald at Saulies-de-Bearn, 1926.

The whirling wooden fan, which cooled the room to a frigid (Stokes termed it "excellent") working temperature, scattered the feather plumes helter-skelter all over the furniture, Dosha and Stokes.

"So sorry for the lateness. Your fault, Dosha, for bringing Fisher's best friend into my life. William set the alarm correctly but it was still on St. Helena, California, time. Confusing. Remarkable fingers Hamilton has, but forgetful.

"Anyway, I'm happy to tell you both what I want. I want a feather to be given to each child who visits the exhibition. I want butterflies flying throughout the hall—and no bird dioramas. Nothing dead. No formaldehyde. All lightness. I want each adult who hasn't found a lover to get three feathers, and those adults who have, to get two feathers."

Nina was spinning around on her toes, like Pavlova, scattering her feathers in the air, blowing on the ones that descended from the ceiling. Her red jersey above her white skirt made her look to Hastings like a revolving peppermint stick.

■ F. SCOTT FITZGERALD: Fisher's best friend—Not Fisher's classmate Hamilton, I assure you. They've both already left Yale. Dosha even. Her paintings, or Zelda's or mine will never be his or mine. Is her best friend Tal? The camps and the War took all from him: Rachel Beller swallowed in the horror of it all. Tal has the "sort of blow that comes from within…he will never be as good a man again."

Fisher's best friend: this novel he is writing. *"It seemed a romantic business to be a successful literary man—you were not ever going to be as famous as a movie star but what note you had probably longer-lived. I for one would not have chosen any other…And then, ten years this side of forty-nine, I suddenly realized that I had prematurely cracked."*

Fisher: my own best friend. His novel: me. One writes one's novel before and after one's death. Writing. Editing and rewriting.

■ GERDA MAYER: Dead—

Say I were not sixty,
say you weren't near hundred,
say you were alive.
Say my verse was read
In some distant country
And say you were idly turning the pages
the blood washed from your shirt,
the tears from your eyes,
the earth from your bones;
neither missing since 1940,
nor dead as reported later
by a friend of a friend of a friend…
Quite dapper you stand in that bookshop
And chance upon my clues.

That is why at sixty
When some publisher asks me
For biographical details,
I still carefully give
The year of my birth,
The name of my hometown:
GERDA MAYER born in '27, in Karlsbad,
Czechoslovakia…write to me, Father.

■ RABBI NAHUM OF CHERNOBYL: Student—For the teacher here to become the student is a simple thing. For the student to become a teacher is even simpler. *"How can a person be exalted by means of the Torah? Only by coming to the hidden light, that one might see by means of the hidden light what is to befall the world from one end to the other…this means that both the present and the future are the same to them…and so Rabbi Simeon ben Yohai was able to say in the Zohar what Rabbah bar bar Hana was to say several centuries after him. Similarly Moses, our teacher, peace be upon him, was able to see Rabbi Akiva who lived thousands of years after him. Through their learning, they came to the hidden light, where there is no distinction between present and future, for it is a place where what is, is on a par with what shall be."*

◆ SIMHA BUNAM PADAWER, DOSHA'S GRANDFATHER: Student—In America, everything is upside down. The young person is the professor and the old person the student. The young professor doesn't need the student and comes to school whenever he wishes. The older person, the student, comes early to class. The older student sits. The young professor stands. Here the student is in his seat, and the professor hides behind the door. Where will it all end? The professors will get younger and younger? And the students older and older? In the end of days, neither will be able to talk, each will be hidden from each other. If it wouldn't be my granddaughter, I would laugh.

■ ANNIE OAKLEY: With one motion, behind a door—Nina. As like me as two drops of water. Though a bit taller perhaps. But moving with one motion. It's all in that one motion. If it's broken, you're broken.

Behind a door, she is, like me, a lady. What the world thinks of her should be of no concern.

Buffalo Bill, what do I think of him?

"I traveled with him for seventeen years…. And the whole time we were one great family loyal to a man… His words were worth more than most contracts."

I wouldn't be quick to judge Nina, behind that door, not if I were Stokes, Dosha, or the world. Seeing is not always believing. Even with an eagle's eye.

"Slow down, Nina. Slow down. The idea of giving feathers is great. The Mayor, who promised to come to the opening, will love it. But school kids, how will they learn some aerodynamics from birds?"

"Catch their interest! Rivet them! Say I'm the teacher and you, Hastings, are my student. I begin my lecture: When a bird is in flight, its legs are held close to the body—"

With one motion, Nina threw herself behind an open door, hidden from both Stokes and Dosha, and kicked off her sandals. They landed with a heavy clump just beyond the door.

Stokes and Dosha heard a fearful rustle of clothing. Had Stokes heard the band around her white shirt snap? Was she removing the skirt, exposing her tanned, long legs?

"—aerodynamic advantages. The large contour feathers also help give the birds' angular body a more streamlined shape."

Nina was running her hands up and down her thighs, continuing to talk, though slower.

■ BUFFALO BILL: Running her hands up and down her thighs—The beautiful baby is running her hands up and down her thighs. It all depends on who you are and where you're standing. Lord knows, Stokey-boy thinks she's running her hands back and forth playing piggly poo. If there is a Mrs. Stokes, though I'd bet my last pair of Parisian-made britches there isn't, she's sure Stokey-boy's feet are running toward her.

Dosha, her young friend, would she see where Nina's hands are and what they are doing? Of course, she's got an eagle's eye. Does she care what Nina's hands are doing? No, never and never ever. Like Annie Oakley, she's a lady.

Finally, one small point, for Nina, for Stokey, for Dosha, Annie and for Lulu Cody, my century old wife. Nina's thrown herself behind an open door. Hidden from us all.

And don't they all just throw themselves behind an open door? Bessie Isbell, always clanging my Buffalo's bell. "Oh Miss Isbell," I looking finer than the devil himself would explain, *"She's often in my chambers discussing business the press of it which often occupies me virtually the whole of the day and night but Miss Isbell is the finest of press agents for the finest of Wild West shows in all the world."*

When I sued for divorce from my darling Mrs. Cody, in Cheyenne in Feb. 1905, Johnnie Claire, my valet, set it straight: *"He saw Miss Isbell in her room. She was clothed in a loose-fitting wrapper, or Kimono, and the Colonel was asleep in her bed. There was but one bed in Miss Isbell's room."*

They're all of a piece, Stokes, the Colonel, Miss Isbell, Miss Nina, and it doesn't matter none if the door is open or shut, and where they're standing for they're all thinking about just one thing, day or night, young, old, or in their graves.

◆ RACHEL TAL, TAL'S MOTHER: Still in the crook of the doorway—This young woman, Dosha, soon will leave the museum. Walk through the park and wend her way home. She will leave at four and arrive in her apartment house at five-thirty. Or, if she takes the train, at four-thirty.

My son Abraham will be waiting, still in the crook of the doorway of their house at 551 Hudson Street.

All afternoon he has been studying. Perhaps the words of our teacher, Isaac Luria:

"It is taught in the Holy Zohar Rabbi Simeon said: 'Jacob was a complete man, dwelling in tents.' It is not written 'dwelling in a tent' but 'dwelling in tents.' That is two. The patriarchs are the sum of all, and Jacob is the sum of the patriarchs."

Abraham has read the entire day; even while walking about his apartment house, he carries a book. He remembers each page he reads, always did, even in Antwerp, but each page is mixed with a page from the book he read from previously.

He dwells in two tents, my son does, in his own and wherever this Dosha is. That is why he waits for her from half four to half five. For if she takes a train, he fears he may miss her.

Without her, he is merely Abraham, and he dreams of being Jacob. But she will never be his Rachel. For she dreams of telling Fisher all, though Abraham tarry, in the crook of the doorway, forever and ever.

One travels from Antwerp to New York, one cannot return to Antwerp from New York. Certainly not after the War.

■ CHIEF SITTING BULL, THE HUNKPAPA: Visible—In this peaceful land of museums everything is visible. But upside down. Like reflected trees on a still lake. Here the women are the warriors. They have all the eagle feathers. The half man does not go into battle, is Stokes a Winkte? He is so skilled at decoration.

Nina appears like the wind. Like Crazy Horse, she will not work for a living. *"You tell our people to work for a living,"* I told a government official, but the Great Spirit did not *"make us to work but to live by hunting. You White Men can work if you want to. We do not interfere with you, and again you say, why do you not become civilized?"*

Nina is as Crazy Horse, charging forward. No bullets will fell her. Dosha is Chief, and Stokes, well, his long hair reminds me of the Colonel, Buffalo Bill.

"Because of this, many birds are capable of very rapid flight. Am I getting your full attention?" She touched the buttons on her jersey as she continued lecturing.

"The fastest, such as the peregrine falcon, have baffles in their nostrils to protect their internal organs from all the air pressure that builds up as a result of their speed.

"In addition to their lungs, birds have air sacs that extrude through the body and into their hollow bones." More fearful rustling. It must be that she's opening her jersey, sliding it down her back to reveal her flat stomach, thought Stokes. Out flew a shimmering red brassiere, landing right on Nina's sandals a foot from the door.

"As well as its light skull," continued Nina, still in the crook of the doorway but only partially visible to Hastings and to Dosha, who was looking at Hastings more than at Nina. How would she describe this to Fisher?

"—and bones," continued Nina, "a bird makes many other concessions in the interests of keeping its weight down."

◆ ISAAC TAL, ABRAHAM TAL'S FATHER: Light skull—When this young woman returns to her house on Hudson Street, she will repeat to my son Abraham word for word what her friend Nina has said.

Abraham will nod after each word, his lips moving as though completing each of Dosha's sentences. He will sway backward and forward while Dosha recounts the day.

But Abraham is not listening nor is he repeating. Already he has changed the words "light skull" into "white skull." Dosha his Vital and Nina the Holy Ari, Isaac Luria:

"It is taught," Abraham is whispering more to himself than to Dosha, *"when it became the intention of the white head, the all merciful, to act gloriously for the sake of its own honor, it prepared and established and produced from the spark of blackness a single ray. Then a single strong skull was prepared…By means of the spirit concealed in this skull, fire extended on one side and air on one side, and pure air remained above it on this side and pure fire on that. Into this skull drips dew from the white head, which remains full of it. And because of this dew, which is shaken down from its head the dead will come to life again…The dew comprises two colors: whiteness and a white crystal, in which both white and red may be seen…This is the meaning of Isaiah 26:19 your dew is as the dew of lights. And this dew that drips drips every day into the apple orchard is in the form of colors, white and red."*

My son will speak all this, lecture all this, quote all this, to Dosha who will laugh, he will tell her that Tal is the word for dew and he will think that instead of wasting the day in his apartment he is actually working side by side with this young woman.

Gian Lorenzo Bernini, *Kneeling Angel.*

SHipped by the Grace of God in good order and well conditioned, by *mee John Mendes da Costa*

in and upon the good Ship called the *Williamson*

Voyage *Capt Richard Warner* whereof is Master under God for this present

Buar of Thames and by Gods grace bound for *Port C George* and now riding at Anchor in the

to say *one box containing Corral Beads valued*

one hundred & twenty Pounds, to bee delivered to the Honourable 88 Team

before & m Elihu Yalle: for them to deliver the same to m: Daniel Chardin

& Salvador Rodrigues,

A M
N° – 1
being marked and numbred as in the Margent, and are to be delivered in the like good order and well conditioned, at the aforesaid Port of *Port S George* ——— (the danger of the Seas only excepted) unto *the above named Persons* ———

or to Assigns, he or they paying Freight for the said Goods *the freight being allready Paid to the Honourable East India Company* ———

with Primage and Average accustomed. In witness whereof the Master or Purser of the said Ship hath affirmed to ~~three~~ Bills of Lading all of this tenor and date; the one of which ~~three~~ Bills being accomplished the other ~~two~~ to stand void. And so God send the good Ship to her desired Port in safety, Amen. Dated in *London* the *2 of January 1686. Insides and concern not known.*

p Rich: Warner

Nina, Stokes and Dosha, the three of them together having tea. And who should arrive but…

Pity for Dosha, Nina and Stokes, that Chitten Coggeshall Jr., a child really, always, ever a Junior should arrive at tea time.

Where will it lead? Shall they invite him in?

Nina is late. Stokes is just on time for the tea party, for his watch is stopped twice and every twenty-four hours, is he not right on time?

Nina's watch loses but a minute a day. She is only punctual once in two years. Dosha, dear Dosha, doesn't wear a watch.

Should these three admit Junior Chittenden, yet can one hope to exclude an important guest? Alice could not be denied entrance in England; surely in America, master Chittenden will not allow his way to be barred.

And what time may he enter? The right time, 10 o'clock of course. You may go on to ask how will Stokes know 10 o'clock comes if his clock will not tell him?

Alas, Stokes' eyes are not on his clock.

Nina started to gyrate the upper part of her body and extend her tanned left arm inches beyond the door, moving her index finger. "There are no sweat glands, which would only moisten their feathers and make them heavy. Female birds have just a single ovary. Outside the breeding season the sex organs of both females—"

By this time, Nina was shouting.

"—and males atrophy!" Suddenly a pair of fiery red panties flew through the air and parachuted down atop her bra and shoes.

"Oh my G-d!" screamed Hastings, moving his eyes to the open door, and practically leapt across the transom.

"Chit, you're here!"

Bewildered, Chittenden Coggeshall Jr. stood like a statue in the doorway looking at all the feathers on the floor.

"I thought I heard Nina's voice."

"Oh no Chit, that was Miss Padawer. Nina's not here. Oh no, definitely not here."

"Wait a second," Professor Horn said to me. "Are you saying that there is nothing material at all?"

"*Well, the Jews lived a thousand years in Poland, and what are the signs that they were there? Graveyards and texts. And so it is in texts that even the non-religious must go to find their essence and their history… Recognizing ourselves as Middle Eastern, that our roots and sources are not Eastern or Western but Middle Eastern can help us in matters of identity.*"

Nina is the Orientalist fantasy in Stokes' mind. Dosha can see the dance and feel the pulse of it all and though she does not speak any language of the Middle East, surely her children could. "*Learning Hebrew is essential. All citizens must renew their relationship with the Hebrew language. Hebrew must be studied seriously in the Diaspora. The language that Jews will use to speak to each other cannot be broken, primitive English.*"

"*We writers have to reform the Hebrew language which is still a language with twenty-two consonants and no vowels. We will establish vowels in the Hebrew language in order to ease the way to learn the language.*"

Chittenden Coggeshall Jr., he is in the museum for he is hoping to close the great rift between American rich and poor.

Which we in Israel must do and not just within our borders but beyond ourselves, an Israeli-Jewish learning corps could resemble the Swiss with the Red Cross.

Chittenden Coggeshall can see beyond the room, the dream for social justice. But he cannot see Nina's dance.

Bill of lading bound for Elihu Yale, Daniel Chardin, and Salvador Rodrigues, 1686.

■ VIRGINIA WOOLF: Into the Park—Nina and Dosha. Nina invites. Nina has the key. Hadn't Uncle Charlie given Vita a master key to the Knole. Vita roamed about, having the place entirely to herself. "*The only person alive in the world, Vita was, with the Uncle Charlie skeleton key*."

But Nina wants company. She beckons Dosha into the garden. When they walk in the public park it is a garden to the both of them, for their eyes only.

"*I'm interested by the gnawing down of strata in friendship; how one passes unconsciously to different terms; takes things easier; don't mind hardly at all about dress or anything; scarcely feel it as an exciting atmosphere, which too, has its drawback from the 'fizzing' point of view; yet it is saner, perhaps deeper. I lay by the black currant bushes lecturing Vita on her floundering habits with the Campbells for instance*."

The two, Dosha and Nina, a path trod on by Vita and me—Knole and Sissinghurst, England or America, *ça ne change pas jamais*.

■ Chang Wei, 8th century Chinese aesthete: Door—Chittenden Coggeshall's grandfather was a wealthy merchant. His father was a lawyer and his mother an owner of vast lands. Chittenden is an official. "*It is fine to be an Official. You lock your door and shut yourself in. Quietly you drop a hook in the water and from time to time you catch a little fish*."

Chittenden has accidentally caught his cousin Nina, a little fish, but he is puzzled and she, as always, wiggles away from him and remains free.

■ VITA SACKVILLE WEST: Let's go into the Park—And where but into a garden shall Nina take her Dosha?

A tired swimmer in the waves of time
I throw my hands up: let the surface close:
Sink down through centuries to another time,
And buried find the castle and the rose.

My poem: and who better to dedicate it to than Virginia? And the Sissignhurst gardens: who better to walk in the garden first with but Virginia? Central Park—Sissinghurst. All begins on rubble and nettle. Rocks hauled. Dreams of past faded gardens—of gardens in the future —which once blooming provide walkways for lovers to dream yet again of future gardens:

To be sketched, seeded, watered, crimped, coddled, bent over, fondled, gazed at, overcome by, undone by. Gardens that slip into sand running between one's fingers, back to the ever receiving, thirsty and hungry earth.

"I see," said Chit, puzzled. "Anyway, the Board would like to hear the plan. Come across the hall with me right now and make sure they don't see this crap on the floor." Chittenden Coggeshall strode across the hallway with Stokes behind him.

Just before Stokes entered the Board Room, he turned and said, "Miss Padawer, see to those feathers! And send me a memo re: color."

As soon as the door closed, Nina stepped out fully dressed. She calmly placed her bra and panties inside her necessaire.

"My G-d, you're mad," Dosha said.

"Well, Mama always told me never to travel without a change of underwear," said Nina dryly. "Last minute, my boots. I was listening to you two jabber for forty-five minutes. It's already close to tea time. Let's go into the Park for a stroll. Leave the feathers to Hastings.

"And you, Nina, decide the exhition wall color."

Before the two left, Dosha went to the blackboard and wrote:

In Honor of Our Lady's Skirt: White.

■ JULIUS MEYER, DOSHA'S GREAT GRANDFATHER'S BROTHER: Let's go into the park for a stroll—My brother Max, though, when he would speak to me he would always say "Son" and then pause and say, "Let's go into the park for a stroll."

Walk we would, around and around. He would talk about all the big plans—another store, not two blocks from Farnham. Why have a warehouse use up half the building on Farnham. Have the whole structure—M. Meyer and Brothers—selling to the general public. Pianos, watch cases, all my curiosities. He could never mouth the words: Indian, Chinese and Japanese, and certainly never could utter the word Wigwam. Once I sputtered, "I don't live in a home, I live in my Wigwam."

I thought he would strike me, but he knew I'd leave. By G-d, I'd go back to Blomberg with nothing rather than be whipped, even by a brother. Especially by a brother.

All he could talk about, Max, was "move this there" and "we'll have the biggest" and "ours will be the best."

"The salesman have no place on Farnham." Over and over. I'd try to reason with him, tell him tales of the real Omaha or get my brothers Moritz and Adolph to tell him that the great outdoors was far greater than M. Meyer & Bros. on Farnham. The biggest part of nature he could imagine was Hanscom Park. But by G-d, do I miss those strolls with him. If only I could, once again, go into the park for a stroll with Max, or even with Moritz or Adolph.

◆ EMIL FISHER: Waiting, just outside…wants you to reply immediately—I was waiting just outside the consul Hiram Bingham IV's door in Marseilles. 1940. All the refugees were waiting, barely standing upright outside the American consul door. Standing by the hour, by the day. One waited but the American consul never came out. There were two exits in Marseilles—one leading into the hall just inside the consulate and the other outside in the back.

He was impossible to miss. His *"towering height and prematurely white hair made everybody else in the lobby look insignificant."*

But if I were inside the lobby and he left by the outside exit, what to do? I told my cherie, Lotty Johanna, waiting at the end of the line, outside in the cold, though pregnant: "Either he will see you or he will see me. Of course she said, "Better you wait, Émil, inside the consulate. If the American consul comes out into the inner lobby, he will want you to reply immediately. I'll wait outside. It's freezing and if he leaves by the back exit, he'll see me immediately. I'm so pregnant. He'll stop for sure." There was no arguing with my wife, ever. "Ma cherie," I said to her. "What will I say to him? Here Mr. Rockefeller—for that's what he looked like—here are our immigration papers, all 62 of them, for our family, sign our exit visas so that we may leave. It's crazy. I don't know one word to say, Cherie."

"Then hold the papers in your hands and say nothing," my wife said with a shy smile. As G-d is my witness, I waited for four hours inside the consulate. And suddenly, who do I see but Mr. Bingham Rockefeller himself, stooping down and holding Lotty's hand. He seemed twice as tall as she. "Mr. Fisher," he said with the polish only original Yankees from the Pilgrims' time have, "Might I see these documents?" My hands were shaking. Before I knew it, he was reading them intently. "Ah, I see your family is French, Belgian or Polish. I'll call them all 'important political figures.' Excellent. These will do." And suddenly he looked down at Lotty and said, "So I understand you have two girls, what are your wishes for your coming son?" "How do you know it will be a boy?" my wife asked, startled. "Oh, my father Hiram Bingham III and my mother had so many sons, I can see one coming. So, what will your son be in America?"

"Oh," said my cherie, looking directly at Mr. Rockefeller, "I'd like him to be you."

Bingham laughed. "So it shall be Mrs. Fisher, so it shall be." The laughter echoed in my ears through all the voyage of the Serpa Pinto, from Marseilles to Portugal, to Staten Island, even on the stop when we were searched for 3 days in Bermuda until on March 30, 1941, we arrived in America. I heard Bingham laugh: but my left hand which held the papers never stopped shaking.

CHAPTER 5

"WHITE Russian, three fingers, dear, straight up," said Walker Percy to his wife Bunt.

"And what's his name?" Bunt replied with a trace of annoyance.

"Dr. Richard Padawer, dear. It says so right here on his medical prescription slip. Well, this Dr. Padawer's waiting just outside the driveway. He wants you to read his letter and reply immediately. Don't they all? All your readers. All your Binx Bollingses, all your solitary moviegoers. Tired of watching the movie alone, they arrive at our door step. Lonely. They want to get into the projectionist's room. To see if there is in fact anyone there. The popcorn is not to their liking. They've seen the movie before—because it's a musical entitled "My Life" and it's sung off key so they are restless to the point of panic. And if, Lord knows, there's no one in the projection room, well then, who and what in G-d's name started the movie in the first place? What will they do when the show, their show, is over?"

"Dear," said Walker Percy, looking up at his wife, thin and with slender hips, like an early Ming vase. "What have you been drinking?"

Why is she bringing him a letter? Shall not his servant run and fetch it? And why is his wife to prepare his drink, again a servant's chore? Beyond reckoning. He looks at his wife, skeletal, a lifeless vase, once containing luxuriant flowers, fragrant, drawing his eyes and mouth toward her, much like Hieronomya drew me. Yet his vase is Ming from a long-dead dynasty, rulers of China, once seething with life, now forever gone. Better a wilting flower than a marble, albeit royal, sepulchre. I swear by all that's holy, Hieronyma was ever flower and never sepulchre to me. In Fort St. George and even in fairer London and I ever rushing liquid to her, even in my dotage. Ever India, never China.

■ SHITAO: Ming vase—Walker is in exile. Far from his native home. Even his wife is from another time. Ming. More a place than a time.

> The ten thousand li of Dongting's water
>   Are blurred, lost in the dawn half-light.
> A sail floats at the foot of the sun,
> Waves upon waves have washed
>   away the mountain's roots.
> White feathers scatter in all directions,
> An old wutong tree remains, weeping.
> The sound of soldiers shakes the ground;
> I gaze, heart broken, into the distance.

"This poem expresses my feelings as a young man at losing my family and nation. I wrote it when I was stuck at the Yueyang Tower, waiting to cross [Lake] Dongting, and now I have sketched an illustration. I found [the poem] in an old book, where 'the tattered edges added another layer of melancholy.' I have imitated that effect [in the painting]."

Walker too is in exile. He sees his wife as from another time. A flower within a Ming flower vase. Perishing within fragility. When he is gone, even friends from long ago will not be a comfort—for his mind has placed all humans in a vase of the past—Ming—shattered yet not fallen.

■ SHITAO: Bada Shanren (1626–1705): Ming vase—This is not the first letter Dr. Padawer has written to Dr. Percy. Even I can see they are both doctors. They are both artists pretending to be doctors for they must cure each other, if either is to live. Certainly both Shitao and myself cannot survive delicate as we are, watered within a cracked Ming vase.

Did you not write to me:

"I have received several letters from you, but I have not been able to make a reply. This is because I have been troubled by illnesses and have found myself inept in entertaining and corresponding with people. I am not like this with you alone. People on all sides know about this shortcoming of mine. It makes me a laughable person….The picture you were kind enough to send me some time ago was too big. My small house cannot hold it. Please do not refer to me as a monk, for I am a man who wears a hat and keeps his hair, and who is striving to cleanse everything…the sickness of old age is with me. What is to be done? What is to be done?"

Dr. Percy does not wish to be seen as a monk. But if he sees his wife as a flower in a Ming jar, how can we not say that he is a monk? Even if he finally replies to one of Dr. Padawer's letters, still he will not be cured—any more than my cousin Shi Ta'o's was, when finally he responded to me. We are all, Percy, Padawer, Shitao and I, all flowers, miracles really, watered so long ago, contained in our Ming memories. What is to be done? What is to be done?

■ ELIHU YALE: Wife—As his wife is his servant, shall we not assume with safety that his servant be his wife?

Cordially Yours
Blind Lemon Jefferson

You can't ever tell what a woman's
got on her mind
Man, you can't tell what a woman's
Got on her mind
You might think she's crazy
'bout you,
she's leavin'
you all the the time.

Mighty fine, this Bunt. Calling up her man's promises to her. Years before. Smart too. Says she'll drink with him before six. When he should be writing. Keepin' his promise long before in Louisiana. If he starts drinking then she starts drinking. And what worked for them? Who knows now? But Louisiana? Was it there?

I was raised in Texas, schooled in
Tennessee
I was raised in Texas schooled in
Tennessee
Now sugar you can't make no
Fat mouth out of me

Never did see Tennessee
As a young boy. But if it sings it sings.
If they made the promise to themselves in
Texas, and she sayin' Louisiana
What the difference?

The words not the place count. Walker's no fat mouth. Once she starts to drink before six, no tellin where she'll end up.

Yeah a woman act funny quit you
for another man
She ain't gon' look at you straight
But she's always raisin sand.

■ GROUCHO MARX: Projectionist—I would sit in Sheky Siegel's projectionist room while he watched the reels of *Horse Feathers* unwinding. I had gotten Sheky his job by saying to the Moldovan brothers that he was my cousin from the old country. So Sheky wasn't about to say "Groucho, no one's allowed in the projection booth during the movie."

It's me [Groucho].
Have we got a stadium?
Faculty: Yes.
Me: Have we got a college?
Faculty: Yes.
Me: Well, we can't support both. Tomorrow
we start tearing down the college.
Faculty: But Professor, where will the students sleep?
Me: Where they always slept. In the classroom.

Sheky would roar with laughter. Nothing beat it. Sheky was a professional. If he liked my movie, imagine what was going on downstairs in the audience.

"Nothing, but I will if you will. Walker, you know you promised, by all the joy we had together our first year in Louisiana, that you wouldn't drink until six o'clock, when you would stop writing and start courting me.

"But if you're going to start drinking during your writing time, and what's more have the effrontery to ask me to mix your poison, well then so will I. But no, Walker dear, I haven't started drinking just yet. But yes dear, I will if you will."

Walker Percy stared at the thick envelope, unsealed, covered with a blank prescription page stapled neatly onto the envelope. "The fellow wants me to answer him right here and now. He doesn't want to come up and meet me face to face?"

"Oh no," exclaimed Bunt. "He said he wouldn't dream of imposing on you. Just a brief answer is what he wants."

"So what's all the speechifying about, Bunt? The projectionist and the popcorn?" He walked toward his wife, resting his hand under her right shoulder so he could feel the warmth of her breast. It was just as thrilling as it had been a decade before when they'd gone fishing on Lake Ferguson—Shelby Foote and Liber Wood and she and Walker, vodka and orange soda for the men and fishing for the women. Then and now. "Who's the novelist dear? You or I?" asked Percy.

■ THE YUD, a Hasidic Rabbi: To come up— When I was a child, my father showed me in the prayer book the Hebrew letter "Yud." He told me that when the two letters—Yud— stand together, they form a word by themselves. This word is the Holy name of G-d.

I asked Father: suppose one letter "yud" stands just above another "yud" does this also form a holy name?

"'No,' my father told me.

"*Then and there I learned a lesson: When two Jews (Yuden) associate on an equal footing and discuss a subject of the Torah, the Indwelling Presence of G-d is with them. But when one of them holds himself superior to the other, G-d is not there.*"

Here Dr. Padawer doesn't want "to come up." Is he afraid? Or shy? Or too tired after his journey?

But Dr. Percy must reach out and lift Padawer up. Though Percy is not a Jew and Padawer is, Padawer comes to him as to a Rabbi.

If Dr. Percy accepts being a Rabbi, Padawer will listen to him. Percy will invite him up, speak with him, and raise Padawer to his level.

The Indwelling Presence of G-d will be with them. Even when they part.

■ ALFRED BINGHAM, brother of Hiram (Harry) Bingham IV, son of Hiram Bingham III: A Jew—Over and over my brother Harry would ask me: What is it about Yale that so captivated Father? Sometimes I'd say, Father enjoyed the leafy New Haven Woodbridge Cemetery where he'd walk often at midnight to "clear his head," where as a freshman he had brought his father's bones to be interred.

"Not Yale the college, Alfred. The man, Elihu Yale!" Harry would barge in. "Well truth to tell I thought it was a simple tale. A poor Welshman marries a wealthy English widow of a wealthy Fort St. George East India Company servant in 1680. Much like Father married the Tiffany fortune, or part of it, so he could study, write books, learning was what fascinated all the Binghams.

Certainly all my years at *Common Sense* made me feel that economics is the blood of it all.

But I knew Harry well enough to know that he wanted to hear that Elihu Yale was a politician first and foremost. Didn't he establish the corporation in Madras? Didn't he deal with Huguenots, Hindus, Muslims, Jews and Armenian Catholics? All things to all men he was. Service to England. Finally riches and then a burst of philanthropy to buy his way to heaven. Money was really not that important to Harry. Service was: "whom to serve is to reign." Our Groton School motto. He didn't wish to see Father through the spectacles of Ben Franklin, two pennies earned a penny saved, happiness. A soul saved: happiness. A thousand souls saved: Bingham bliss. Certain for Bingham I, II, III. How much more so for IV. All those souls saved by Harry.

Yet Harry wouldn't speak of his wartime heroism. Of those he saved. He would grumble and grouse and remain livid with silence about the shoddiness of the State Department that had betrayed him—but would not talk of his accomplishments:

One day in my "*long and expensive series of sessions with psychotherapists*" I mentioned to my therapist how Harry was haunted by why Father had written a biography of Elihu. "What was the biography of Elihu called?" asked the therapist. "*Elihu Yale: The American Nabob of Queen's Square.*"

It came to me then and there. My father chose to see Elihu as wealthy beyond dreams, of English aristocracy in public appearance.— yet Yale founded a seat of learning to last forever. Father would exploor Elihu Yale's forgotten life.

"And what didn't your father's biography of Yale reveal?" the therapist asked. "Well, he didn't do his usual thorough search '*finding beyond the monumental archives*' information about one figure in Elihu Yale's past. Of course the therapist didn't press me. I answered myself. "Elihu Yale's mistress, the mother of their illegitimate child, Hieronyma de Paiva. A widow, Portuguese and a Jew."

"What's got you in such a hostile twit?" asked Percy again. He looked at the blank prescription page:

"Dr. Richard Padawer, 44 Finch Court, Naperville, Illinois." Something clicked inside Percy's mind. He could hear his wife protesting, "I'm not in a twit: Normally, if that is a word I might use, visitors know someone in our circle and get an introduction. They come on by when we can see them. Occasionally they telephone and then you meet them in the waffle shop. They write to your publisher and then the letter is forwarded *tout-de-suite* and then you invite them on a Tuesday evening and tell me just after they ring the garden bell. But to arrive on foot, with no car and expect me to deliver this letter to you and fill out Padawer's prescription letter while he waits. You're not his doctor, and I'm not his nurse. In all of Goshen, this is odd, Walker, don't you think?"

"Fix me the drink, dear, and go tell him I'll answer with the promptness of Abraham. Bunt, is he a Jew?"

"Walker, how should I know? Ask him yourself."

"What do you mean he has no car? Did he walk from Naperville?"

"Dear, he's wearing the whitest of white suits, dark socks, and a tie with little white polka dots on a noble blue background. That's all I know. He looks like a Yankee Mark Twain."

All Father could say was "*With additional capital from the widow Hymners, Elihu became a specialist in precious stones. The diamond trade was particularly profitable…One of the diamond merchants in Fort St. George was a Portuguese Jew, Jacques de Paiva, who was highly thought of in London. His wife attracted Elihu. They may have given the young factor some hints.*"

I remember how I went silent. The next session too, I was silent. Then just before session's end, I said simply. "A Jew. Father didn't research the records of Jacques da Paiva, of Jacque's partner in London. He didn't uncover de Paiva's last will and testament. Nor Hieronyma's, if it exists. Father only mentioned the tombstone of their child, Charles, in Capetown.

"*Here lies Charles. Fashionable, virtuous, even elegant, loved by all*" erected by Jeronima de Paiva. With the curious addendum in stone: The only son of "*Lord Yale, once Governor of Madras, but not of Hieronyma.*"

Father did not go to Capetown to view the gravestone with his own eyes. He relied on a Dutch naturalist's reports. Father, who had to see everything with his own eyes—even Machu Picchu hidden by the clouds.

"Why do you think Father didn't view the tombstone," asked the therapists.

I knew full well what my therapist was thinking—he was an émigré from Vienna.

"No, Doctor. I know what you're thinking. It's not that she was a Jew."

"It's that Father had fallen in love with Suzanne Carroll Hill, a Maryland congressman's wife. And he wed her after mother divorced him to marry her concert accompanyist." Sweet and simple.

He and Elihu—a dark secret. Secret sharers. Father dedicated his biography of Elihu Yale to S.C.B. Suzanne Carroll Bingham. He posed by the tomb in 1937. Photographed by Suzanne Carroll, no less. Brothers under the skin. Father and Elihu. "And what did your brother Harry think of this theory?"

"I haven't spoken with him yet," I answered meekly—knowing to Harry service to G-d by serving mankind would be his answer to the genesis of Elihu's biography by father.

■ VAN GOGH: Dear Doctor—Who is the physician? Padawer is a physician. He is coming to be cured by the sun. The warmth. A remedy to be offered by Dr. Percy. For does not Dr. Percy live in the sun of the south? He is an artist.

I had written to Bernard in March 1888: "Quite a number of artists who love the sun and colors might settle in the south," echoing my words to Rappard in 1885: "If any painter…should come here, I should be glad to invite him to my house and show him the way."

Did Rappard come? No. Did Bernard come? No. I could not ask Gauguin to come. But Theo could for me, so I wrote Theo: "I could well share the new studio in the yellow house with someone, and I should like to. Perhaps Gauguin will come south?"

The truth is if one must ask another to come, it comes to nothing. One comes through despair or not at all. If Dr. Percy bars the door, Padawer will crash through the window. But the true physician is the sun. And art.

■ DORA DIAMANT, Kafka's last love: Jew—Jiri Langer's letter arrived as suddenly as the answer to my Franz's letter from Father asking for my Father's permission for Franz to wed me: Franz had written to Father that: "Although he was not a practicing Jew in Father's sense, he was a repentant one, seeking to return." When my brother Avram sent the Gerrer Rebbe's answer to Franz's request —the letter flew to my hand. Light as air it was— logical for it contained but one word of the Rebbe's: "No." I knew afterward, Franz, devastated, had asked Jiri to go to Belz to ask his Rebbe for permission. As Franz put it, we are all Jews. We are all sick. Do we all not ask another specialist for a "second opinion"? Sick. A sweet word. But death is what we are asking about. Dear Franz, Jiri wrote. The Belzer listened. I spoke of you. Of Marienbad. He remembered our meeting. I spoke of your writing. He listened and listened. If I tell you Franz, that I spent two hours there telling of my life and yours in Prague, speaking of what this marriage could do for you for Dora, for me—for you too are my Rabbi. Can not a friend be one's Rabbi? Franz you wrote me "a yes from Yissachar Dov of Belz would revive you, and a no can not worsen your condition more than it is." By all that is Holy, I tell you that though I wept and pleaded, the Belzer Rebbe said neither yes or no. He remained silent. What can I tell you, dearest Franz? Now I must show Jiri's letter to Franz. Even in Ger we had a saying: "The whole world journeys to Belz." I had heard a story from my tateleh. A neighbor of his in Bedzin was a follower of the Belzer. "When his son's wife became pregnant, when it came close to the ninth month, the father took his son and went to the Belzer Rebbe. It was close to the time, and it was customary that the Belzer should give a blessing. The father told him of the circumstances, but the Belzer did not answer. He repeated it twice, "I want a blessing," the Rebbe said something, but he just mumbled. The child died. When the man's daughter became pregnant the second time, the man and his son-in-law went again. This time when they told the Rebbe, he took a terrific interest, told them which hospital to go to, which doctor to take, to go at a certain time, and he assured them everything will be perfect. To them it was it was a miracle. It was a sign that the Rebbe saw that the first child would not live and he did not want to say good luck, to give his blessing." Franz does not know this story. Jiri Langer does. The Belzer is silent. Franz is dying. We will not wed. And what of it? The Gerer is dying too. And the Belzer. And I too. But Franz and I together, we will never die. "Put your hand on my forehead for a moment to give me courage," Franz asks me. I do. And I lift Franz's hand from his 100 pound body and place it on my forehead, to give me courage, and it does. Forever.

"I bet he's a Jew. *Of course he's a Jew. As much as I'm of the Jewish sect: Catholicism*," Walker spoke nonchalantly.

"Tell him I'll have his answer soon, and bring that White Russian, dear, and of course take a healthy sip yourself." Without looking up at his wife, Percy started to read the letter from Dr. Padawer:

"Dear Dr. Percy, or Walker if I may presume. Like you, I am a physician. Although I was trained at the University of Chicago, I believe my true college was the city of New York, where I lived just after graduation. Thus I believe that you and I are classmates.

"Several weeks ago I was sitting upon my American Harvester Home Garden Model #582 lawn mower mowing the lawn late on a Friday afternoon. There is something extraordinary in mowing a lawn. Grass grows. We shape, we cut; the bouquet of our work is overwhelming.

■ BILLUPS PHINIZY SPALDING: Catholic—My cousin Walker wrote me after Will's death:

"Will used to speak often in admiration of the Catholic Church—of her wisdom, noble tradition, esthetic beauty, etc. but he would not have regarded himself as a believer. That is to say, he did not believe that G-d actually revealed Himself in time, through the Jewish people, through the Incarnation, through the Catholic Church. He would regard the Jews as a peculiar people whose mysterious role in history could be explained by natural cultural causes; he regarded Christ as a great ethical teacher (and he would frequently list him along with Socrates, Gautama Buddha, St. Francis, Robert E. Lee, etc.); he regarded the Catholic Church as a purely human institution with a noble history and a great store of wisdom."

■ SITTING BULL THE GOOD, Ogalala Sioux: A Jew—Dosha's father: a Jew, like the White, Julius Meyer in Omaha, 1875 who had Red Cloud photographed standing next to him. And also Swift Bear and Spotted Tail, seated. All in dark, dark suits. Almost like White men they looked. Not I. I would go to Washington. I would accept a gun from the Great White Father. I too would sit for a photograph. I was the Good Sitting Bull, though they, the whites, could not distinguish between me and the Bad Sitting Bull, the Hunkpapa. In 1874, the Indian agent wrote the Great White Father and read me the letter: "Regarding quelling of disturbance of the agency—Sitting Bull is not the Hunkpapa but an Oglala, the nephew of Little Wound, Chief of the Kiosces, noted among the Indians for his courage and daring. During the late war [Sitting Bull] was a bitter enemy of the Whites. Since the treaty he has been friendly and a warm friend since I have been on the agency. He is a head soldier of the Head Bands, of which Young Man Afraid of His Horse is chief. I have made him leader of the soldiers whom I have armed with the permission of the department." So we went to Washington and stopped at Omaha. Red Cloud and I, Swift Bear and Spotted Tail. In Omaha, Julius Meyer, who spoke the language of the Whites but also the language of Ponca, Brule Sioux, Omaha, Winnebago, Pawnee and even my own language, Oglala Sioux. He knew my heart. He had seen the twin horns of the lying Buffalo, of the Bear's Lodge that the Whites call the Devil's tower—they should know—and Bear Butte— where Crazy Horse was born. Meyer also knew the other Sitting Bull, the Hunkpapa, the bad Sitting Bull, who would not sit with the Whites nor join them. I will sit with them, but will not dress like them. And Meyer knows that. He is my friend. Strange. This Jew approaching in a white suit. He reminds me of Julius Meyer, should be of the same tribe. I trust him, although he seems as lonely and lost as Julius. I would trust his children too.

■ WILL PERCY, Walker Percy's uncle: A Jew—My they make a pair— Padawer and Percy. If Padawer stays past lunch, they'll be partners for sure. My nephew Walker chants this psalm to himself each day:

"In this age of the lost self lost in the desert of theory and consumption nothing of significance remains but signs. And only two signs are of significance in a world where all cats are gray. One is oneself and the other is the Jews. But for the self that finds itself lost in the desert of theory and consumption, there remains only one sign, the Jews. By the Jews I mean not only Israel, the exclusive people of G-d, but the worldwide 'ecclesia' institution by one of them, G-d-become-man a Jew."

95

Vincent Van Gogh, *The Yellow House (The Street)*.

נפטר י"ג אב תקפ"ט ל'

פ"נ איש נבון וחכם
תם וישר וירא אלקים
והגה תורה ה' לילות וימי'
זקן ושבע ימים ה"ה
איש צדיק תמים הרבני
מ'ברוך יעקב בן מו"ה
אברהם שלמה ז"ל

■ LORD RAGLAN: Prescription—Dr. Padawer is visiting Walker as a writer, not as a fellow physician. He is not coming for a prescription—for he himself is writing a note on prescription paper.

Walker is a novelist—and Padawer knows that his life—albeit not the subject for a non-fiction study—can be sauce for Walker's novelistic stew.

"Any fact about a person which is not placed or recorded within a hundred years after his death is lost."

Padawer knows that he is denied fame—so immortality or at least notice is what he is craving.

■ DEBORAH ABOLAIS DUARTE, wife of Manuel Levy Duarte: Letter—When the letter arrived at our home, I instructed Rachel to bring it without a minute's delay to her father's office.

She must accept our decision. Or shall I say my decision. For Manuel would do whatever she wished if G-d willed me an early death. Alone he could not manage her. Nor the diamond trade. As sweet as he is, for the world is not made for the likes of him, nor Rachel at 19. By my Duarte blood I know it. Jacques, as handsome as the moon, but as changeable too. If he had agreed to stay in Amsterdam he could have had it all, the Duarte name, the house of Levy and Athias—all the Antwerp treasure pictures of my Uncle Diego Duarte. Is not Rachel, the only child, of ours and Athias childless and my uncle childless.

But the Indies, never, for Hindustan would finish everything. Either Jacques would perish, or would lose our faith or Rachel would perish.

Then let him have Hieronyma—radiant—they are a match in beauty, but what lies beneath those glistening eyes of hers, the devil's own can guess.

But to send my Duarte daughter to the Indies. Never. Only a father could deliver such a message to a daughter less than twenty.

"If you don't deliver these instructions Manuel, and if our daughter suspects they are my words, I then whispered to him, to the palace of my uncle Diego we go, and you are no longer a Duarte. And he did, and his daughter didn't. Wed de Paiva. Nor go to Hindustan.

"One has the sense of work, for what is work but ordering, knowing full well that time will return us to disorder. The truth is, Walker, my lawn in the back of my house has been undone for two years—much to my neighbor's distress. It was the lawn in front of my office complex I was working on. My fellow doctors prefer I not cut the lawn during office hours. As the eyes, ears and throat specialist Edward Cuffe says, it is odd for 'a professional' to do such work, and Lawrence Gottlieb says what Cuffe means is that it's too Jewish—too mean to save the $42 per month 'Henderson dream garden while you sleep' fee.

"Now as to being personally too Jewish, I find that exceedingly odd for I am a Rabbi's son, and a Rabbi's grandson and a Rabbi's great grandson etc., surely of all my sins, by their standards it may not be said that I am too Jewish.

"But that is for another day's discussion and another night's prescription. To return to my American Harvester, suddenly Mel the postman comes running across the office lawn shouting, 'Doc, a letter from your daughter.'

"There it was, a large envelope with carefully drawn butterflies sketched in color, one wing reaching from the front to the back of the envelope.

"How did I know it was from your daughter? Simple," said Mel as I stared at the envelope and him. "The name is Jerusha Padawer and she's not your wife, because wives rarely write and never draw butterflies. Gee, it's beautiful. Sign here. You're my last stop."

■ MANUEL LEVY DUARTE: A letter from your daughter—21 October 1687. Antonio Rodrigues Marques posted me a letter in Portuguese from London.

"Pataca coins have now risen to 64d because the two ships from Cadiz have not arrived and orders are increasing. As far as the insurance for the return voyage from India goes, I think it sufficient to make it 10 January 1688 for diamonds coming on a ship or ships. You will by now have received and paid the two bills drawn on you. Please write to Jacques de Paiva, who merits some rebuke for his brashness, and let me see what you write. His saying you will make 70% to 75% and some Englishmen too, has upset Pedro and Peter Henriques…they told me that they would only make 25% and wanted to cancel the deal."

I then wrote de Paiva from my heart, always mindful of my daughter Rachel. But seven days later, 28 Oct. 1687, who should be standing by my side—Rachel's hands shaking—handing me another letter. "It's from your daughter," she said, pointing to the name on the outside: de Paiva. I took the letter from her and opened it, and read it aloud in Portuguese: *"The letter to Jacques de Paiva is excellent and the courtesy of sending it open is appreciated. It will go with mine."*

"You are my dear daughter," I said to my Rachel. "This is from London from Antonio Rodrigues Marques and the name de Paiva on the outside of the letter is there because it refers to Jacques de Paiva—and not to Hieronyma de Paiva. And in any and all cases, you are my daughter and not she."

■ RACHEL DUARTE SALVADOR: From your daughter—One must not scream at one's father. Neither in Portuguese, in Hebrew, nor in any tongue.

When I saw the name on the letter, the name that should have been mine, for what did I care if Jacques de Paiva were to go to the ends of the Earth—farther east than Ft. St. George, more easterly than all of Hindustan—would I not have been happy? Anywhere, in his gaze.

Father would not hear of it. No, I must stay in Amsterdam with Mother, with him, with my Amsterdam husband to be, Salvador, he said over and over again. Not only with Abraham but with the entire house of Salvador, the brothers of Abraham: Jacob, known in England as Francis, and Isaac—himself—fled to Golconda as Salvador Rodrigues—all of them diamond traders.

If Father has found a bride for my beloved Jacques, our cousin Hieronyma, surely she must be his daughter, not I.

But fathers do not listen to daughters and wives do not plead their daughter's cause. So I was wed at 19 to Abraham Salvador, a not very young 35. My beloved Jacques is in Hindustan, with voyage-money, dowry, cousin bride Hieronyma, everything lost—to the Indies. Planned and paid for, by my father. How can he say I am his daughter?

■ DYLAN THOMAS: One of us very happy. Not the same one but always one of us—Between the University in Chicago and where he is now Richard Padawer was a poet and Susanna was his parchment. She was a poet and he her foolscap. One of them very happy, not the same always. But always one.

Caitlin and I, dancing round each other. Starting our lovemaking at the Eiffel Tower Hotel in London, rolling onward through Richard Hughes' castle in Laugharne. Caitlin spoken for by Augustus Johns and I by all who returned my glance.

"We'll always keep each alive." Love is always sung in person, and written when apart. I am always happiest when writing to, about, and always for my dream of Cait. And Cait, of what did she dream? Her Irish father? Of London's Augustus Johns, or of me and Laugharne?

How could I see her when my hand gripped the paper before me as I wrote to Caitlin, even as I slept in her arms.

Caitlin Thomas: one of us very happy, not the same one always but always one of us.

She may be happy only if her father is unhappy.

"My father's not man but monster," she told me. He horrifies every pore in my body. I hold myself apart, and meditate in silence."

Caitlin's father's wine cellar, the best in all of Ireland—she waiting at Father's narrow bar in Ennistymon and painting and writing poetry.

"This place, Father's Ennistymon Crown Hotel, is totally beautiful and corrupt—yes—G-d will guide me."

Father guided the hand of Augustus John while he painted Caitlin. Father guided Augustus' other hand while he spun her on the wheel of his lust.

Caitlin's diary: "What is the magic that pervades the air? I wrote in my first immortal poem, and nothing would persuade me that it was not immortal; I could feel the authentic throb and tingle running down my spine and I chanted it."

Caitlin, too, Muse and Poet herself. Writing and chanting, sings with one's tongue and with one's fingers. One of us very happy. Not the same one always but always one of us.

"And I did and the letter, summarized, said: 'Dear Dad, Mother might as well be in Chicago for all that I see her or talk to her or understand her.'

"The truth is, Walker, Susanna, Jerusha's mother, and I are not together. Susanna was extraordinary looking. She lived across the street from me, studying sociology at the University of Chicago. We met when she had to carry two huge boxes of placards down to the Union headquarters and her then boyfriend Henry Holland, I believe, failed to show up. I had an autopsy course which I cut, pardon the pun. One thing led to another as they inevitably do in one's twenties and shortly we were living on Waverly Place in the West Village under a skylight with one of us very happy. Not the same one always, but always one of us. To return to Jerusha. She is not a pilgrim, named after—'verily shall I give you this land as an everlasting (Jerusha) inheritance'—but rather the Lithuanian version thereof. Dreaming of Zion. My father was a Rabbi, teaching in Slonim, 'Jerusalem of the West' refusing to follow his children to America. In those days, I was Reuben, not Richard, and with my brother and sister—deigning to live in my mother's brother's house—but of course where else could we live once we had left Ellis Island and trekked to Chicago?

■ GAUGUIN: Susanna had to carry huge boxes to the Union headquarters—I was conceived in Paris and born in the revolutionary year of 1848. My father, Clovis, editor of the *Le National*, laughed at the ridiculous humbug himself, Napoleon III. Third rate in everything. My grandmother too, Flora, could smell wealth a boulevard away. And see poverty even further.

I like Susanna. She had to carry boxes of placards down to the headquarters of the union. Not because she was made to but because she made herself do it. What was she to do? Or I, or grandmother Flora or father? Close our eyes to misery? Everywhere. La Belle France, Martinique, en brèf, le monde entier. Even then we would smell poverty. What were we to do, close our nostrils? Still we heard cries. Even if we all, Father, Grandmother, Susanana and I, did not see hear or smell. Still Millet would wake us from our sleep and in our nightmare we would act. I to paint, the others to act. It is all one.

■ LEONARD WOOLF: Extraordinary —Virginia could see from one end of the world to the other. As broad of vision as her father was shortsighted. But she could not sit still for Duncan Grant or any other. Duncan told me that "he had to work swiftly or she might just get up and walk out."

Duncan saw her fear of being pinned, frozen forever, much as he pinned butterflies on trecle spread on tree bark. Her father only saw her through his madness, ever shifting, through countless emendations of those great Victorians who passed through their house as guests, her father, sometimes lion of fame, sometimes weeping without warning at the dinning table.

And I her husband, her lover, her publisher, her widower. I saw her always as I saw her first: she and Vanessa, chaperoned by their cousin Katherine Stephen when they came to their brother Thoby's room at Trinity College—in June of our millennium, 1900. "In white dresses and large hats with parasols in their hands. Their extraordinary beauty literally took one's breath away."

◆ SARAH PADAWER, DOSHA'S GRAND-MOTHER: Goldeneh Land—Simha and I would come after dinner to Reuben's house and he and Susanna would just be finishing their dinner with Jerusha. G-d forbid we should be invited for dinner together with them.

His wife would always be rushing in and out of the kitchen shouting "Richard honey bunch" or "Little dumpling" or some *meshugah* food name. "We have to rush, we're late, the movie starts at 8:10." Always she knew the time to the minute, G-d forbid she would start eating ten minutes early and eat like a *mensch*.

"Oh, I hate to leave you with the dishes, Mrs. P.," she'd shout. "But Richard and I are running."

"Maybe next week you could join us, but I never know what dishes you'll eat, Mrs. P.," sticking the knife into us. If we kept kosher in the Beloruss forests during the War, surely in Brooklyn it wouldn't be such a miracle.

And she'd blow a kiss to Jerusha while dragging Reuben out the door, like a *Golem* he was, saying almost nothing, just following her.

Jerusha would walk to the window, looking outside at her mother and father as they walked down the street and even for a long time afterward.

Then she would slowly walk toward the table, and take her parents' two dinner plates, one her father's with no food left on the plate and one her stupid mother's—"you can never be too rich or too skinny," Susanna would say—with half the food uneaten, and take them toward the sink.

With a tiny voice, Jerusha would say, "Tell me a story." I'd look at Simha but I could see he was about to cry and all I could say is "How do I start?"

Jersuha would answer: "Once upon a time in a golden land there was a little girl with a mother and father. They lived all by themselves far from anyone else…"

I don't remember how I was able to think. The Angel Gabriel himself must have put the words in my mouth. Praised be G-d forever.

I grew up without parents but with a parental admonition that when I wed, the first girl should be named Sarah after my mother. But if, please G-d, mother was alive then the girl should be called "Jerusha," "the inheritance," "the land," unforgotten Jerusalem, the eternal gift. We would all go there, I, my wife, our daughter—no mention of the possibility of a son. With Mother and Father still alive and a faulty testimentary letter that became an astonishingly precise precatory predictor that we would meet in the Holy Land. No mention was made of my mother's brother. Pfui. He would stay in the "Goldeneh Land" of Chicago.

"But to return to Jerusha. She wanted me to visit her in New York. She said it would do us both good. I should stop "running away" and she felt if not now, when? The truth is that the reason I left was that two years ago I was diagnosed in New York with severe arrhythmia.

"My heart had already been broken on Waverly Place—there was a limit to how many times I could visit my parents' grave in Monte-fiore Cemetery in Ardsdale, New Jersey. I simply had left. I am not a novelist nor was meant to be.

"The 'invitation' suggested I meet my daughter at 12 o'clock the following Friday on the American Museum of Natural History entrance steps in front of Central Park. Jerusha only worked half of Friday at her new job at the Museum and we could picnic and talk.

◆ SIMHA PADAWER: Dosha's grandfather—Jerusha: She understood everything: the past, the present and the future.

Rabbi Johanan said: "Since the temple was destroyed, prophecy was taken from the prophets and given to the foolish and to babes."

Jerusha knew the story of the future. She recited it all: "Once upon a time, there was a little girl with a mother and father and they lived in a land all by themselves far from anyone else."

When I was in Slonim, I remember sitting with my *havrusa*—the brother of my Sarah—before my wedding.

Reb. Weinberg asked me to explain the passage in Yoma.

"*On Yom Kippur, it is prohibited to engage in eating and drinking, in washing oneself, in anointing oneself with oil, in wearing leather shoes and in cohabitation. The king and the bride may wash their face and a new mother may wear shoes.*"

But before I could answer, my learning partner spoke. Each word he explained. Surely the king must wash because he must always present an attractive appearance, as it is written in Isaiah 33:17: "*Your eyes will behold the king in his splendor.*" A bride remains a bride even for thirty days following her wedding, and she must remain beautiful for her husband so a warm relationship develops between them.

A new mother wears shoes so that the cold floors, according to Rashi, will not harm her body. And on and on he went. For more than an hour.

"And what do you say, Padawer?" the Rosh Yeshivah asked me. I replied simply, "Failure to afflict oneself on Yom Kippur is punishable by spiritual exile."

Reb. Weinberg smiled and said: "You both speak well. Your study partner is an Ashkenasi, every word explained on each level. You, Padawer, a Sephardi, you have squeezed it all into one sentence."

Shall I comment on Jerusha's tale. As Rabbi Nahman teaches us, the way things start is the way they end.

My study partner, Kleinhaus, Antwerpener would say, "The little girl has a mother but she doesn't have a father. But rather she has a Father. For is not the heavenly Father of us all with us at all times? And in all places." "Once upon a time," which occurs again and again, over and over, but I, who am I to comment on my grandchild's story?

Doubly exiled, is she and my wife and I for are not the mother and father living in a land all by themselves? They will not afflict themselves on Yom Kippur. And are they not in spiritual exile from their beloved Jerusha, from me and Sarah, and far from anyone else?

But which grandfather can speak these words to a granddaughter? In Slonim, we would say: "G-d could not be everywhere, so He created mothers." In America, you can see, G-d could not be everywhere so He created grandmothers.

Thank G-d for my Sarah, she could speak to our grandchild.

Cut-stone inlay of a lotus flower on the side of the Taj Mahal.

◆ SIMHA PADAWER: Bless her soul—My son Reuben is blessing my granddaughter Jerusha. Her innermost heart: her soul. He is singing his Mosaic blessing to his tribe: "Let Reuben live and not die."

But surely these are his last words to her. Spoken not written. Yet Talmud Gittin teaches us *"the words of the dying person are as valid as if they were written down and registered."*

Jerusha has vowed to wed and has received Reuben's blessing. The Holy Zohar teaches us when the children are blessed, the parents by this very token are blessed.

My son has journeyed far. In a suit of white. His day of atonement. He has come to his American Rabbi, the Doctor Percy who says "Amen" with all his heart.

"An energetic amen is said to open the gates of Paradise, to win for children a place in the world to come."

This Dr. Percy knows. For my granddaughter has given the Doctor's book to her father and she has sent her father to him. Just as we, my dear wife Sarah and I, were brought *lehavdil* to the Rebbe at 770 Eastern Parkway after the War.

Now nothing is greater to the Blessed Holy One than "Amen," says Midrash Devarim Rabbah, and *"Greater is the one who responds Amen than the one who blesses."*

We all need partners. I, Jerusha, her father, my Reuben and Doctor Percy, all of us.

■ VIRGINIA WOOLF: How she would spend the rest of her life?—How shall she, or I, ever know that unless one *"has gone too far to come back?"*

Dosha, fresh from her Cambridge studies, is wise enough to know *"it is vain and foolish to talk of knowing Greek."*

And I, my Cambridge was Father's library. The books he wrote and the books he read.

"Women have served all these centuries as looking glasses possessing the magic and delicious power of reflecting the figure of man at twice its natural size."

Dosha has already been at University. She will choose: painter, poet, naturalist, housewife, mother or counterfeiter, a list well ordered, from real to unreal.

But she is on firm ground.

Cambridge for me: a durbar parade-ground passing in review before Leonard, Thoby, and all the rest. The torch of my beauty to be admired. By all, by each, but by myself?

"Surely it is time someone invented a new plot, or that the author came out from the bushes."

Dosha will an author be, or move the hand that will pen her, different she is. If only I'd her father.

"I arrived on Thursday night, checked into the Hotel Olcott, slept well, and on the dot of 12 o'clock I met Jerusha. She giggled, bless her soul, at my white suit. These were the points that she made:

A. Not all couples were made for each other.
B. Her relationship with her mother was her business and had nothing to do with me.
C. My relationship with her was excellent; therefore, it made no sense for me to live in a distant city.
D. I should stop trying to stop asking her whom she was going out with and admit that I would "kill to know."
E. That, yes, she would wed.
F. And that, yes, I would like the "lad."
G. And that she had no idea of how she would spend the rest of her life. As a painter, a poet, a naturalist, a housewife, a mother, or a bank note counterfeiter, but that I would always be a part of her choice (except counterfeiter because I was weak in the keeping secrets department). Because I had always supported her and had always given her the assurance that she would be special because she was special.

"The points I made to her were:

A. Not all couples were made for each other for all time.
B. Her relationship with her mother was her business.
C. That I never dreamt any daughter could be as generous to a father as she was.
D. That she looked radiant, was probably in love, and from now on I would ask her openly whom she was dating.
E. And that I gave her my blessings now and forever, in each and everything she did or dreamed of.

"But when she pressed me to move back to New York, I began to weep. I couldn't speak of my arrhythmia. I hugged her that afternoon, just before the Sabbath began, but I felt I couldn't bring myself to tell her how short a time I had left.

■ DIAMOND JIM BRADY: White suit—It isn't the white suit that makes daughter Dosha giggle. Her father might as well be Lot, naked he appears, without sporting so much as a diamond, ruby or even a sapphire to offset his choice of suit. Generally *"the trouble with our American men is that they overdress. They do not understand that beauty unadorned is adorned the most. Now, I take it that I am considered a handsome man and one who would be called well dressed. Never by any chance do I permit more than seventeen colors to creep into the pattern of my waistcoat. Moreover, I consider that twenty-eight rings are enough for any man to wear at one time. The others may be carried in the pocket and exhibited as occasion requires. A similar rule applies to the cuff buttons and shirt studs…three of them may be worn without entirely covering the shirt bosom. Diamonds larger than door knobs should never be worn except in the evening."*

■ DUNCAN GRANT, Bloomsbury painter: Points —Dosha's points, as finely drawn as Virginia Stephen's face before the Woolf was at her door.

Not all couples were made for each other, but all Bloomsbury couples fantasize that they are made for each other. Virginia is looking beyond Leonard, beyond Vita and backward again through Vanessa all the way to Mr. Leslie Stephen, president of the London library, a very grand honor it was for Tennyson and Carlyle before Tennyson had been so honored. To think of it, Mr. Gladstone was but vice president.

These *"great people"*—Virginia would confide in me—*"always talked much as you and I talk; Tennyson would say to me"*—Virginia would prattle—*"pass the salt"* or *"Thank you for the butter."*

She is musing, Dosha is, on how the rest of her life will be spent and mispent. It will not have Virginia's mix, for Vanessa was to be the painter and the mother, Thoby was to be elected the poet, leaving naturalist and wife to Virginia. All images of Father Leslie Stephen imprinted on his children's foreheads, like playing cards forever shuffled during the after adult dinner games that parents forever play while their children are half asleep.

Dosha is alone and she needs to be all in all: poet, painter, wife or mother, fantasy or genuine or counterfeit. A version of them and all acceptable to the extent of the openess of her father's heart. Dosha's father weeping by himself; Virginia's father weeping at dinner in full view of the children.

■ SHELBY FOOTE: *The Moviegoer* by you, Walker Percy—Walker summoned me down in early July to Covington with an imperial message: "We are desirous to discuss the worlds of art and music with you." Walker knew full well I was neither Cardinal nor he Pope. We were just two boys, friends since thirteen when Uncle Will approached me at the country club swimming pool in the spring of 1930.

"Some kinsmen of mine are coming here to spend the summer with me. There are three boys in the group and two older boys are about your age, young Shelby. I hope you'll come over to the house often and help them enjoy themselves while they're here."

There we were, Percy and I, both with no fathers living, and Walker asking me a million questions about my mother—Morris Rosenstock's daughter, Walker would call her. And come over to Uncle Will's house I did and often and didn't stop talking or dreaming with Walker for thirty years. Walker indicated the subjects to be discussed when we would meet. "Art," he said. I brought him an illustrated book on Vermeer, his favorite painter, and when he said "music" I brought him Mozart's *Requiem*, but I knew he wanted to talk about literature. On the last night of my stay in Covington on the dot of midnight, Walker said to me: "I'm writing a novel, Shelby. Do you think Vermeer was a Jew?" The question wasn't meant to be answered. Walker followed it up with, "I've been listening to your offerings: Mozart's *Requiem*. Do you think if he hadn't lived in Vienna, let's say he was a country boy, just like us, originally from Greenville and living in Covington, Louisiana, do you think he could have written the *Requiem*?" "Walker, is that what you brought me down here to discuss? How should I know?" "Well," said Walker. "You are the grandson of Morris Rosenstock, a Viennese Jew and an accountant by trade who came to the Mississippi Delta in 1892. Do my theories add up?"

"Well, Walker," I said with half-irony that only men can have who have known each other through their teens, high school, proms, courtship, marriage and divorce with a soupçon of "both of us are going to change the world." "What you're really saying, Walker is you're about to show me your novel that you've been working on since 1920 when we met. Is it about Vermeer or Mozart?"

"That it is Shelby, but I don't dare mention them by name and New York wants me to change it, to change it and to change it. If you breathe a word of the men from Delft and Vienna, I'll tell the world what you did and didn't do to Tess during the War."

"Deal," I said. "But Walker, no one, *NO one should ever monkey with a writer's manuscript. These articulate people who can put their finger on the trouble and tell why are archfiends incarnate."* Deal, I repeated, "but send me your novel, not New York's novel."

■ STANLEY KAUFFMANN, Percy's editor: *The Moviegoer* by Walker Percy—Unless you judge a book by the cover, of course, Walker was the author. But if you're an American, and aren't we all, I simply drew a thin line through the proposed title *Carnival in Gentilly: Confessions of a Moviegoer* and wrote above it: *The Moviegoer*. Gone: Confession. Gone: Gentilly. And what remained? *"The other day a sociologist reported that a significantly large percentage of solitary moviegoers are Jews."*

"As we parted, Walker, I asked her as I always did, 'Read any books lately?' She reached into her knapsack and handed me *The Moviegoer*. 'I love you, Dad. To be continued?' she said and we parted.

"I stayed up all night in the Olcott. I've read your book three times, Walker.

"That's why I'm here. What do I do? Please fill out my prescription."

Walker Percy looked at his desk. A quiet had settled over his lawn. He could see the sun setting over Lake Pontchartrain, well beyond Covington.

He noticed the White Russian Bunt had placed before him. He sipped it and reached into his drawer. There was a note pad from his Columbia days: Walker Percy. He wrote in scriptural block letters: "REUBEN, YOU HAVE SUFFERED AS THE FIRST BORN. BUT YOU HAVE NOT LOST THE POWER TO LOVE. YOU HAVE ALREADY SPOKEN TO YOUR DAUGHTER. NOT WITH WORDS BUT WITH YOUR HEART. SHE UNDERSTANDS."

■ ANGUS CAMERON, Percy's editor at Knopf after Kauffmann: *Moviegoer—The Moviegoer* by you, Walker Percy. But it wasn't by you, Walker Percy, not if Mr. Knopf had anything to do with it. He had everything to do with it if Knopf's imprimatur was on the book.

■ AUTHORS: first Will Percy and then Walker Percy, uncle and nephew, both Knopf authors: *"I tried to tie this book up, and not in any way that's invidiously comparative either, with the two outlooks of two generations of Southerners which Alfred A. Knopf has had the pleasure of publishing."*

■ ELIZABETH OTIS, Percy's agent at McIntosh who submitted *Moviegoer* to Knopf: *Moviegoer*—Dr. Padawer is far more preceptive than he appears. Why does he not mention *The Moviegoer* alone, without the words "by you, Walker Percy." Because Dr. Padawer senses that Walker did not really write the novel.

Padawer is correct.

Who wrote the novel? Padawer doesn't know, for he's not the book's agent. I am. I know. Stanley Kauffmann wrote it. Or fashioned it. Or shaped it. Or brought it into being. Or. Or. Or.

Kauffmann was 43 years old in '61 when I sent him Walker's typescript and a novel's not a novel until it's edited, contracted for, laid out, printed, promoted and sent to the stores to be handled, fondled, passed over, purchased, remaindered. Until it's crowed over, despaired over, ignored, reviewed, destroyed the sleep of, in short: a novel's created, still-born, ever growing, forgotten, missing in action, soon to be Messianically revived, till the end of time. Only the agent knows its supposed author and its whereabouts.

Kauffmann was 19 in '61 and I daresay he was 61 in 1943. No fool, and definitely not born yesterday.

He wrote and told Walker Percy in no unmincing northern words: *"It's not that The Moviegoer's structure falters here [in the middle] because it never had a strong structure; it begins to assume a structure, a purpose, almost an obligation to have a more conventional plan and resolution. Particularly weak was the use of a death [Binx's uncle] as the immediate cause of Binx's rengagement with the world." "At present,"* Kauffmann noted, *"it is as if someone had suddenly switched on a lot of rosy lights."*

Presto, no Novel.

Finally, on July 20, 1961, with Kauffmann's hand, I believe guiding Walker's though I think after Percy's friend Shelby Foote's encouraging visit, Percy penned the following to Kauffmann.

"I am going to have another go at it, at least another hard look—and—think, because your acute criticism (and Miss Otis's which has been much the same as yours all along) only confirms my own misgivings. I mean to say that all I can hope to do is please myself, so if you should see it again you need not worry that I have tried to fix it up to pass Knopf."

Kauffmann, myself, Shelby Foote, and a host of others, right on the palimsest cover of *The Moviegoer* just under the putative author's name.

Vermeer, details from *Girl Reading a Letter at an Open Window*.   105

◆ SARAH PADAWER: Opened the door…reading his note—When we lived in Brooklyn after the War, Simha rarely went out. To visit the grandchild, Jerusha, of course, yes. But to go to Chicago, to see my brother, Simha flatly refused. "He's rich, your brother," said Simha. "He can afford to come to us." "He's offered to send us the train tickets," I said. "I don't need his *tseddakah*," said Simha sharply. "He's rich," I said, "He can't afford the time to come. "That's what rich is in America," said my husband. To get him to go anywhere was impossible. I remember when I pushed him to go to that Yiddish novelist Singer. "I'll go on Hanukah, but not again, never on Purim."

"What's the big deal, really? It's in Yiddish. It's a story. We'll see Mrs. Mermelstein. She lost her husband, and it's only right to go. Her grandson is leading the program on Jewish novelists."

"I'm not interested in novelists. I'm interested in serious books—a *sefer*," said Simha.

My son Reuben, a genius really as like his father as two drops of water, and who is he visiting: his Rabbi, Dr. Percy, who opens the door from his study to him. My son is reading what his Rabbi writes. With the same expression, Simha would look at a note from the Stoliner. Here, the paper is different. The words are different, so different. But the expression on the face, the same.

■ STANLEY KAUFFMANN, Walker Percy's editor: Reading the note—Walker wrote to me in long hand. Tightly packed majuscule, somewhat medieval. A monk in Iona, he was, at the edge of the darkness preserving the light.

Not at all easy to read, his notes. But easy, so easy to look at. Beautiful. If he had colored his capital letters and written on parchment, it would have been the Lindisfarne Gospels or perhaps a page from the Book of Kells.

"Walker, you're a doctor," I protested to him once, in a rare phone conversation. Percy didn't feel comfortable on the phone. "I can't read your prescription-writing script."

"Oh, Stanley, you've read before, again and again, it's engraved on your heart.

Go forth from your native land and from your father's house to the land that I will show you. I will make you a great nation, and I will bless you. All the families of the earth shall bless themselves by you."

"*Abraham saw signs of G-d and believed. Now the only sign is that all the signs in the world make no difference. Is this G-d's ironic revenge? But I am on to him. You are on to him. Pax Vobiscum"*

Walker opened the door of the study and called out to Bunt, "Please take this prescription to Dr. Padawer at the gate, and invite him in if he wants to come."

Bunt walked down the winding garden path to Dr. Padawer, opened the gate and handed him the envelope with her husband's note taped onto the envelope.

Walker Percy could see his wife pointing to the house. And the man reading the note intently and nodding his head.

As he turned to leave the Percy property, Richard Padawer waved to the house.

Walker Percy waved back, thinking of the blessing of Abraham.

Percy's eyes followed Padawer's as he meandered down the side of the valley. When he reached Thomspon's bend, the last Percy could make out was the back of his suit—a shimmering dot of white.

◆ SIMHA PADAWER: Reading—My wife Sarah dragged me to her "holiday book club." Twice a year they met, the Wednesday during Hanukkah and the Monday after Purim. They called it *Mittevoch und Donnershtik.*

"Simha, after the War, you haven't read a single story, a novel. It will do you good to come."

"Before the War, I didn't read a single story. I studied the Talmud," I thought but I didn't correct her. Of course, I went. Sixty-two women and thirty-six husbands. In America, the women survive the men. That's why they call it the *Goldeneh Medinah*, the Golden Country.

Isaac Singer from Warsaw had just read in Yiddish an excerpt of a short story and Sadie Mermelstein's grandson (Already a Phd Doctor at 22!) who spoke two words of Yiddish fluently—mazel tov—was the interviewer.

Isaac, you say: "*If there is such a thing as truth, it is as complicated and hidden as a crown of feathers,*" said Mermelstein, not realizing this sentence occurred nowhere in what Singer had read, but nothing follows anything in America, land of complete freedom, "Is there someone in the audience who would like to ask a question only it has to be a man first. Let's have a little fun," smiled Mermelstein junior junior. "Please say your name first."

Next, I see a man, very elegant, European 100%, stand up, "Emil Fisher. Professor Singer, I'm a feather dealer, Meletz born, lived in Paris. Which feathers do you talk of as the truth, fancy feather for ladies hats or bedding feathers?"

All the men laughed, and the ladies laughed twice as hard. "Since you are a man, Mr. Fisher, I say fancy feathers. But if a lady, and I don't see many, asked the same question, I should say bedding for sure. That's where the truth lies, Mr. Fisher."

Mermelstein immediately asked, "Permit me Isaac a question. Why do you write in Yiddish?"

Sarah whispered to me: "Not enough *tsuris*, this writer has. Should he write and talk in Greek for us?"

But Singer answered: "*When the Messiah comes, the dead from Europe will be raised, alive. Once they walk from the cemetery, they will all ask in Yiddish, 'Read any good books lately?' And then my Yiddish novels will sell and sell and sell.*"

And what were we, my Sarah and I, dead or living?

■ SØREN KIERKEGAARD (1813–1865): Join—*"Truth is power. But one can see that only in rare instances, because it is suffering and must be defeated as long as it is truth. When it has become victorious, others will join it. Why? Because it is truth? No, if it had been for that reason, they would have joined it also when it was suffering. Therefore, they do not join it because it has power. They join it after it has become a power because others had joined it."*

And who is joining whom? Is youthful Dosha joining Nina? Nina is hungry because of her longings for Thompson—but Thompson is only an assistant. To whom? To the teacher of us all: men, women, even children. The teacher who though he speaks to us each and every day, we hear him if we allow ourselves to. Still, we cannot approach him.

"Between G-d and man there is an infinite, yawning, qualitative difference." A difference so great that the closer Nina or Dosha come, albeit only a distance of an extended arm the distance isn't bridgeable other than through an intermediary.

But Nina's heart is open. She thirsts and hungers for the word. She cannot sleep. The heavenly gates are never closed to her or her companion Dosha.

■ SAMUEL CLEMENS (Mark Twain): A palace—These are the royals. A palace scene. The upper of uppers. It's night and they want breakfast fruit. A four piece jug band is certainly creating a lot of wind. The boys are drinking before starting Four-handed Poker. The ladies will have to wait for the game to end before the games can begin, but they'll know exactly when because they're looking through the peephole in the harem floor. In Persia, the peeping Toms are Tesses.

But how does the artist, Mr. Ali, know what is in the harem? Same as I did. In the Prince of Palitana's harem's rooms, Livy and Clara visited and told me all. The only trouble, said my wife to me, *"was that she was as great a curiosity to the harem ladies as they were to her."*

All the same, men, women. From Hartford to Hindustan. When *"I think of man, and how he is constructed, and what a shabby poor ridiculous thing he is, and how mistaken he is in his estimate of his character and powers and his place among the animals,"* I weep and sniff and laugh at the same time.

I agree with Mr. Ali, who's at the top of the palace heap, an artist. Ali and me, each of us: a little puppy wagging his curly red tail at the sight of it all.

■ SU DONG PO (1037–1101), Sung Poet: In the center—*"Originally I did just the tree, but some exhilaration was left over so I did the bamboo and stone on another piece of paper."*

In the center, quite properly, is a blossoming tree. Quite properly, too, a bud resting on the ground. More than these, I fear, the paper—always fragile—cannot support.

Is paper so dear that musicians and wine drinkers cannot enter on another manuscript leaf?

Or is the artist so weary from seeing so much and perhaps himself drinking with his figures that he has not the strength to stop painting and not the will to begin another page?

C H A P T E R   6

"WHITE. The grace of white." Cary Welch had lectured Dosha, her six Radcliffe classmates and one entranced tutorial assistant. Welch was more than a professor, he was an autodidact of Far Eastern art. "This is white. This is truly white. This white," said Professor Welch, pointing at an ivory colored dog squatting squarely in the center of a 16th century palace in a Persian miniature. "How would you describe the white, Miss Padawer?"

Dosha stared at the painting. What was Welch's eye searching for She hesitated for two reasons: Professor Welch would immediately answer his own question, and Dosha was feeling waterlogged.

She and her roommate Nina Abigail Coggeshall had stayed up half the night talking about Nina's infatuation with Thompson, Cary Welch's tutorial assistant. At 2:15, Nina had proclaimed: "Thompson makes me hungry. Join me for a bite to eat."

"Everything is closed, Nina," said Dosha. "Let's get to sleep."

"The I.H.O.P. never closes its doors," Nina protested.

"The International House of Pancakes!" Dosha cried. "Pancakes at this hour?"

"Early breakfasts make pulchritudinous girls, my Dad always told me. We've got to be wide awake for Thompson's Far Eastern art seminar. 10 o'clock is just minutes away." "It's not Thompson's class, it's Professor Welch's," Dosha said.

■ Isaac Luria: White, white—Dosha: A white rose. Nina: a red rose. *"Rabbi Abba was on a journey and Rabbi Isaac was with him. As they were going along, they came across some roses. Rabbi Abba picked one and went on his way.*

"Rabbi Jose met them. He said the Shekinah must be here. I can see from what is in Rabbi Abba's hands that I am going to learn great wisdom because I know that Rabbi Abba picked it for the sole purpose of teaching wisdom.

"Rabbi Abba smelled the rose. He said: 'It is scent alone that sustains the world, for we have seen that the soul survives only through scent…' 'My beloved is mine and I am his, who feeds among the roses (Song of Songs 2:11).' A rose is red and has scent, and if you heat it, it turns white, but it does not lose its scent. The Holy One, blessed be He, rules His world in this way; for if it were not so, the world could not survive human sin.

"The sinner is called red and it is written 'though your sins be as scarlet they shall be white as snow (Isaiah 1:18).' He brings his offering to the fire, which is red; around the altar he sprinkles blood, which is red; the attribute of judgement is red. The offering is heated, and smoke arises, which is completely white. Then red changes to white. The attribute of judgement turns into the attribute of mercy…red and white are always offered together and the scent rises from them both. Therefore He rules His world with roses, which are both red and white." Dosha and Nina, white and red roses, intertwined forever.

■ LOUIS CARTIER: What was he searching for?—It's all here. A night-time in a 16th century Tabriz palace. Harem ladies, courtiers drinking. Vegetable merchants weighing and vending fruits, and music wafting throughout the halls—drums, a Tabrizi-stringed lute, an enchanted bowed musician—all in a Tabriz night, 1525 I should think. But what's Mir Sayyid-'Ali searching for anyway? To see everything but never joining in? And I, in Paris. Pierre and Jacques allowed me to place my collection of Moghul and Persian miniatures in our private conference hall where we went to before lunch each day.

"No music, Louis," they said when I had asked for a sitar player to play each morning in our shop. "This is Maison Cartier, not a harem." Pierre exclaimed, using his American wife's pronunciation of the word: Hay-Ram.

"Oh but Maison Cartier is a palace, the Taj Mahal itself, a museum, a merchant's bazaar and even a harem," I insisted. But my brothers were two and I was one. Better a portrait of a musician's song played two hundred and eighty years ago, than no portrait of music never played.

I observed through Mir Sayyid-'Ali's eyes—the courtiers, the women, the music, the jeweled colors of gorgeous fabrics, the sounds of the artisans—enough for a lifetime.

Yet Mir Sayyid-'Ali, after Tabriz and Humayum's court in Moghul Hindustan, after an audience with Akbar, what was he searching for?

Mecca. When he left India in the prime of his life that is where he headed. Mir Sayyid-Ali, a *"beloved white hound,"* observing everything, chasing his own *"hennaed tail"* from Tabriz to Kabul to Hindustan to Mecca, and then to where? I, too, an *"erstwhile puppy"* observing all, in Paris, now in Cambridge, looking at these young Radcliffe students, while they gaze at me. Mirror upon mirror across time.

■ Lois Orswell, art collector and donor to the Fogg Art Museum at Harvard: There she was in class—Nina was in class before she was in class. As she walked the corridors of the Fogg with the Sufis ascending the stairs. The art in her mind. Collected by others—in a dream—to be enjoyed by these students. "Purer white, a white free of any admixture of color," her professor is chanting—along with the paintings that have sung to her, she but half awake, still dreaming.

The white of Cézanne, to me more sensuous than the blues and greens with a hint of brown.

"I for some reason do not wear colours much except touches…white silk blouse and pearls for forays into the city."

Cézanne's canvas, my true dress. Nina's too, both of us wee peas from the same pod: *"Anglo-colonial revolutionary Puritan religiously unaffiliated sexually unknown pro-choice for everything pro-aesthetics anti-deconstruction animal mad square musician financially trembling on the edge female having lots of fun."*

Nina might as well walk out of class and stroll by the Fogg's sumptuous necklace of paintings, radiant gems snaking along the walls up and down the museum staircases even. But Nina's not in class to study, she's there to dance. Thompson's a Harvard man—he's the vision.

"It's all so simple really. All you have to do is look and meditate on a work of art, if you want to, and do your own feeling and tell everyone else to stop talking. If you really want, it comes."

Best of all. Why not ask Thompson to retrace Nina's steps backward, out the classroom, past the Fogg's treasures: Wertheim's jewels—Van Gogh and Gauguin–not talking Nina and Thompson—but more alive than life, forever.

"Ages ago, there was a shop on Tremont Street that sold short vamp high instep and enormously high heels for three (3) dollars. And I tramped about Beacon Hill and its old brick sidewalks thinking I looked marvelous." As did John Codman, my beau. His photograph, along with a snap of Henry James, framed picture treasures by my bed always.

Marriage? Does it matter? For Nina or for me? *"In 1927 John committed the conventional Boston act of marrying a distant cousin and daughter of a Harvard man."*

Tutor Thompson will vanish. But if Nina and he walk the Fogg together, Nina will dream of him forever. My Cézanne will chaperone the next generation of Harvard lovers and all who wish to saunter and pray in its halls.

Paul Cezanne, Study of Trees (Arbes, Winding Road).

"Only dear, art history is in the eye of the beholder. Let's invite Tancy for blueberry pancakes. I'll knock on her door."

"She's been asleep since 10'clock."

"Why should Tancy be the freshest daisy in the meadow?" Nina stretched the phone to the hallway and dialed Cambridge Cabs. "Shepard Street—to the I.H.O.P." She slammed the phone down. "Constance, are you dozing, dearie? No, this is serious. What? You don't want to eat? Oh well, see you in the morning in class in the Fogg Museum, Chez Thompson."

There she was in class, Nina staring beadily at Thompson, Professor Welch staring at Dosha, Dosha staring at Nina, and Constance not having slept a wink since having been awakened by Nina at 2:15.

"As you were about, no doubt, to comment, Miss Padawer," said Professor Welch, "this is an ivory white, a white almost free of any admixture of color. Quite different from the imperial white in Shah Jahan's beard in this miniature—painted possibly by Chitarman—as the Emperor thinks of his wife, lost, the Taj he has built and his future ever more dim. Payag's Sufi whites are more nuanced. Here he has constructed a staircase for Sufis to ascend to Paradise. First at the invitational stairs, one is drawn into the picture. One passes the Mullahs on the left but one is stopped by the hand of the Mullah on the right."

■ Abraham Joshua Heschel, The Apter Rebbe (18th–19th Century): Eat—*"If it were in my power, I would do away with all the afflictions, except for the affliction on the bitter day, which is the ninth of Av [in remembrance of the Roman destruction of Jerusalem]. for who could eat on that day? And the afflictions on the holy and awesome day, Yom Kippur, who needs to eat on that day?"*

■ Annie Oakley: White—More French than English. More English than American, this class at Radcliffe. The professor and his assistant coolie eyeing the women. Little difference from the Universal Exposition in 1889 with Buffalo Bill's Wild West Show in Paris.

Without my English Schultze gunpowder, my shooting would have been worse than bad. But a lady has her ways. Underneath my dress with a bustle, I smuggled the powder in a hot water bottle. French Customs looked at every inch of me but dared not touch me.

Nor my other conspirators, all lady shooters, with Schultze powder hidden in water bottles under their bustle dresses.

Saved the day, that English powder. But not right away. President Carnot and Mademoiselle Carnot just gawking at me. I, riding about in my white hat, firing pistols, rifles and shotguns. At glass balls, clay birds, what have you.

Shooting is a language everyone understands. *"When you feel like changing your nationality and profession there is a commission awaiting you in the French army,"* the President of France told me.

More gallant the French President, though less on the bull's eye than the King of Senegal who offered Mr. Cody one hundred thousand francs to buy me to rid his land of wild tigers—and do a little housekeeping as well.

That's all these girls are as well, riders before presidents and kings, preparing their powder for just the right targets.

111

■ JOHN FLATTAU, American photographer and explorer: The viewer is frozen—The owner of the miniature, the collector, is frozen. The Moghul prince is frozen. Mir Sayyid Ali, the painter, is frozen, for all art is photography—and all photography but a self-portrait of the viewer.

"When you accept that every photograph is a self-portrait, and then believe that a self-portrait is an attempt to preserve who we are, and what we look like to others as well as to ourselves, images become a visual path to the past. Memory, the confirmation of a past, has no sense of time…a specific event, when recalled, is as recent as any other part of the past; all moments exist in the presence of a memory without boundaries…Memory exists in an emotional context; one incident can resonate more than another…A specific incident cannot exist apart from a collective memory. What we possess is this single, collective memory with different facets, as a single diamond has many sides…Is memory a poetic form of expression? Poetry often fragments sentences and grammatical construction into a series of words and images that link through emotional interface…Memory, like poetry, also fragments reality to provide, through ambiguity and suggestiveness, a deeper meaning, an emotional richness that the exactitude of words cannot convey. Its strength exists in suggestiveness, not logic, for the ambiguity allows for individual identification, personal meaning to import a certain significance to an image…Memory, a past, runs through these pages. It moves, changes, amends, yet never explains itself…There is only an emotional continuity which is clear; there is a personal reality which remains hidden, but may be discovered."

Dosha is seeing Nina out of the corner of her eye. Mir Sayyid Ali too. In Mecca, his memory of Hindustan. Fisher, too, frozen. We all remember each other as we discover ourselves.

"The viewer is frozen. The owner of this miniature has told me that he often finds himself leaning toward these figures, uncertain if he can gain entrance.

"On the other hand, in Mir Sayyid Ali's portrait of the palace, the viewer is seated within the edifice."

Suddenly, Nina Coggeshall's hand shot up. "Who is the owner of this painting, Cary? I've seen it before, I believe, in Philadelphia."

"Nina Abigail," said Professor Welch sharply, "I'm not at liberty to discuss that here." Professor Welch paused dramatically. "But within a year or two, Inshallah, I'd be delighted to, and in any case, it is Miss Padawer who has the floor."

Dosha could see out of the corner of her eye that Nina had brought a dance card written in Jeffersonian hand: "Tutor Thompson: Your room, my room, the Brattle Street café, the cemetery off the Square, now, at midnight, anywhere, or everywhere? N.A.C."

Before Nina could pass the note to Thompson, Dosha reached across and inserted the words "International House of Pancakes" after "cemetery off the square." Good-looking he is, Thompson, just Nina's type, shy, she thought to herself. But a bit on the thin side.

■ SØREN KIERKEGAARD: Frozen—*"It was early morning. Everything had been made ready for the journey to Abraham's house. Abraham took leave of Sarah, and the faithful servant Eleazar followed him out on the way until he had to turn back. They rode together in accord, Abraham and Isaac, until they came to the mountain in Moriah. Yet Abraham made everything ready for the sacrifice, calmly and quietly, but as he turned away, Isaac saw that Abraham's left hand was clenched in Anguish, that a shudder went through his body but Abraham drew the knife.*

"Then they turned home again and Sarah ran to meet them but Isaac had lost his faith. Never a word in the whole world is spoken of this, and Isaac told no one what he had seen, and Abraham never suspected that anyone had seen it."

The viewer is frozen, are we not all Isaac watching our Heavenly Father about to sacrifice us. Or is it Abraham, our earthly father, not frozen in terror but filled with apprehension, the slightest shudder coursing through his body.

There are pretty pictures of our lives, a map summary of our choices. Simple voyage charts.

Date Born: in…place. Died in…in…place. With all the intermediate *caravanserei* stops of our spirit, clearly visible to our Lord. This classroom, a cathedral really. With works of beauty its catechism. Faith just beyond the fingertips of Dosha and even Nina.

■ VAN GOGH: In Western terms...And why is the sage not addressing Dara directly?—In written terms, the sage cannot address the pupil directly. Certainly not by speech alone. Perhaps by writing a letter or even better, a book. Certainly Harriet Beecher Stowe's *Uncle Tom's Cabin*—a book— is *"one of the strongest proofs of the existence of something transcendent in which Millet believed"* that man *"cannot be destined for worms."*

Best of all, a painting. A sage in a painting showing a pupil. Dara Shikoh in one generation, Gauguin in another, a university student in another, all not daring to gaze at the sage's face themselves.

So I painted my Western message on Eastern cloth for my pupil Paul—sent it to Gaugain as an offering, along with words from my heart: *"I've painted a portrait of myself, all ash gray. The ashen color—which results from the mixture of emerald green with orange lead—on a pale green background, all in harmony with the reddish brown clothing. But exaggerating my own personality as well, I instead looked for the character of a bonze, a simple worshipper of the eternal buddha. It caused me enough pain."*

Our yellow house's school room would be the center of the *"art of the future,"* even the *"church of the future."* I am painting myself *"like a Japanese"* more acolyte than sage. For which true sage is not a pupil of his pupil?

■ YASUNARI KAWABATA, Japanese novelist: Pale white, purest white, more than the sky—Professor Welch is playing with all of them: Nina, Dosha, Miss Constance Holden. Mr. Thompson, who is coaching all the American ladies in their game with him.

He talks of the Indian Payag, and his one hairbrush of pale white, pure white, more than the sky, but what he is speaking of is the moon—the one connection between the Master of Go—which Professor Welch is, and the young woman's heart.

"Shusai, Master of Go, twenty-first in the Honnimbô succession, died at Atami, at the Urokoya Inn, on the morning of January 18, 1940. He was sixty-seven years old by the Oriental count.

"January 18 is an easy day to remember in Atami. 'Remember in years to come the moon of this night of this month,' said Kan'ichi in the famous scene from Kôyôs melodramatic novel Demon Gold, the parting on the beach at Atami. The night to be remembered is January 17, and the Kôyô festival is held in Atami on the anniversary. The master's death came the following day."

Professor Welch speaks of whiteness, for he knows that being young, they have seen the full moon the night before. Not a pale white moon but the purest of white. But he is enough of a Master of Go to know that he can discuss that whiteness only through the passages of the Oriental miniaturist's hand centuries before. He is playing with his students, but they are holding their own.

Nina looked down at Dosha's emendation and mumbled sotto voce, "Ah jilting me for my Thompson mania, eh?"

"Miss Constance Holden," said Professor Welch. "Please share with us your trance-like wisdom...What do the values of Payag, and I believe it is Payag's painting, declare? I know you will say the Hindu Payag's one-haired brush has assigned a pale white on the cotton rug covering, and where is the purest white? Why, directly on the hat of the sage! More than the sky, the heaven—in Western terms—ah yes, for the Sufi sage's head contains wisdom. And he is instructing his fellow sage in the true path, and young Dara is bolt upright.

"And why is the sage not addressing Dara directly? In the same way that I were to address you, Constance, directly. There would be what our dear Sufi master, Sigmund Aben Freud, would call resistance in your dream-like state. "No, we must address a fellow sage in a manner that our pupil-devoté may glimpse the light, musn't we, Mr. Thompson?"

"William," bellowed Professor Welch. "On your feet!" From the deepest of his reveries, Thompson jumped up. He stood shyly before a stunning Ming Chinese scroll painting. Nina looked excited.

■ PAUL GAUGUIN: In Western terms—In Western terms, the sage is not addressing Dara directly. With Vincent, as with me, it was all indirection. Angles. With Mette and with me, endless circling around, above, below, across from me. Sage, pupil, devotee—all faraway thoughts, losing so much on their weary travels to the west. Better to leave and examine it all—far away.

Van Gogh's portrait placed before my feet as an offering. Penance. Sustenance. His brother Theo would commit himself to me as *"the first dealer-apostle."* For was I not as trumpeted a *"very great master...absolutely superior in character and intellect."*

There we would be, stranded on an island of sunlight, in the warmth of the south in a little house at the very center of the *"Art of the Future."* Vincent, Bernard, the apostle Theo, myself and *le Bon Dieu* knows who else.

Forever? What would we live on, oranges from each other's canvasses? Where would we rest? On tiny beds in others paintings?

There we would be, sage and pupils—till the end of it all—if we didn't, according to Vincent, *"turn into worms."* And never, never would we Westerners gaze at each other, for then our dreams would shatter.

■ SHAH JAHAN: Payag's one-haired brush... where is the purest white?—Where is the purest white to be found? Surely in the reflection of the neck of Mumtaz on a pale moonlit night. As we sat by the Jumna River, awake long after all in our palace slept. Now she is dead, my Mumtaz. Yet the moon still climbs disrespectfully each month, not mourning with myself and all of Hindustan my love's passing.

How shall I paint my love's likeness again and yet again? With Payag's one-haired brush I plant my moonlight garden—the Mahtab Bagh—of my heart. My fragrant red cedars rise majestically and sing to the cypresses that my hand waves into existence. I dine on the fruit of the jujube and eat my portion of nuts, carefully hiding my Mumtaz's portion in the folds of my garment, until we two again shall dine together under the ever-full moon of Paradise. The *"night-blooming white flowers"* on the red cedars reflect the white marble slabs erected by 20,000 laborers each day, day by day, year by year—twenty years in all. Finally on both sides of the Jumna the glorious lotus opens each morning and closes each evening, revived and nourished and sustained by my tears alone.

It is We that sent Sechina
[tranquility] into the hearts of the believers
that they may add faith to their faith
for to G-d belongs the host of
the heavens and the earth;
that He may admit the believers,
men and women alike,
to the gardens of Paradise, beneath
which rivers flow,
to dwell therein forever.

■ ELIHU YALE: Payag's white gradation… Persian's Platonic white—A Welshman teaching them all, daughters of titled rich they appear to me, one with the name Nina though her given name be Abigail.

G-dspeed, that ship, *The Abigail*, brought me nothing if not grief, my bulse of diamonds taken and John Chardin waiting for the goods at Dockside in London.

Three little maidens at sea, Constance Holden, Nina and Dosha, being shown miniatures, small as diamonds with a fleeting glimpse of their future husbands in a facet on the crown of the gem.

They will flee from their Welsh professor as quickly as the snows of Denbighshire melt before April's sun. Did they not all flee from me? Mother remained with me in the Americas when I was but two. Father gone back to Wales and London. Only to have her leave to his arms but a year later. I bundled off to Hindustan not yet a man at twenty-two. Widow Hymners first abandons her dead husband's memory, and then the *"ill natured toad that loved nothing so well as her bottle"* decamps to England, shouting curses at Hieronyma, at shrewd Mrs. Nicks, my partner in almost all things and at every woman, alive or dead, in Fort St. George. Hindoo or Muslim, Armenian, Huguenot or Catholic, dead or seemingly alive, cursing at me as her ship departed the Fort. Cursing at me until the ship left India, cursing at me the day I returned to London, wealthy beyond any promise I ever made her. All women save Hieronyma abandon all men. For a snake, a child, a lover, a dream, a house in Wales—for anything. Still, I have memories—Hieronyma's Portuguese Tazza filled with her glistening sweets—my partner, the good Mrs. Nicks whose accounts we balance between the bed sheets, and dreams of sweet stickiness and warmth, that no betrayal can banish even in the fires of hell.

"Miss Padawer," continued Professor Welch, "has made the implicit comparison between the subtlety of Payag's white gradations and the Platonic white—Persians ever idealize—the impossibly white Persian cat.

"Platonic, I say, Miss Coggeshall," said Professor Welch to Nina, who seemed about to ask the tutor to jitterbug.

With her eyes still on Nina, Dosha dug her nails into her palm. The gesture had always stopped her from laughing when her mother, thinking of gurus, revolutionaries and friends, asked for a fork when it was sitting right in front of her. Set to the right of the plate by her mother herself, for it was too "bougie" to set the table by ordinary Western standards.

"Yes, Tutor Thompson, what of the white wild plum blossom? Speak to the class of Liu Shiru, the Chinese 16th century master roughly but not quite contemporaneous with Mir Sayyid Ali."

■ HIERONYMA DE PAIVA: White gradations versus the Platonic white—Salvador Rodrigues, the brother of Abraham Salvador in Holland, the one whom Levy Duarte married his daughter, young Rachel. Better a son-in-law who is dead at home," Levy Duarte declared, "than one who dies in Hindustan." Though how could he have known my Jacques would go to the Fort, to Golconda, cough up blood redder than any ruby he purchased from Devendra's cousin in Burma? How could even Manuel Levy's wife, that shrew, Deborah Abolais, have known my Jacques would perish—simple spite prevented her from giving her Duarte's daughter's hand to Jacques—I second best always, for I did not have Rachel Duarte's fortune. Shrewd he was, Levy Duarte, pushing his son-in-law Abraham Salvador to pay his brother Salvador Rodrigues' passage across the waters, six months on a ship, to lose his faith in India more Hindu than Jew at Golconda and paying my dear husband's wages for a year and a promise of riches in commissions on all goods sold. When my Jacques died, where should I travel to? Back to Amsterdam, to another arranged marriage by Manuel Duarte, I was second choice, first time around, no thank you. Would my thieving brother provide the voyage money? I would not leave without my husband's estate, and would play the sweet game with my Lord Elihu of Madras until I pry what was mine out of Elihu's hands. Salvador Rodrigues would come to me every three months and solemnly place in my fingers the best of the uncut Golconda diamonds he had purchased at the mines. "These are your husband's share and my sister-in-law's share, Rachel Duarte Salvador and Marques' share." "And Elihu's share too," I would reply with a wink of an eye. "I do not ask what you barter these stones for with Lord Yale of Madras," Salvador would reply with the swiftness of a Haham. "And I do not ask of your Hindu wives how you obtained these, my dear cousin," I immediately countered. Salvador looked down at his feet and mumbled, "Golconda's stones made me crazy. Do not bury yourselves in Jacques' Golconda grave, flee while you can." But I did as I always did. I placed the four best pieces of Salvador's rough stones on the Portuguese tazza dish that Jacques and I brought from Antwerp, one that Jacques' father, Isaac Zagache, had rescued from Portugal. Elihu could sense when I had a shipment. He would arrive more Muslim than European on his favorite elephant, Jimnu, at the garden house. "I could smell the sweets in the governor's chambers," he would shout and dismount Jimnu and bound off to the dining room just off the veranda. Elihu would have all the servants away from the house—heaven help Mrs. Nicks if she were about—and Elihu would gaze at each of the four rough stones. "And what have we here?" he would ask, white grading off to pure white. With his right hand he would pick up the white Golconda pebble, notched at the point, which trapped a rainbow within it. With another flourish, he would remove another river white crystal with his left hand. "Ah," he would exclaim. "the arms of Yale." Then without being able to restrain himself, remove the two remaining stones from the sides of the tazza—my two Portuguese partners, Salvador Rodrigues and Manuel Levy Duarte. "My but Salvador doth laugh as should I if I dallied with a score of Hindu princesses and my doth Duarte look dour, and so should I, if I were chained to Constancia Duarte." Then Elihu would pause and look through the cut 4 3/4 flat Golconda, the one that Manuel had given my husband Jacques in Amsterdam: "You have brought the rough Indian stone that my brother Francis cut last year in England. Take this, Jacques with you and when you have sent us back to Amsterdam enough stones to make us a riviere of this quality, you can return a rich man to Amsterdam, to London, to Antwerp and if you are a fool, to Lisboa." I placed the cut Golconda stone that my dear Jacques had left for me in the middles of the tazza. "Ah, but do my eyes deceive me? Is this not the most delectable sweet of all?" I never failed to laugh at Elihu's love of this game. And when I said, as always, "What doth my Lord Elihu think of today's collection?" he would always reply, "We must taste of it inside." Together we would go to the interior of the garden house, to the one room whose only window opened above to the sky.

■ HARRY BOBER, Assistant Professor: Professor—An assistant, a young man for almost all seasons. Brim full of knowledge, of Eden's nature, the wild plum symbolizes winter and purity. *"For the plum blossoms while snow covers its branches but the flickering white—the feibri—the flying white of the plum blossoms."* Are they not overlaid with spring's green? Along with pine and bamboo, plum is one of the three friends of winter—sanyou suihan—green the year round. Tutor Thompson, a humble scholar. But Professor Welch, a professor! A man for each season, a peony in spring, a lotus for his summer school devotees and a bright chrysanthemum each fall.

A professor of the heart with knowledge of the heart, a Renaissance man born each fall yet again.

■ GROUCHO MARX: Professor—Why is the professor interrupting the assistant professor as he starts to translate? Because he's going to leave things out. He's looking at the students not at the art.

"GROUCHO: Jameson, take a letter to my lawyer. Honorable Charles H. Hungerdunger, care of Hungerdunger, Hungerdunger, Hungerdunger, Hungerdunger and McCormick, semicolon… now read me the letter, Jamison.

ZEPPO: Honorable Charles H. Hungerdunger, care of Hungerdunger, Hungerdunger, Hungerdunger and McCormick.

GROUCHO: You left out a Hungerdunger. You left out the main one, too. Thought you could slip one over on me, eh? All right, leave it out and put it in a windshield wiper instead. I'll tell you what you do. Make it three windshield wipers and one Hungerdunger. They won't all be there when the letter arrives anyhow."

The professor's not so smart. If he were he'd be the assistant professor.

Thompson was standing next to Professor Welch. "Read and translate the inscription, William. Show your stuff." Professor Welch pointed to the gorgeously calligraphed lines in the upper left hand corner of the scroll.

Smiling with a smile that only a 30-year-old assistant professor on a tenure track could have—unattached, with two years of tabla training with Ali Akbar Khan. He translated fluently: "A green dragon…"

A green dragon, it rears up high
And seems to reach for
The Milky Way,

Like jade butterflies, in irregular
patterns, unsoiled by mud.

Suddenly the Wind G-d Fengyi gives
Forth a wild whistle

And the splendor of spring is scattered
All over, east and west.

"Thank you, Tutor Thompson," said Professor Welch. "You have somewhat redeemed yourself. What I would not give for your language skills. What should Miss Padawer say to you if you asked her of the color values of Liu Shiru's white blossoms?"

With a surprisingly agile motion, Professor Welch slid Thompson's chair next to him. "Sit down here before your acolytes at the right hand of G-d, Mr. Thompson. While Miss Padawer permits me to interject: Wang Siren, 1575–1646, I believe, if memory serves, asserted that Liu Shiru painted plum blossoms for eighty of his ninety years.

■ SHITAO, 1642–1707: Painting and calligraphy—During an autumn in my fiftieth year of life, I lost on a boat wreck more than my life itself: my luggage, my poems, my books, my collection of scrolls.

Here they sit, teacher and student. A miracle. Far from China. All survivors clutching onto a hanging scroll, floating since Ming times.

"There are seven types of calamities that can happen to painting and calligraphy: 1) When prices are too high, they are above the reach of the common people. As a result, the works of art all go into collections of the wealthy, where genuine works of art are lumped together with the spurious. 2) When a noble family falls and its property is confiscated, the collections all go to the Imperial Court where they are eaten by moths and insects and can no longer be seen by the people. 3) Vulgar people collect art objects for reputation and professional dealers compete in raising the prices, without regard to their intrinsic worth. 4) Great, powerful dealers trade them like goods and are willing to part with them for a profit. Then the works go into the possession of the vulgarians. 5) The works are locked in rich mansions, their cases covered with dust, while the owners gorge themselves with food. 6) Uneducated heirs of fortune do not care a bit about these family possessions and seem totally unconcerned in case of fire or theft. 7) The works are sometimes spoiled through bad, unskilled mountings, and facial features are destroyed, or substitutions are made, causing disputes."

How I marvel to see Liu Shiru's Blossoming Plum Scroll survive these calamities.

■ JULIUS MEYER: White—Black and white. The photograph of my Indian friends by Currier. Black and white. Forever. Cost me more than $800. I even threw in two ponies for each Indian chief to pose.

You could tell a story that would last an entire night looking at the black and white. Me with my silk brocade jacket from the Chinese. Red Cloud with a chief's coat towering above the two Brulé.

As he did, and Swift Bear and Spotted Tail knew it. Even if the Whites replaced Red Cloud he would always tower above Spotted Tail. But Spotted Tail was shrewder. More clear-sighted, knew when to blend.

But my favorite, always and ever, Sitting Bull, the Oglala. Ever himself, no White Man's costume for him. No, thank you. One eagle feather. No more. None needed. "I'll give you four ponies and more than all the rest," I said in Oglala to Sitting Bull "If you'll gift me your chief's feather."

"I'll give it to you for nothing if you earn it, Box-Ka-Re-Sha-Hash-Ta-Ka.

I had many pictures made. Myself with Chief Standing Bear, myself with the Good Sitting Bull. Currier always had to rearrange the picture. "Just a tad," he'd say. "Slip into this, my boy." And I'd have to switch into White Man's clothes. "They can wear any darn thing," the photographer said, pointing at Sitting Bull.

Foolish the Whites to call the Oglala the Good Sitting Bull and the Hunkpapa the Bad Sitting Bull. In the end, it was all the same. Killed by the army. Or by scouts. Or by half-breeds. Or by starving Sioux or Pawnee.

And all that remains are my dreams, my memories, my black and whites. Alive to me, forever.

"Hence the poem. Hence the green dragon. Hence Time's continuing seasons forward, a mixture of green and white. Hence the assignment for next time: Color values and M&M's.

"Miss Athern and Miss Buxton and Constance Holden in M, that is Ming, to report to tutor Thompson, to alphabetically split the class. Mademoiselles Rosenwald, Smythe and Watson in the other M&M—the Moghul, to be handled by yours truly. That leaves Miss Padawer and Miss Coggeshall. The center of the world. Joyce's Omnaphalus. The alphabetical epicenter of our constellation of stars.

"Any suggestions, T.T.? What to do with Miss Padawer and Coggeshall?

"Does Nina join Chinese Ming and abandon her study partner and roommate Ms. Padawer to myself and the Moghuls? Or does she join Miss Padawer and ourselves in Moghul? And abandon young Thompson?"

Nina had risen to her feet, staring imploringly at Professor Welch. Tutor Thompson and the rest of the class were also standing. "Class dismissed," said Professor Welch. "Nina Coggeshall, let me, if I may, put words of decision in your mouth: 'Make mine Ming.'" Professor Welch smiled at Abigail.

"Tutor Thompson, I'll see you in the faculty lounge at half three, as they say at Eton. Miss Padawer, bide a while. I wish to discuss your putatively brilliant performance in class today." Barnes, Buxton, Rosenwald, Smythe and Watson filed out, followed by Thompson.

◆ SARAH PADAWER, DOSHA'S GRANDMOTHER: Study partner—When my granddaughter Jerushalleh brought us to the Lubovitcher after the War, she was only eight years old. Simha was so tired he couldn't sleep. Night after night. For weeks on end. He barely ate and never spoke. When the Rebbe stretched out his hand to Simha, he said "*Fin ven kimt a yid? From where does a Jew come?*" I could not see the expression on Simha's face. I was standing behind him and Dosha was in front of me, her tiny left hand balancing her grandfather's hand on her palm. It was almost as if she was supporting him.

I heard my husband say, in a voice drained of emotion and strength, "*Ich bin a pushette litvak fin Slonim. I am a simple litvak from Slonim.*"

And then the Rebbe looking at Jerusha who spoke no Yiddish asked, "Why have you all come together here?"

I answered the Rebbe: "All through the War, my Simha would say—in Byten—in Belorusse—we go together."

And then I remember like today, the Rebbe quoting from Abraham's bindng of Isaac: "*And Abraham took in his hand the fire and the knife. They went both of them, together.*" I understood the Rebbe. In the war, thank G-d it was that Simha and I went together. But in America, when Simha lost the hope that Reuven would walk together with him in his path, I understood that Jerusha would be his study partner. Now my granddaughter is no longer Jerusha but Dosha—but is she not the same person? And her study partner, according to this American professor, is her friend Nina.

The Rebbe blessed Simha and me that "*in multiplying I will multiply your seed as the stars of the heaven… and in your name all nations will be blessed.*"

For as my father would say in Slonim, "*If there are no kids, there are no goats; if there are no goats, there are no flocks; if there are no flocks, there are no Shepherds.*"

Thus will Jerusha's—or Dosha's—true study partner in years to come fulfill the Rebbe's blessing to Simha. In America, the way is even more crooked than in the forest of Belorusse.

Julius Meyer with Indian Chiefs Red Cloud, Sitting Bull, Spotted Tail, and Swift Bear.

■ F. SCOTT FITZGERALD: Nina winked. They are all—Nina, Dosha, the good professor Welch—first-rate intelligences.

If Miss Coggeshall is to attract the tutor she knows she must encourage him to tempt her. Thus she must flip the Golden Delicious apple to Professor Welch instead. Catch if he can, the professor, but old enough he is, with a generation of Radcliffe students behind him, to recognize the apple offering is not meant for him.

"The test of a first-rate mind is the ability to hold two opposing ideas in the mind at the same time."

Dosha knows that Coggeshall's wink to her means that Coggeshall would like nothing better to do than spend the rest of her life boarding with her, flirting, coming and going *"like moths among the whispering and the champagne and the stars."* At the same time Nina is already sprinting, albeit with a brief layover in New York City, to a comfortable, cossetted sleep in the arms of a Philadelphia beau.

I, did not I choose the same? To lie with Lily Shiel and Sheilah Graham, not quite the same arms at one and the same instant, and of course, Heaven forbid, not abandon mad Zelda at Christmas holidays, '38, while still holding the idea on my mind of nurturing Scottie at The Walker School in Connecticut, preparing to enter Vassar. How could I simply post my daughter, holiday express, to the Obers. Elementary, I would spend Christmas in '38 in Hollywood, New York and inside Zelda's mind in Asheville at the same instant.

■ RED CLOUD, Oglala Chief: Alone—The whites will fix me a drink. But who knows what will be in it. In 1856, at Ft. Laramie, I was expecting some big chiefs. I *"went to the post surgeon and asked for a bottle of whiskey."* I gave him my two wonderful buffalo robes. When the chiefs arrived I gave each a drink from my bottle. Each drank but with a sad expression. Only when the bottle came to me did I understand. The cork had two drops of whiskey on it but all the rest was water. The surgeon's officer had fled the fort by the time I reached him. Even when I got more gifts from him, it was too late, already I was called *Two Robes* in memory of my having given fine robes for a bottle of water. Never did the white man give good whiskey. Only water or bad whiskey. Even my father was killed by their bad whiskey in 1825, when I was a little child. But my sister alone brought me up. Only I was able to defeat them and pour all their bad whiskey and water over them.

Nina winked her left eye at Dosha. At the door she reached into her Bokharan fabric knapsack, retrieved a Golden Delicious apple and flipped it to Professor Welch, whispering: "Died and gone to Heaven. Thank you, Cary, from the bottom of my heart."

When the seven sisters and the tutor had departed, Professor Welch closed the door behind them. He propped up the miniature of Dara Shikoh on the chair vacated by the tutor, and on the chair just vacated by Nina Coggeshall placed Mir Sayyid Ali's masterwork, "Night time in the Palace."

Between them was the "Branch of Blossoming Plum," a Ming ink on silk, Liu Shiru's work.

"In which miniature scenes would you care to dwell next month, Miss Padawer?"

"Well, Professor, let's first say in which one would I not—for at my age I know what I don't want.

"Spending even a night in the Palace would be maddening. The dog seems more alive than the people, isolated from each other as they are.

"Where would I want to be alone or able to rest? In the Blossoming Plum with its Thompson translated jade butterfly inscription, I find its winter not cold enough, not vivifying enough.

"I would sojourn in the space within the white-capped triangulation of the two Sufis, if they would have me. I would sit directly in the center of the portrait and listen, listen, listen.

■ JAMES JOYCE: Apple—Not the seven sisters studying the muddy tale of the Welsh professor but she alone, Shaun and He, Shem *"and that's the He and the She of it."*

He has whispered to her Cara Mia, *"The best authenticated version, the Dumlat,"* and she alone has *"read the Readings of Hofed-ben-Edar, has it that it was this way."*

She has read ben-Edar's words: *"And when the woman said that the tree was good for food, and that it was pleasant to the eyes, and a tree to be desired to make one wise, she took of the fruit thereof and did eat, and gave also unto her husband with her and he did eat."*

A golden apple of Sammarkand has her weekday husband accepted. Not for one instant does the Welshman conjure: *"Heva, naked no naval—never G-d forbid a woman brought sin into the world."*

As he looks, she flees to celebrate her weekend. *"There's no sabbath for the nomad."*

■ MARY CASSATT: Nina winked her left eye at Dosha—She is able to communicate with each of her limbs separately. To each of her family members and friends. The world is her audience. Coggeshall winks at Dosha with her left eye. With her right eye, she regards her five sororal rivals. No rival to Dosha she is, rather confidante, late night whisperer, guardian of Dosha's secrets bartered freely, friends until death and well beyond. They will always speak to each other, even when not in each other's presence. Coggeshall is a Philadelphia Coggeshall, till death do we all part. Like Lydia and me, more friends than sisters. Her body an entirely white strand of Nature's pearls glowing from within. For all an opera house to see. Paris, her audience, when mother and Father brought her in '79. Radiant really, lighting the entire Parisian hall. Yet I knew she was always and ever Philadelphia. She cared not a fig for her operatic Parisian audience. "Why can't you be more like Lydia?" was my mother's unasked question. And my unanswered reply: "Better a death in Paris than a life in Philadelphia."

Coggeshall will live, perhaps in New York, even Paris. With Dosha, visiting Dosha, working with Dosha, but she is Philadelphia. That's where her sails tend to.

◆ SIMHA PADAWER: Teacher—It was a saying in Ladino in my family from when we lived in Padua: "Woe to the children whose teacher has quarreled with his wife." But Talmud Shevi'it makes it clear. "*A man from whom others learn must be strict with himself.*"

Professor Welch sees all. He has come to the class, calm from his house. He is strict with Tutor Thompson, looks at him closely as he watches his seven students.

For the tutor is the professor in time's mirror. "*Just as the mirror should be more polished than the gazer, so should the teacher be more brilliant than the pupil.*"

Tutor Thompson is becoming. Not a present. But a future. What does my granddaughter wish? What we all wish. A blessing, a hope, an uplifting hand. She is far from home, from me, from my Sarah.

The professor is giving his benediction. And how shall we judge his blessing if not from Talmud Berahot: "*From a man's blessings one may know if he be a scholar or not.*"

The professor can see that a winter's white which hid me in the black nights of Belorusse will become a blessing, ever blossoming, for my Jerusha.

■ DONN PENNEBAKER, Director of *Don't Look Back*, a documentary about Dylan's tour in England: Art flows—I'm the professor and Dylan and Neuwirth are the students. Don't look back, here comes Kerouac and Cassidy. Certainly Albert Grossman is not the professor.

"Albert didn't have the slightest idea what he wanted to do. He never even mentioned the words "movie" or "feature." He simply invited me to England to do some filming. But Dylan dreams of James Dean and Marlon Brando.

"*The first idea Dylan came up with knocked me for a loop. Bob wanted to open the film with a song, only he wouldn't be signing it. It would be a track from one of his albums during which he'd flip over cue cards displaying snatches of lyrics.*" It was fantastic, exhilarating. He'd be acting out his own life. Changing and evolving. I'd be the not-entirely dispassionate observer. There was drama coming on. I could smell it.

Who's the director here? Professor Welch or Dosha? She's flipping through the flash cards. Chinese script. Payag's Mullah's hand. They too mirror writing. Art excites Dosha's epiphany. I could film her. Or she me. Filming her. Art flows in every direction.

Just as I come to the Fogg each Wednesday 15 minutes before class, I would think of the bonze Van Gogh we saw on a class trip in New York in Wertheimer's apartment and pay my respects as well to young Gauguin, not yet starving but starting as an artist. Vincent, Paul, you: my Trinity. A weekly epiphany."

Professor Welch smiled. "Why did you not say any of this in class, Miss Padawer? Is your roommate's note to Tutor Thompson more interesting than our class discussions?" Dosha blushed and said, "However did you…"

Professor Welch interrupted. "In Mir Sayid Ali's painting, a courtier is at an 80 degree angle, offering sweet meats to a prince. Payag's Mullah's teaching hand is at a 10 degree off the horizontal. The Chinese script flows and flares outwards Bustrikon, mirror writing. Art moves in each and every direction. Art excites the eyes. The mind. Every limb and pore. Part of the charm of teaching Nina and you. You're to be in my Moghul tutorial. Be in my office tomorrow evening at 7:00 with Buxton and Holden and please bring some paint so you can match the whites of each of these."

"By the way, which of these paintings would you inhabit?" Dosha asked her professor. "Miss Padawer, you will be a great teacher." He paused. "At my age, I both know what I don't like and what I like. 'The Blossoming Plum'—with its winter of white. Oh it's more than vivifying to me. Life itself. I'd live here." With a flourish Professor Welch placed a portrait of Shah Jahan just to the right of the Liu Shiru.

"Or here," he added quietly, "and I'll give you my benediction: before long, not more than a decade, you too will inhabit a painting—and it won't be with the likes of Nina's Tutor Thompson—but with another—not a painter mind you, too many cooks spoil the broth—perhaps an extraordinary novelist, ever blossoming in a wintry night of white."

■ REMBRANDT: You're to be in my Moghul tutorial—The students teach the teacher. The teacher teaches the students. The students teach themselves. The professor is the professor's professor.

Had the Dutch East India Company offered me a place in Persia, I would not have hesitated to go to the court of Shah Abbas II.

Instead, they sent Hendrick Boudewijn van Lockhorst, the one with the big nose. A merry chase Hendrick led the Company, till they could lead him like an ox back to Holland. The big nose, the director's said "*zichzelf niet gouverneren kan en door luxurieus, ongebonden leven de Compagnie veel schande heeft aangedann. He cannot control himself, and by his luxurious living has caused the Company great embarrassment.*"

If they had led me by the nose to the Hindustan court of Shah Jahan where beggars boasted better clothes than princes here, would the court not have been my Moghul tutorial? But Saskia did not travel well. Nor Titus. Nor any of the mouths around my table. So my collection of curious Indian miniatures would have to be my models. Even if my miniatures were stolen, sold or burned. Alphonso Lopes' costumes, Ephraim Bonas' face, any of the naçion, my neighbors, would serve as well. And finally, G-d prevent such a calamity—should my Hindustan miniatures vanish, the Jews yet again disperse, my own sketches of Lopes' paintings disappear, I could remember my mother's bedtime reading to me, stories of Father Abraham. That, even in the dark, would be my Moghul tutorial.

■ ASSADULLAH SOUREN MELIKIAN-CHIRVANI: Mir Sayyid' Ali—Stuart Cary Welch looked into Louis Cartier's treasure. To him, it is a gift of his student John Goelet to the Fogg Museum. And to Cartier, the master of jewels, it was a Moghul gift, starting in Royal Persia, brought back by Humayun in Kabul. A journey leading to Shah Jahan's fabled peacock throne and all the jewels scattered through the centuries to sweeten the dreams of gem fanciers everywhere. Now Welch's student Dosha has understood that Mir Sayyid Ali's eye contains all corners of the world within its palace walls.

Dosha has performed her ablutions before Van Gogh and paid her respects to Gauguin before viewing Mir Sayyid Ali's picture. She well knows that Mir Sayyed 'Ali is more poet than painter. So too her love to come, Fisher, more novelist than painter. But Fisher will not be writer if she be not painter, and in the end, is not all done by one brush? Painting in Kabul, in Hindustan, in Paris, even in Cambridge.

Into one grain, there came a hundred harvests
A whole world came about in the heart of a single
grain of millet.

Rembrandt van Rijn, *Shah Jahan.*

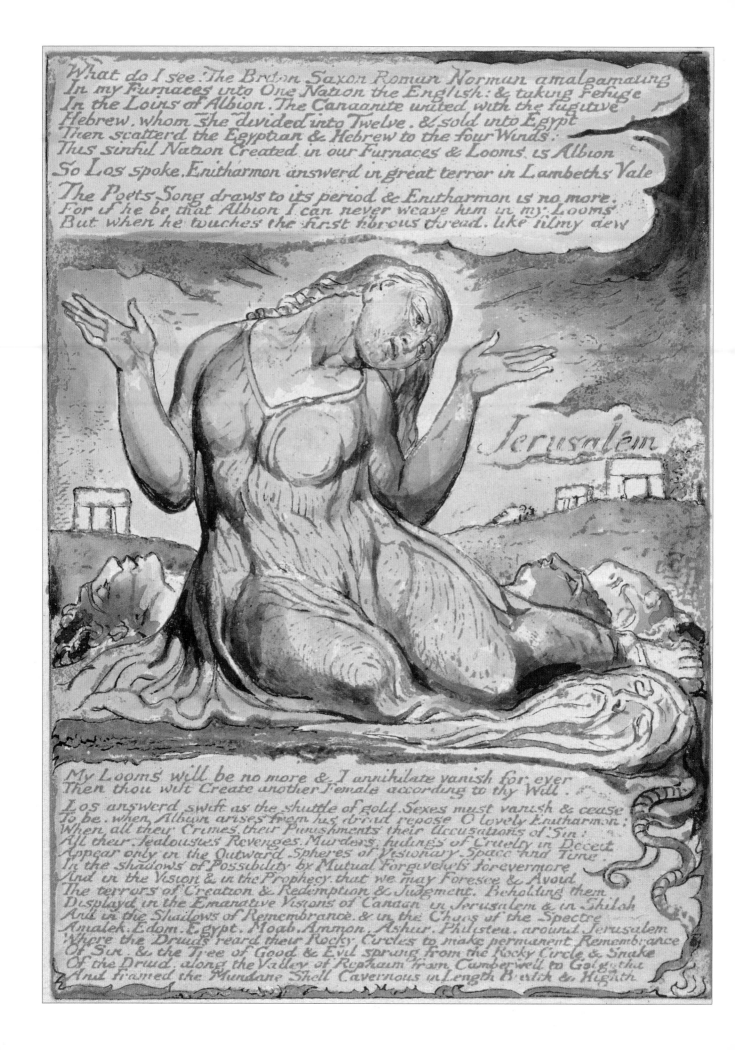

What do I see? The Briton Saxon Roman Norman amalgamating
In my Furnaces into One Nation the English: & taking Refuge
In the Loins of Albion. The Canaanite united with the fugitive
Hebrew, whom she divided into Twelve, & sold into Egypt
Then scatterd the Egyptian & Hebrew to the four Winds:
This sinful Nation Created in our Furnaces & Looms is Albion

So Los spoke. Enitharmon answerd in great terror in Lambeths Vale

The Poets Song draws to its period & Enitharmon is no more.
For if he be that Albion I can never weave him in my Looms
But when he touches the first fibrous thread, like filmy dew

Jerusalem

My Looms will be no more & I annihilate vanish for ever
Then thou wilt Create another Female according to thy Will.

Los answerd swift as the shuttle of gold. Sexes must vanish & cease
To be, when Albion arises from his dread repose O lovely Enitharmon:
When all their Crimes, their Punishments, their Accusations of Sin:
All their Jealousies Revenges. Murders. hidings of Cruelty in Deceit
Appear only in the Outward Spheres of Visionary Space and Time.
In the shadows of Possibility by Mutual Forgiveness forevermore
And in the Vision & in the Prophecy, that we may Foresee & Avoid
The terrors of Creation & Redemption & Judgement. Beholding them
Displayd in the Emanative Visions of Canaan in Jerusalem & in Shiloh
And in the Shadows of Remembrance, & in the Chaos of the Spectre
Amalek. Edom. Egypt. Moab. Ammon. Ashur. Philistea. around Jerusalem
Where the Druids reard their Rocky Circles to make permanent Remembrance
Of Sin. & the Tree of Good & Evil sprung from the Rocky Circle & Snake
Of the Druid. along the Valley of Rephaim from Camberwell to Golgotha
And framed the Mundane Shell Cavernous in Length Bredth & Highth

◆ ISAAC TAL, ABRAHAM TAL'S FATHER: Jerusalem—Why does Abraham guide this young woman's hand in the alphabet of exile? She knows more English than he. I could understand it if my son chose to tutor this woman in aleph bet. In all the Hebrew day schools in the City of New York, in Manhattan and Brooklyn, Abraham has not found a classroom to teach in. Instead, he would teach at night, to a class of one, and not a jot of our holy tongue. Speaking of salary, why is it that all my illustrious Abraham can dream of doing is paying his student to study with him. Some fancy private school!

■ RABBI ISAIAH HURWITZ: Jerusalem—"In 1621, in Damascus, two distinguished men from Safed came to me. They welcomed me and approached me with requests on behalf of the community to settle in Safed and become their head. I answered them that I had to go to Safed, and that we could take council there. My intention was, however, to proceed to Jerusalem…. On the same day Rabbi N. brought a long letter from the inhabitants of Jerusalem with an offer according to which they appointed me the Ab Beth Din (head of the Rabbinical court) and head of the Academy until the coming of the Messiah, and they gave full power to Rabbi N. to grant me a salary according to my wish. He was not allowed to withdraw his hand from mine until I had agreed to accept that offer. They were much afraid of the people of Safed. I praised the Lord and thanked Him that He had found me worthy to spread the Torah in Israel and Jerusalem, and influence men to serve G-d in truth and sincerity…. I answered the Rabbi that I did not wish to accept a salary from them, as they were so overburdened with obligations because of our many sins. I told them that they should grant me only a good and comfortable lodging. This is a great thing because there is a considerable shortage of apartments in Jerusalem, because the community of the Ashkenazim in Jerusalem is twice as big as that of Safed and increases in numbers every-day. There are also many remarkable scholars of the Torah in the community of the Ashkenazim in Jerusalem.

"Although Jerusalem lies in ruins now, it is still the glory of the whole earth. There is peace and safety, good food and delicious wine, all much cheaper than in Safed. The community is situated in a special district of the city. This is not so in Safed, where the Jews live in an open space. That is why many robberies occur there….My beloved children, tell everybody who intends to go to the Holy Land to settle in Jerusalem. Let nobody assume that I give this advice because I shall settle there… the city is enclosed and surrounded by a wall. It is as big as Lwow but the most important part is that it is particularly holy and the gate to heaven."

C H A P T E R   7

"WHITE. How I chose white for my painting?" Dosha asked Tal in his advice shop. "Why didn't I choose red? Too unsettling, Tal. Even Dreamboat and I must sleep occasionally. Can't have red floating around our palace, as you call it so quaintly?"

"And blue, why no blue? Our foundation is blue. Right down here in your advice shop," said Dosha staring at her own blue stenciled letters.

England! Awake. Awake, Awake
Jerusalem thy sister calls!
Why wilt thou sleep the sleep of death,
And close her from the ancient walls?

"Right behind you in glorious blue, I might add. Dreamboat's and my blue foundation stone. Definitely more blue than green, dear Tal."

"We shall speak of green later," said Tal. "Does Fisher like your use of white in every one of your canvasses?"

"I'll answer you with a joke you've told me, Tal. A poor Polish Jew is approached by a farmer who wants to sell his wagon. 'I can't buy your wagon,' says the poor Jew, 'for ten reasons.' 'What is the tenth?' asks the farmer."

■ ARYEH LEIB BEN EPHRAIM HAKOHEN (1616–1678), Fisher's mother's ancestor: Jerusalem—Why does Tal speak of Jerusalem? Not of Safed where he is tending. Soon, sooner than Dosha realizes. While my blessed father Ephraim ben Jakob Hakohen was with me, he too spoke only of Jerusalem. Of the Jerusalem where his father had been a dayan eighty years before. Before Vilna, before Ofen. Of the Jerusalem to which he was returning. And I too, to write with Aaron my blessed brother's son, my father's responsa. I too would speak of Jerusalem to my father, to my dying brother Hezekiah, to my saintly mother. I too would speak of Safed. When the Messiah shall come the dead shall be raised. First in Safed. Tal speaks of Jerusalem with this young woman, Jerusha. For is not her daughter, Ariel, to inherit the heavenly city as her birthright? And do not our children inscribe our tombstones with their good deeds?

So Tal and I too in our hearts murmur of Safed while our mouths sing of Jerusalem.

■ WILLIAM BLAKE: Stenciled letters—A child: Dosha. Heavenly and heaven sent, albeit a child. Better Tal's own free hand lettering even by candlelight than Dosha's stenciling. But Tal has not the strength to recognize his own Seraphim. Raphael's study partner: Gabriel. So he purchased color paints and stencil, insisted on Dosha's use thereof. Yet it is our Lord who steadies all hands, causes our fingers to move, our joints to strain and at the end of our days, before our journey backward and upward, closes our eye lids violently for some, peacefully for others. Tal is blinded by the light. So close they all are to Heaven's very walls. He calls his neighbors Fisher and Dosha and does not recognize they are Raphael and Gabriel. Child's play, even for a child, to write in letters of shimmering blue this handful of my lettered lines.

I, backward, slanting and chanting, a hundred plates of Jerusalem, and I defy any of the heavenly hosts to find so much as a jot of a dot of error.

■ BERNARD ZUCKER (Binyamin Zucker): Grandfather living in the house—My grandfather no longer lived in my house. He had moved just two blocks away to Eighty-Ninth Street. All the books from his house in Antwerp, more than 2,000, all in Hebrew save one German concordance, survived the war. They arrived in long white pine boxes, coffin size, while my grandfather still lived with us.

"Each book now labeled on the outside—Hidushei Abrach—New Commentaries of Abram Abish Rheinhold on the Shulhan Aruch clearly labeled on the outside (volume 61) in the handwriting of the librarian who had been hired to catalog all my grandfather's books. Shelf after shelf. With far away titles *Petach Ha'Gan*—the opening of the garden—all sitting like soldiers, survivors from the War, waiting for my grandfather to come over and lovingly caress their spines, open up the book yet again and dream of Antwerp, of Tarnov, of Cracow, of Riglitz, and further back, of Vilna, of Prague, of Saloniki, of Constantinople, and further back still, of Zion: The Opening of the Garden. Safed, Tiberias and Jerusalem.

What could I do on Parent's Day when my mother asked me to ask Mr. Nemerov if I could, as my father was away, bring my grandfather to school to see my progress.

"Of course," my teacher said. The weekly Parsha portion: The Chapter Noah. These are generations of Noah. Noah was the just and righteous man of his generation. "And why, Benjamin Zucker, does the Torah use the words 'Noah was a just, righteous man?' after 'these are the generations of Noah'?" asked my teacher. I answered bright as a button. "Because Rashi tells us that a person's good deeds are his true children."

The next day, into the classroom of Ramaz my mother led my grandfather, both sitting along with other class parents in the back.

My teacher nodded at my grandfather and said in Hebrew: "Children today we will study the portion of the week, the story of Noah. And what Benjamin Zucker, does Rashi tell us about the phrases: 'These are the generations of Noah, Noah was the righteous man of his generation.'"

Suddenly I could feel my grandfather's hand around mine. I could see my mother calling me into the kitchen for breakfast. I was frozen. I could not say a word.

"Binyamin, why?" my teacher persisted. Still, I could say nothing. "Strange, Binyamin. Yesterday, you knew it perfectly."

That evening when we returned to my grandfather's house, I not hearing a word and my mother not saying a word until we entered grandfather's library. Bless your grandson that he will become a scholar. My grandfather placed his hands on my forehead and gently said, "If Benyamin will study, he will become a scholar."

So spoken, his 2,000 volumes from Jerusalem to Antwerp, served as witnesses.

■ BENNELLE ZUCKER: For when his grandfather lived in his family house—I was four with Grandfather living in my house. Also my family: Mother. Dadda. Margot. Nikki.

Into my grandfather's room. His white beard above the sheets. On his back, he slept. Easy to awake him. Pull on his beard.

"Are you awake?" I would ask him. His smile so simple. "I am now," his eyes would nod. Next thing I would stand next to him. He would be praying by the window, swaying so slowly. I could feel the breeze of his arms moving, back and forth, back and forth. I could feel the tefill-in, black and smooth, on his left arm as he leaned down holding my little hand in his.

I looked beyond the window, my eyes just above the sill, at the building across the way, the lights starting to go on, as 6 o'clock early morning white light streamed into the apartment.

Then the prayers would be over and a hissing sound from the kitchen filled my ears. The door swung open into the living room and next my mother handed me a glass of milk. "Drink Bennelle," she said softly, and put her warm hand on my fingers as I lifted the cold glass to my lips.

■ BERNARD ZUCKER: Grandfather living in my house—The Great American Novel used to be the secular Grail of every university student from Hanover, New Hampshire, to Princeton, New Jersey. It can be written in the Pacific trenches, dreamed in a Greenwich Village basement, composed on napkins in a French café, recorded in a Saigon safe house—venue not important. Even on the road between cities or towns or villages or bus stops. Every writer dreaming to capture the title: Great American Novelist. All roads lead through the shortcuts of one's arteries and ventricles. And mine: In my first year at Harvard Law School, 1965 LLB, my little lovely book, a grandfather, Rabbi, beard as snow, sent away from his Chicago accountant's home, in his grandson's first year at Yale, generational crevices.

What shall I call my book? None other than: *res ipse loquitur*—The Great American Novel. No matter that William Carlos Williams has already written and so named it; no matter that Philip Roth will write and so name his.

Thy Will be done, in heaven as it is on earth.

"'The tenth reason is that I have no money.' 'Forget the other reasons,' says the farmer. The tenth reason Fisher likes my use of noble white is that it's my favorite non-color."

"But Dosha, I'm not a Polish farmer. What is the first reason he likes the color white?"

"Ah," said Dosha, patting Tal's hand. "His grandfather's—Tuviah Gutman Gutwirth's— beard was as white as the light of a heavenly morning. Fisher was four when his grandfather lived in his family house. It's an early memory. Grandfather praying. Young Fisher by his side. Gentleness itself. Dispensing a familial and priestly blessing upon Fisher. All these reasons, white for me, and white for the groom."

"What! He asked you? Our plan to get Fisher to ask you to wed worked?"

"Not our plan, Jones," said Dosha.

"Who's Jones?"

"Just a figure of speech, Tal, relax. Who's 'our'? It was your plan."

■ BENJAMIN ZUCKER: Grandfather living in my family house—They are all there together. Mr. Borges, Maimonides and my grandfather. Borges: "*When I think of paradise, I think of a library.*"

Maimonides explains: "*In heaven, the righteous sit with crown on their heads. They study Torah for time everlasting.*"

My grandfather sits in the same large hall, with a spacious ceiling, open to the heavens in the center of the hall.

All his books are at his fingertips. Pardes Rimonin sitting on his study table in front of him. I can feel my grandfather's hand on mine. I can hear the murmur of his lips as he and Maimonides converse, Borges moves his head, back and forth between them. Though gone, Grandfather is living in my family house. While I paint his words in hues of blue, green and white.

Picture of a Young Boy, photographer unknown.

tattered copy of *The Devarim Arevim*, published in 1903, I read:

"A certain countryman, who knew it is right to eat and drink heartily on the eve of the Holy Day of Yom Kippur, said to himself, 'I will eat and drink until after the afternoon prayer. Then I will get on my horse and will reach the city in a short time.' When he concluded his meal, he mounted his horse. But he got lost in the forest, and could not find the way. The sunset and the night of Kol Nidre arrived. He saw that he would have to remain in the forest all the night and all the day of the holy and awesome day. He had no festival prayer book with him, for he had already sent ahead those he had to the city with members of his household.

"The countryman wept long and bitterly and said, 'Master of the universe, what shall I do? But there is a verse, the word of the lord can be combined (Psalms 18:31). I shall recite the alphabet and you, O master of the universe, must combine the letters into syllables and words.' So he recited all the letters of the alphabet.

"Now this recital made a great impression in heaven, for the countryman drew many other prayers to heaven after his."

Dosha has recited Tal's alphabet. Fisher has heard. This has made a great impression in heaven. Their wedding day fast will be their great Day of Awe. Fisher's novels, soon to be written, will be his prayer. Please G-d, may it be accepted.

"Pure and simple. Each letter. A.B.C. Each line. Down to the locket. Yes, he's asked and it's complete. Sealed, signed and delivered."

"But it's not final without a Rabbi."

"I don't get it, Tal," said Dosha. "Paradoxical training. First you ask me to say I'm a gypsy. And now only a Rabbi will do. Where will this end?"

"Not well," said Tal. "Not well unless you listen to me precisely. Now you both must be married by a Rabbi. With a Ketubah. A normal wedding. A Ketubah with witnesses. The whole ten yards."

"Not ten, Tal. Nine." Dosha patted Tal's hand again.

"OK. OK. You've gone one yard already. Now the whole other nine yards."

"You know, admitting mistakes is not your forte."

"Who are you, my brother?" said Tal. "You've got to go to a Rabbi. This is not so simple. This is very, very, very not simple." He started to pace around the room.

"What's so complicated? Go upstairs to your apartment and get a phone book and come down here and dial a Rabbi and bring him here and get your brother as a witness."

■ MU XIN: Pure and simple. Each letter. Each line—Dosha is an artist. She does not stand alone. Tal is her teacher. His lessons are pure and simple. Each letter…each line.

Fortunately she is able to speak with him face to face. Even after his passing still will they converse. Her children's children, too.

Leonardo was *"my early teacher."* I sat in his class in my cousin's village hidden library, Mao Dun. His private library open to me, paradise beyond dreams. The cacophony of voices, Pascal, Rousseau, Tolstoy, Dostoevsky, all speaking at once to me—Cezanne and Van Gogh, Rembrandt, Vermeer, Shitao, Bada Shanren, Ni Tsan, images more like movies playing at the very same time, day and night, but unseen and unheard outside the enclosed garden of my library because the madness encircling it was overwhelming. In Mao Dun enchanted space, *"I enjoyed reading all of the masterpieces of world literature, when war and chaos ruled outside."*

■ BADA SHANREN: Listen to me precisely—Tal the ancient asks the young woman, as he asked the young man, Fisher, to listen to him precisely. But not to listen to him alone, rather to the Ancients:

Shushua Tongyuan: Calligraphy and painting are of the same origin. This the Ancients taught.

The calligrapher Fisher and the painter Dosha must listen to this precisely. This I taught Shitao, though we did not meet, ever. I did not speak, so that Shitao could hear me, two thousand *li* away, precisely.

Surely Tal does not speak of marriage, even less of normal marriage. For he and I must be dumb on such a topic. *"What promise did I break?"* Or probably the promise neither Tal nor I made. Could make. Neither of us may speak of normal marriage. Still we can teach the lessons of the Ancients.

◆ SIMHA PADAWER: Here—My granddaughter is willing to wed immediately. No discussions between her family and the bridegroom's. No renting of a hall. Here. No preparations. Just a surprise on her intended life partner. Is this custom in America? My Jerusha knows that just across the river, in the same shtetl she lives in, two thousand Hassidim danced at a wedding just the other day.

In Talmud Kiddushin, we read: R. Ashi set a problem. What is the law if he said: "*Your daughter and your land can be acquired with a perutah (a penny)."* Does he mean your daughter with a half a perutah, and your land with half a *perutah*, or perhaps he means your land with *hazakah* (as of right). How can it be that in former times even the barest minimum, the smallest coin, was agreed by our sages to allow a man to marry a wife whereas today it's yet more simple. Almost half of nothing. My granddaughter demands half of nothing for her wedding day! Yet what did our sages teach us of Reb. Ashi's words: "*TEYKU— Tishbi yetaretz kushyot ve-'ibbayot. The Tishbi (the Messiah) will resolve this difficulty and all problems."* What my eyes see now, my mind cannot make sense of. G-d, send the Messiah to explain all of these puzzles.

■ VITA SACKVILLE-WEST: *I can be dressed in white—11 November, Friday morning, 1927. "I have been so really wretched since last night. I felt suddenly that the whole of my life was a failure, in so far as I seemed incapable of creating one single perfect relationship. What shall I do about it, Virginia? Be strong-minded, I suppose. Well, I at least I won't create any further mistakes! My darling, I'm grateful to you; you were quite right to say what you did; it has given me a pull-up. I drift too easily. But look here, remember and believe that you mean something absolutely vital to me. I don't exaggerate when I say I don't know what I should do if you ceased to be fond of me—got irritated—got bored…*

"Darling, forgive my faults. I hate them in myself, and I know you are right. But they are silly, surface things. My love for you is absolutely true, vivid and unalterable."

Shall I dress like Dosha in white and await my Virginia? Seasons will pass. Summer followed by summer and never a spring for us. For in all Christendom none to marry we two. Perhaps a Rabbi will do for the likes of us.

But you will be mine, Virginia, and I'll be yours forever white. If not at Knole, then Seven Oaks. If not under the Long Barn, then in Sissinghurst, — but in the earth with you— I, dressed in white—my "courtyard not rectangular but coffin-shaped." You shall swim along my moat, walk with its supporting walk, slide by my "minor crookednesses," up my axial Northern enclave, resting forever in the most intimate surprise of my small geometric garden.

"And when Fisher comes back tonight from *Time* magazine, I can be dressed in white and the Rabbi can perform the ceremony and you and your brother can sign on as witnesses and I'm sure you'll be able to explain away my being a gypsy yesterday and a *frummie* today."

"Not here, not here. Here won't last an eternity for you.

"Alright, not here in your advice shop—we'll do the ceremony on Hudson and Perry. Didn't I read that just the other day over 2,000 black-hatted Satmar Hassidim celebrated a wedding in the streets of Brooklyn?"

"Not Satmar—Belz," Tal said dreamily. "Not here, but there."

"Where?"

"In Jerusalem. In full view of her ancient walls. Yes, it's that simple. You'll wed in Jerusalem."

■ VIRGINIA WOOLF: And when Fisher comes back—Friday night, 11 November 1927, 52 Tavistock Square. To Vita Sackville-West. *"Dearest Creature, You make me feel such a brute and I didn't mean to be. One can't regulate the tone of one's voice, I suppose; for nothing I said could in substance make you wretched for even half a second, only that you can't help attracting the flounderers…And I'm half or 10th part jealous when I see you with the Valeries and the Marys: so you can discount that.*

"And that's all there is to it as far as I'm concerned. I'm happy to think you do care, for often I seem old, fretful, querulous, difficult (tho' charming) and begin to doubt…Berg."

When Fisher comes back he will be like every lover, expectant, not without a trace of nervousness, certainly with more than a soupçon of jealousy. For radiant Dosha is more than one person's dream. She wanders at night in Tal's head and even in his brother's mind. While she sleeps, she too flies across celestial roads touching Fisher's body which sometimes has Tal's head on it and sometimes even his brother's. All our eyes rest on all we see. Little magicians, our fingers and eyes are, continuously making everyone we experience appear and disappear in our arms.

All the Marys, the Valeries, the Tals even young Fisher and Dosha, a river of desire in an endless springtime. Bits and pieces of Vita descending the heavens, fine as dew.

■ R. LEVI YITZHAK of Berditchev (1740-1810): Here…Jerusalem—The woman wishes to be wed immediately under the laws of Moses and of all Israel. Her teacher, sage and Rabbi, Abraham Tal, is insisting on Jerusalem.

Each of their words must be counted and weighed for they are discussing yet a higher question. Why must Elijah, the Messiah, be required to solve all unsolvable questions. The TEYKU problems, in the coming of the Messiah.

Surely Moses will be among the resurrected dead and will he not be *"better equipped to solve these problems than Elijah? In every problem there is something to be said for each side, otherwise there would be no problem. The decision depends on the spiritual needs of the times."* Hillel's decisions stressing mercy are followed today because today the world needs the element of mercy. Moses *"having returned from the dead will have no voice in what these spiritual needs are since he no longer belongs to this world at all. But Elijah, who never died, belongs to this would still and can render the decision the age requires."*

Dosha is dealing with the present world. Her Rabbi Abraham Tal is preparing for the messianic world of Jerusalem. And we all say: Amen.

The White Garden, Sissinghurst.

■ M.K. Heeramaneck, painting dealer: Fine—My grandfather P.K. always told me, "*Do not contradict an Englishman to his face. But do not agree with him when he is wrong.*"

Who was I to say to the keeper of drawings of the Victoria and Albert Museum, in 1914, war was clearly coming. I had to get back to India.

I had spread out my three finest Indian paintings, two Kangra paintings, and one extraordinary tinted drawing, early Moghul. "We are not now purchasing Kangra paintings. What are you asking for this drawing?" said the keeper evenly. "It is very fine, sir." I looked down carefully at the drawing. "Excellent condition," I mumbled half to myself. I moved my head from elephant to elephant, slowly, as though seeing the elephant heads for the first time. I rested my eyes on the half-lion, half-elephant, the gaja-simha lifting the seven elephants off the ground. I bowed my head to the Simurgh reverentially so as to acknowledge its royalty, but I didn't say another word.

"Well, Mr. Heeramaneck, what are the damages to be?" insisted the keeper. "Sixty-six pounds, sir," I answered with the quietly authoritative voice my grandfather P.K. always used. "Sixty-six pounds, sir." "What!" cried the keeper, bolting out of his seat. "How do you reckon that peculiar sum?" "Three pounds an elephant, sir."

The keeper looked at me incredulously. "What do you charge for the simurgh and the gaja-simha?" "Nothing sir. They are unique and imaginary and it is difficult to calculate their worth."

The keeper burst out laughing and pointed slowly to the elephants counting out loud, "One, two, three," and ended with "sixteen." "Well then, what we have here is sixteen elephants. Surely you don't expect the Victoria and Albert Museum to pay for barely drawn, only one-quarter represented elephants." "That makes sense, sir," I said. "But this elephant in the second row, far right, is two-thirds visible." "Fine, Mr. Heeramaneck. Make it forty-eight pounds and two pounds for two-thirds of an elephant. Fifty pounds total. And throw in the two Kangra." "Excuse me sir, but I understood you to state clearly the Museum was not interested in Kangra paintings at present."

"That is quite right, but his Majesty's museum would be delighted to obtain them as a gift. Fifty British pounds, Mr. M.K. Heeramaneck."

"As you wish, sir," I said. "And a fine farewell to my sixteen and two-thirds elephants," I said with a flourish, thinking of my grandfather P.K.'s injunction: "It is always vital to leave a good taste in a customer's mouth."

"Out of curiosity, how do I explain this to Dreamboat? That our secular ceremony at Centre Street, perfectly valid by American, New York State standards, and recognized internationally, is not really valid."

"But what about your grandchildren?"

"OK, for the moment we'll leave that possibility of future generations open.

"But in the eyes of the world, by those unborn, how do I tell Dreamboat we must to Jerusalem?"

"This week. You must go this week," insisted Tal.

"It's freezing, Tal. This is not the season for travel to the Holy Land. It's damp in Jerusalem, I'm told."

"Who's talking of weather, Dosha? I'm talking about your share in the world to come."

"Fine. But how do I broach the topic to Fisher?"

■ Tuviah Gutman Gutwirth, Fisher's grandfather: What about your grandchildren?—Tal is closest here to being a Rav. So he is asking the question. The right question. At the right time. In the right country. For a marriage to be accepted in every country in the world does not make it acceptable. Legal. Binding. Just. And for a marriage not to be recognized in every nation in the world, does it become invalid where the grandchildren are concerned?

I was born in Riglitz in 1874. Travelled to Antwerp before the century turned. Fled to neutral Holland in 1914. And back to Antwerp before the crash of the Credit Anstaldt Bank. Fleeing Antwerp hoping to come to America in '40. Crossed the Atlantic toward New York, only to have our ship turn back before an attack by the evening's U-boats. Thank G-d, reached South Africa, and able to purchase kosher meat in Laurenzo Marques. Then to Cuba and finally on to New York. Driven by the hand of Providence. To see my grandchildren in New York. To live with them. And always dreaming of the Holy Land. All these passports, identity papers. Papier de Naissance, recognized internationally but were any of these papers valid? France did not recognize Belgian papers. Belgium had no confidence in Polish documents. America was a law unto itself. And even if every nation on earth recognized my papers, would I not be without a true home?

Tal knows this. He can see ahead. He can see the children's children to come. The answer is awakening the young woman. She will awaken my grandchild. But Tal must be the responsa to his own questions—though G-d pity him, he be without grandchildren or even children.

The world has passed through fire and the embers still render warm the pavements of all the capitals of the world. Warm. So warm that we must all wear shorts, though the ground we stand on, all of it, is holy.

■ Chaya Gutwirth, Tuviah Gutman Gutwirth's wife and Fisher's grandmother: —Over and over in Riglitz, in Tarnov, Antwerp, in Scheevening and again in Antwerp, Tuviah would ask me: What about your grandchildren?

As though they were not both ours. As much Rheinhold as Gutwirth. I would answer him softly in the middle of the night, "Look at the children yourself, each more clever than the next. Baruch and Hessiah, Anna quick as fire. Aron and Hendrik. Sheindele so remarkable even at six, and Malkah almost her twin." Before Malkah said a word, Sheindel would prepare what she wanted. That went for me also and for Tuviah too. Look at the children, Tuviah, yourself. Who should look, me? I was growing more blind by the year. The children knew it. Tuviah knew it. Perhaps the rug dealer Eknayan, who would come to our house every six months, would not know as I touched the silk rugs in various parts, and asking him how he would compare the colors of the Bokhara to one I bought last year—but everyone else knew it.

Look at them Tuviah, they are your blue-white diamonds. They are rough stones now, but G-d Himself will polish them. We will build a house, beautiful with antiques and the finest art, solid beyond argument. And Tuviah will repeat over and over, but what about your grandchildren?

The *Simurgh* attacks a *Gaja-Simba* carrying off seven elephants.

■ FERDINAND DE ROTHSCHILD: Advice—Take advice from everyone. For I was Austrian born. A Jew before birth and a Jew after death. But with the world of advice I took, still I could not become *plus anglais que les anglais*. We were guests at Gladstone's house, Ponsby—the English diplomat—and I. *"The conversation turned to the question of how many books constituted a good gentleman's library."* Ponsby polled the group at Prime Minister Gladstone's house and announced grandly, *"Twenty thousand was the ideal number."* I am told that Ponsby, the good Queen Victoria's private secretary, smiled when I immediately made a note. Odd. To the English a number could be remembered or forgotten or mistaken or counted twice. Not I. I was to be *plus anglais*. And my manor, Waddeston, to be my everlasting home, more mausoleum than palace. Of course I paced about my *"salle des curiosiés"* in the west wing in my private apartments. I did not need to place my hands on a Renaissance jewel for I could feel the texture with my eyes. And my father's eyes. Father *"used to rise at 6 o'clock and remain on his legs until dusk…shopping and sight-seeing. I wish he had handed his constitution down to his sons. In Father's museum, he spent many a happy hour puffing away at his cigar, and making the catalogue of his collection in the company of one Plach, an Austrian dealer."*

As a child, Father would allow me *"as soon as the swallows made their appearance,"* before we moved to our Grüneburg summer villa, *"to place some of the smaller articles in their old leather cases and then again in the winter to assist in unpacking them and rearranging them in their places. Merely to touch them sent a thrill of delight through my small frame."*

When one is young, one needs to touch. When one is old, one touches with one's eyes. The lapis. The gold. The pointed diamonds. The flat, impossibly cool white table cut diamonds surrounding Hilliard's miniature of James I. The Lyte jewel. King James's eyes resting on the blue enameled roof of my Renaissance wedding ring. All my treasures. *"Old works of art are not…desirable only for their rarity or beauty but for their associations, for the memories they evoke, the trains of thought to which they lead, and the many ways they stimulate the imagination and realize our ideals."*

These treasures by my will and bequest —from the Lyte jewel to Jamnitzer's Nürenberg Bell, its lizards, insects and flowers, all cast from life—a gift to the nation. I too, my spirit contained beneath the cool blue enameled roof of my Jewish betrothal ring. I am in my objects, resting forever in the British Museum. All of us *plus anglais que les anglais*.

"You, never heard of the word honeymoon?"

Dosha jumped up from her chair. "Dear Tal, if I weren't me, and you weren't you, I'd have both of us committed."

"Didn't my advice on the locket and the proposal work?" insisted Tal. "Trust me. Trust me, as they say in this country. You'll tell him now. Dear, honeymoon!"

"Fine, I'll say that and then he'll say when. And I'll say—oh it must be within a week. It's a gypsy custom to travel to our Holy Land within a week of the wedding vows.

"And just one little point. What do we do for, as my father would say, *pinonza*? Dough-re-mi-gelt-ducati etc. Dreamboat is down to zero, that I can assure you. And I have none on my butterfly's salary."

■ SAIDA-YE GILANI, JAHANGHIR's head of goldsmiths Kharkhana: Butterfly— Place the picture here, Nader-al-Zaman. Just before my wheel. For today I will finish the line. Or the line will finish me. Neither heat of the day nor the coldness of the night will grant me a reprieve.

Paint me a picture of a flower in Kashmir with a butterfly that floats above. My hand must be light today, my fingers nimble. I am writing on a butterfly's emerald wing.

■ MANSUR: Butterfly—Write for me Sayid'ah, a single word on a gem page.

My hand floats across my paper.
What shall remain of me, of my hand's work,
My manuscript paper well-watered by
My tears. Crumpled, lost
Orphaned by time.

■ DAVID LINSAY, later Earl of Crawford: Land— *"Baron Ferdinand, whose hands always itch with nervousness, walks about, at times petulantly, while jealously caring for the pleasure of his guests. I failed to gather that his priceless pictures give him true pleasure. His clock for which he gave 25,000 pounds, his statuary, his china, and his superb collection of jewels, enamels and so forth ("gimcracks" he calls them)—all these things give him meager satisfaction: And I felt that the only pleasure he derives from them is gained when he is showing them to his friends… However, it is in the gardens and shrubberies that he is happy. He is responsible for the design of the flower beds, for the arrangement of colour, for the transplanting of trees: all these things are under his personal control and I am astonished at the knowledge he displayed…It is only among his shrubs and orchids that the nervous hands of Baron Ferdinand Rothschild are at rest."*

I watch him from my window facing the garden. The Baron is already up at 7:00, walking among his orchids at seven. A footman at my door asks:

Tea, coffee, chocolate or cocoa, sir?"
"Tea, please," I reply.
"Yes, sir. Assam, Souchang or Ceylon?"
"Souchang, please," I reply.
"Yes, sir. Milk, cream or lemon?"
"Milk, please," I again reply.
"Yes, sir. Jersey, Hereford or Shorthorn?

I am speechless. Only in England. But are we in England? We are in quite another land. We are in the mind of a Rothschild.

Sculptural relief of a lotus flower on the side of the Taj Mahal.

Charm—*Oh Scott had it. The main criterion I had to marry him. He was:*

1. *Good looking.*
2. *Best company.*
3. *Famous.*
4. *Made a good living.*

And I wouldn't have traded him for anybody as so few people have so many of the desirabilities. "Don't you think I was made for you?" I asked Scott. "I feel like you had me ordered. And I was delivered to you to be worn. *I want you to wear me like a watch-charm or a button hole to the world.*"

Young Fisher, all charm to Dosha. Like my Scott. Who was the most charming person in the world simply because he described me, his wife, as "*the most charming person in the world.*"

Simple. Dear Scott. At the center of us all, the light ever behind him, prancing on an elephant while all of us, me on a rooster, Scottie on a horse, Tara, our butler, on a turtle. George Jean Nathan, leonine, and all of us moving round-and-round on our merry-go-way through villa St. Louis, Juan-les-Pins, Bear Lake Yacht Club, White Minnesota, Ellerslie, Delaware, the Plaza Hotel, Capri, the Villa Marie at St. Raphael, the Spanish Steps, the house in Westport, riding around and around each other, catching the light and living only on charm.

■ HIERONYMA DE PAIVA: It's not too late—My G-d, the nerve of Elihu. Though I suppose it was half his charm. He'd ask anything of the devil himself. If he saw the Angel of Death approach to take him, he'd argue he was not Elihu Yale but rather John Nicks, or even me, if he were darker complected.

"Never surrender and never confess," was his motto. Must be the Welsh in him. First he would grant the right to my dear Jacques and our people to purchase the land for a Portuguese cemetery for our people in Peddenaipetam. Then when poor Jacques died, Elihu said he must first probate before burying Jacques and before probating, he must write to the company and beg their permission. "What if I were to move to your house, Lord Yale," I asked him, "would you waive the probate process?" "Ah, Madame de Paiva, that would greatly influence me." "And what if I were to tell you that I have decided Lord Yale, to immediately leave for London, if you do not bury my husband before nightfall in our people's graveyard." I could feel his breath upon my face and knew exactly what he was thinking. Never had Jacques or I been in his presence that he failed to look at me like a smiling fox, waiting to pounce. He was no fool, Lord Yale, and he said: "I waive the formalities and beg my Lady's indulgence to allow me the protection of my home so that she may arrange her affairs and settle her accounts. I pray it is not too late for my Lady to dwell amongst my family and recover her balance."

Bury Jacques I did. Enter Governor Yale's house, I did. Bed my Elihu, I did. Roust his virago of a wife, I did. But to agree to share my Lord's bed for all eternity. Never. Each night I prayed that G-d would give me strength to live. For if dead, Elihu would not hesitate to plunge me in the cold earth, and lie on top, or on the side, or under me forever. In a Welsh grave or an Anglican Indian churchyard or even the devil take him as sport in an emperor's Muslim white sepulchre. Live I would. Follow Elihu back to London, I would. But it was too late to rest beside him forever. Jacques would never forgive me.

"That's simple," said Tal. "One phone call and I'll have the money."

"And the Rabbi?" asked Dosha. "Can you call him too? It's not too late? It must be ten in the evening in Israel." Tal picked up the phone and dialed slowly. When someone answered, he spoke in Hebrew, then English:

"Wednesday night is excellent," muttered Tal. "Excellent."

"Are you completely wacko? Where am I supposed to meet the Rabbi? At the Western Wall?"

"Yes, yes, at the Wall."

Dosha sat down in her chair. Her head was spinning. Tal had his ways. She'd always be a sucker for charm. For obsession. For the secret collector. The late-night Kabbalist. The unseen figure. The lost map. Plot complications delighted her.

■ F. SCOTT FITZGERALD: Charm—Dosha is a sucker for charm. For the secret collector, the solitary figure. The late night Kabbalist. The reflection of Zelda through Time's hourglass.

"*My wife is the most charming person in the world…that's all. I refuse to amplify except she's perfect.*"

"You don't think that," Zelda answered with a languidness that only a Montgomery Sayre can muster. "You think I'm a lazy woman."

"*No,*" I said. "*I like it. I think you're perfect. You're always ready to listen to my manuscripts at any hour of the day or night.*"

Ditto Dosha. Plot complications delight her as much as Zelda.

But for Zelda, the unexpected ever came.

■ ELIHU YALE: It's not too late—"It's not too late," I would taunt Hieronyma in the middle of the night. If you wish, it is not too late to talk. To plan. To scheme. To buy, to sell. To whisper. To laugh. To love. And she would talk. Plan. Scheme. Buy from me and sell to me. And sell with me. And laugh with me and love with me throughout the Indian night.

But sometimes if it had rained all day, or the monsoon air befouled the fort, she would lie still, almost dead, she seemed. She moaned: "It's too late, Elihu it's too late," over and over.

I would try to bring her around. Clutch her to me. But on those days, the black days I called them, nights when there was no room, I would tease her. "If you will not lie with me now, will you lie with me later?"

She knew what I meant by the word: "Later." One could hear it in my voice. My father would tell me in Welsh. "A young man may die, an old man must die." Hindustan turned all men into old men. The average Englishman died after but a four years stay in the East. I was of hardy Welsh stock, G-d be praised, but I could see my reflection in Hieronyma's eyes. I was old.

Her husband, her precious Portuguese Jewish diamond dealing graveyard purchasing Hebrew Bible chanting Jacques de Paiva. Did he not die in less than three summers here? And her cousin Salvador, were not his Hindu princesses soon to finish his soul too?

"It is too late for my Lord to lie beside me when I die," my love said rather formally to me. Though it excited me more than if my Sovereign would address me. "Why not? Did not Shah Jahan build a white tomb, the Taj, to lie in next to Mumtaz his bride and a garden across the river? To gaze at her tomb preparing to join her while he dreamed of her, night and day. "But I am not Muslim," she laughed and added lightly, "and no Jew will suffer you to be buried next to me in our graveyard at Peddenaipetam."

"Then come lie with me in the courtyard of St. Mary's in the fort. Or in Wrexam Cathedral in a good Welsh grave." "But my Lord, I am not a Christian." "Then meet me halfway to the garden and we shall drink, make merry and carouse. Wink at all in the gloaming of our lives, enter paradise together, and bed in a white tomb forever."

She laughed but by G-d I knew she would never agree.

■ J.P. MORGAN: One phone call and I'll have the money—1924. "*First class business in a first class way.*" Harry Davison used to say it simply: $400 million was all my partners could handle without diluting the Morgan style. 23 Wall was private. A private bank. No deposits from the general public. Only larger corporations, honorable banks and foreign governments. No deposits. No interest paid on amounts less than $7,500 and heaven forbid, no deposits less than a thousand dollars. One phone call to any of my 14 partners at 23 Wall and you'd have the money. Simple really. If you keep it small and tight.

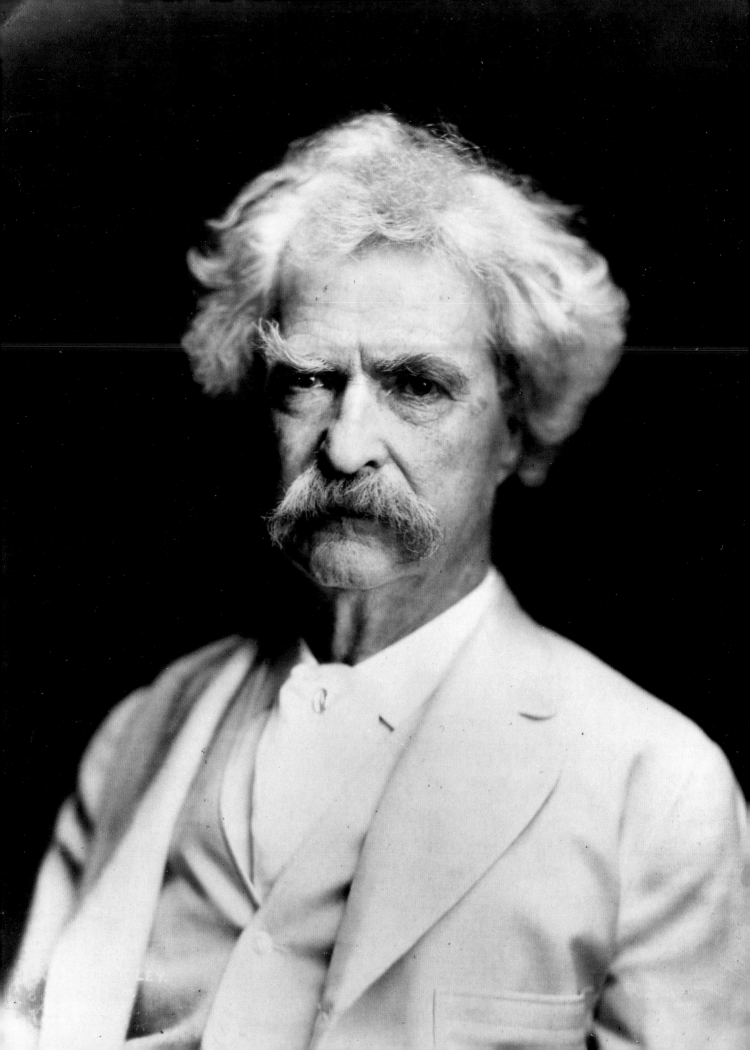

◆ ISAAC TAL, Tal's father: Tal had dialed only seven digits—In front of this young woman my son Abraham makes no sense. He stacks books by "the Americans," as he calls them: Melville, *Moby Dick*, all editions paperback, hard back and illustrated. He has Mark Twain's *Huckleberry Finn* and *Tom Sawyer*. He has Classic Comic versions of *A Connecticut Yankee in King Arthur's Court*, all used to prop the door of his apartment open so that Dosha will notice: he is an intellectual in Hebrew, Aramaic, Ladino which he mumbles to himself in Operatic Italian, English and now American comic book talk.

Does she care? With his mouth he encourages her to marry; with his child's eye he dreams of sweeping her off her Walt Disney glass-slippered feet, with his hands he dials too few numbers. He didn't add up in Antwerp and he doesn't here, certainly not with one half his age.

■ SAMUEL CLEMENS (Mark Twain): She had what she wanted—She has what she wants. Dosha. Fisher. Together in each other's nocturnal arms. "*We catched fish and talked, and we took a swim now and then to keep off sleepiness. It was kind of solemn, drifting down the big, still river, laying on our backs looking up at the stars, and we didn't ever feel like talking loud, and it warn't often that we laughed, only a little kind of a low chuckle. We had mighty good weather as a general thing, and nothing ever happened to us at all.*"

They lie together on the banks of Hudson Street, Dosha and Fisher. Tal is tempting Dosha to saunter from her Eden. Tal preaches to her: Go forth as a pilgrim to the Promised Land with "*the confidence of a Christian with four aces.*"

"*There are several good protections against temptations, but the surest is cowardice.*"

Nothing frightens Dosha. She will leave for the Holy Land. Whither she goes, Fisher will surely follow. He's stucker than stuck.

But she had what she wanted. Her long-shot dream. And now Tal, her neighbor, was telling her to put all her chips on number 32 a second time.

Easy probability. If it worked, it worked. If it didn't, it didn't. Either she would voyage to Jerusalem with Dreamboat, or not. It didn't really matter. It seemed so surreal, it had to be real.

"Now I'm calling the Rabbi." He dialed the number. "Reb Shlomo, please," Tal said triumphantly into the phone.

"I thought you said the Rabbi is in Israel," said Dosha, noticing that Tal had dialed only seven digits. Tal covered the mouthpiece.

"That's the problem. He lives here but he's got to go to Israel."

■ ABRAHAM OF SACHATZOV: Neighbor: It will be recited by Tal's neighbor Fisher. For his neighbor and his neighbor's wife-to-be Jerusha have learned from him that "*there isn't a person to whom a miracle doesn't occur every moment but the person is not aware of it.*" Fisher has learned from his teacher Tal what I have learned from my father-in-law the Heilege Kotzger Rebbe: "*There is a book of remembrances in which each miracle is recorded. And in the distant future it will be made clear to each person what miracles happened to him.*"

Fisher is writing his own book of remembrance. A *kaddish* for Tal and for many, many others.

■ RABBI NO'AM ELIMELECH of Lizhensk (1717–1786): Neighbor—In Leviticus 19:18 we read: "*Do not take revenge nor bear a grudge against the children of your people. You must love your neighbor as you love yourself. I am G-d.*"

"*The Zohar tells us that the soul wears the body like a garment, pervading all its limbs and organs. The soul yearns to love the Holy One, blessed is He, but our carnal body stands in the way. In a figurative sense, the Torah instructs us in the above-mentioned verse to love our neighbor, meaning G-d (as in the verse, 'Do not forsake your friend and your father's friend,' Proverbs 27:10) as we love ourselves; just as your soul loves G-d, with a perfect all-embracing love, so must you, its corporeal counterpart, love G-d with a true love, so that body and soul will be in complete harmony.*"

Tal, Dosha's neighbor, can see this voyage to the Holy Land will unite the souls of the bridegroom and groom with the Holy One, blessed be G-d.

■ HERMAN MELVILLE: Jerusalem—"'*Oh! Ahab,*' cried my Starbuck, '*not too late is it, even now, the third day, to desist. See! Moby Dick seeks thee not. It is thou, thou that madly seekest him.*'"

Tal lives here but he's got to go to Israel. I too, to Jerusalem must go. "*Warden Crisson of Philadelphia—an American turned Jew—divorced from his former wife, married to a Jewess here. Sad.*"

An old Connecticut man wandering about Jerusalem, stooped beneath the religious tracts, "*knew not the language, hopelessness of it, his lonely bachelor rooms, he maintained that expression Oh Jerusalem! Was an assignment proving that Jerusalem was a bye-word, etc.*"

Starbuck and Queequeg, the Rabbi and I, all sailing toward Jerusalem: We are boarding Dosha and Fisher.

"*The rising sea forbade all attempts to bale out of the boat. The oars were useless as propellers, performing now the office of life preservers. So, cutting the lashing of the waterproof match-keg after many failures, Starbuck contrived to ignite the lamp in the lantern; then stretching it on a waif pole, handed it to Queequeg as the standard bearer of this forlorn hope. There, then, he sat, holding that imbecile candle in the heart of the almighty forlorness. There, then he sat, the sign and symbol of a man without faith, hopelessly holding up hope in the midst of despair.*"

Tal hopelessly holding up hope, for Dosha. Will not her children's children be rescued by the good ship Rachel?

les misérables
à l'ami Vincent
P Gauguin 88

◆ ISAAC TAL, ABRAHAM TAL'S FATHER: "What, he's not there? He's in Israel?"—My son Abraham is not speaking into the phone. He's covering the phone with his hand. Or he's covering his eyes with his hand. He's not here. He's there. Always was. As a child. As a man. In Antwerp, he dreamed of Israel. "When are we going to the Holy Land, Father?" he would ask me every day before the war. I would smile, try to loosen him a bit. "Ask Tuviah, Abraham," I would answer, "you always claim he makes up our mind for us." "No, it's Mother who makes up your mind, Father." "Then ask her." "No, she will say, 'Ask Father.'" "Then ask Tuviah," I persisted. "No, he will wink at me and say, 'Who is we? You and your intended, Rachel Beller? Or mother, father, you and I, my dear brother?' Why should I ask Tuviah when I already know his reply?" "Then ask yourself, Abraham. And you answer." But he thought he should not answer so could not answer though the truth was his mother would have done what he wished and I would have followed Rachel anywhere at any time and Tuviah would have followed me. Abraham had the key in his hand. Always. But in truth he was already "there." Because he was never "here."

◆ RACHEL ABENDANA TAL, Abraham Tal's mother: There. He's in Israel—All I heard before the War was "Israel, Israel, Israel." "Are you asking me or telling me, Abraham," I said to him.

Of course he didn't reply. "When are we gong to the Holy Land" meant one thing to Tuviah, one thing to Isaac and G-d knows what it meant to Abraham.

If Tuviah was right, Abraham wanted me to tell him: "We, your intended Rachel Beller, your father, Tuviah and I are going to the Holy Land."

Not so simple. If it is to be a Sephardic match, then we should choose the bride. If it is to be an Ashkenasic match, then a matchmaker should come to us. But Abraham has chosen Rachel, pure and simple. Not us. Not Rachel's father, simple man that he is. But sweet.

If it is to be a "modern" match, Abraham must walk to Rachel's house, ask her father with downcast eyes, looking at his newly polished shoes, which he must scrub himself, come back to our house, with Rachel, and her father and announce to his father, to Tuviah and to myself, whom he has decided upon.

But I will not polish his shoes for him. When I'm gone, at their very first fight, in the middle of the night, Abraham's Rachel will whimper to him: "You never wanted to marry me. Your mother even shined your shoes before you walked over to propose." And Abraham, dear Abraham, will be child enough to believe her.

"What, he's in Israel? He's in Israel?" Tal shouted into the phone. "Mrs. Carlebach, I can't hear you. Your son is in Israel? Oy, OK. OK. I'll call back in an hour. I have an important wedding for him to perform. Very important. Very, very. But I insist on paying before he goes. Also the tickets…in two days…I'll call back. I'm on the road, unreachable, Rebbetzin." Tal put the phone down.

"Tal, are you telling me that you're flying me to Israel? Fisher to Israel? The Rabbi to Israel? What about you and your brother? Are you both coming to Israel?"

"I should have gone years ago. With Rachel. Now it's hopeless. Everywhere I made mistakes: Antwerp, New York. Oh no, I'm not a Peeping John. I know where I'm not wanted, G-d forbid. But speaking of my brother, I'm settling this immediately." Tal dialed the phone once again.

"Tal please, this is Tal."

In less than a minute, Tal's face dropped.

■ GAUGUIN: I insist—My self-portrait. "One of my best things," I insist. My nose and eyes, "a complete abstraction." I insist: "The color is far from anything in nature. Imagine a distant memory of my stoneware twisted by intense heat. All the reds and violets streaked with bursts of flame, as though from a glowing furnace radiating from the eyes, the site of struggles is the painter's thoughts."

Do I care if Van Gogh understands me? I will go to Arles until the time is right to launch myself. When I leave, if Van Gogh chooses to come with me, he comes at his own risk. At the moment of his own choosing. We are both pilgrims. But neither of us Pope. Nor any man. Rabbi. Pope. Guide. Nor map, to me.

● RABBI AMIEL, ABRAHAM TAL'S RABBI in Antwerp: He's in Israel—Why they came to me I do not know. They went, all the Abendana cousins, and Isaac Tal and his sons too, to the Sephardic shul.

But Abraham was special. "We will only speak to you, Rabbi Amiel," said Isaac Tal. "Believe me, Rabbi, my wife will make it worthwhile for your synagogue if you can talk some sense into my son. Abraham wants to know when we are going to Israel."

What could I say to Tal? Thank G-d I had everything I needed. Except life. Life in the Holy Land. I came to their house at the appointed hour. "Come at five sharp," they said.

I did, and Tal senior was there. And Tuviah his son also. I never saw a son who followed his father about as much, almost a shadow. Of course the mother, an Abendana, was there, but in a corner of the library, in the shadows. Her family, originally Abolais was the Sephardic name, living in Antwerp 500 years before as Marranos under their Portuguese name, Duarte. They brought the diamond trade to Antwerp, they said.

I spoke to Isaac Tal, but I was looking at the mother's face in the shadowy corner of the room. "Where is your son Abraham? Am I not here to speak to his question, when you are going to Israel?"

I could see Rachel Abendana Tal sigh. No different a sigh from a sigh I saw on my mother's face, a mother's sigh, no different an Ashkenazi's sigh from a pure Sephardi. Probably no different from any mother's sigh. "G-d could not be everywhere so He created mothers," my father would say in Yiddish.

"But let us begin," I said. "When will you go to Israel, Isaac Tal? When will Abraham go? Let me answer from my mind and then from my heart," I continued.

"Our Rabbis taught in Tractate Kiddushin: 'If one has to study Torah and to marry a wife, he should first study and then marry. But if he cannot live without a wife, he should first marry and then study. Rav Judah said in Samuel's name: The rule is a man first marries then studies. Rabbi Jonathan said with a millstone around the neck shall one study Torah! Yet they do not differ: The one refers to ourselves [Babylonians] the other to them [Jerusalemites].'"

Suddenly the door flung open. Abraham entered. "Rabbi, speak to me from your heart."

He must have been standing outside the door. Abraham was a bit crazy but more than a bit brilliant. "From my heart, Abraham, I tell you that each morning, I awake here in Antwerp counting the minutes. This is not a life. Though I be married and, thank G-d, study Torah. Abraham, let me speak plainly. Marry Rachel. Come with me to the Holy Land and we will study together."

"But Rabbi Amiel," said Abraham. "You are going to Tel Aviv and I must go to Safed."

What could I say? Or what could his mother or father or even his brother say? His voyage was to Safed. May G-d give Abraham a speedy and safe journey.

Paul Gauguin, *Self-Portrait with Portrait of Bernard*, *Les Miserables*, Pont-Aven.

143

■ SHITAO (1642–1707): What do you mean? —"*Bada Shanren and I are one thousand lie apart, but we are two of a kind.*" Two prince-painters. Cousins. Cheng Jinge is our agent. Not so much to present our works to collectors but to guard us from the ever foolish, always asked question: What do you mean?

When Du Jin, our master, painted the scholar Fu Sheng transmitting the "Book of Documents," what did he show: a blank page. Every scroll blank, to be filled in by the owner, the viewer. A fellow painter. For if the scroll is filled in, still the viewer, the owner, another painter will think that he thinks that he knows what is meant by the lotus on the page. Then the owner, or the viewer, or the painter will write his dream on the page. And we will have two dreams. Far, far from the white, blank, empty, cold scroll. "In the Spring of 1696, Bada Shanren was commissioned to write out Tao Qian's "Essay on the Peach Blossom Spring.""

I received the calligraphy in Yungchow. Bada Shanren was wise. Silent. He spoke of "*the person who will do the painting.*"

For I, his cousin, a prince-painter, a "*thousand li*" apart from him was honored to be asked to complete the scroll. Who was I to my cousin? Or to myself?

A jade leaf from a golden branch,
An aging remnant subject?
Or
An empty-eyed monk in the
Tushita heaven…
A former incarnation.

I do not ask a question. My cousin does not answer. My cousin does not ask a question, I do not answer. "*Bada Shanren's calligraphy and painting are the best in the entire country.*"

Cheng Jing'e, our agent, will be our mountain refuge from the howling wind of words.

"What do you mean, he'll call me back? I'm not the to-be-called-back person. This is life or sudden death. You tell my brother that I'm not getting off or I'm getting off and I'm coming down to the office immediately… That will raise him from the dead," said Tal, winking at Dosha.

Suddenly Tal started to shake his head and roll his eyes.

"Such stupidities. Talking, talking, talking. Over and over. As though I'm hearing this for the first time."

"Tal, he can hear you. You're not covering the phone."

"So he can. You don't think he's heard me tell him that before? Of course he has." He seemed confused as to whether he was talking to his brother or to Dosha.

■ BADA SHAREN: What do you mean?—I, a descendant of the Ming Emperor. The dynasty fallen. My father dies within a waning of the moon. "What do you mean?" Kung Hsien asked me. "Do you mean your father could not survive the end of the Ming, or do you mean the Emperor had to die or your father would have been immortal?"

Foolish such a question. I answered Kung Hsien simply: "I am becoming a monk outside of time." My father never died and the Ming Emperor never died. No one dies. Certainly not an Emperor. Nor his offspring.

"What do you mean?" my Buddhist master asked me. What could I say but nothing? Ever. Simply dumb. Instead of stammering, I remained silent. But shouted in my silence. My father was silent all his life. If he hadn't died, should I too not remain silent? If I had stammered during the time the Emperor sat on the auspicious throne, should I now speak?

But eventually my silence was too loud for the monastery. I began to travel, laughing and crying as I wandered.

"What do you mean by your laughter?" asked the innkeepers who took me in.

I would simply take out a scroll and write with a running hand and laughing fingers. When I cried I was asked, "What do your tears mean?" I answered with a pictorial flourish, a plant drawn, a single bamboo shoot placed on a hanging scroll. Two birds, one crying, one laughing, singing to each other.

In all China, there was but one who never asked me: "What do you mean?" Shitao, for he was my cousin, a Ming emperor's descendant too. "*A thousand li away from me*": so did he not know me far better than my neighbor or my Buddhist master?

■ CHANG FENG (c. 1640): children—
Of the greatest living calligraphers of
San Yin, Wang was the greatest.
The children, I am afraid, are
Ignorant of this.
A Wang-addict, I am prone to
Being wine-rapt;
Waking up, I would try my hand
A little.

Tal and his brother, still children—always.

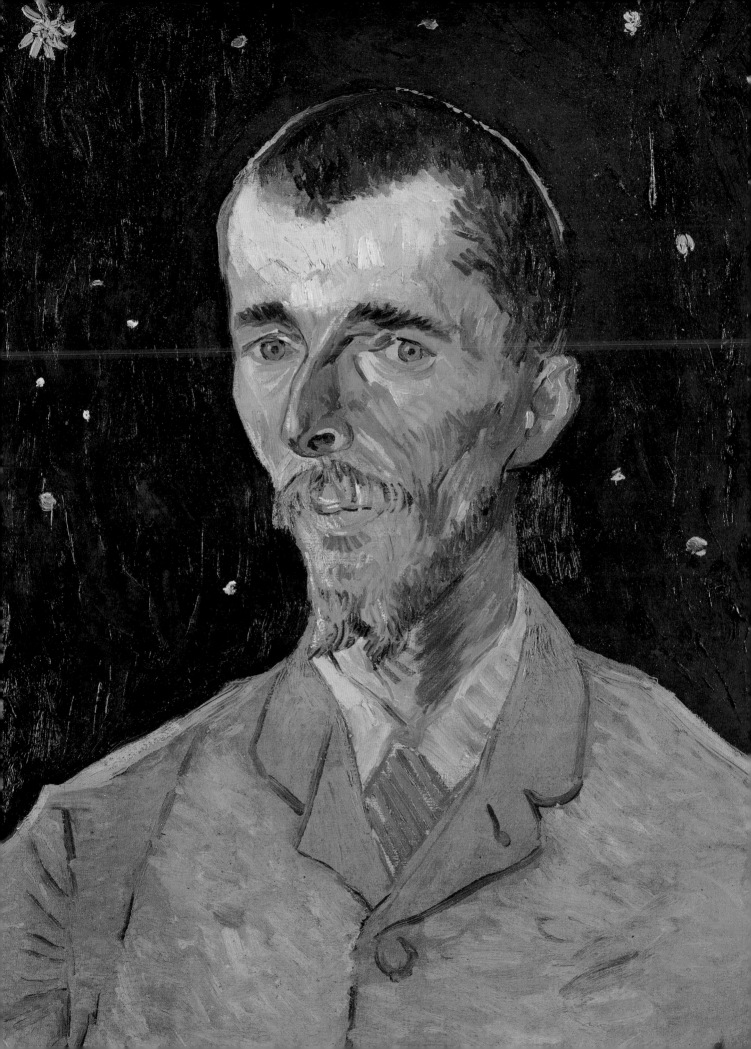

◆ ISAAC TAL, ABRAHAM TAL'S FATHER: Screamed, Tal...muttered— Why is my son screaming over the phone at twice normal volume to Tuviah and muttering to Dosha, a woman less than half his age? If his brother, my Tuviah, were present still, would Abraham talk too loud?

I understand why my son whispers, murmurs and mutters to Dosha. He is not hiding anything but hoping that a passerby, an acquaintance, even her boyfriend sees them. He lives in a dream, Abraham, hoping to fool himself and others into believing that she and he are in love, soon to elope, to the Holy Land naturally, and there to wed—as though that would solve his problems.

Why involve his brother Tuviah? Tuviah knows and I know that there is no such Talmudic concept as "ketubah money." If he is speaking of a dowry—from a father or, G-d forbid, for a fatherless bride let him tell Tuviah outright that he, Abraham Tal, is reminding Tuviah of their mother's ancestor Rachel Abolais Duarte who left the greater part of her fortune to poor orphaned brides— so that they could enter under the wedding canopy with joy and honor. But no, Abraham shouts nonsensical non-Talmudic orders to his brother. After he has misled the young man Fisher to believe he is marrying a "gypsy" he will entrust the woman with making all the wedding arrangements in the Holy City, entrust her with his mother's Abendana Abolais' family blue-domed wedding ring, Rabbi, ketubah, even cautioning her to fast before she and Fisher walk together to the Huppah, of that I'm sure.

A real Kol Nidre, vows made, vows not kept, fasting, atonement, all will be forgiven according to Abraham's dream quite angelic. Amazing.

■ HERMAN MELVILLE: Fast—Dosha is promised to Fisher: "A fast-fish belongs to the party fast to it."

"What is a fast-fish? Alive or dead, a fish is technically fast, when it is connected with an occupied ship or boat, by any medium at all controllable by the occupant or occupants, a mast, or oar, a nine-inch cable, a telegragh wire, or a strand of cobweb, it is all the same."

Raphael the younger has claimed young Dosha. What matters if it is Dosha's hand guided by Father Abraham that rests on Fisher's hand that caught her?

Father Abraham himself, a loose fish. Fair game for anybody who can catch it.

What shall we say of a "loose fish which bears a waif, or any other recognized symbol of possession. The party waifing it, having long since disappeared."

Lost. Forgotten. Missing. In an Antwerp sea. Far from the ocean, in a Polish grave. What shall we say of Father Abraham and his Rachel? Long gone. Abraham holding fast to her arms, but loose to all the world for all eternity.

That Dosha be fast-fish to Fisher, the party fast to her is dear to me. For "the American fishermen have their own legislators and lawyers in this matter. They have provided a system which for terse comprehensiveness surpasses Justinian's pandects and the by-laws of the Chinese society for the suppression of meddling with other people's business." Abraham Tal, president.

"Listen Tuviah. I know you don't want to waste my time.

"My neighbor, Dosha Padawer, is traveling to the Holy Land to marry Fisher. Yes, yes. I know you've already given me money toward their wedding. I know, I know. But now I need the Ketubah money. Reb Shlomo will also be there. Anyway, the main point is that I know we're seeing Mr. Fisher tomorrow at 12 o'clock. But 9 o'clock sharp, I want you to see Dosha. I've hired her as a $3,600 consultant on the Taj Mahal Emerald.

"What!" said Tal as he raised his voice and cupped the cupped the phone. "He's having a fit. Don't worry, he'll calm down in a hundred years."

He danced around his desk with the phone, holding fast to the cord.

"Of course she knows about the emerald. She studied jewelry arts under the world's most famous Indian art expert at Radcliffe. I promised her $3,600 on the spot. Cheap at any price. And then at 12 o'clock, Fisher, he's Yale. And I don't want Fisher to know about my payment."

◆ RACHEL ABENDANA TAL, ABRAHAM'S MOTHER: Raised his voice— Once I was walking toward our home on the Van Eykelei in Antwerp and I saw Abraham and young Rachel Beller in front of me. You could not call it walking, so slow they moved. You almost sensed they were wandering two steps backward, two and one half steps forward. Abraham was muttering. You could not call it talking, for Rachel's head was not inclined toward his, but rather bobbing slowly up and down as though she were trying to pump the words out of him.

And follow them I did for more than an hour. A space of less than two blocks, until I grew weary and passed the couple (though could you call them that?) on the right and mounted the staircase on the Eykelei into our house.

Eventually Abraham came home. And of course he knew that I knew that he knew I had walked behind Rachel and him. "Why were you muttering?" I asked, staring straight at him. It was in September, just before the Days of Awe, before Yom Kippur.

"In the Mahzor Vitry it is written: 'The first time the Reader chants Kol Nidre, he ought to chant in a very low voice, like a man who is amazed at entering the palace of the king to ask for a favor, and is afraid of coming close to the king; and so the Reader speaks softly, like one asking for something. The second time the cantor ought to raise his voice a little higher than the first time. The third time, he ought to raise his voice higher and higher, like a man who is at home and accustomed to being a member of the king's household.'"

That is all Abraham said. My son. My poor, little, earnest, hesitating Abraham. To Rachel and to this young woman Dosha, he mutters. To her intended, young Fisher, he speaks louder, and to my other son, who both understands and will not allow himself to understand, raises his voice higher and higher. For poor Abraham, each day he is standing and speaking to our Heavenly Father. Vowing the Kol Nidre vows, fasting, for is not his wedding day this very day— my poor Abraham, he is not speaking to me, to his Rachel nor to Dosha, not to young Fisher and certainly not to Tuviah. His whole life, night and day, is a conversation with the Ineffable Name.

■ VAN GOGH: Art—Two paintings hung above my bed in the yellow house at Arles. Eugène Boch: the poet. Millier in uniform: the lover. Behind each portrait stood Gauguin. Behind the stars, behind the dark violet blue universe behind the cool gaze of Boch, Gauguin cooly peered at me. Passion had to be withheld and hoarded, doled out only occasionally for "weak, impressionable artists' brains to give their essence to the creation of our pictures."

Two paintings, not visible to the world, hang above Tal's bed: the novelist poet: Fisher and the lover: Dosha. Peering behind the two paintings at him lies his virgin lover Rachel Beller, softly speaking to him from their Antwerp garden walks, calling to him from the unmarked grave she shares with her father and hosts of hosts of others.

■ LOUIS CARTIER: White—Once Patiala agreed to our House's terms to reset all His Majesty's fabulous emeralds or should I rather say, once we had agreed to all of Patiala's terms, I communicated through Imré Schwaiger our jeweler who communicated through His Majesty's treasurer Kassim that His Majesty had finally conquered Paris with his army of jewels. Would His Majesty come in person, favor us with a visit to review his green triumph?

His Majesty duly communicated through Kassim who had summoned Schwaiger and instructed him as follows: "His Majesty is delighted to visit the House of Cartier and the city of Paris. As to finally having "conquered Paris," his majesty wishes it clearly understood, not by letter or by cable, but by Schwaiger coming directly to Paris, and speaking in person to the House of Cartier, all brothers in the same room, at the same time, with a special message."

Schwaiger was in our study but eight days later, white as a Golconda from having stayed up and drunk Pernod day and night aboard the English ship.

"His Majesty Bhupindar Singh of Patiala wishes me to respond to the kind invitation of Monsieur Louis Cartier." Once Schwaiger said my name, Pierre fixed his gaze on his shoes, which he proceeded to buff up with a tiny silk handkerchief, ever present in his inner vest pocket.

"Monsieur Louis Cartier spoke of my green army conquering Paris, words which I do not accept for I always have a vision of Patiala, my father, my unwordly self, my future son and heir, generation after generation, invited to Paris as guests of France.

"Did not my father, Rajendar Singh, purchase the first motorcar in India? A Deboin Bouton from France. (Its number plate Patiala zero.)

"Did not my father travel to the Paris Exhibition of 1889 and outride a group of Pawnee Indians brought by a merchant from Omaha who spoke their language? Did not my father buy the largest diamond from the Kimberly mines, 428 carats in the rough. 228 carats after being cut, when my father commanded the owners cease cutting or he wouldn't purchase it, lest it get so small he lost sight of it in his gem caskets—a 'pale, shimmering diamond'.

"And my heir, when I to Paradise am summoned. Which color shall it be that he purchases while a guest in Paris.

"For all the world dreams of a journey to Paris. But if you insist on terming my jewels as conquering soldiers, please be assured I will look with favor on a gift of a general's gem medals, all colors: Burma reds, cornflower Ceylon sapphire blue, Golconda white will do." Schwaiger suddenly went silent, as though exhausted from carrying Patiala's message.

I suddenly saw Pierre's head shoot up, and with a sardonic laugh, he leapt to his feet and lectured me for an hour. With Imré, our employee, in full view. Quel idiot!

■ VINCENT VAN GOGH: A face, pallid, more translucent than she had noticed before, with a cadaverous shade of white—Above my bed, my painting of Lieutenant Paul-Eugène Millier hanging on a nail. Behind the painting, the window pane silhouettes the crescent moon, but Paul-Eugène billeted at the Caserne Calvin, en route from Tonkin to North Africa has lit the crescent moon on fire. A face more pallid, more translucent than I'd noticed before, with a cadaver's shade of white slipping out from his chest, rising toward his skull, riveted my eyes. Gauguin by day, and his Zouave-self at night. Never a moment alone—though could I bear it if I were granted a separation from him?

Though of course Gauguin and the Zouve are but billeting for an instant in the Caserne of my heart. The trumpet of the tropics sounds for both. For they are one. And Boch, the poet too, is one with Millier, the lover and the pair of them—one with Gauguin. Tal too, a pair with Dosha and Fisher. My studio of the south, but south for an instant, and north to where each will depart. We are all but compass points, wildly spinning on our fleeing lover's body.

"Yes. Yes. Your payment. What's the difference? Yours, mine. We're brothers. We're partners. Anyway, tell Suleimani to come tomorrow. At 8, or he won't be there at 9. And bring the jewel. I've brought Radcliffe and Yale. Believe me, the rest is easy. Father would be happy. Imagine another couple we've brought together."

Tal covered the phone as his brother spoke again.

After a brief time, Tal interrupted. "Yes. Yes. Who knows, maybe. Who knows." Tal put down the phone and looked up at Dosha. "Be at my office on 47th street tomorrow at 9 sharp."

"Tal, how did you know I studied Indian art at Radcliffe?"

"I'm not so foolish as you think I look," he said with a weary look. "I'll see you tomorrow."

He strode out of the advice shop, leaving Dosha thinking about his face. A face, pallid, more translucent than she had noticed before, a cadaverous white.

■ PIERRE CARTIER: All the same, these princes. An appetite for everything. Scottish women. French Ali Baba jewels. And a purse dwindling dangerously. But Patiala was the record holder: Hors de concours, champion spender and imperial debtor. Louis had been forewarned: His Highness Patiala's grandfather (who my American belle called His Lowness), already set the family tradition.

Imré had briefed us carefully: the English writer, Rudyard Kipling wrote: "When the current Maharajah of Patiala's grandfather, Narendar Singh died, he owed various Calcutta trades people close upon nine lakhs of rupees, and had, during his life, dealt with them three or four times that extent of cash. (These were all paid by the Council of Regency.) The Maharaja's method of purchase was peculiar and expensive. Walking into a shop, he would take all on that side of the counter, or all in the shop, as his royal fancy moved him, and after his decease his purchases formed the Patiala museum."

Rajendar Singh too, no different. He took a liking to his British stable keeper's sister, and decided on making Mins Florry Bryan his wife. Renamed her Harnam Kaur. C'est fini "though Lord William Beresford had told him of the Viceroy, Lord Lansdowne's views: An alliance of this kind, contracted with a European far below your rank, is bound to lead to the most unfortunate results. It will render your position both with Europeans and Indians most embarrassing…In the Punjab, as you must be well aware, the marriage will be most unpopular."

I suppose I lost myself, but I'd be damned if I let Louis continue in his folie à deux with Patiala.

What meals are we talking of as gifts to His Highness? Do we give him our stock of gems we've assembled in Paris. Perhaps Patiala wishes you to deliver "Andrée-Caroline who was eight years old at the 1889 Exhibition in Paris and wore minireproductions of the Jean-Philippe Worth dresses with the House of Cartier jeweled accessories." Perhaps this Patiala wishes whatever his dear father saw before, chrystaline yellow diamonds, and pale Andrée-Caroline to model the gem in the Punjab highlands.

What further honey do you intend us to give the House of Patiala before we are all fatally stung? Perhaps what Patiala wishes is you, Louis and you Jacques, and even me, embalmed, crated and displayed in the Patiala museum. With young Schwaiger dutifully polishing the museum case each day.

Louis stormed out. Jacques, that fool, could not stop laughing. Imré Schwaiger just stood there. When I told the story that night to Elma, she smiled and said with her American certainty:

"You are right. But Louis will prevail. For he has Jacques in his pocket. They're both boys lost in Alladin's cave."

■ PRINCESS LABANOFF: Jewel—Both the Tal brothers know the Russian proverb: "Land and jewels never betray one." They and Suleimani know it in their bones.

◆ RACHEL TAL, Abraham Tal's mother: Boss—"*When a father gives to his son, both laugh, when a son gives to his father, both cry.*" Suleimani, my husband's biggest customer would quote Pollak's Yiddish. "*Az der tate sheynkt dem zum, lakn beyde az der zun sheynkt den tatn, veynen beyde.*"

With Suleimani, unless you quoted the original language, the proverb or incantation had no power. Pollak would laughingly correct Suleimani's pronunciation. "Not *there-tah-tea but der tah tuh.*" By the time the proverb reached me, it had changed for the thousandth time. But Suleimani was the childless father, giving his uncut diamond rough to be polished into crystaline, river-white polished stones. Just like a father to Suleimani Pollak was. Suleimani, like Pollak, childless, gave these rough stones to Abraham, who would hand them to Tuviah, who would mark them, with India ink, provided free, always blue, by Suleimani, the rough covered with Bukharian and Yiddish proverbs. Pollak would make perhaps 5%. "No more," he said to Suleimani. "What does an old man need money for?" Pollak would wish me luck: "Better an ounce of luck than a pound of gold. *Besser a loyt mazl eyder a funt gold.*"

Believe me, Mrs. Dear Tal, I only added pennies to the cost when I gave away the rough to your genius son Abraham. So by now you may be sure Tuviah has already marked the goods and mark my words, get it Mrs. Dear Tal, your family is to make another fortune. You will see it on Mr. Isaac Tal's face when he comes home tonight.

"But why do you come here to drink tea and tell me all this? Why not tell it directly to Isaac?"

"Because I like to speak to the boss directly." Pollak was right. Father and son, Pollak and me. Me and Abraham. All of us laughing.

And Abraham and Tuviah. And then I, crying.

CHAPTER 8

WHITE-FACED from talking with Abraham Tal, his brother, whom he left slumped in his leather chair—their father's chair, the chair Isaac Tal had sat in on the Pelikaanstraat in Antwerp before the War. Not the Great War—as their father Isaac would call it, but the Second World War—or The War as Abraham would call it.

And what was he doing, Abraham Tal, hunched over in Father's chair, muttering to himself. "He's going to give the Ring of Blue to my Isaac," thought Tuviah Tal.

Belda, Tuviah's secretary—or "the boss" as Abraham called her—interrupted them without so much as a knock to tell them that Miss Padawer was here to see a Mr. Tal.

"It's for you, Abraham," Tuviah had said, but Abraham didn't interrupt his wandering monologue about Isaac, Kaddish and of course Rachel—always Rachel.

Tuviah told Abraham to his face, "I'll wager you the $3,600 that I'm supposed to pay Miss Padawer that she's a straggly-haired West Village hippie."

■ REB. YECHIEL (Rabbi Nachman of Brelsov's brother): Brother—Once I visited my brother, the Rebbe. He was seated in his seat all Shabbat evening. Speaking words of Torah. All night facing his Hassidim and talking. At the morning meal, the people at the table spoke to the Rebbe about a number of worldly matters not connected to the Torah.

I was shocked. I went to the Rebbe and asked him: "Is this the lesson your followers have learned from being with you all night?" My brother looked directly at me and asked, "'*Do you remember all the things they spoke about at the morning meal?*' I didn't.

"*My brother said, 'I remember everything.' He went and locked the door of the room and started going through all the topics one by one, explaining a little of their deeper implications. He spoke to his brother all day, through the night and into the morning hours. The windows were shuttered so that only when he looked at the clock did he see that it was already time to recite the morning Shema and he ended the conversation.'*

"*I went from my brother weeping. For several days, I could not eat or sleep. So moved I was, I bound myself to my brother, my Rebbe, with the utmost intensity.*"

They are speaking, the brothers Tal, they are binding each other, each to each, for generations to come.

■ TK'WAY THUNDERHORSE, a Munsee Chief: Village—Abraham has come from the village, our village. North of the Mannetta where the river turns into a swamp. Under the grounds of Abraham Tal's house on Hudson Street. He has taken the old Sapohannikan trail north to the office of his brother.

It is winter. It is dark and his brother Tuviah knows that Abraham has journeyed far and on foot to tell a story.

"*Sky woman had a daughter. She told her daughter, 'Whatever you do, don't go toward the setting sun!' But she went west anyway. The west wind was meant to be her husband at a future time, but she was still too small and it knocked her down, and in doing so, made her pregnant.*"

Tuviah knows his brother Abraham's tale of the West Village, Dosha and her lover Fisher. For this Lenape tale is known to all. It is the Lenape story of the creation of the human race.

Tuviah knows that three is the number "*of the father sky, mother earth and ourselves, a baby.*" Six, "*gut-tash, is the six colors of red, white, yellow, black, green and blue.*" The six directions of the spheres within the spheres we all lie within.

Abraham will accept the three and the six and he will present them with a blessing to Dosha: "Ay-dja-djan-wah-nee-shee. Wherever you go, may the way be beautiful for you."

Abraham still had not moved. Tuviah was exasperated by his brother—My husband would hold up the *Afikoman* matzoh at our seders in Antwerp before the War—shaking a little, even then he had a slight tremor, though only in America did we find out what lay behind my husband's weakness and trembling, especially in his left arm, and he'd say very slowly: "*This is the bread of affliction that our fathers ate in the land of Egypt. Whoever is hungry, let him come and eat; whoever is in need, let him come and join in celebrating the Pesach festival. This year we are here* (in Antwerp he would whisper); *next year may we be in Israel* (he would say loudly). *This year, slaves. Next year, free men.*"

Then my Isaac would hold the matzoh and ask looking at Tuviah, "Why do we say whoever is hungry?" Tuviah would say with a laugh, "Because we're all hungry, Father. We burned the *Hametz* at 11 and we start to eat only after we have recited the *Haggadah*."

Then Isaac would look at my Abraham and say, "But why does the *Haggadah* seemingly repeat itself and say, whoever is in need?"

Abraham would answer. "The Rabbis teach us that the true hunger is a spiritual one."

Then Isaac would put back the Afikoman matzoh behind his back, under his pillow. Afterwards, Tuviah would stare at the pillow longingly but Abraham would ask me, each year, "Mother, did your father Abraham Abendanda put the matzoh behind his back or would do what some of the Ashkenasim do in Antwerp, hide it themselves and let the children search for them." I would tell him that I wasn't sure. But I did say what my brother had told me. We must search carefully to remove all hametz from the house. "*The soul of a person is like a divine light searching all the chambers of the body.*"

We must try to remove all the imperfections from our heart. Once we eat the *matzoh*, baked in haste, we must eat it with zeal and a full heart.

Until he received this answer from me, Abraham would not move toward stealing the *Afikoman*. Tuviah was exasperated by his brother. Unless Abraham distracted my husband, Tuviah could not even think of attempting to capture the *afikoman*.

Belda retreated, rolling her eyes. "What should I tell the young lady?"

"Tell her anything. One of us will be out in a minute," said Tuviah.

Abraham still had not moved. Tuviah was exasperated by his brother.

"Alright. Alright. I'll see Miss Padawer. I'll pay her the $3,600 for G-d knows what advice she'll give me about the Suleimani Green Paradise-on-Earth emerald that we've only paid half a fortune for already. You'll go to Safed, and you'll give the Ring of Blue to Isaac." Tuviah paused. He couldn't speak. The thought dawned on him. Abraham's crazy, but he is no fool. He's giving me nine replicas of our family treasure. And I'm deeding to him absolute right to the Venetian original. I'm giving him the ring and I gave him $1,800 for that young *pisher* or Fisher or whatever his name is.

Now I'm supposed to give to this Dosha or Moshe or whatever her name is. Does every name rhyme in their village *shtetl*.

Tell her anything—"*For there is a spot the size of a shilling at the back of the head which one can never see for oneself. It is one of the good offices that sex can discharge for sex—to describe that spot the size of a shilling at the back of the head.*"

Tell her anything, says Tuviah. It doesn't matter much what for. One of us, one of another sex, will be out in a minute. It will not be Tuviah, for he is not truly in the picture. It cannot be Tal—a winter bear—for since Antwerp, Lisbon and the War, he speaks but to the dead. It will be Fisher, like Dosha an elephant. He can see that spot behind Dosha's head. He can talk to her in words: He can describe her longings: a life of friends, laughter in the afternoon, painting from daybreak on and family in the evening, love at night. Never easy, almost impossible, to balance all with a jeweller's scale one must hold oneself bolt steady even as one grows old.

Tuviah, Tal and Fisher, all doctors to Dosha. Examining the spot the size of a shilling piece hidden from her. She too, with her longing for friendship, for family, for love, and for art, looking for her reflection at the backs of their heads…"*No two of them ever alike…each bound on some private affair.*" All of them, all of us, one long, endless interconnected ball of white string.

Replica—Either the neighbors of my beloved tower predicted that it would topple upon the houses in Trocadero, or they feared like the editor of *The New York Times* that the Paris weather patterns would be altered by its great height.

Everyone wanted a replica of what already existed. Haussmann built Paris. One cannot improve on perfection, they all thought.

Either Paris's magnificent palaces would be obscured or the tower would not be built in time for the Paris Exposition of 1889. Or the costs would tower above the pockets of the government so that, after I became bankrupt—had I not agreed to deliver the Eiffel Tower for a sum certain 1,600,000 francs at a date set, March 1889—all Paris would be bankrupt.

Either it would crumble, a vain edifice of wrought iron decreed by a mad Pharaoh. Or it would prematurely disfigure the body of Paris. Guy de Maupassant laughed at my "*Tall, skinny pyramid of iron ladders, this giant and disgraceful skeleton…which aborts into the thin ridiculous profile of a factory chimney.*"

De Maupassant laughingly said "*he often lunched at the tower's second-level restaurant because it was the only place in Paris he did not have to look at the tower.*"

I delighted in his misery. For did I not own the restaurant for twenty years? When Maupassant left for Aix—so that he could get away from La Tour Eiffel—I wished my neighbor, Maupassant, Bon Voyage.

26 Décembre 1888   20 Janvier 1889

■ TUVIAH GUTMAN GUTWIRTH, FISHER'S GRAND-FATHER: He's been preparing for death—"From making a will you don't die. From preparing for death you don't hasten your end." On his death bed Simha Bunam of Psyscka's wife cried. "Why are you crying?" he asked her. "My entire life was devoted to learning how to die." Still, Simha Bunam was given yet more time to live, more than his doctor, who was permitted to examine him at the insistence of one of his wealthy German hassidim predicted

■ HIRAM BINGHAM III: Abandoned—Elihu Yale. Abandoned by his father. Why did every tale resolve itself like that? Elihu's Welsh father, after emigrating from England to New Haven, married a young woman, Ursala, ten years his junior. First child, Elizabeth, lives only a few months. "David Yale and Ursala moved to Boston and lived on the north slope of Beacon Hill…David Junior is born into the sumptuous house…In 1646 David Senior appointed attorney for the Earl of Warwick." He was fined for his "remonstrance and petition" addressed to the governor for he felt "all of the kings subjects had a right to become citizens of the colony."

Perfectly reasonable to David Yale, not so to Governor Winthrop of Massachusetts. The governor placed in parallel columns:

The Magna Carta

The Common Law

The Fundamentals of Massachusetts

And what did Governor Winthrop write of David Yale? "Yale is little acquainted with commonwealth affairs…" Adding "we wait daily to heare of him in Jerusalem." Fine, 30 pounds.

News of the execution of Charles I reached David Yale. Elihu, not a common Welsh name, was born in America on April 5, 1649. He was not a resident of Boston for long. When Elihu was two, his father left alone for Cromwell's England—only a year and a half later could Elihu and his mother (and his brother and sister) see his father again.

Abandoned by Father, Elihu thought. Only trust in mother. Should I, Hiram Bingham, abandon my family for this passion of exploring? See the truth of history? Should I let my career—publish or perish—take me away from my sons and wife? I sail off on June 8, 1911 on the Yale Peruvian Expedition? Heartbreaking really, with my wife Alfreda holding "little Harry [my Hiram Bingham IV] by one hand and waving frantically with the other." I can see the look in my son's eyes. He will carry my name as I carried my missionary father's name, and he before his father. Hiram Bingham IV, myself: Hiram Bingham III, then Bingham II. And backward to I. Ducks in a row. I have flown away to serve.

What if all this talk about Tal's Kaddish is just the same old lament? He's been preparing for death since he was eight. The "young Bar Mitzah boy tragically taken from us" as he ascended the *Bimah* to give his *drasha*, killed in his prime before turning 18, couldn't consider, even think about a marriage proposal, for he could feel that his heart was not 100% normal even after three specialists from Louvain and one Viennese crackpot tested it. Abraham's been preparing to abandon us and die for more than half a century.

What if this is what he's working for? He and this Village neighbor of his. My brother's going to give him the ring. And they're going to give her the ring. And they're going to Israel to wed on my $1,800 and her $3,600 consultancy fee from me.

And do I really care, Tuviah wondered.

■ RED SHIRT: Talk—Rocky Bear, Featherman and I went up in the elevator at the Eiffel Tower during the Paris Exhibition of 1889. Higher and higher. Louder and louder, as we rose. Everywhere we went white men followed us.

A man with a pencil slept outside my hotel—whenever Featherman or I went for a walk—who could sleep at night in Parisfrance—louder than a passing train and brighter than any afternoon in the mountains—the "reporter" would follow us. Once to play a joke on him, I went one way and Featherman went another. The fool raced back and forth across Parisfrance trying to see where each of us was going.

Of course we knew when we got into the elevator, the reporter would be there. He would talk all the time, even when we had ridden in an elevator in Omaha and one in Chicago too—but this was much louder, louder than thunder. Featherman said in the middle of the ride upward when we had gone above a cloud, "I am about to go crazy."

The reporter shouted above the screech of the elevator that Featherman is "positively showing the white flag."

But I understand Featherman. He was afraid of no man and certainly of no machine. He was in "a rejoicing state of mind." When the elevator stopped at the top, Rocky Bear and I held Featherman over the side. Featherman pointed his hand and shouted: "Over there, people," and "Over there too, tiny, tiny people moving. Moving like young rabbits. Smaller even like caterpillars."

"If people look so little to us up here, how much smaller they must seem to One [Wakantanka] who is higher," I told him.

■ Søren Kierkegaard: What would Mother say, Abraham—Abraham Tal's brother poses the question. Were Tuviah Tal able to ask the question himself, and answer, he would be a philosopher. If Abraham Tal would be able to ask: "What would Mother say?" he would ask and he would answer and he would be both novelist and himself and even a philosopher.

For though Tal "*may have extraordinary talent and remarkable learning…an author he is not, in spite of the fact that he produces a book…*" albeit unpublished, that lies in his drawer *written, half-written, outlined or about to be started. "No, in spite of the fact that the man writes, he is not essentially an author; he will be capable of writing the first…and also the second part, but he cannot write the third part— the last part he cannot write. If he goes ahead naively (led astray by the reflection that every book must have a last part) and so writes the last part, he will make it thoroughly clear by writing the last part that he makes a written renunciation to all claim to be an author. For though it is indeed by writing that one justifies the claim to be an author, it is also, strangely enough, by writing that one virtually renounces this claim. If he had been thoroughly aware of the inappropriateness of the third part—well, one may say, si tacuisset, philosophus mansisset [if he had kept quiet he would have remained a philosopher!]*"

It is the young man Fisher who will be the novelist. "*To find the conclusion it is necessary first of all to observe that it is lacking and then in turn to feel quite vividly the lack of it.*"

Dosha will be Fisher's observing eyes. Abraham Tal's eyes alas—would have been Rachel Beller's. As far as Holy Isaac's question: "What would Mother say?" Father Abraham, no novelist, answered, "Faith."

"*It was early morning. Abraham rose in good time, had the asses saddled and left his tent, taking Isaac with him, but Sarah watched them from the window as they went down the valley until she could see them no more.*"

Sarah saw that Father Abraham could not allow himself to hear what Isaac's mother would say.

What would Mother say, Abraham off to Safed to wed a woman half his age, though more mature I'm sure.

Good luck to him. Finally he can choose. If they have children, they will be my problem—he's my problem anyway—and if they don't have children who cares anyway. Better a taste of life together than never. Certainly Mother would say that. And Abraham certainly doesn't care 1% what I think. Truth to tell, he's a genius and I love him, but I cannot understand him. Not in a thousand years.

"Mr. T," bellowed Belda. "We're keeping the young lady waiting."

"Alright, I'll be out in a minute. Show her into the diamond room." Tuviah turned to Abraham and said tenderly, "Then everything is signed and accepted. You will be what you have always wanted to be, completely free of me and completely alone."

■ Israel Friedman, the Riziner Rebbe (1797–1850): Show her into the diamond room—Why has Tuviah instructed his Shamas, his factotum, Belda, to show Dosha into the diamond buying room—because she herself is a diamond.

Psalm 104:2 teaches us: "*You are clothed in glory and majesty, wrapped in a robe of light.*" "*Inside each person there is a spark of holiness, but its brightness varies according to the individual. For example, if you encase a bright diamond in a wall, it will not sparkle. If you remove it from the wall, it will begin to glow and glitter. Then if you polish and burnish it, it will shimmer and gleam even more. Finally, when you set the diamond in a gold crown, it will radiate in its full glory. That is the meaning of 'You are wrapped in a robe of light.' The spark of G-dliness, man's soul, is wrapped in man's earthly garment, his body. The luminescence of this spark depends on how man treats it: how much he polishes and refines, purifies and perfects his deed.*"

It is before Yom Kippur. We read Hosea's words: Return, O Israel, to the Lord your G-d. Tuviah, through his brother, is transporting this diamond and her groom Fisher to the Holy Land—Both of the brothers Tal are chanting to them: "Return O Israel to the Lord your G-d."

I too, whose first name is Israel, I too am chanting. "You, Israel, return to the Lord your G-d."

■ Wallace Stevens: What would Mother say, Abraham to wed a woman half his age— Dosha. Song itself.

Since what she sang was uttered word by word
It may be that in all her phrases stirred
The grinding water and the gasping wind;
But it was she and not the sea
We heard.

That's what Mother would say. Old Abraham to wed a woman half his age. Or bed a woman half his age. Or create a woman *de novo ab initio.*

Shall not the rule of strict law beget equity? "*Poor Mother,*" I broke with her because of Elsie, my poor wife, my conscience.

Blessed Abraham Tal.. No office for him. He lives in his library. Cursed me. "*I certainly do not exist from nine to six when I am at the office. There is no everyday Wallace, apart from the one at work—and that one is tedious. At night I strut my individual state once more…*"

What would Mother say: if I departed in the day time: "Bravo, Wallace." Better alive at 80 than dead at 40. If I fled at nighttime, surely she would smile. Abraham is fleeing across the sea. She will be signing, uttering her song, word by word, if not for him, for another. Mother would accept, even if she would not, could not understand.

■ MAX MEYER: Brother—Julius, my younger brother, always stuck out like a sore thumb. We could be the Rothschilds if we hung together. "You are the smartest thing my sweet younger brother," I'd tell him.

But he was always going off to the Pawnee. To the Brulé. Across the North Platte to G-d knows where. Adolf had good sense, why not stick together. In '69 he took his music business and jewelry (good profits but it needed more money to keep a good inventory selection than even the Rothschilds had) and moved in with me to Farnam and Eleventh. We called it Max Meyer & Bro.

Moritz understood just one thing: smoke. If it burnt, he loved it. So we teamed up together and called it Max Meyer & Co. Moritz and Adolf knew the tune. I wasn't going to be around forever. With my Rabbinical beard and ways, I looked a hundred years older than Julius. They could change the store's name just after they lowered me into the ground.

But Julius couldn't stomach it. Julius Meyer's Indian Wigwam it had to read. His store. His trinkets he sold to the Pawnee. Ponca, Omaha, Ogalala and Brulé Sioux. Even the Winnebago… most often he took back trinkets from them. They didn't have money. "Who needs money," said Standing Bear, "When you're buying from a brother."

"Get Julius into insurance with you. Get him a wife, get him fixed in Omaha and get him into our store. Adolph, you're the only one he'll listen to." All Adolph could do is hem and haw and say, "I'll try. I'll try, Max. But my brother's not himself today."

If we had stuck together after the store burned down in '89 we would have made it through the depression of '93. But all my younger brother could think to do was to take his Indian brothers to Paris, France and dance in front of the Eiffel Tower. No wonder there's no darn Rothschild Brothers in Omaha.

■ SØREN KIERKEGAARD: Abraham—"There was once a man; he had learned as a child that beautiful tale of how G-d tried Abraham, how he withstood the test, kept his faith and for the second time, received a son against every expectation. When he became older, he read the same story with even greater admiration, for life had divided what had been united in the child's pious simplicity. The older he became, the more often his thoughts turned to that tale, his enthusiasm became stronger and stronger, and yet less and less could he understand it. Finally, it put everything else out of his mind; his soul had but one wish, actually to see Abraham, and one longing, to have been witness to these events…this man was no learned exegete, he knew no Hebrew, had he known Hebrew, then perhaps it might have been easy for him to understand the story of Abraham."

Again and yet again. Abraham is in his tale. Each generation. Less and less do we understand the tale. Stranger and stranger does it become in each generation's retelling and seeing it yet again. Before our eyes. Dear G-d. We, witnesses, longing to begin. To start, to understand: Abraham, Isaac.

White-faced, he moved toward the buying room. Dosha was already seated.

Tuviah was stunned. It was not simply that Dosha was beautiful—her hair, knotted in a chignon, interwoven like a Ghent lace pattern he remembered from the Hague where the Tal family had fled in 1914 when Belgium was attacked and Holland remained neutral. Rather it was her wide-open eyes, barely blinking, judging him and yet smiling.

Tuviah did not extend his hand, so at a loss was he as to how to proceed.

"Miss," he said, forgetting her name. "My brother Abraham is not himself today or lately. He'll join us in a while."

Dosha laughed. "If he's not himself, who is he? And what is he when he is himself?"

Now it was Tuviah's chance to laugh. "That's remarkable. You sound like our mother. But I guess it's because you and my brother are neighbors and I imagine he's already filled your head with her ideas."

■ ADOLF MEYER, DOSHA'S MOTHER'S GRANDFATHER: My brother's not himself today—1889. "My brother is not himself today," I said for a week after the fire on Sixteenth Street just off of Farnam destroyed our store. Our stock: books, microscopes, telescopes, pianos, 10,000 Havanas which we hadn't paid for. Two years credit we had with Upmann in Cuba. Diamonds, in the show cases, along with every watch case a Westerner might see in New York or Philadelphia and want to buy in the Middle West. And couldn't. Even the diamonds in the safe were cut and mounted by our goldsmith working in the basement. All the diamonds, when we finally jimmied open our four Henderson safes, had turned to carbon-like black sand.

Julius sat inside his store: *Julius Meyer, at 163 Farnam*, unable to open the store or close it for a week. Not eating. Not sleeping more than an hour a day.

"Heck, Julius, we'll open an even bigger store. We'll be the biggest in the West, bigger than San Francisco."

But Julius didn't say Bobitty Boo. I stood outside his store for a week, turning away each customer. "Sorry ma'm. The Julius Meyer store is closed. My brother's not himself today." "No sir, Julius Meyer's not open. My brother's not himself today." Over and over. Julius hearing and seeing the back of me. Not moving a jot.

■ JULIUS MEYER: My brother's not himself today—"My brother's not himself today. 1889. Store's closed." All day long Adolf saying to every customer who came back. What a fire it had been. Everything they had up in smoke. All the white man's trinkets: banjos, harmonicas, gold watch cases, diamond rings, even bracelets. Sample lines for 12 traveling salesmen who worked the road from the Dakotas to Wyoming.

Adolf just didn't get it plain. With the insurance money he, Mortiz, Max and I received, of course they wanted me in, they would build bigger and better, biggest in all of America. Maybe bigger than Paris.

What was I going to say? To take insurance money and try not to pretend the times had passed us by—and build bigger only to see it all topple down. Did Max ever listen to me? For one day? I was nothing but a younger brother. More Pawnee than kin.

So I decided then and there to say nothing, take Standing Bear and my Indian brothers to see Paris where they were building the biggest teepee of them all, the Eiffel, and let them all mumble: "My brother's not himself today."

◆ RACHEL TAL: Abraham should leave them—The night of June 5, 1940, was the worst night of my life. Belgium had surrendered to those whose name I will never utter. More than half of Antwerp's Jews had fled when the Belgian campaign started but we did not leave our house on Van Eyklei. Isaac and Tuviah insisted that all the stones from the office be kept in the walled safe in my father's room. Should we have to flee "like our forefathers without having time to let the dough rise," as my husband put it.

On the night of June 5, I looked out our window and could see at least two hundred of their soldiers marching toward our house across the park.

They seemed to grow as they crossed the park, louder and more huge each one under their iron helmets without eyes moving left or right. My husband and I trembled. "Rachel, let's go back to sleep. They're not coming here, G-d forbid."

Then and there I took Isaac's hand and marched to Abraham and Tuviah's room directly above us. The boys too were cowering by the window. Abraham was weeping, Tuviah icily quiet.

"We're leaving, Isaac," I said firmly before my boys and husband. "Next time they will not turn down Van Eyklei, next time they will come directly here."

Isaac looked at my boys and asked, "Do we leave or stay?" Immediately, Tuviah said, "Papa, we stay." And Abraham blurted out, "Mama, we leave."

The silence that followed reminded me of the quiet before a tempest in Knokke. "What to do Rachel?" Isaac pleaded. "Wake your brother, ask him if you won't listen to me."

Isaac went upstairs and I could hear my Uncle Jacob speak for the next half hour. "Before the war, there were 50,000 of us here in Antwerp. In the last month more Belgian Jews were in Paris than here. So great was the fear. Now we are told all will be well. Trachtenberg. Morgenenstern, the Woolf Brothers, Jonah Hellman, even Abraham's so-called fiancée family the Bellers came back from France. Danger over. They all say they need the diamond trade here. They want us Jews to stay. When Jerusalem fell, prophesy was given to fools. Last month they fled and now they've returned. Last month I said, stay, but Isaac, if you really are asking, we should leave. Now. Immediately."

I heard my husband say: "Of course, Mr. Abendana, I shall follow your words and Rachel's." Down the stairs he walked, carrying my Uncle's amazingly small suitcase. We all had our bags packed for a month and we silently followed my Uncle to the car. Down the avenue, off the side street, we stopped at a light on Schupfstraat when suddenly Abraham bounded out of the car toward Rachel Beller's house, scampering up the stairs. In the next moment I could see the light on the floor and I could see Abraham raising his hands, both drawn into fists and gesturing wildly toward the end of the street. Round and round the apart-

"Actually I'm quite serious, Mr. Tal. Who is your brother when he's himself?"

"Since you ask, I'll give you a clue. He's confused. My twin son Isaac is ten minutes older than my other twin son Ephraim. Still, Abraham keeps referring to Ephraim as my 'elder' son. Abraham should leave them as they are, twins."

Dosha stared at Tuviah. Cut to the chase, she thought.

Tuviah knew for certain, by her self-composure, that this young woman would never marry, run off with, or even dream of Tal, although he also knew that she would never treat him lightly, and never, ever forget him. "Do you know who Rachel is?"

"Yes. His mother. Or your mother, I should say. And yet another, his..." she paused. "Yes, his girlfriend. Fiancée. The one who was destined for him before the War, the one who was sick with tuberculosis. The one, the one whom he should have...the one who was killed. May the killers' name be blotted out forever."

Suddenly Tuviah composed himself. "Here is your fee..." Dosha raised her hand to refuse the payment. "Here is your fee before you start talking. Tal & Sons do not bargain. At least about consultancy fees." He pushed the crisp Tal & Sons' check across the table.

■ BOB DYLAN: Who is your brother when he's himself?—Tal's brother doesn't have the foggiest idea of who Abraham is. Nor Abraham of who Tuviah, his brother, is. For they are not themselves. *"Something is happening here and you don't know what it is, do you Mister Jones."*

My father Abraham, walks into Pennebaker's movie studio in New York and says *"Mrs. Dylan and I came to New York for a brief stay and everyone's been so nice to us."* I haven't seen *Don't Look Back* but my friends have and they all commented that *"his son Mr. Dylan used a lot of four-letter words and would the director take them out."*

Pennebaker tried to explain to Father Abraham the people "who the film is for would be disappointed if they heard me talking in a way they knew I shouldn't."

Mr. Jones something is happening. How should Dosha know who Rachel is when Abraham Tal himself doesn't know who Rachel is, or which Rachel. Lover or mother.

Your sons and your daughters are
beyond your command
your old road is rapidly agin.'

So why is Tal offering an offering to Dosha? Because she is: Here. Now. Long gone. And always in the Future.

She takes just like a woman, yes, she does
She makes love just like a woman, yes, she does
And she aches just like a woman
But she breaks just like a little girl

ment he paced. Finally, Isaac said, "Abraham should leave them." He walked into the house and practically carried Abraham in his arms to the car.

June 5, 1940, each year after that, on June 5, Abraham would come to our house. He would read in Hebrew in a slow voice 22 verses from Genesis. *"And it came to pass after these things, that G-d did tempt Abraham, and said unto him..."* Each year, I would try to reason with my Abraham. There was not enough room in our car for Rachel and her father. That Mr. Beller would never have gone with us. That Rachel would never leave her father. That had we not left, none of us would have survived. No words could comfort Abraham's tears, nor mine, even though no one could see me weep.

◆ ISAAC TAL, ABRAHAM AND TUVIAH'S FATHER: Abraham's a wise man—My wife never ceased to build up her Abendana past, her Yichus. Her ancestors in Holland, Abigail and David Abendana who lost—"pray G-d it not happen to us" she would whisper—their two sons dying while children because of David's sin of not being circumcised after arriving through the mercies of the Lord to Amsterdam in 1598.

And of Isaac Sardo Abendana the great diamond expert in Madras—he knew more than the Indian merchants—a buyer and adviser to Diamond Pitt, Governor of Madras, after Elihu Yale told him in London in 1701 he would make his fortune there and not be afraid to travel to Ft. St. George with his wife, for the climate was fine for women. And of the other Isaac Abendana, teacher of Hebrew at Magdalen College, Oxford.

And the Hamburg Abendanas, Manuel and Fernando (Abraham) after whom her own father was named. She spoke too of Manuel Pereira Coutino's father's other children—his five daughters, nuns who served the rest of their lives in the convent of La Esperança, while the other Ibn-Danan flourished in Amsterdam. And her mother's branch—the Abolais-Duartes—all linked by learning and diamonds.

Linked also to the Ibn Danans of Morocco, Maimon who was known as the Rambam of Fez. If I had a dollar for each time my Abraham asked if we were truly related to Maimonides, my children and grandchildren would not have to work.

Once when Abraham was nine and Tuviah ten, we were walking across the park toward our house on Van Eyklei when we ran into Pollak, who asked, "What are you boys going to do when you grow up? Help your father in the diamond business?" Before Tuviah could answer, Abraham said, "Oh, I will sit in the synagogue and study all day long like the Talmud tells us to do. And Tuviah will help father." Pollak knew his Talmud like he knew his rough diamonds. He laughed and said, "It is true the Talmud teaches us that every Jewish community should have "ten men free from work," but Maimonides denounced this custom. The Talmud does not say idlers without work, but "men at leisure from their work." "Well, then I'll work with Tuviah, but not every day," said Abraham.

When Pollak looked at Tuviah and said "What do you think young man?" Tuviah said with the same seriousness he has today "We'll see. We're not there yet." All Abraham could say after Pollak left was "Are we related to Maimonides, Father?" I said, "Ask your mother." And Abraham said, "You know she never talks of the Abendana family to us." It was true. With the boys she sighed as though they were still in Portugal, too dangerous to talk. I was supposed to tell Abraham and Tuviah of the glories of the Abendana and Abolais Duartes.

"We're not there yet," Tuviah would say, and now they are. Abraham working with Tuviah but not "every day." I don't know whether to laugh or to cry.

Tuviah reached into his pocket, pulled out a shimmering white diamond paper and put it on top of the check. He opened the gem paper deftly and revealed the 141 carat, 1 1/2 inch wide hexagonal carved, pure green Columbia emerald.

"Here it is. The Taj Mahal emerald. What can you tell us about it, young woman?"

Dosha looked at the stone for a long time. Three flower heads were carved on the face of the emerald: a lotus, a meconopsis and an amaranth—arranged in a triangle, resting on a scrolling acanthus leaf. The motion of the petals sang to Dosha of Mansur's Kashmir, of Shah Jahan's Taj Mahal. "Why do you ask me?" she asked Tuviah.

"Because Abraham, a wise man, told me to pay for your words of wisdom."

"Let me start with your words. A man. The design of the emerald is by a man, not Mansur. Probably Payag."

"Who's Mansur? Who's Payag? How do you know this? Did you read this in a book?"

"I know this because when I was a young woman I saw a painting in a book. And the inspiration for this is a young woman—Mumtaz."

Tuviah persisted, pronouncing the names differently. "Who's Payag? Who's the other person, Mansur?"

■ LOUIS CARTIER: Here it is, the Taj Mahal—There are collectors. There are salespeople. There is myself. There is Pierre. Tal is one of the subspecies of collectors—a would-be collector, temporarily without funds. His brother Tuviah, definitely a variety of the sales phylum. Look how he pauses after he speaks the word "here." The heavenly green gem almost visible through its white paper outer garment. Then another pause, reverential almost before the words: the Taj Mahal. What are we to think? He is going to present the mausoleum: the Taj Mahal itself. Simply uproot the structure in the palm of his hand and carry Shah Jahan and the divine Mumtaz all the way to 47th Street without waking the long-sleeping couple. Then the coup de grâce—emerald. Not spoken loudly, but with a whisper. He is practicing his drummer's voice on the "young woman," as he calls her.

Tal would present the "Merveille" as I always called it to Pierre. He would have the gem already out of its gem paper. Out of its mummy case. Breathing. Alone on a white background. The flowerheads, lotus, poppy, and acanthus leaf shimmering as do the celestial inlaid and divinely carved flowers rest on white skin of the marble Taj Mahal itself. The young woman would enter the chamber together with Tal. Both would look at the Merveille. No glass between them and it. The petals of the flowers somewhere between life and death, not swaying in a breeze, yet moving to their connoisseur's eyes.

For an instant the two would possess the emerald itself, together. For what are museum goers but pilgrims rummaging through the cases of Ali Baba, viewing their dream treasures, before they are routed so rudely from their sleep back into the so-called "real world."

I understood this. Pierre did not. For a while, Jacques kept the proper balance between. We did not part with the Merveille. But for the Tal Brothers, alas, no Jacques exists. Tuviah minds the store. To his credit, Tal has given the celestial pleasure of viewing to the young woman and her beau. Collecting need not be done with one's hands but with one's eyes.

But where is the Taj Mahal itself? In which Moghul painting? A great puzzle.

■ MARI SANDOZ: fiction/nonfiction writer about Native Americans in 19th and 20th centuries: Pronouncing—*"About the hostiles: I've never heard it pronounced with anything but a long "I" as a noun meaning the hostile Indians, while they were effectively hostile. Curiously, old army men who fought them sometimes changed the "i" to a short one when they were captured. I recall old General Brown at Denver once speaking of the 'captured hostiles'—short "i"—immediately after he had spoken of them with a long "i" while out under Crazy Horse at the Rosebud. I'm certain he wasn't conscious of this change in pronunciation."*

IMRÉ SCHWEIGER, Cartier's buying agent in India: Mansur—Louis Cartier would imperiously telegraph me: "Fetch me the Taj. Where is the Taj Mahal?"

At first I thought him mad. Receiving these cables in Delhi in summer. Once I cabled back in response to his Cartier message:

"Mr. Schweiger, you've located for me everything. Please return to Paris House of Cartier immediately with my heart's desire. Where o where is the Taj?"

The brothers Cartier would wire me no end of instructions. Which gems they required. Shapes of rubies. Diamond rondels. Not so yellowish white like the last lot. Not so whitish white so as to shock. Also orders for fabrics, muslim, Moghul velvet, for wives, daughters, customers, and for the devil knew who in Louis' case. But my replies had to be the soul of brevity.

"We are a commercial house, Mr. Schweiger," Pierre would caution me. Mr. Louis was more gentle. "Better not to write too much, words are best in the inner sanctum," as he would call the office on the second floor where only Les Frères Cartier and I were allowed to enter and only I if I had brought back a treasure. Jacques too liked succinct correspondence or shall I put it differently, more than twenty written words put him to sleep. So I answered catching the sprit of the house.

"Mission successful, Louis. Taj found in Agra. Please advise."

Jacques later told me that Pierre couldn't stop laughing when the cable arrived. Louis started to scream. "That's it! We must fire Schweiger." He ripped up the telegram, storming out and not returning for three days. Pierre glued up the pieces and carried it in his wallet for a few months, showing it to his set at the Jockey Club. It was touching. What Louis wanted was a drawing. A painting, a scrap of paper showing the Taj Mahal edifice itself. "How can it be that never have you seen a miniature painting of it, Imré." Louis would grow filial with me when we looked together at a miniature I found for him. "A representation of the most magnificent, haunting, gorgeous, lovely, seductive of all Moghul creations, the tomb of Mumtaz, the Taj Mahal itself." I tried to placate him with a drawing by Mansur of flowers that looked as though they had carefully caressed the walls of the Taj itself. I tried to please him with other gemstones with celestial flowerheads. I argued with him on the plains of philosophy: it is a dream so bright and white that the artist's eye, even the wonder of the age Nader al-Zaman, is blinded when looking. Yet like an unrequited lover, he kept asking, "Where is the Taj? Where?"

His fidelity was touching, much more than Pierre, who could only see what he knew he could sell. And Jacques, who thought he had seen it all.

Dosha took the check slowly from underneath the gem paper, wrote her name on top and on the bottom left in small letters, "Mansur-Payag-Mumtaz-Shah Jahan."

She stood up. "I believe you're speaking to my boyfriend later. I'm going to speak to your brother. I've got to get to work in ten minutes. Fisher's got time for this."

"Fisher's got time for this?"

"No, Fisher's got Time for this," and she left Tuviah in his office.

Entering the next room, she found Tal staring at the Ring of Blue. "Here is the Ring, Dosha, I'll need it back as I discussed. It's all set. I've got the Rabbi. He'll see you in Jerusalem. By the Wall. Did you get the check?"

Dosha waved the check at Tal and left the room. As she exited, Tal could see her signature and small Indian names at the bottom. Tiny scratches of blue on the check's background white.

■ KALIM, the court poet to Shah Jahan: Shah Jahan—Here he sits: His majesty, Shihabuddin Muhammad Shah Jahan, the king, warrior of the Faith, may G-d perpetuate his kingdom and sovereignty. Here he sits on the peacock throne holding a flower, alive forever, painted by Govardam. "Born in imperial atelier."

Here he sits on the peacock throne, studded with white Golconda diamonds, rubies from Burma and emeralds from across the waters.

Here he sits on the peacock throne in Delhi on the day that Nauruz and the feast of fast-breaking have fallen together while Govardham paints. My pen writes:

*The rays of the throne's rubies and
emeralds fall on diamonds
like lamplight playing on a
water cascade.*

All flow together, the waterfalls rivuleting by the throne. The flowers forever blooming—Govardham's amaranths: my verse and His Majesty, Shihabuddin Muhammad Shah Jahan, may G-d ever perpetuate his kingdom and sovereignty.

■ STUART CARY WELCH: Mansur-Payag-Mumtaz-Shah Jahan—Not just a pretty face, Dosha or Jerusha Padawer. I remember her well. None of them at Radcliffe or Harvard or at the Fogg, simply pretty faces.

For we were all of a piece. The miniatures, the ones the Fogg owned and mine too, that I would bring in to share with my students train their eye, so I could see the miniatures through fresh vision, their vision.

Ownership influenced them. My students always wondered how a collector acquired a painting. All people did. "Whose miniature is that," Nina Abigail Coggeshall asked with that abrupt off-handedness that all the *comme-les-enfants-sont bien elevées*—Philadelphia Mayflower descendants had.

Why should I reveal that Payag's sumptuous drawing of a Sufi Mullah instructing a prince was mine or John Goelet's or that I was dickering to buy it in New York, or that I would part with it in less than a decade or two, teaching those delicate Radcliffe flowers—doesn't keep one alive forever—even I knew it.

Mind you, it was all a miracle, the chance to hold up Govardham's painting, tiny really, to look at the flower in Shah Jahan's hand, to look at the flowers still blooming in the borders. Or Balchand's painting: Shah Shuja's beloved, with hyperthyroidic eyes—passion and shyness at once.

I dying slowly to be sure but still dying, amidst the youth of my students: "You should add to your vision of the Moghul world, Mademoiselles Padawer and Coggeshall, by visiting Govardham's other portrait, a companion piece if you will of the Dying Inayat Khan, which is now on display at the Fine Arts in Boston. A trip outside Cambridge will not kill either of you."

I remember speaking those words to them so clearly. Why should only I hear death's march and back they came, Dosha and Nina, like the good soldiers Schweik with Mademoiselle Coggeshall chirping. "Thanks for the lead about the dying Mr. Khan. Professor, now we know how you feel after reading our term papers."

Crazy she was, but not at all stupid.

■ GAUGUIN: What did they want of him?—Fisher. A plaything for his lover Dosha. For Tal. Her dead father now risen. Or is Tal the father and her father merely a ghost? What do they want of him? Nothing and at the same instant everything.

What do they want of me? Theo and Vincent. Theo: nothing. A small nothing Theo writes me in late October 1888. *"I have sold your Breton Girls Dancing so that you and Vincent can frolic about in the sun for months to come. Northern nocturnal led to endless Southern drenched days."* "Oh yes," Monsieur Theo adds, *"another small thing, a nothing. The buyer wishes you to correct the hand—a bit more life—nothing really, a painter's right hand stretched a bit more toward a Breton girl's hand. See she is already meeting you and I and the client more than half way. Fifteen minutes work. Maximum."*

Nothing and everything. For Vincent can finish a sun in the space of five minutes on his mad clock. The hour hand broken and the minute hand circling feverishly like a dervish.

Vincent, what does Vincent want of me? *"In general Vincent and I do not see eye to eye, especially as regards painting. He admires Daudet, Daubigny, Ziem and the great Rousseau, all men I cannot stand. And on the other hand, he detests Ingres, Raphael, Degas, all men I admire; I answer 'Sergeant, you're right' so that I can have peace. He likes my paintings very much, but when I paint them, he always finds that I have made mistakes here and there. He is a romantic and I am rather inclined to a primitive state. As far as color is concerned, he favors the accidents of impasto as in Monticelli, and I detest messing with brushwork."*

Vincent has placed me gently on an empty green throne. Dainty, apart from the dozen jute apostles' chairs in the guest bedroom. What do they want from me, Theo and Vincent. Nothing. And everything.

CHAPTER 9

WHITE snowflakes clung to the green vines dangling down the Western Wall. Like shadows of Chinese bamboo brushstrokes across a white canvas, each stone a scroll by itself, thought Dosha.

Fisher hesitated before the Wall. Much, much more impressive than he'd imagined. Each stone almost his height.

Or was it his sudden fatigue? What did they want of him—Dosha and Tal?

Fisher had asked for her hand in marriage. Asked whom? Her? Her father? The one she claimed lived in Chicago? The one who had died?

Her mother? Whom he had never met and probably wouldn't: "Past always being guide to the present," witty Tal always quipped.

Had he asked Tal for Dosha's hand—Tal *"more than Kin, less than kind."* What day was it anyway? Certainly not Tuesday, for then he'd been in the Tal & Sons' office on 47th Street.

■ LAURENCE STERNE: Like shadows of Chinese bamboo brushstrokes—Pilgrims, the two of them. Woman leads. Everyman, almost blind, follows. I, led by my Elizabeth: *"My dear Lawrey, I can never be yours, for I verily believe I have not long to live but I have left you every shilling of my fortune. Upon that she showed me her will—this generosity overpowered me—it pleased G-d that she recovered and I married her in the year 1741."*

This I wrote to my daughter Lydia. Is not the body of the beloved paper on which one writes one's novel? What is a novel but a memoir for one's daughter to be read by one's daughter's daughter? Onward till time shall dance no more. Fair Dosha sees the shadows of Chinese brush strokes across a white canvas. Each stone is a scroll by her Fisher. Shall he not hesitate before the mountain of the wall before him: a lifetime to be spent before he can put on paper what she has traced on his mind.

But much as Dosha will paint on his eyelids her pretty pictures of his dreams, still will he hesitate. My own wife Mrs. Sterne fancied herself the Queen of Bohemia. Shall *"Tristram, her husband to amuse and induce her to take the air, proposed coursing in the way practiced in Bohemia."*

Or shall I dally with Kitty Fourmantel writing: *"I am a giddy foolish unthinking fellow for keeping you so late up—but this Sabbath is the day of rest—at the same time that it is a day of sorrow—for I shall not see my dear Creature today—unless you meet at Taylor's half an hour after twelve—but in this do as you like—I have ordered Matthew to turn thief & steal you a quart of honey.*

"What is honey to sweetness of thee, who are sweeter than all the flowers it comes from. I love you to distraction Kitty—I will love you on so to eternity—so adieu & believe what, time only will prove me, that I am. Yours."

My dear sweet mad wife Elizabeth. My dear honeyed Kitty. Still we hesitate. Before the wall.

Kitchen—Fisher, by now a novelist. His dream to create but really to recreate. What has not yet happened but will because the pen has written it. He shivering, the words flowing into him. Byzantine in his inspiration. He writes of the kitchen but not of food eaten. "*It is a curious fact that novelists have a way of making us believe that luncheon parties are invariably memorable for something very witty that was said or for something very wise that was done. But they seldom spare a word for what was eaten. It is part of the novelist's' convention not to mention soup and salmon and ducklings, as if soup and salmon and ducklings were of no importance whatsoever, as if nobody ever smoked a cigar or drank a glass of wine.*"

Tal's influence no doubt on Fisher. His apartment is filled with books, even on the stove, a dreadful fire hazard if Tal ever cooked in his own place instead of hoping to be invited to "family," as he quaintly calls Dosha and Fisher. Or he sits alone in a café, lost in dreams of his past.

Here, however, I would "*take the liberty to defy that convention and to tell you that the lunch began with soles.*"

Perfectly acceptable even with Rabbi Tal, but Fisher will have none of it, just a kitchen with Van Gogh's rickety chair—smoke but no cigars—a kitchen with no food.

■ RED SHIRT: Sky—When I returned home after travelling to Paris, after Buffalo Bill and the Wild West Show, I told my story over and over. We all did. I heard from my friend Featherman that even the miserable Pawnee whom Julius Meyer the White Man brought to Paris bragged of everything they had seen. Claiming the sun never set the whole time their voyage lasted. Why should they not lie of what they did in Paris if they do not tell the truth on our lands.

One day after Paris, I saw Julius Meyer walking toward me slower than I remember him walking, not like Bufallo Bill who moved quickly to hide his age—and then looked twice as old. "Red Shirt, do you miss that sky-high teepee the Eiffel as much as the Pawnee do," he asks sadly.

I looked at him and said simply, "The teepee was not as high as the sky. The sky cannot be taken from me." "Yes, but the Whites will never give up trying," Meyer said sadly. A good man. A man.

"That is what I hoped the Pawnee would see," he said so softly I almost could not hear him. "And what of Featherman, does he miss the great teepee we saw?"

"Featherman is no longer in this world. He is looking down on us. All of us. He is happy," I said and I could see that the White Man too would soon be with Featherman. For he was a man. A good man.

■ VAN GOGH: A rickety jute chair placed by the door leading into the kitchen—I bought twelve chairs. Simplicity themselves. Jute. And Gauguin's chair. Ever present, day or night. "*Take, eat, this is my body.*" Blue, green and white. Its arms outstretched to all of us. I, a rickety jute chair placed by the door leading into the kitchen. Only a true artist can sit before the throne of G-d on Judgment Day. Painted in one night. Our Lord's throne and my rickety jute child's chair. No family name. 20 November 1888.

Has not Our Lord risen? Will He come again? I paint on the dry paint this time a pipe and tobacco pouch. This I will smoke when He returns. But we both know, He, the Father, and I, the child, that he never will

■ JULIO CORTÁZAR: Waiting for him—Fisher does not know where he will find Dosha. If he did she is not a woman who would wait for him. Fisher does not know where Dosha will take him. If he did, surely Dosha would not be the woman of his dreams. Nor mine. Give me La Maga anytime. In Buenos Aires or Paris.

"*Would I find La Maga? Most of the time it was just a case of my putting in an appearance, going along the Rue de Seine to the arch leading into the Quai de Conti, and I would see her slender form against the olive-ashen light which floats along the river as she crossed back and forth on the Pont des Arts, or leaned over the iron rail looking at the water. It was quite natural for me to climb the steps to the bridge, go into its narrowness and over to where La Maga stood. She would smile and show no surprise, convinced as she was, the same as I, that casual meetings are apt to be just the opposite, and that people who make dates are the same kind who need lines on their writing paper, or who always squeeze up from the bottom on a tube of toothpaste.*"

Dosha had waited for him in front of the skyscraper offices of TimeLife. "I've got the tickets, honey," she had said with the innocence of Hansel and Gretel's Inn Keeper—"Hop aboard."

He hadn't gone home, hadn't showered, he'd just followed her into a taxi—she who never took a taxi. Those Meyers, they still had the first dollar they made in Omaha selling Pawnee artifacts on Farnam Street.

Fisher had sat scrunched up in his taxi seat as uncomfortably as on that rickety jute chair that Dosha had placed by the door leading into the kitchen—"Darling, that chair's only for a true painter."

"Where are we going?" Fisher asked.

"Honeymoon," Dosha replied.

"It's Cambridge, isn't it? Back to the Harvard haunts. Or is it High Street for another look at your Yale art gallery Hopper and then higgledy piggledy to the Guilford Islands."

■ BADA SHANREN (1626–1705), Ching Painter: End of story—Beginning of story. My name. Zhu Da. Member of the Ming Imperial family. A descendant of the Prince of Yiyang. The story continues. In our garden in our princely mansion in our city—Nanchang.

I, full of humor just like this young woman. Teasing my friends. Full of puzzles and riddles and jests. Then my birthday present. All the Chinese Kingdom's present. No more Ming Dynasty. No more birthday speeches. In fact, no more speech. Stillness. Silence. No more guests, no more friends and no more parties for birthdays. My door marked dumb: And finally for me, no more Nanchang. In the monastery, in the Fengxin mountains outside Nanchang I cultivate my own garden. Watering my lotus pond with my tears.

I order about my 100 gardener-pupil-servant devotées with shouts and grimaces. We plant at night. I paint lying down, on my side only by moonlight. The eyes of my mad verse:

"There is a guest at Nanchang gate,
I pretend to be mad and talk
To the flying swallows."

They are flying just above my body as I lie on my side painting a narcissus by moonlight. Each end of the scroll is held by the hands of my followers. The scroll trembles as I paint the narcissus in a single stroke. I laugh at the swallows squawking.

The swallow wrenches my scroll out of my pupil's hands. The swallows are flying with my narcissus still leaning but now bending toward my royal Ming cousin Shitao. I am screaming. Shitao will write what I have painted. I have written what he will paint.

This young man Fisher writes the beginning of the story. His moonbride, Dosha, paints the end.

"Long rain falls, my boat has nowhere
to go,
Clouds move on, at my studio in the lotus
At this time, I exhaust my view of
the south
It is already this picture of
Bright Mountain."

We write our beginnings, paint the end of our tale. We all dream with the same brush.

"No, dear," said Dosha. "Passports are required, I'm afraid. Are you still in?"

"To the ends of the earth," replied Fisher.

"Good girls like me don't come cheap." Dosha jibed. She reached into a *New Yorker* canvas bag— filled with rolled up clothing, including Fisher's underwear. Must be her Julius Meyer Indian trader genes, thought Fisher.

"All our gear, Dreamboat, is in this little canvas bag." Dosha waved their passports at Fisher as they pulled into the El Al terminal at Idlewild. Fisher protested, "Where did you get my passport?"

But Dosha wouldn't answer: We're married now. Beginning of story. End of story. And she's chosen the honeymoon, thought Fisher.

"What's a nice gypsy like you doing in a place like this?" Fisher had said to Dosha as soon as they landed at Lod Airport. Fisher had hardly slept on the plane.

"Over there's your taxi cab," Dosha said, waving it down as they passed the outside gate.

■ SHITAO: Beginning of the story—Bada Shanren is the beginning of the story and I am the end of it. The young man is the beginning of the story and the young woman is the end. For Dosha is patting his hand as though he were the child. And the child is the beginning of the story.

But no. The mother is the beginning of the story. Dosha is like the beginning of the story. The child does not remember the beginning of the story but the mother reminds the child of the beginning. Li Tianfu said that Bada Shanren was older than I. Eighteen, when the "*long rain fell and his boat had nowhere to go.*" And I was a boy of two when a jade leaf, the golden branch and all of the palace of the Ming fell.

Bada Shanren began as a child and became a youth. Playing with other princes in his Nanchang garden. He abandoned his home and ran to the Fengxin mountains.

I myself entered this world. I became the beginning. For he became silent again. Though he could walk, he would not speak. Though he could speak, he would not. Who was the youngest child then?

Who was my mother then? The attendant who hid me in a barrel on the rickety horse wagon? I died and became the leftover man of Jingjiang.

Bada Shanren too, died at the age of less than 60. He wrote out: "*Scripture on the Inner Phosphors of the Yellow Court.*" His signature seal changed. It read "*immortality is attainable*" (Ke de shenxian).

He and I. Neither of us children. Neither of us old. Both of us dead. Both reborn. We are the beginning of the story. We are the end.

Chen Ding is right. "*Ba Da means the eight great ones. Ba Da, the four chief and the four secondary points on the compass. In all I am great and none is greater than I.*"

Bada Shanren's former Buddhist incarnation seal is mine too. "*I am the Kugua of former years.*"

Bada thinks I am still Buddhist. I think him to be a Taoist. The young man, Fisher, looks to the young woman, Dosha, to bring him to the story's end; the woman pats his hand so the story may begin. The beginning and the end circle around each other with childlike glee forever.

■ GAUGUIN: What's going on? Are we on a magic carpet?—Fisher is dreaming and in his dream he is asking Dosha what is going on.

His feet can feel the magic of yellow flowers tightly seeded, an Indian silk carpet, magical to walk on, flowers forever alive, vivid. Dosha has unfolded the panorama of their life together now and in the future. Shall I place a dwelling in her picture? Yes.

No. It is her picture. Her carpet. Her flowering gift to Fisher. What I have painted, I can unpaint. Erase. What I have painted, Dosha can overpaint. It is her life and Fisher's. Ah, Dosha: "Vous y passerez, la belle!" Your turn will come, pretty one."

■ MU XIN: Raphael. I too trust him. Because he trusts himself. Beyond thinking. Which will be the foundation of the art of his novel. "Art is never the result of thinking. One day, Rafaello Sanzio was painting in the church and he saw Leonardo da Vinci, approaching him. So he stopped what he was doing and greeted Leonardo, who asked him: "Do you think when you paint?" Rafaello replied, "No, I don't. If I think, I won't be able to paint well." Of course there was no one around to record this dialogue, but the exchange perfectly fits the personalities of both men. It would be beneficial to establish a methodology in aesthetics, namely: thinking exists before and after a painter is created, but it goes without saying that in the moment of painting thinking stops. But I didn't finish my story. Leonardo looked at the handsome face of this young artist and said to himself: "He is right. It seems that I have been thinking too much." A painter creates with the infinite laws of painting itself. All the principles of paintings are owned and used by the whole world; they resist such distinctions as East and West or the ancient versus modern."

They are finished thinking. Raphael and his Dosha Vinci. They have begun to create.

Fisher yawned. "Does that man know us?"

Dosha leaned forward and shouted, "Yes! Yes!" Fisher did not move. Object. Question. He trusted Dosha more than himself. In small things and big. Dosha knew it. If she spoke, he listened. Simple as that. No one she'd known had ever acted like that. Certainly not her mother. Her father didn't second guess her but Dosha could always see him puzzling her out. Raphael Fisher's trust relaxed her. Captivated her. "Yes, yes," she repeated. "Take us there now."

The Israeli cab driver stared at them in the rearview mirror throughout the ride. Ascending beyond the green cedars planted by congregations from Buenos Aires to Boston.

"Dosha, what's going on? Are we on a magic carpet? Where are we racing to?"

■ VIRGINIA WOOLF: Man—Dosha and Fisher are getting in a taxi. In New York. In Paris. In London. In the Holy Land—Jerusalem. Everywhere. Anywhere. In courtship. In marriage, even after death.

"Certainly when I saw the couple get into the taxi cab the mind felt as if, after being divided, it had come together again in a natural fusion. The obvious reason would be that it is natural for the sexes to co-operate. One has a profound, if irrational, instinct in favour of the theory that the union of man and woman makes for the greatest satisfaction, the most complete happiness. But the sight of the two people getting into the taxi and the satisfaction it gave me made me also ask whether there are two sexes in the mind corresponding to the two sexes in the body, and whether they also require to be united in order to get complete satisfaction and happiness. And I went on amateurishly to sketch a plan of the soul so that in each of us two powers preside, one male one female; and in the man's brain, the man predominates the woman, and in the woman's brain, the woman predominates the man. The normal and comfortable state of being is that when the two live in harmony together, spiritually cooperating. If one is a man, still the woman part of the brain must have effect; and a woman also must have intercourse with the man in her....It is when this fusion takes place that the mind is fully fertilized and uses all its faculties. Perhaps a mind that is purely masculine cannot create, anymore than a mind that is purely feminine, I thought."

Dosha is firmly lodged inside Fisher's mind. He and she, forever in a taxi together. Both creating as they voyage.

■ Harold Nicolson, Vita Sackville-West's husband: White—We wrote to each other in a language of flowers. For that was all our fingers could bear to do. But our hearts penned our messages to each other, even when our memories dreamed of another.

On 12th December 1939, Vita first dreamed her white dream and wrote to me for words as these spoken by her in my presence would have melted before reaching my ear.

"The lion pond [in the Lower Courtyard] is being drained. I have got what I hope will be a really lovely scheme for it: all white flowers, with some clumps of very pale pink. White clematis, white lavender, white agapanthus, white double primroses, white anemones, white camelias, white lilies including giganteum in one corner, and the pale peach coloured Primula pulverulenta."

But Vita was not dreaming of the Lion Pond alone. Draining it, the water coursing outwards beyond the bedded borders, irresistibly dissolving, soon to be visible across the world itself. From our Leonine shore all the way west to the Argentines east to India's Taj itself. What to do as we ourselves were being drained, pulled down, impossibly toward the earth's breast itself. Vita's solution always a love letter addressed to Virginia, who was being drained, day by day, before her heart's eye. So after a night for me not squandered on sleep. Time enough for that later and ever. I wrote Vita the language only lovers understand:

"I love your idea about the Lion Pond. Only of course it gets no sun. You know that. You are a horticulturist. It is impudence on my part to remind you that the Lion pond gets almost no sun. Just a beam at dawn is all it gets. We have the Japanese anemones which do well. We know that the blue Agapanthus flowers, so why not the white? But what about the clematis, the camelia, the lily, and the giganteum ditto? But you know, only it is such a good idea that I want it to succeed…of course there is not much room…yes it is certainly a good idea."

The whole of the language of my lady's flowers, of touch, of memories longing, of the heart's desire, is a letter written in the cipher of love. Even a love note written to another by my lady would I treasure and press to my lips.

Dosha nestled in Fisher's arms—they might be courting in a hay wagon, so secure and radiant she looked. Suddenly they were in front of the Western Wall. "This will do, Mr. Ezekiel, this will do," Dosha said to the taxi driver before Fisher could ask her "What's the damage?" Her father's favorite expression when a bill arrived in the Chicago of his youth.

But where was her father? When did he disappear? Or was he here?

Fisher had seen picture after picture of the Wall at setting sun. At daybreak, by moonlight. But never like this—covered with a white sheet of snow, invisibly set with cut, polished radiant stones. Stretching from the Earth, upward, continuing beyond his vision.

Fisher was wearing his Oxford blue shirt and blue slacks, which he wore each day to Time Incorporated. No tie—"I won't wear a tie to your brother's office," Fisher had insisted to Tal. "If I have to wear a tie, I won't come."

"What's a tie?" said Tal without smiling.

■ Vita Sackville-West: Snow—He caught the fragments of my tune perfectly. Perfect pitch, my Harold's ear. His eyes too could see me through Virginia's flesh, whiter than white itself, smaller than me. Yet all over each and every one of her pores, over my eyes, Virginia calls me *"a picture maker,"* my love does. The Lion Pond is draining and the British sun setting from the Argentine to the Indies. Virginia is draining, sinking, drowning. The Taj Mahal itself is moving into an eclipse: world wide it is. I am writing a love letter on the whitest paper I can find, glowing white even in winter. A thousand winters, even a thousand thousands. *"Of course I realized the Lion Pond was in the shade,"* I addressed my reply to dear Harold. *"And I chose things accordingly. Primulas and Giant Himalayan lily simply revel in a north aspect. I have been rather extravagant, I fear, on the principle of 'Let us plant and be merry, for next autumn we may all be ruined.'"*

And of course my Berg, my sweet Virginia, received my white hot letter penned all over the hard whiteness of her body. I have been ruined by my extravagance over her. And I would plant her again and again, forever if the Heavenly rains permit.

■ Virginia Woolf: White—Dec. 17, 1939: in my diary. *"Oh! The Graf Spee is going to steam out of Montevideo today into the jaws of death. And journalists and rich people are hiring aeroplanes from which to see the sight."* Our lion is bellowing, we can hear halfway round the world and I am draining, sinking, drowning, clutching at a letter written on the whitest of foolscap—from Vita. I am sending her my body itself:

"And this is the only scrap of paper I can find. But my dear, how nice to get your letter! How it heartened me! And how I long to hear from your own lips what's worrying you, for you'll never shake me off. No, not for a moment do I feel ever less attached. Ain't it odd? And so I didn't write but waited—Yes, do, do come. What fun, what joy that'll be."

All of our white letters of love penned to each other, messages folded in the bottles of our bodies, floating on the vastest of seas—all of us, Dosha, Fisher, Vita and I. Writing and not writing. Waiting, waiting, all for love.

AQVI ESTA SEPVLTADO O HONRADO
VSE AO YMANVEL ABOLAIS QVE SE
FINAN? EM 24 DO MES DE NISAN
A° 5392

ESE VE O IO YMANVEL ABOLAIS F EM 5 DE YA?
A° 5421

MANVEL   RACHEL
ABOLAIS   ABOLAIS

QVE YA ES AN? H VILDE & VE
VOZ   RA?   OLAIS SVA
SHER OVE POY AGO   GLORIA
29 DE SIVAN AN 5416

■ RACHEL LEVY DUARTE: Death—My father, though I would wager my life it was with my mother's words, came to me in 1687 with the news that "Jacob de Paiva had gone to his death at the mines of Hell itself—so hot it is in the Indies. A great blow has been dealt all of us—though foreseen—still great. For he was a fine man—with the broadest heart I have ever met."

Why did Father have to speak of "Jacob de Paiva"? That is not how I knew him. And Father too, and did he not call him Jacques in his letters to Louis Alvares. As to de Paiva or de Payva, to me he was a Zagache and to Father too. As a Zagache he was born—but in the world he could only live as a de Paiva.

But all of that is but a grain of sand on the shore of a sea—it matters not where it is—for only its ultimate source is of importance. For now my Jacques Zagache is with our Heavenly Father—to which even we Duartes and certainly we of the Abolais family must also voyage to. Yes, Father, he was a fine man, and yes he had the greatest heart of any man you, and certainly I, have ever met.

And eyes too, the finest eyes, though Mother was enough of a woman not to put those words in your mouth to be chewed over like a babe and spit back to me. For you would have agreed and would be thinking of Jacques's skill as diamond sawyer. How his eye could separate a box of rough stones in an instant. I would have thought far different things about Jacques's marvelous G-d given eyes as you delighted in mentioning as you filled out the membership in Antonio Rodrigues Marques's syndicate—and sent enough Spanish pieces of eight—one thousand pounds of them—to suffocate dear Jacques—if the Indian Ocean didn't drown him —or the heat of Golconda didn't finish him— or if she, that Almanza woman, didn't find a way. For even Samson is but sugar in the mouth of Delilah.

What was I to say to your parental aside: "A great blow though foreseen."

For years my Jacques had come to our house, and spread his diamonds on the table in our garden amongst the tea cups—for we all knew the servants should be sent out of the house and not see such treasures. One never knew: "The eyes can speak," as my grandmother Rachel Salom Duarte would say.

Should I speak of the walk I took not so many years before with Abraham Zagache. I pleaded with him to persuade Jacques to marry me. At dusk, between Rosh Hashannah and Kippurim it was—I walked Zagache to my grandmother's tomb and he read the words on her gravestone silently: "HAZ LO QVE QVIZIERAS AVER HECHO QVANDO MVERES." "ALWAYS DO THAT WHICH, AT THE MOMENT OF DEATH, YOU WOULD HAVE WISHED TO HAVE DONE." I did not have to open my mouth, but I asked with my eyes. Tears were my witnesses before G-d almighty. How could Zagache allow Jacques to be promised to that woman Hieronyma—when my heart could be bound for all eternity to him? Abraham Zagache, who loved Jacques no less than Father Abraham did his son, traced his fingers on the letters as though he were writing them fresh. He sighed, "It is already settled, my dear Rachel. No one can reason with your mother, she is a Duarte." And he too began to weep. Then with a weariness I shall never forget, he murmured, "Though it will be the end for me, for Jacques, for his sister, it is settled, it is settled." And so it was. In that order. So what shall I say father to "your news" but: "Always do that which, at the moment of death, you would have wished to have wished to have done."

Fisher's blue slacks were sticking to his legs. "Walk over there. I'll watch over you," Dosha said, pointing at a folding chair not twenty yards from the Wall.

"Walk me to the chair, darling."

"I can't," said Dosha.

"Why not? Because you're a gypsy? And gypsies need not apply?" said Fisher sluggishly.

He could joke in his sleep, in his dreams, probably even after his death, thought Dosha.

"No, because you've got to go the last ten yards alone."

Fisher sauntered over to the chair and looked at the wall. His feet felt impossibly heavy as he lowered his body onto the chair. Asleep, he dreamed a child's dream of his housekeeper who watched him when he was five years old.

■ MANUEL LEVY DUARTE: Death—Deborah Abolais was an Abolais in her dreams but once her eyes opened she was all Duarte.

Over and over she told me, "No daughter of mine will live in the Indies." No daughter of ours. Soul of simplicity. One marries a Duarte, one becomes a Duarte.

"What of de Paiva," I asked my wife. "You brought him from Antwerp to Holland. We taught him the diamond trade. We supplied him with goods. With recommendations. We guaranteed his purchases in Paris."

"Yes. And you, my dear Manuel, filled his head with dreams of Hindustan."

"And you," continued my wife, "invited him into our home, where he saw your daughter, and, more important, Rachel saw him."

"That is why it must not continue. Or it will end as all voyages to India end for all of our nation of Portuguese. We can live as Jews for a hundred years by Portuguese candlelight but we cannot survive three summers in India. Either we forget or we die. Not a great groom for my Duarte daughter."

"But he is one of us and Abraham Zagache is not a man of the streets—G-d forbid—he is gabbay of our community."

"Then I will speak to Abraham. For what will it gain him in his old age if he loses a brother to the lure of Hindustan?"

"If diamonds make men mad, what shall we say of Golconda—the mother of the greatest of all gemstones? And had I chosen to travel to the East, would you still have agreed to marry me?" I asked my wife Deborah.

But a Duarte knows that not all questions need be answered—Rachel was her mother's match in silence—neither Deborah answered my foolish question nor Rachel for the longest time after I told Rachel of Jacques's death at the mines of Golconda barely three years after he had left Amsterdam with his new bride Hieronyma Almanza.

Jacques' marriage was not a match made by my wife. She was far too shrewd for that, but let us say the dowry Hieronyma provided far exceeded even her remarkable beauty and certainly her Almanza pocket. When I heard Jacques had died at the mines, my heart went out to his wife. She was of our nation, after all, and I suggested that we send her passage money to return to her native Antwerp or settle in Amsterdam. "You are a fool, Manuel. With our Rachel now married to Abraham Salvador—let us send Hieronyma so much money that she and her worthless Almanza brother will sink in their own soup."

When I protested, all my wife could say is: "Did I not tell you that either de Paiva would perish or take leave of his senses in the East. What would you have for my Rachel: an abandoned daughter or a widowed wife?" And when I told Rachel, my dear daughter, Jacques had gone to his death after what seemed to me a lifetime of silence she murmured her grandmother's epitaph words: "Always do that which, at the moment of death, you would have wished to have done." I could see in her eyes—that my poor daughter would have walked through fires of Hell itself if only she had been at Jacques's side.

■ RABBI NACHMAN OF BRESLOV: Grass—"*Know this, every single blade of grass has a unique melody all its own. And from the poetry of leaves comes the music of the heart.*"

Fisher's mother walks with him in the Park. She sings to him and he listens. The housekeeper too walks with him to the Park. All the while, every leaf, every blade of grass is singing to Fisher, to his mother, to his companion. Shall such a beautiful song, G-d forbid, be forgotten?

Once heard, the song echoes softly. One note hummed by one who loves Fisher will bring back the entire lullaby of his youth. For each blade of grass has a unique melody—and each person hears that melody in his own unique fashion. "*G-d never repeats himself.*"

Dosha, a Levite's daughter, is opening Fisher's ear to the song of his childhood garden.

■ CHIEF RED CLOUD: His English—This medicine man speaks English. But his English is not Fisher's English. Fisher is tired. He has traveled far. He is trusting his woman to translate for him. To explain. The medicine man, like all medicine men, speaks many tongues and can write in many tongues too.

"*In 1868 at the Council of Fort Laramie, men came out and brought papers. We are ignorant and do not read papers, and they did not tell us right what was in these papers. We wanted them to take away their forts, leave our country. Then we would not make war. They said we had bound ourselves to trade on the Missouri, and we said, no we did not want that. The interpreters deceived us.*"

In 1866, what did I know of Colonel Henry Carrington's language? The white man wished the Sioux to agree to safe passage for travels. But all the Oglala, understood what he meant. I left with my people. For two years we fought. In the winter, Fetterman and his troops were killed. The White Men had built two forts: C.F. Smith and Phil Kearny. But what is built can be burnt. If the Great Father desires it.

I would not go to Ft. Laramie but sent my fellow Chief Man Afraid of His Horses. When the forts along the Powder River were no more then I would come. Not for a paper. Not for a word. But when the soldiers walked away from the forts. And they did. I burnt the forts to the ground and with the ashes still in the air in November of 1868, I and the Brule signed the treaty.

Roman Nose, Little Wolf, Dull Knife, Hump, Rain in the Face, Crazy Horse and I had defeated them. The whites called the war Red Cloud's War. I could defeat them, but I never understood them. Nor their language. Someday I knew they would change my name from Chief Red Cloud (Makhpiya-Luta) to plain Red Cloud. They did and Spotted Tail became chief. He imagined that he understood their paper. Their words. Fisher must depend on Dosha to translate. Not with her tongue but with her heart.

"Oh I'll watch him well. Don't you worry, Mrs. Fisher," the housekeeper would reassure his mother when she took him just two blocks away to play on the grass and ride the Riverside Park swings.

Dosha fingered the small canvas bag and sat on it like an Ellis Island refugee. Suddenly she was aware that behind her was the man, the "officiating official," as Tal called him, the Rabbi.

Dosha heard him say behind her, "Miss Padawer, I presume."

She turned and saw the Rabbi dressed in black baggy trousers with white in his beard, white hair springing helter skelter from his head.

"You must be tired."

"Not really," said Dosha.

"It's been so far for the both of you," said the Rabbi. His skin was so pale she thought he must have never seen an Eastern European summer. His English was more like Yiddish, accented with a Viennese cadence.

"I'm not so tired. I slept all the way. Fisher, on the other hand…"

"I know, I know. He's been tossing and turning in his sleep since New York."

"How do you know that?"

■ ABRAHAM SALVADOR, RACHEL DUARTE'S HUSBAND: It's been so far for the both of you—I should speak to my treasure, Rachel Duarte, and tell her that Jacques de Paiva has perished at the Kollur mines by the Krishna river. I should hold her hand and comfort her. How can I mention Jacques' death in our house for he, to dearest Rachel, will never die. Three years ago, Immanuel Levy Duarte came to me, put his hand on mine, and said, "My son, I wish to give to you in marriage the greatest Duarte treasure."

Of course I knew his words were not his own but those of his wife Constantia Duarte.

"Is not the 'Greatest Duarte Treasure' married? Your wife, Constantia Abolais Duarte?" I asked him, without a trace of a smile, though my heart was simply not in my body and my hands were shaking.

"Do not jest with me, Abraham!" Immanuel shouted. "You know full well I speak of my daughter Rachel, and 50,000 florins is to be her dowry."

"Is not the Duarte's treasure promised to Jacques de Paiva?" I asked though how I spoke the words I do not know.

"If it were so, would I be offering my daughter to you, Salvador?"

But I was no fool and I held my ground. "But I am too old Imanuel. I am 35. And your treasure is but 18," I persisted.

"So is de Paiva. He is also 35," Immanuel blurted out.

"What does de Paiva have to do with it," I pressed.

"Nothing," sighed Immanuel. "Nothing and everything. It is our wish the husband shall be you in Amsterdam and not de Paiva in India. We do not wish for a son-in-law in Hindustan, like Domingo do Porto, or Alvaro da Fonseca so eager for diamond dreams. They have left their wives and children for 'just a while' soon to return, of course, with a great, great treasure. We Duartes wish to view our treasures nightly."

"Then make my dowry 40,000 florins and give me the pleasure of seeing your wife's face when she learns of my suggestion of a bargain for the Duartes."

"Make it 30,000 then," laughed Immanuel in reposte. "And you'll see a miracle on my dear Constantia's face."

"No, Father-to-be," I said. "Let's stabilize it at 40,000."

"You are no fool, my son," Immanuel laughed and clasped me to him tightly. So it was, but three years after Jacques left and Rachel and I wed, and bed, Jacques is dead.

Immanuel pleaded with me: "You break this tale of India and Jacob to Rachel."

But I could not. And would not. And should not. And Immanuel knew it.

■ ABU SAID, Sufi Mystic (967–1049): When Fisher awakens—Fisher has been sleeping for hours. For days. Months. Years. The first step to take on a spiritual voyage is *"the breaking of ink pots and tearing up of books."*

He has not begun to write yet, so the breaking of ink pots will be simple. In any case, all the books he will need are in the room next door to him, his master Tal. His companion Dosha will provide and decorate his inkpots, create them from the earth's clay, turn them on a wheel, round and round and yet round again, like at Konya. She will fire them, glaze them all with her heart's hand.

But they are not there yet. Neither master Tal nor his guide, not Fisher himself yet. In an instant he will awaken.

First they must fast. Are they not both on a pilgrimage? They have arrived at the Holy City. Wisdom's words themselves hang in the air. No one has uttered them. All can hear them.

The important thing is not to be awakened. One must awaken oneself. What time should the guide be there? When time has started. When the sleeper opens his eyes. And the bride *"dazzles him in the darkness."*

■ ALFRED BINGHAM: Don't you remember—I asked my therapist "Don't you remember when you asked me to ask my brother Harry about Father's sketchy mention of Elihu Yale's paramour, Hieronyma de Paiva?"

He remained impassive. "Well, as you would imagine," I continued. "Harry remembered Father slowly sailing away from Mother, but all he said was: "Father had to serve, had to sail. We all knew that.""

Of course no word from my analyst. In any case, I know what you're thinking. "What does this have to do with me?"

"I'm a Yankee too, don't you remember? I was on the same plane. One row behind. 36J, as Mr. Tal insisted."

"Why didn't you speak to us?"

"Well, when I wanted to say a hello, you were sleeping. And once you opened your eyes, he seemed asleep and…" The Rabbi lowered his eyes, "I couldn't talk to you alone on your honeymoon. It's not done. I'm a Rabbi. A Rabbi's son, and Rabbi's grandson also a…"

"I get the picture," said Dosha. "So what do we do now?"

"Well, when Fisher awakes—and it's essential that you don't wake him, the Talmud tells us it's a sin to awaken a sleeping man.

"So we wait," the Rabbi continued. "When Fisher awakens, walk with him around the city. And go to the windmill. At dark. But don't eat and don't let Mr. Fisher eat. Even a morsel of food as big as an olive. I'll meet you at Mishkenot, as planned."

"What time should I be there?"

■ HIRAM (HARRY) BINGHAM IV: I'm a Yankee too—Alfred, my brother, adored Father. Everything Father did. Father would throw us up in the air and spin us head over heels, singing "I'm a Yankee Doodle Dandy."

And Alfred would stand before father imploring him to throw him up in the air along with the rest of the Bingham boys, stuttering "I'm a Yankee t-t-t-too."

He never changed, Alfred. Father wrote about Machu Picchu, Alfred wrote about Father conquering Machu Picchu. Father wrote about Elihu Yale. Alfred read and reread Father's biography of Elihu Yale. Not only that, he'd read portions of the book to his Freudian analyst. One day Alfred asked me point blank: Why hadn't Father been more thorough about Elihu Yale's Jewish Portuguese paramour and partner: Hieronyma de Paiva?

"Why ask me, Alfred?" I parried. "Why not ask Dr. Freud? Oh Harry, my analyst asked me to ask you."

"Well, in that case, I believe Alfred we must start at the beginning. Father. What can I say about him? 1911. Grandfather Mitchell dead, resting near the end of Folly Point. Mother watching her slowly sinking, yet Father as Father must sail on. I could be a Father to you, Alfred. To all of our younger brothers: Charles, Brewster, Mitchell and Jonathan. But how could I be Father to Mother? Mother who had the determination to give Father $1,800 he was lacking to sail off with the Yale Peruvian Expedition. Whom to serve is to reign. Alfred knew as I knew that our Father lived to serve. He must set sail. Mother holding my little eight-year-old hand while she *"waved frantically with the other."*

Alfred stared at me, wild-eyed, "You never gave Father an inch."

Suddenly Alfred gazed at his watch and said much like Groucho Marx "Oh my G-d, I've to get to my analyst. Can't wait till he hears this."

How could one not love Alfred and Father too?

THE MAGGID OF DUBNO: Vilna—The Vilna Gaon: The way things begin is the way they continue. The way they continue is the way they end. For me, for all of Israel, even for him, Elijah, the Gaon of Vilna, solitary, alone in the corner of the synagogue—his *Klois*. Year after year, I came. Elijah would wrap his arms around the Torah scroll, binding it with a white cord—*gelilah*—on Rosh Hashanah. All the eyes in his synagogue would be on him and his arms would be around the Torah and his eyes peering down as he wrapped and wrapped and wrapped the Torah yet again.

Then it would be just a moment before the Gaon blew the *shofar* (he did not permit anyone else to blow).

Year after year, he ushered in a New Year for all the world from Vilna, our day's Jerusalem, to the farthest shores of wherever our people dwelled, may they return to our hearts' Jerusalem. Suddenly, one year I could see, as even and only a child could see, that Elijah, the Gaon of Vilna's face, drained of color, whiter than white, paler than the moon, straining to sound the *shofar* and awake the world.

Yet no sound emerged. After three attempts, his son Abraham simply took the *shofar* from his father's hand and handed it to whomever cared to blow.

Who should blow the shofar but Mendeleh Shtum, who would sit in the back row each year. Mendel raced toward the front row and as he blew with the ease of a Yeshivah boy picking up a bag of *shaloch manot* on Purim. I could see a tear on the Vilna Gaon's cheek, white on white, water on water.

I knew it would be but a day before I would be summoned by his son Abraham, who silently walked me into his father's study and left as Elijah began: "Does G-d no longer desire my *tekioth*? Is Mendle Shtum, a simple, uneducated man, worth more to Him than I?" His eye penned a letter that asked the same question. The question that I was summoned with years before:

"Come my friend, to my house and do not delay to revive and entertain me."

The same tear, whiter than white, hung on his cheek and I began: Telling a tale:

"Once in a land far distant from here, beyond the great ever-flowing rivers, a mighty king possessed a diamond crystal larger than a man's fist, whiter than the moon on Pesach's first night. The king desired to have the diamond polished and cut. Because the rough stone was so large and pure, only the greatest diamond cutter in all the land could be entrusted with the task.

"The most skilled diamond cutters in the land beyond the great river were summoned and an enormous reward was offered."

"Any time after dark. Then it will be the fourth day of the week."

Tal's words exactly, thought Dosha. Fourth day of the week.

"Start counting the week when?" Dosha had asked Tal.

"Starting after the holiest day, the Sabbath bride," replied Tal.

"But what time?" asked Dosha.

"Slonim time, Vilna, Cracow or Padua time?" said the Rabbi.

"How do you know of Slonim? Tal's favorite Yeshivah." Dosha wondered.

"Who does not know of the *Heilege* Reb Weinberg and of the Slonim Yeshivah," answered the Rabbi without waiting for her question.

■ C: "The next year, G-d be praised, I could hear Elijah's shofar blowing. I was standing in the back row, unbeknownst to all, listening as he once again lifted his *shofar*, light as a feather, and blew and blew directly into my body, every part of me, giving my feet a lightness to walk through all of the towns and villages far from Vilna, from Velodawa, Zilkiew, Kalisz and Zamosc.

"Blessed are you Hashem, our G-d, King of the Universe, who has sanctified us with His commandments and has commanded us to hear the sound of the *shofar*. And what is the mitzvah but to hear, and if, G-d forbid, one sounds the *shofar* but cannot hear its sound, he has not performed the commandment."

■ B: "To the astonishment of the king, each and every one of the expert diamond cutters—each cleaver, each bruter, every skilled polisher refused to attempt—all felt the stone to be beyond their skill. Suddenly, a simple diamond girdler, from a small country town, who had never heard about the stone, but happened to be in the palace at the time, visiting one of the master cutters(who was his relative) offered to do the cutting and polishing.

"When the young diamond worker brought back the stone, the whole court was astonished for the perfect rough crystal had been fashioned into a gem of astounding whiteness, and symmetry. The king thanked the young man and wanted to present the promised reward but the cutter refused. *"The reward belongs not to me but to the youngest of my apprentices. It is he who did the actual work."*

"The king was baffled. It seemed extraordinary that a young cutter, unknown, was able to fashion such a diamond, but to imagine that a mere apprentice could create such a stone was inconceivable. The king summoned to his palace courtyard each of the master craftsmen, the cleavers, the girdlers, the bruters, the cutters, the master brillianteers that he had at the beginning offered the opportunity to work on the rough crystal. Passing the stone from expert's hand to hand, the king asked: *'Why is it that you, the most skilled diamond cutters in my kingdom, should have refused to perform a task which it seems that even a village jeweler's apprentice could complete with such remarkable results?'*

"The head of all the jewelers bowed his head before the king and spoke softly. "We experts know a great deal about all manner of precious stones. When we saw this rare stone, we knew at once that to bring out its true beauty and brilliance would be a most formidable task. Therefore, our hands were paralyzed with fright. We did not dare touch it. Not so the plain cutter from the country and his apprentice. They never realized the importance of the owner nor did they understand the true worth of the stone. To them it was just another diamond to cut and polish. So they set about their task without fear and remained at it until the work had been completed to their own satisfaction."

"I looked at Elijah the Gaon of Vilna, his shofar that roused me and all Israel, year after year, and I whispered: *"You are a man of great learning. When you put the shofar to your lips, you were so overcome with awe so that your strength failed you and you could not perform the task. Not so the plain man from the back row of the synagogue. He knew only that there was a simple piece of work to be done, namely to blow the ram's horn and knowing that his lungs were healthy and strong, he felt no fear and could sound the shofar clearly and with ease. He did not know enough about this sacred rite to be overawed by its momentous import as was my illustrious master, the Gaon of Vilna, the most learned of Rabbis, who is fully aware of the deep meaning of the sounds of the shofar."*

Roman diamond ring, 3rd century.

Eyes—Standing Bear was alive to everything. Paris to him was greater than all the lands of the Oglala. The tower built by Eiffel, taller than Bear Butte. We would walk all day along the endless promenades, always starting at the base of Eiffel's tower, past all the ladies wearing umbrellas to shield themselves against the sun, past the Nicaragua pavilion and the Portugal pavilion by the river's edge. Standing Bear would dangle his feet in the Seine and if we walked with Has No Horses and White Star, we would attract every child under ten that could escape from their Parisian guardians.

Standing Bear would always glance back at the tower to make sure it was still standing. I had written my brother Adolph that Gustav Eiffel was so sure of the construction of his building that he paid for two-thirds of the construction costs in exchange for becoming the sole beneficiary of the tower for twenty years. When the neighbors of the building site during the construction became panicky about the tower's safety, Eiffel himself insured the project.

Round and round, down the Champs de Mars, all day long, even after dark, I'd plead with the chief: "Let's go to our hotel and get something to eat and go to sleep." "We can sleep, Box-Ka-Re-Sha-Hash-Ta-Ka when we return to our land. Let us keep our eyes open. Let us eat." We would walk to Volpini's café where I would play orchestral music with one dozen women violinists and a single male cornet player.

The Omaha would either be jumping in their seats or lifting each other to look at the French paintings hung high on the walls. I remember one of the artists coming over to me and pointing to my hat saying something. Volpini translated as he always did: "Monsieur le peintre Gauguin says he will give you a painting in exchange for your magnificent cowboy chapeau."

"Tell him Volpini, I'll give him my hat for nothing. I'm in the Indian treasure business. What am I going to do with a French painting?" By G-d instead of thanking me, Volpini translated what the crackpot said next: "What do I do if I lose your cowboy chapeau?"

"Well my boy, on the inside you can see my address: J. Meyers's Wigwam 169 Farnam Street, Omaha. You can come by and purchase one. I'm sorry, one to a customer. House rules."

I wonder whatever did happen to that French painter. Or my hat. He never did drop by.

Dosha heard nothing. She felt her grandfather's hands on her forehead before Yom Kippur evening. Could this Rabbi have studied with her grandfather? Impossible. He must only be Tal's age.

And none of Slonim had survived, her grandfather always told her, or at least almost none. But the story always survives if it's true. If it is from the heart, said her grandfather.

Suddenly she heard the Rabbi say, "Padua time would be 18 minutes after sunset. Why miss a day in the holy of the holiest," the Rabbi continued. "Slonim in the middle of the night. And Yankee time, the stroke of midnight. Anyway, if he made it this far, I'll be there, G-d be praised. Sweetest friend, the rest is simple."

With that, the Rabbi turned to Fisher, who opened his eyes and turned toward the Rabbi who intoned loudly while waving at Fisher:

■ P. JENOT, a French naval lieutenant who knew Gauguin in Tahiti: Eyes—*"As soon as Gauguin disembarked at Papeete, he attracted the stares of the natives, provoked their surprise, and also their jeers, above all from the women…What focussed their eyes on Gauguin above all was his long, salt and pepper hair falling in a sheet on his shoulders from beneath a vast, brown felt hat with a large brim, like a cowboy's. As far as the inhabitants could remember, they had never seen a man with long hair on the island…that very day Gauguin was renamed Taata Vahine [Man-Woman], which the natives made up ironically, but which provoked such interest among the women and children that I had to chase them from the entrance to my cabin. At first Gauguin laughed when told of this…"*

■ VIRGINIA WOOLF: A story always survives if it's true—Dosha knows it as only a painter can know. A story always survives if it's true. If it is from the heart. That knowledge is her gift to Fisher: her novelist beau, who sees everything and is writing their story's first draft with his eyes.

My sister Vanessa knew it as only a painter can know. Painting me after Roger's Post-Impressionist show. Brilliant she was, my left eye gazing inward. Inside my skull words streaming about, sucking my whole self inside, while outside my right eye viewing the world through a window—although I was weary again under the weight of it all. Vanessa could see all, even more than she understood.

Strange about painters—Roger too understood it less than he could paint it. *"Art,"* he said, *"is significant deformity."* What fun for Vanessa and me to drape ourselves in *"gaudy draperies"* over precious little else at the Post-Impressionist Ball.

As sensational and equally disliked by *toute Londres* as the paintings by Gauguin and Van Gogh that Fry hung at the Grafton Gallery. *"Pornographic"* the one. *"The work of a madman"* the other.

"Cézanne had shown the way; writers should fling representations to the winds and follow suit." Dosha knows this. She is a painter. A Cambridge don, Fisher is. Most fortunate to sit in her eternal tutorial. Dosha is but a painter and I for one thought, and still do: *"The furious excitement of people…over their pieces of canvas colored green or blue is odious."*

■ GAUGUIN: Pulled himself up from his chair—First we sit. Dream. Then we paint. Vincent's chairs. Mine and his. But both painted by him. Even as I sat in my armchair, curved but never comfortable, for Vincent always placed at least two books on it "Just in case you have a minute, Paul." "Vincent, I'm painting. I can't read." Vincent could see behind his back, he could gaze at the sun itself. He would say, "Paul you are sitting and if you have a minute…"

I'd cut him off sharply: "When I sit, Monsieur Van Gogh, I think. When I think, I paint." "So then, do it all at once, Paul. Sit, think, read and paint. It's all the same."

Of course I knew Van Gogh was right. I would pull myself up from my chair and stumble. To where? To get away from Vincent. To go to Paris. To walk about the Exposition Universelle. 1889. Paris. The gamelan players in the Javanese temple. Clever, Schuff, to have convinced the restaurateur Volpini to hang my paintings—higher up of course than Bernard's and Schuff's canvasses in his Café des Arts on the Exposition grounds.

Everyone came to the restaurant. Even that American cowboy Monsieur Julius with his Western hat and Pawnee Indians. Long hair down the length of their necks—one would sit on the other's shoulders so that he could look at my canvasses while Monsieur Julius explained French painting to the Indians and how one shouldn't touch them but just look with one's eyes, and the Indian, Standing Bear was his name—saying in his tongue, which Monsieur Julius explained to Volpini in English who translated me into French: "*These little women look as alive as birds on a tree. I want to see if they will move if I touch them.*"

I was overcome by the Angkor Indo-China Temple at the Exposition. Why not apply to the Colonial Office? "*The west was rotten but a man with the character of Hercules could gain new vigor like Antaus out there by touching the ground. And after a year one comes back strong and toughed up.*"

Stumbling out of one's armchair. But Van Gogh's eye is ever upon me. Though my chair, his painting is already covered with a shroud. Even when I got to Tahiti—even when I waltzed around the streets, looking for the face to frame in my painting, the lost face of Eve, the postcard from Java sent by my mother so that I would be able to finally sleep in the moonlight. Did Van Gogh's eye still shine in my bedroom? Even when Montfried shipped me those sunflower seeds from the south of France which sprouted as I removed them from the box in my very hand so powerfully did I yearn for the yellow house. Even these seeds could not darken my room forever lit by Vincent's fiery eye.

Paul Gauguin, Sunflowers on a Chair.

"*Blessed art thou O Lord our G-d, who has kept us fully alive, has sustained us and brought us to this time.*"

Hearing the words "this time," Fisher thought of the first time he met Dosha. The touch of her skin as he brushed her hand, the moment when Dosha tried to correct the first page of his novel and he told her he loved her but he'd be the writer and she'd be the painter and she kissed him and said, "Yes. Yes. Yes." All this flooded his mind. He jumped to his feet, held Dosha's hand, saying "Amen" loudly to past times and to all the future with Dosha, who *sotto voce* but audible to the Rabbi, answered Fisher's "Amen" with an "Amen" exactly as she remembered from her grandparents' house.

As soon as the Rabbi uttered these words, he walked briskly away from the Wall.

Fisher pulled himself up from his chair walked toward Dosha.

"Honey, I don't feel so hot. Let's go to a hotel and get something to eat and fall into bed."

"OK, Dreamboat. I'll be porter and you be *memsahib*." With those words, Dosha hoisted the bag on her back like a knapsack and held Fisher's arm as they walked along the stone path, up and down trails for what seemed to Fisher like hours.

Finally he saw a windmill glistening in the snow.

"A windmill," he blurted out. "Don Quixote, we must rest a while here." He collapsed on a stone bench, resting his head on Dosha's lap.

Her hands were kneading his back. Slowly her hands moved over him.

◆ SARA PADAWER, DOSHA'S GRANDMOTHER: Snow—In the beginning, my granddaughter's intended feels the snow. The cold. The chill of the night as Simha did when we hid in the snows of Belorusse. Did the winter never end until the War's end?

His whole body shaking, no matter how many blankets we slept under. But then as I touched him, he would lift his head above the blanket, staring at the snow lit by the moon, and kiss my hands, and whisper: "Come and see," over and over, as I caressed him, and he, me.

Turning the cold night above us into a warmth that exploded inside of me—white heat, I could not open my eyes. From the beginning of my granddaughter, Jerusha's, marriage, this angel Raphael is bringing the moon's white light to her. If Jerusha asks him the meaning of all his whispering and moanings, he will answer as my Simha would. "*The question is half the answer. Without a question, there is no reason for an answer.*"

■ JEREMY KALMANOFSKY, AMERICAN RABBI: Amen—R. Yose's teaching: "*Greater is the one who responds Amen than the one who blesses.*"

What are we to make of Fisher's thunderous, "Amen." He does not accept this man as his Rabbi, but, because he has responded, "*he has, according to R. Bahye of Saragossa, the thirteenth-century Bible commentator, become a second witness (the Rabbi is the first) that the Blessed Holy One is the source of blessing.*"

Fisher is no longer weary. On the contrary, he is more alive, ready for life, hoping for life—a life with Dosha.

But is Fisher the only one saying Amen? No. Dosha too has said Amen. She too is greater than the Rabbi who blesses. She too is fully alive, waiting to accept and to give love, to wed and nourish Fisher.

"*One human being alone can't make a true blessing. We need partners.*"

◆ SIMHA PADAWER, DOSHA'S GRAND-FATHER: Rabbi—In 16th century Padua, where my ancestors came from, Rabbi Meir ben Isaac Katzenellenbogen, the head of the Academy of Padua, read in a letter from Rabbi Elijah Capsali: *"There is an ancient custom in the city of Candia. When the portion of the Book of Jonah is to be read on Yom Kippur only the first three verses are in the Holy tongue, Hebrew. The rest of the book, from beginning to end, is translated into the secular Greek. Afterwards they skip to the book of Micah, where they read three verses, and translate the balance of the reading in the same way into Greek. I, Rabbi Elijah Capsali, feel this is not according to the Law. Blessed Rabbi Meir answered Rabbi Elijah to turn him from his purpose. In truth this is a puzzling custom, but it is not right to rest entirely upon our intelligence, and abrogate an ancient custom. It is necessary to find an explanation for it. That is what our early sages did whenever they came across a puzzling custom."*

Jonah is on a voyage. Not to Nineveh but to Tarshish. Fleeing from the Lord, not even going back to his home, simply boarding a ship in a different direction.

If my granddaughter, barely speaking the Holy tongue, were she told the story of Jonah in Hebrew, what would she understand of it? But praise G-d she has booked passage for Fisher and herself, they are moving toward holiness.

Nothing is beyond the will of G-d. Cannot Jonah be delivered from the belly of the great fish in any language? Cannot my granddaughter's grand-daughter teach the tale in the Holy tongue?

"I'm so tired I can't move a muscle," he said but, in fact, he suddenly felt refreshed.

Last year, when Fisher said that to her, thought Dosha, then and there she decided that he was for her.

Hours before, she had flown into a rage—a funk—every painting in their apartment—the studies in white, the newer "red" experiments, they all looked so horrible to her. She had ripped the half-finished canvas, "Taj White," off her stretcher and smashed her palette on the floor. It was in the middle of the afternoon. Fisher was still at Time Inc. She felt so groggy she fell asleep. When she awoke, there he was beside her, stripped naked, saying "Darling, please get me some water. I'm so tired…I can't move."

When she staggered into the kitchen, she found his gift: a new palette. He had found the wreckage, gone to Pearl Paints, and bought her a new palette. All that night until morning, he talked her down from total despair to starting again.

"We'll see about that," Dosha said, and playfully slid her hand down his chest.

"Dosha," he said, seeing a figure in front of them, "who's that?"

"A Rabbi. I'm a Rabbi. Don't you want a Rabbi?" said the figure.

"No!" yelled Fisher.

"Darling, we do want a Rabbi. That's why we came here," Dosha whispered.

■ VAN GOGH: Tired—Dosha is a master painter. She can see all surfaces and feel them too with her eyes. He need not tell her he is tired. Her eyes can see this. She is painting Fisher's portrait as he speaks. I am talking to Gauguin. He is painting my portrait. The thinnest of thin brushes in my hand. *"It is really me, very tired and charged with electricity as I was then."* Sunflowers drinking moisture from my palette. I am drinking my own paint and being reborn, Lazarus from the dead.

Fisher, the thinnest writer's pen in his hands. Dosha painting him, breathing life into his lips. His fingers are starting to move, to compose not only one novel but three, the story of Dosha, of his neighbor Tal, the voyage to blue-domed Jerusalem. His fingers are already sketching the outlines of their daughter Ariel, even their grandchild, yet another Rachel.

Novels of his teacher who sang to him—his Dutch mother—novels of Paris, of the far away Indies. Dosha is painting him as he is writing his white dreams of blue and green while Gauguin is painting me and the sun explodes before my hand extended toward the white canvas finger of G-d.

■ BADA SHANREN: Painting—Van Gogh is painting with the side of his brush top—*cefeng.* Gauguin is holding his own brush upright. The fine tip of his brush—*zhongfeng*—dances across his painting.

Fisher is a broad brush portrait of Dosha as she, more even and angular than he, paints him. I started wearily painting pine trees, *cefeng* and lilac, brush ever upright, shall I not be mad?

◆ RACHEL ABENDANA TAL: He's no Rabbi —How like my son, Abraham, is his pupil Fisher. Poor Abraham, before each Yom Kippur fast, even on the day itself, Abraham would quote the Talmud Yoma, (The Day of Yom Kippur): "Seven days before Yom Kippur they sequester the Kohen Gadol, the High Priest, from his house to the Parhedrin chamber and they prepare for him another Kohen—High Priest—as his substitute lest he become disqualified. Rabbi Yehuda teaches: they also even prepare another wife for him lest his wife die, for it is stated regarding the Kohen Gadol on Yom Kippur 'And he shall make atonement for himself and for his household.' His household, this refers to his wife. Thus we learn the Kohen Gadol must be married. Said the sages to Rabbi Yehuda, if so we have to prepare for the possibility that the second wife might die. But that was not done—for there is no end to the matter."

My poor Abraham, he could not accept these words. What would happen if the second wife did die, he would ask my husband Isaac, even when we sent him to our Rabbi, Rabbi Amiel—and all said "There is no end to the matter," Abraham still shook his head.

Today Abraham has selected the Rabbi. Fisher has fasted and his bride Dosha has, too. All their sins are forgiven on this day. They themselves are forgiveness for us all. Fisher worries that not all the proper preparations have been made.

"He's no Rabbi," Fisher exclaims. But praise G-d, Dosha is not my son's Rachel. She and Fisher will wed.

He's no Rabbi," said Fisher, waving his hand at the spectre.

"Honey, if it looks like a Rabbi and sounds like a Rabbi, where I come from, it is a Rabbi."

"How much is this going to cost?"

"It's on the house," said the figure in black.

"This can't be a Rabbi, Dosha. I think I've seen this guy somewhere. He's some creepy Peeping Tom."

"Excuse me, Rabbi. Where will you perform the ceremony?" Dosha didn't even look at Fisher.

The Rabbi waved toward the row of low 19th century houses before them and said, "No place like the present."

He pushed the door directly in front of them. A room revealed itself, not large but with a chair and an enormous piece of paper on the desk.

■ RACHEL ZUCKER, poet: House—
Largely a house myself I have, when seated,
A kind of balance and from my gray chair are
　　everywhere windows and color
and in the distance the thin blue promise of
　　what I know must be another coast—

■ GAUGUIN: The figure in black—The Rabbi is approaching Le Juif Errant. In Jerusalem, no less. Though he has been sighted in Avignon, in Paris certainly, walking for thousands of years.

I, a figure in black, or brown, but always in dark tones, walking to Pont Aven, Martinique, Tahiti, to Paris even if only to see the Exposition of 1889. Easy for me to dine on and dream of primitive art, those French barbarians. I was not searching for Courbet's ridiculous patron but rather a map to my heart.

Only a Breton peasant, an Arlesienne or a Tahitian, will be able to draw my map, especially considering all my torturous turns, cul de sacs and blind alleys of my heart's passionate highways and byways. The oceans of my desire.

But I'll sail on "with all the tactlessness of a sailor," as Father Pissaro spoke of me. "I'm troubled by all the fathers that have been attributed to me." Thank you very much. I'll sail alone and walk alone in brown searching for the true, natural, unspoiled chart of all that is inside my boiling body and brain. "Bonjour, Monsieur Gauguin," all will greet me and I will tarry but not stay long and will politely bid all adieu.

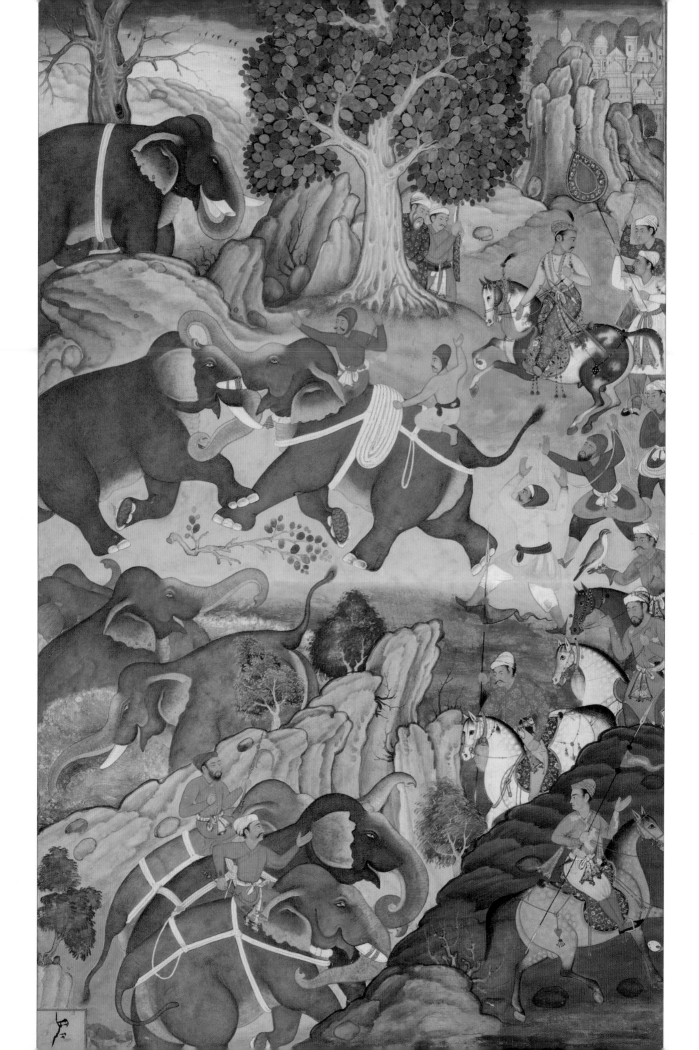

■ LEONARD WOOLF: Miss P., my friend—When I returned from Ceylon in 1911, I was struck by the extraordinary degree to which my family, my friends, London indeed all of my country had changed.

"The social significance of using Christian instead of surnames and of kissing instead of shaking hands is curious. Their effect is greater, I think, than those who have never lived in a more formal society imagine. They produce a sense, often unconscious, of intimacy and freedom, and so break down barriers to thought and feeling...to have discussed some subjects or to have called a (sexual) spade a spade in the presence of Miss Strachey or Miss Stephen would seven years before been unimaginable."

The Rabbi is the agent of Mr. Tal. Or shall I say Abraham. Speak to the point he does: "Miss P., my friend."

For Dosha must marry Fisher. She is a painter and only he can enable her to paint, to create in the widest sense of her world.

She with canvasses filling, year by year, with her embrace of him—warming her in a world growing increasingly cold. She has given Fisher—only she has the imagination to meld the two worlds of first and last name—the courage to eventually attempt his novel which will include them all. On paper, stumbling slowly, but eventually shepherded into Book form. Tal? My Strachey. I could not face Miss Virginia Stephen directly, so I telegramed Strachey. *"Do you think Viginia would have me? Wire me if she accepts..."* And Strachey, bless his soul, wired me back in August 1909: *"You must marry Virginia. She's sitting waiting for you, is there any objection? She's the only woman in the world with sufficient brains; it's a miracle that she should exist; but if you're not careful you'll lose the opportunity. She's yours, wild, inquisitive, disconnected, and longing to be in love. If I were you, I should telegraph."*

A light touch they both have, Tal and Strachey.

"Don't we need witnesses?" asked Dosha.

"The Lord will provide, Miss P., my friend."

How does he know her initial, thought Fisher.

The Rabbi snapped his fingers, and two bell boys—or were they angels?—appeared with wine and a *hallah*.

The Rabbi began to write on a brilliantly white piece of vellum.

"What are you doing?" asked Fisher.

"I'm the *sopher*, the scribe. I'm writing the *ketubah*," said the Rabbi.

"I thought you said you were a Rabbi," snapped Fisher.

"These days you can't just be a Rabbi."

■ VIRGINIA WOOLF: The Lord will provide, Miss P., my friend—*"On or about December 1910 human character changed."* The clergyman is caught between two worlds. "The Lord will provide," he intones.

"I am not saying that one went out, as one might into a garden, and there saw that a rose had flowered or that a hen had laid an egg. The change was not sudden and definite like that. But a change there was, nevertheless; and, since one must be arbitrary, let us date it about the year 1910...In life one can see the change, if I may use a homely illustration, in the character of one's cook."

Now Dosha and her fiancé have shared the same digs. The Rabbi knows it and doesn't know it. He accepts it and feigns no knowledge.

At home Fisher cooks for Dosha on weekends. Luxury: croissants, fresh sunshine-filled orange juice, eggs at midnight.

Dosha cooks an adventurer's lunch for him. Lord Sandwich's sandwich always with, "What do you wish today, my love?" He answers always and ever, "Surprise me." She does as he stares at his lover's offering (which he placed directly on the blank page of the unbegun novel he is trying to write each lunch hour at *Time* magazine). Today they fasted, which very much concerns our Rabbi.

"The Victorian cook lived like a leviathan in the lower depths, formidable, silent, obscure, inscrutable; the Georgian cook is a creature of sunshine and fresh air; in and out of the drawing-room, now to borrow the Daily Herald, now to ask advice about a hat. Do you ask for more solemn instance of the power of the human race to change? All human relations have shifted—those between masters and servants, husbands and wives, parents and children. And when human relations change, there is at the same time a change in religion, conduct, politics and literature. Lets us agree to place these changes about the year 1910."

Of course Miss P, if pushed, would argue on or about a half a century later, say 1960, human relations changed. Will not her children's children also state: that on or about a half a century later, say 2010, human relations changed?

■ Talmud Yerushalmi Yoma, 3:2:III: Blue… white—"A. One time R. Hiyya the Elder and R. Simeon b. Halapta were walking in the valley of Arabel at daybreak. They saw that the light of the morning star was breaking forth. Said R. Hiyya the Elder to R. Simeon b. Halapta, "*Son of my master, this is what the redemption of Israel is like—at first, little by little, but in the end it will go along and burst into light.*

"What is the scriptural basis for this view? Rejoice not over me, O my enemy, when I fall, I shall rise; when I sit in darkness, the Lord shall be a light to me (Micah 7:8)…Mordekhai was sitting in the king's gate (Ester 2:19)…Haman took the robes and the horse, and he arrayed Mordekhai and made him ride through the open square of the city proclaiming, thus shall it be done to the man when the king delights to honor (Ester 6:11)."

And in the end: "*Thus Mordekhai went out from the presence of the king in royal robes of blue and white, with a great golden crown and a mantle of fine linen…while the city of Susa shouted and rejoiced (Ester 8:15). And finally, the Jews had light and gladness and joy and honor."*

Fisher the groom, Dosha the bride have fasted. Their day—*Yoma*—their sins attoned for. The night and day too, a day of redemption and joy, their Purim. And Tal's too, through them and through their children's children, his name will be blessed. And all of Israel too.

■ Bob Dylan: Soon—Soon it won't be night and the Rabbi won't be there. The witnesses will vanish. They never stay for long. The moon on Dosha's shoulder isn't flickering. It's morning, Dosha and Fisher can see it. New morning.

Can't you hear that rooster crownin'?
Rabbit runnin' down across the road
Underneath the bridge where the water
*   flowed through*
So happy just to see you smile
Under the sky of blue
On this new morning, new morning
On this new morning with you

It'll be gone. All too soon. The Rabbi, the witnesses, the ring, the night, even the moon. But the song, their song will be heard forever.

Suddenly the Rabbi jumped up started to chant.

"*Soon there will be heard in Judah and the outskirts of Jerusalem the voice of joy, the voice of gladness, the voice of the groom.*"

Fisher felt himself lifted off the ground. He wasn't in Jerusalem. He wasn't in Israel. His feet weren't in New York. His mind wasn't in New Haven. He wasn't anywhere in his past. He was dancing around and around Dosha, sometimes in step with the Rabbi, sometimes with the witnesses. But they couldn't keep up with him. Soon he was dancing in front of her, doing a Cossack dance, the *Kazatzka* that his father had taught him, arms and feet extended. Dosha's eyes fixed on his just as they had on Hudson Street when they met, in the White Horse when they talked till 2:00, or on Centre Street in the marriage courthouse where she had said, "Yes."

Dosha, radiant, more beautiful than he had ever seen her, holding in her hand a ring of blue with a domed roof of blue enamel, lending blue to her greenish blue eyes, now green, now blue, danced around and around.

Then, in an instant, Fisher found himself lying on the cot in the corner of the room, Dosha in his arms, and directly on her shoulder, not flickering, the moon: perfect, round, eternal, white.

■ Rabbi Hiyyah ben Joseph, Talmud Yerushalmi, 9:6 III: Witnesses—"*A youth sold his property, and the case came before me and R. Yohanan, since the relatives claimed that he sold the property as a minor and had no power to do so.*"

I ruled that "*The prevailing supposition is that the witnesses signed a deed for a person of mature mind and the purchaser has the advantage.*"

Rabbi Yochanan ruled: "*Since the purchaser has come to remove property from the family, it is his burden to bring proof that the youth was of mature capacities when he made the sale of his property.*"

Is this the wedding ring that the bride Dosha is holding? If so, it must be the property of the groom Fisher. If it is the property of Fisher, was Abraham Tal allowed to sell his family's ring. And if no sale was effected, what of the marriage?

I rule a sale was effected—Tuviah Tal to his brother Abraham. Rabbi Yochanan rules that the groom must bring proof that Tal was of mature capacity when he made the sale of his property. The ring has traveled from the Diaspora to the Holy Land. I too, from Babylonia from the city of Sichna to Tiberius. My wife, left behind, and only later, escorted by three Torah scholars, joined me. This ring will again return. And return again, through the children's children, praise G-d to the Holy Land, all the families: Tal, the groom and the bride, shall be one family. Amen.

■ Rabbi Kalonymus Kalman Shapira, the Rebbe of the Warsaw ghetto: The Rabbi jumped and started to chant—Why does the Rabbi jump? Because he must. As a Jew. "*Just as one must fast on Yom Kippur, whether you like it or not, because G-d decreed it, so must you be joyful on Purim, whether you are in the mood for it or not. You simply have to, because G-d decreed it!*" This is what I said in the ghetto in Warsaw, Purim 1941.

And why does the Rabbi start to chant? Because he is a Rabbi, he must teach. I am still singing, praise be to G-d, though I have lost a son. An only son. Still singing for all Israel, for every human, for all those who will open their ears and hearts.

■ ELIHU YALE: India—The painter could not have been more than twenty-one. Full of chatter he was, a million questions. All turning on one point: cash. What would I pay for the portraits? "Four portraits in one," he claimed. Quite a joke. He reminded me of myself. Brash. Welsh. Off to India to make my fortune. I already had spent it all on the voyage over. "Move your hand more toward the lad, my Lordship. Let your Golconda ring sparkle. How much do you reckon it, my Lord Yale?" Of course I wouldn't tell him. "Would my Lord give me the ring instead of the wages for these four portraits?" "Worsdale, I've commissioned you to paint but one." "O no, my Lord. There is the portrait of your Lordship and the portrait of Master Yale and the portrait of Fort St. George and the portrait of the diamond that made all this possible." Crazy, this Worsdale, but not stupid. Would do well in the East, I thought. "Reckon as you wish. Do I care how you tally the parts, Worsdale—at sunset it's the total that I'll pay—as to a swap of my diamond for your wages, throw in a duke for my daughter's hand and we'll seal the contract immediately." On and on, Worsdale, an Irishman, repeated himself, badgering me with questions.

◆ SARAH PADAWER: Ask—My granddaughter Jerusha has asked Tal how she can get Fisher to ask her to wed. Fisher could not ask my son Reuben for his daughter's hand—for this is America. So Fisher has asked Tal how to ask Dosha, for Tal did not know it was America. He still lived in Antwerp before the War. And could not ask for his intended's hand.

Now Jerusha has wed in Jerusalem and as day follows moonlit night her daughter Ariel has wed Benjamin. Tal's question, the one he could not ask himself aloud, has been asked by his brother Tuviah's grandson.

What matter who asks a question: And in what generation, either by voice or by thought. As my dear Simha would tell me, over and over, as though my mind was like the fingers on my hand—as I held them up to the rain water pouring between them: *Come and see. The question is half the answer: without a question there is no reason for an answer.*

Now Benjamin's daughter Rachel, my granddaughter's granddaughter, herself an answer to Tal's unasked question, is answering this ten-year-old boy's question.

C H A P T E R   1 0

"WHITE elephant. You ask if a white elephant is real. It exists in India," said Rachel. She was in her early thirties, dressed in a simple white blouse and a no nonsense blue skirt.

"Where's that?" asked the ten-year-old boy, looking across the room, whose walls were covered with drawings and photographs of elephants. Alexander, Rachel's young student, kept looking for India.

"Is it over there?" he gestured with his whole hand, revealing his gnawed fingernails.

"No, as a matter of fact, it's over there," said Rachel, moving his hand toward the East, beyond Beersheva's new university district. "It's over there, beyond your home on King David Street, beyond Beersheva, beyond the sands of the Negev. We could go there together."

"Now?" Alexander blurted out.

"Well, I told your mother that I would walk home with you after our lesson so I don't think we can go to India just now."

"What are the prices of stones today at the Fort? What does a three carat rough, fine water, command in Amsterdam? Do only Jews trade on the bourse there?" Worsdale had a fine eye and when the young, "Master Yale" jumped at the word 'Jew,' Worsdale barked "Be still Master Yale, I see a bit of the Portuguese in you, or am I mistaken? Don't move a tick, Master Yale. I'm teasing with you." How much this Worsdale knew, I knew not. As soon as young Master Yale left the room, the Irish painter would ask me: "Who is this young Master Yale to you? I must know for this is how I will best paint the likness of the love you bear for him." "My heir," I answered laconically. "Your heir, my Lord, to all?" Worsdale had the impudence to ask. To all, to all I took from Madras. To all I spent my life working for. To all I have here, I mumbled to myself. But I knew as clear as the diamond buttons on my shoes what Worsdale was asking. Was Master Yale my son? My dead dear son David had perished and was buried on 25 January 1687. But three years old. Shall I speak of our darling Charles? With my eyes and Hieronyma's silken Portuguese skin, softer than any china shawl. Or shall I speak of David, my cousin from New Haven who might be my heir? For I have seen everything in Hindustan. Half the British dying. Young male babes perishing. De Paiva at the mines. Everything in Hindustan is possible. A son is everything. Daughters I have. Gifts to their lordships. All British, of course, who deign to accept my Welsh girls if wrapped in Indian gold. But one son buried in St. Mary's churchyard and one son half-Hebrew so who will call him my son? If all perish, by G-d, who will my Lord provide to keep my name alive and ever green? I have sat with Hindu merchants for a week and not said one syllable. If one has a treasure, one does not speak of it. A portrait painter is a merchant. I would speak of everything to Worsdale. "You ask, Mr. Worsdale, if a white elephant is real. It exists in Hindustan." I would talk of birds, of the heat of the day, of the garden's cool, of women, of the Muslims, of gold, of the Dutch three-mast warships. But of my heir, I had instructed him to neither smile, nor speak. Worsdale was a snake. Useful. To capture a moment. But still a merchant, and frail is the fabric that legacy rests upon.

◆ LOTTY JOANNA GUTWIRTH FISHER, FISHER'S MOTHER: When we finish the lesson—My father of Blessed Memory, Tuviah Gutman Gutwirth, once said when I asked him, "Can we go outside when we finish the lesson?" "Surely. We can even go now before we finish." "I was so happy. I could not have been more than eight." Barely able to read Hebrew backward or Flemish forward. It was all so confusing.

"You must do your homework under the supervision of your father. He must sign this, Mademoiselle Gutwirth, when you finish the lesson," my teacher Madame Jalou sternly instructed me. I was exhausted. As thick as my glasses were, I still could not see the page. I was crying and begged Papa to walk with me in the park. He held my hand as we walked through the garden paths opposite the Van Eyckelei. "The truth is, Scheindel, we never finish the lesson. Neither you nor I. You will finish mine, and your children's children, perhaps even their children will finish yours. Are not my students too my children? All students one's children. Do not all our children and all students build the world?" I understood my father and didn't understand. But from that evening onward, whenever I did my reading lesson—for the first time without tears, I felt another's hand on mine, a tiny hand—not of my blessed and blessing father but of a child soon to be born.

■ VIRGINIA WOOLF: Before I knew it, Monday passed—Before she knew it, Monday passed for Alexander's mother, Kurshid. For Alexander too, though he did not know it. For childhood is one long Sunday. For Rachel, the teacher, too.

"'Marriage, death, travel, friendship,' said Bernard. 'Town and country, children and all that, a many-sided substance cut out of this dark, many faceted flower. Let us stop for a moment, let us behold what we have made. Let it blaze against the yew trees. One life. There. It is over. Gone out...'"

Monday has turned to Tuesday and Tuesday is now Wednesday. Now a new mother's cookies. Newly baked by Alexander's granddaughter lay untouched by his great grandson. It is Friday.

What has happened? "It is so difficult to give an account of the person to whom things happen."

■ VAN GOGH: Could we go when we finish— We go together when we finish, to finish what we did not finish. Paul and I, just a start in a room 20 shoe lengths by twelve. One window for him and a window for me. "A start in the land of blue tones" speaking together all the time, debating, searching, quoting books we have read and are reading, even as we sleep. Separate rooms with my paintings lecturing him in his sleep and his paintings instructing me in mine.

He the Abbot, I the bonze. Before the end of the studio of the south. Before the start of Gauguin's studio of the tropics.

So short the school term:

Of course, when we finish we shall go together. For we will never finish, Paul and I. Father and I. Theo and I. Millet and I. Even that scoundrel Ingres and Paul.

This woman Rachel and her pupil, Alexander. Even my Rachel and I.

All together. A *weijving* of lovers. Of teachers. Of all who have lived. Even when finished.

"Could we go when we finish the lesson?"

"What will your mother think? She's expecting us for 'cookie-tea,' as she calls it."

Last fall when Alexander's mother, Kurshid, had brought her nine-year-old to school, she had come with two big boxes of cookies. "Not a bribe, Miss Rachel, G-d forbid, just an explanation. The reason I am two days late to apply for entrance for my youngest son Alexander, who can read but is very shy, is that I was baking cookies, and you know how it is with a family of six, four children, a husband who's the biggest baby, and myself."

"Before I knew it, Monday had passed, and here's Wednesday and I have the cookies, so doesn't it make sense to take my cookies, which are better than anything in Beersheva, certainly better than the Russian so-called cookie—'Why not simply put a cherry on a piece of butter and swallow it whole?' I asked Olga the other day, Russian so-called cookies—*pfuii.*" Kurshid held her nose. "Why don't you keep my cookies and my son?"

■ ELIHU YALE: Son—On January 23, 1712. He died. Charles. My son. Hieronyma too, more hers than mine she claimed, for Jews reckon by the mother. But I am not a Hebrew. So, still my son. My last son. David dead in Madras seemingly a century ago. Now all my world is lost. My fairest diamond. The picture, arm in arm with me, his right hand supporting my right. Nice touch by the painter—run off to Ireland I've heard—rogue Worsdale.

But what will any of my pictures do, though I had ten thousand of them? Or a Moghul's ransom of 10,000 diamonds of the finest water, each one a hundred carats or even Heironyma young again, in the garden house. There's a jest, for with son dead shall she come to me now? For she grieves too, our dream lost. Forever.

Damn all, the twenty-thousand I gave my eldest daughter when she married Dudley North. The Glenham fop stole my daughter and absconded with my purse.

Daniel dead, Sir John Chardin's brother, Sir Stephen Evans, I would feign kill. Bankrupt. Took more of my fortune than any one hundred Indian merchants.

Every boy in Christendom will not bring back my Charles, though when I sit in my pew in St. George's Chapel, off of Queen Square in London, for a moment, my boy, my Charles, seems alive.

What of my pledge to the Society for the Propagation of the Gospel? Have I not purchased a building for them? I twitted Hieronyma in a note—if I wed you in the Portuguese synagogue off Bevis Marks, will this wake our Charles?

And she, as full of cheek as under a Madras coverlet, replied, via her rascal neighbor, Mrs. Light, "That's your faith Elihu, not ours."

I left my golden seed to all. "To Christ Hospital in London 100 pounds. To St. Thomas Hospital another hundred." To Good Katherine Nicks, not as good as before, to my wicked wife, to David Yale, my godson, to Conneticote College, 500 pounds.

Cotton Mather has promised me Yale College will be better than "a name of sons and daughters."

That the good people of Yale "will make mention of me in their prayers unto the glorious Lord, as one who has loved their Nation and supported and strengthened the seminary from whence they expect the supply of all their synagogues." All of these benefactions, and all my pictures, all my houses. G-d knows all my substitute sons and daughters. All I would give back, if only G-d would restore my boy, my beloved Charles—and the moonlit night in the garden house with the Portuguese Hieronyma that launched it all.

Vincent Van Gogh, *Road with Cypress and Star.*   **199**

◆ ISAAC TAL, ABRAHAM TAL'S FATHER: How should I know?—Abraham, my son, from the moment we came to America on the boat from Portugal. Actually, on the boat itself, he never stopped asking: How could it happen? Why were we fleeing? Where was G-d? He wouldn't stop talking to his "bride" as he called her—Rachel Beller. Where was she? Why couldn't we take her? And her father, and on and on. Tuviah would talk to him and calm him for a moment, but never really for more than that. How should I know what to say to him? I am not a Rabbi. I'm not even an Abendana and certainly not an Abolais-Duarte. Should I send him to my wife? I'm sure Abraham asks her the same questions, but what can she reply?

Before the War, when he kept asking me questions of ritual. Could he marry a woman named Rachel as his mother had the same name and the Talmud—in his words—"prohibited it?" I asked him to speak to Rabbi Amiel. Then it was possible to reason with my son. Antwerp was Antwerp. Things were black and white. Simpler. Then came the War. Everything upside down. Crazy. For generations Lisbon was a place where our family was hounded. Tortured. Burned alive in Plaza Real. Not a place of safety, a point to flee to, a safe harbor, a stop along the serpentine path to America.

Here too in New York, everything was confused. With Abraham asking over and over: How could G-d allow it to happen? In 1954 he came to my home with a story and a simple weary statement. "Father now I understand." The story was written by a Lithuanian Yiddish writer, Chaim Grade, about two Yeshivah students. Both survive the War. One remains religious. One becomes a secular writer. An all night conversation between them in Paris. Abraham does not ask me if I'm tired. He simply starts to read the entire story aloud. The Orthodox Reb Hersh shouts: "*Your Enlighteners used to sing this tune, 'Be a Jew at home and a man in public. So you took off our traditional coat and shaved your beard and earlocks. Still, when you went out into the street, the Jew pursued you in your language, in your gestures, in every part of you....And the result was that the Jew left you, like an old father whose children don't treat him with respect; first he goes to the synagogue and then because he has no choice, to the home for the aged.'*" I remember the look my son gave me as he read this. How would I know what to say to him? But he continued to read the Rabbi's words: "*Still, not all of you secularists wanted to overthrow the yoke of the law Altogether. Some grumbled that Judaism kept on getting heavier all the time: Mishna on Bible, Gemorah on Mishna...commentaries on the commentaries. Lighten the weight a little, they said. But the more they lightened the burden, the heavier the remainder seemed.*" Of course it followed: "*A half-truth is no truth at all...suppose the Master of the World were to come to me and say, Hersh, you're only flesh and* blood.

It didn't matter, a schedule or no schedule, Rachel had realized from the day she graduated from the Children's Institute in Haifa and came down for an interview with Rivka, the Director.

Rivka had known her father in the army. "If you're half the person your dad is, you'll run the place within five years. Benjamin says you're three times as smart and three times as practical as he is, so you're hired." "When do I start?" Rachel had asked. "Now," Rivka said.

Rachel protested. She didn't know how to teach reading to dyslexic children. She had only taken one course in that field at the University. And where would she live?

"You'll live with my family until you find your own place," Rivka had answered with the promptness of an Israeli sergeant.

If she started today, who was to be her first pupil?

"How should I know?" Rivka shrugged her shoulders. "Whoever is seated there. Don't worry. The child is always the teacher. Just be sure to listen."

The hours had passed in an instant and the seven years in a day. Rachel loved her work, every part of it.

"*Six hundred and thirteen commandments are too many for you. I will lighten your burden...I would pray, Father of Mercy, I don't want my burden to be lightened. I want it to be made heavier.*

"*What point is there to the life of a fugitive? Of a Jew saved from the crematorium, if he isn't always ready to sacrifice his bit of a rescued life for the Torah...All Jews mourn the third of our people who died a martyr's death. But anyone with true feeling knows that it was not a third of the House of Israel that was destroyed but a third of himself, of his body, his soul. And you thought the world was becoming better. Your world has fallen. As for me, I have greater faith than ever.*"

Abraham, my son, was almost shouting these lines from the story. But then he grew quieter and he started to read the secular Jewish writer's response.

"*Reb Hersh,*" I finally said..."*We have been friends since the old days in the Yeshivah. I remember that I once lost the little velvet bag in which I kept my phylacteries. You didn't eat breakfast and you spent half a day looking for it, but you couldn't find it. I got another bag to hold my phylacteries, but you're still looking for the old one.*

"*Remember Reb. Hersh, that the text in my phylacteries is about the community of Israel. Don't think it's easy for us Jewish writers. It's hard, very hard. The same misfortune befell us all, but you have a ready answer while we have not silenced our doubts, and perhaps we never will be able to silence them. The only joy that's left to us is the joy of creation, and in all the travail of creation, we try to draw near to our people.*

"*Reb. Hersh, it's late. Let us take leave of each other.*" I remember like today the last words of the story: "*We are a remnant of those who were driven out. The wind uprooting us is dispersing us to all the corners of the earth. Who knows whether we shall ever meet again? May we both have the merit of meeting again in the future and seeing how it is with us. And may I then be as Jewish as I am now. Reb. Hersh, let us embrace each other.*" My son Tal walked toward me and embraced me. I was so tired, tired unto death. I went to sleep. Abraham never spoke or asked me about the War again. I don't know if he read the story to my wife Rachel, for that night she had not come home yet.

How could it be that the only real discussion of the War, of the horror of it all, the incomparable loss that we lived through, the tragedy and the miracle, all this could only be talked about by my son Abraham to me through the reading of a made up story? But how can it also be, that I did not know what to say to my son? All I could do was listen to him read to me.

◆ RACHEL ABENDANA TAL: Speak—When we survived the bombardment of Antwerp and escaped to Paris, even after we were in Vichy France—and in my opinion, it was more dangerous in Marseilles than on the road south through the French countryside—with the air filled with Luftwaffe bombers strafing the hundreds of thousands walking, crawling, driving along the roads but still you could look up to see the enemy if the sky, praise G-d, was clear. Then you were safe from them and if the sky was black with their planes, you prayed. But in Marseilles you didn't know who was who, who you could speak to. In any café in 1941 you didn't know who the enemy was, the collaborator, who would turn you in for a bundle of francs, which francs were counterfeit, who could save your life with forged papers. People changed sides. For people have hearts that can repent. Finally to escape from France and reach Lisboa with papers to sail to America on the *Serpa Pina*.

I remember it like today. Abraham sees our neighbor, the elderly David Abarabanel Dormido. A miracle. We had heard that David had been caught in Antwerp and sent to the East. But there he was slowly shuffling as he did each Saturday morning toward the Sephardic Synagogue, moving toward the gang plank of the ship, *Serpa Pina*.

Abraham rushed toward Don David: "What does it feel like, Don David Abarabanel, to be in Portugal?" The ancient Abarabanel must have at least 90. He smiled faintly and said, "This time or last?"

But Abraham persisted: "No, tell me what it feels like to escape from here. To America. To life."

Don David looked so elegant, so straight. He was always rail thin and spoke directly to my Abraham but all our ears, my husband's, Tuviah's too, could hear him. Even my sainted Uncle who was two years Abarabanel's senior, listened intently as Don David replied in Ladino evenly and with strength: "*Basta mi nombre que es Abravanel.*" It is enough that my name is Abravanel. Using the old Castilian form of his name.

How should I know how to answer my Abraham when he would ask me over and over again after the War: what I thought of it all, how we survived, did we still believe? He would ask me and every Sephardi. Each Ashkenasi. Each Rabbi. And each and every Jew who didn't believe. Or denied. Or didn't care. Each Gentile too. He would ask a version of that immense, unknowable, awesome question. He was a child who asked the same question over and over: "Why did G-d allow it to happen?" How should I know? We are Abendanas. Duartes-Abolais. Tals. Basta."

Then one day, he came to my house. It was in 1954. Just before Yom Kippur. He had a book of short stories in his hand. Jewish. Edited by an Ashkenasi Professor Howe. Abraham read me a story. For most of it he didn't look down, for he had read it so many times he had memorized it.

One man was an ultra religious Lithuanian Rabbi Hersh Rasseyner and the other was his boyhood friend and Yeshivah student, who had become a writer but secular. After the War, they meet and they talk all night. The secular Jewish writer who loves the Jewish people—philosophers, artists, all people of good faith, Jew or Gentile, speaks slowly: "*But you ask me what has changed for me since the destruction. And what has changed for you, Reb Hersh? You answer that your faith has been strengthened. I tell you openly that your answer is a paltry, whining answer. I don't accept it at all. You must ask G-d the old question about the righteous man who fares ill and the evil man who fares well—only multiplied for a million murdered children.*

After five years, she'd become the head of the Beersheva Nitzan, helping children with reading and writing problems. Of course, it had been somewhat stage-managed, for initially when Rivka retired early, Rachel had refused the position. She adored teaching, and bureaucratic politics weren't her cup of tea. But her husband, Yehoshua, had persisted. He could verbalize what she felt. "Whatever you want to do is fine, darling," he said over and over, but she knew what he really thought.

Rivka had called Rachel's father Benjamin to try to convince his daughter to become head of Nitzan.

"She's already raised heaps of money from Tel Aviv, from Antwerp, from America even—people trust her—you were so right, Benjamin. She's extraordinary. Speak to her." "I told you," said Benjamin. "She's three times smarter than I am. So it's your problem to convince her and Yehoshua." Benjamin got off the phone before Rivka knew what to say.

After hesitating for three months, and finally, after a visit from Ben Belfer, the Mayor of Beersheva, Rachel accepted. She was practical and lucky to boot, thought Rivka. A month later, the Battle of the Elephant began.

■ HUMAYUM: Husband—How did Rachel come to fulfill Rivkah's prediction?

First a good prediction is a blessing in itself. To be ruler of Hindustan, my father Babur predicted for me: the blessing ever before my eyes even when routed by Sher Sherkhan.

Bowing before the feet of the Ruler of the World: Shah Tahmasp. I grasped the hem of his garment and spoke of Babur's foretelling of my rule in Delhi. Even in the midst of the desert, my wife Hamida eight months pregnant, fleeing with me as I rode on a camel—I dreaming to rule Hindustan, and Hamida of a pomegranate.

Doth not G-d provide? Hamida: a pomegranate. Her husband on the plains of Panipat with 7,000 horses to move against Hussain.

More important than a pomegranate, even more important than seven times 7,000 horses: the birth of my son Akbar.

"*The pains of travail came upon Her Majesty and in that auspicious moment the unique pearl of the vice regency of G-d came forth in his glory.*"

Rachel has more than Rivka's blessed prediction—she is among the "*Ahl-I-murad, those who aspire, they include architects, painters, musicians and singers because they are the delight of the world.*" How much more shall we say of the teacher who teaches her pupils so that they too will be "*the delight*" of their world.

■ JAMES JOYCE: Told—Haven't I told you "*a deluge of times…*" says her father. I too, over and over, wrote: "*My dear Kitty told me today that she would dance in a deluge before ever she would starve in such an ark of salvation…dame nature, by the divine blessing, has implanted it in our heart and it has become a household word that il y a deux choses for which the innocence of our original garb…is the fittest nay, the only garment. The first, said she (and here my pretty philosopher, as I handed her to her tilbury, to fix my attention, gently tipped with her tongue the outer chamber of my ear), the first is a bath but at this point a bell tinkling in the hall cut short a discourse which promised so bravely for the enrichment of our store of knowledge.*"

I too would write, over and over, oxen in the sun, the color white, never finished really, the printers took it out of my hands, a Shandean tale, told again and again, stop me if you've heard it and I'll tell it yet again to your children's children always writing ever listening even when I cannot see.

"*If your faith is as strong as Job's, then you must have his courage to cry out to heaven: "Though He slay me, yet will I trust in Him: but I will argue my ways before Him!*" Abraham was crying when he read these words. But he could not stop reading: "*Reb Hersh, it's late, let us take leave of each other. Our paths are different, spiritually and practically. We are the remnant of those who were driven out…Reb Hersh, let us embrace each other.*" And from that day on, he has never asked of the War. But my poor, poor Abraham. By night he dreams he is the secular student at the Lithuanian Yeshivah writing a novel—and by day he daydreams he is Reb Hersh, blazing with religion with fervor, faith, through and through. Preaching to his young neighbors the future of Judaism, a message of G-d, to Dosha a message of humanity—both really a single song at the core. How should I know what to tell my son, my baby to give him peace?

■ LAURENCE STERNE: Squabble—I'll wager you more than two thousand pounds, an African or an Indian elephant. Weighing more than the good mayor, Aronovitz, Mr. Shernavi and the weight of all the children young Rachel teaches at Beit Lotty, I'd double the wager.

Enough for all, really, yet not sufficient for one. Aronovitz, the animal hotelier could have all of the ark's pairs and still begrudge Noah's setting loose a dove. Like my father he is.

"As many pictures have been given of my father…not one, or all of them, can ever help the reader to any preconception of how my father would think, speak, or act upon any untried occasion or occurrence of life…it baffled, sir, all calculations.

"The truth was, his road lay so very far on one side, from that wherein most men traveled, that every object before him presented a face and section of itself to his eye, altogether different from the plan and elevation of it was seen by the rest of mankind. In other words, 'twas a different object, and in course, was differently considered. This is the true reason that my dear Jenny and I, as well as all the world besides us, have eternal squabbles about nothing."

Because I could not understand my dear father, what sense can I make of these professors, all with betterment of the public on their minds, the Mayor, the zookeeper, the schoolmarm, all pulling this way and that on their poor stray elephant of the Indies. Abraham was able to make peace with Philistines but his descendants squabble where to bed the wondrous beast.

The squabble had started very simply. Mayor Belfer had been visited the Blecher family zoo in Beersheva when Aronovitz the Russian zoo keeper had approached the Mayor and said: "Are you setting up a children's zoo in Beersheva?"

"What are you talking about, Aronovitz?" asked Belfer. "Since the last election there's been a freeze on construction."

"Then why the Indian elephant request?" pressed Aronovitz.

"What request?"

"I was just told by Sherbani at the Beilonsohn Zoo in Tel Aviv that a request had come in from that place where they teach children to read—Nitzan—for an elephant, and they wanted to find out if there weren't a mistake, if it was my zoo that wanted the animal. I would dearly love an elephant, but the costs of building a structure are a problem. Indian elephants especially are a problem. I hope you're not going to give Nitzan a birthday gift that by all rights should come to me. The 2nd day of Hanukah, by the way, is actually my birthday!" he shouted with a self-satisfied, gold-toothed smile.

Belfer blanched. "Oh my G-d, I did see the papers," he thought. "I'll clear the matter up," he said quietly. Belfer raced off to Nitzan. That was what started it. Rachel was intransigent. The Mayor's office had signed the permission slip to board an elephant at Beit-Lotty-Nitzan for "educational purposes."

■ DAVID GARETH BIRNBAUM (Extraordinary Connoisseur): I did see—How is it that the mayor of Beersheva, knowing his constituency inside out, knowing the rivalry between the Russian emigrants and the rest of the population, the rivalry between Tel Aviv and Beersheva and finally the fact that Aronovitz's sister had married his wife's first cousin, how could he make such an error after seeing the import papers for the elephant?

Simple as looking at Blue and White. Percival David looked at the slender vase. At least once a day after he acquired it. He would ask each visitor. What do we see? Children would speak of the elephant heads with their piercing eyes and charming trunks. Scholars would read the inscription and marvel at the finest of the pair, one among millions of Jingdezhen. The French scholar Jacques de la Mêre quoted from memory the Jesuit Père d'Entrecolles who wrote of the factory town in 1712: *"The sight with which one is greeted on entering through one of the gorges consists of volumes of smoke and flame rising in different places, so as to define all the outlines of the town…the scene reminds one of a burning city."* And added, *"Of the thousands of blue and white I have seen, this one is the finest."* He ran his hand through the air following the blue serpentine, four-clawed dragon pursuing a fiery pearl through heavenly clouds.

Dealers, collectors, historians, children, all looked only at the blue. But Percival knew the secret lay in the white background. There one separates Yuan from Ming—masterpiece from garden variety.

The Mayor looks at the typed messages but he does not think of the background, the school for learning, the personality of its young new director, the mayor assumes that the more colorful personality is Aronovitz's zoo.

What is Percival gazing at? The elephant, his childhood dream animal, I might add, on his Yuan masterpieces, the earliest—the white tusks, of course. Background. Background.

■ Mu Xin: Happiness itself—What has brought to "Bunam" Belfer the Mayor of Beersheva, happiness itself?

Beersheva is his canvas. He has been painting it for years. The reelection he dreams of, even if he forgets it upon waking, is dependant upon his children's grandchildren's vote—their memory and regard of him.

"Why is it that some humans are Persians? Montesquieu asked this interesting question… what questions am I left with. I venture to view that happiness is so esoteric a body of knowledge that it virtually cannot be articulated. Besides, it is a trick that you can perfect only through trials and tribulations. From such examples as the facial make-up techniques of ancient Egyptians…the design and display of bedrooms in ancient Arabia, and the all too exquisite body language in ancient India, it seems that humanity has tried creating 'happiness' and manipulating it. Historians have put together such stories as certain 'Golden Ages' or 'prosperous periods,' but they have compiled no record of any specific 'happy individuals.' An individual who knows what happiness is, and is good at it, is a genius. The genius of happiness is not an innate genius but a product of deliberate cultivation. I may not be presenting my view in the most lucid manner here, but I do see clearly that such cultivated geniuses once existed in the world but never wrote anything like Methodologies on Happiness. They did leave behind though some mind-boggling cooking recipes, some bizarre stories of spirits and angels, and a few compassionate yet relentless axioms. The legacy from Epicurus seems quite humble, for he proposed 'friendship, discourse and gourmet foods' as the three ingredients of happiness. Can we find a specific case that embodies 'happiness' so that we can see it with our own eyes? Yes, we can, OK, we might ask: what does 'happiness' look like? Answer: It looks like a painting by Cézanne. Happiness is painted one brush stroke after another. Cézanne himself, his wife, they were not happy."

"Rachel," pleaded the Mayor. "I thought it was the zoo requesting the elephant, not a school. I signed, I signed, all right I signed, but I'll be the laughing stock of Beersheva. What are you going to do? Put the elephant in your lap and guide its trunk over the aleph-bet? Teach it to read in a year?"

"You signed. You agreed," said Rachel.

"But," said the Mayor slyly, "I didn't allocate any funds. You'll have to procure, feed and construct a dwelling for the elephant yourself."

"But the slip said, 'upkeep and board and site preparation funding to follow.'"

"Yes, to follow. The Messiah will enter Jerusalem on a donkey and I on an elephant to your Nitzan Institute on the self-same day." He stormed out of her office. "You'll raise the money. It shouldn't be a problem. You've got the elephant permit and your mother was American."

It took a year, but finally the Maharaja of Jodphur himself and the Maharani came to Nitzan. He came on horseback and she on a *howdah* perched on an elephant. Belfer beamed as he showed His Excellency, a Rajput, and descendant of Jodh Bai and Shah Jahan, around Rachel's Institute and, of course, around Beersheva. Happiness itself.

■ Emily Post: It took a year but the Maharaja and Maharani both came to Nitzan—Not an easy choice for what will His Highness, and for that matter, and even more important the Maharani wear? It does not surprise me that it took a year for the Maharaja and Maharani to come to Nitzan.

"The well-dressed man is always a paradox. He must look as though he gave his clothes no thought and as they grew on him like dog's fur, and yet he must be perfectly groomed. He must be closer-shaved and have his hair cut and his nails in good order (not too polished). His linen must always be immaculate. His clothes 'in press', his shoes perfectly 'done.' His brown shoes must shine like old mahogany, and his white buckskin must be whitened and polished like a prize bull terrier at a bench show. Ties and socks and handkerchief may go together but too perfect a match betrays an effort for 'effect' which is always bad."

The Maharaja and Maharani on horseback and on howdah have arrived. He is white linen. On his waistcoat, only the faintest of pink Indian diamond buttons betray any color in either of their dress.

Their outfits look so natural one would guess they lived directly next door to Rachel's institute, Beit Lotty. Royalty sparkles demurely half-way around the world from the Indies.

■ Mikhail Tal: Elephant—In 1960 in Leipzig Fischer determined to beat me, dreaming of a victory as his plane flew over the Atlantic. We ended in a draw. *"If I had lost, Bobby would have said I had played brilliantly."* A year later, on the shore of Bled, in the mountains of Slovenia, *"I lost practically without a struggle to Fischer. As a result of a 'castling' operation I had a difficult position by move 6 and a lost position by the 10th or 12th move."*

Some chess games take an hour, some a lifetime, some a thousand years. Rachel Tal has summoned an elephant from India. She knows the al'Adli's 9th century work on the history of chess: *"Elephants can get into all the squares without collision. But in the form of chess we have taken from the Persians, and which is played now, the Elephants have only half the board."* Her Indian chief will triumph over the Mayor's position. An elegant Tal solution.

Jan Vermeer, *The Art of Painting.*

HOPSCOTCH

a novel

HEAVEN

9
8
7
6
5
4
3
2
1

EARTH

Julio Cortázar

salter

■ JULIO CORTÁZAR: Come out of ancestral child-hood—They are playing together: Rachel, the Maharaja, the Maharani, inviting all the children in—and their parents too and grandparents across the continents, over the ages, ancestral hopscotch. "Hopscotch is played with a pebble that you move with the tip of your toe. The things you need: a sidewalk, a pebble, a toe and a pretty chalk drawing, preferably in colors. On top is Heaven, on the bottom is Earth. It's very hard to get the pebble up to Heaven, you almost always miscalculate and the stone goes off the drawing. But little by little you start to get the knack of how to jump over the different squares (spiral hopscotch, rectangular hopscotch, fantasy hopscotch, not played very often) and then one day you learn how to leave Earth and make the pebble climb up into Heaven, childhood is over all of a sudden and you're into novels, into the anguish of the senseless divine trajectory, into the speculation about another Heaven that you have to learn to reach, too. And since you have come out of childhood…you forget that in order to get to Heaven you have to have a pebble and a toe." Rachel and the Maharaja, they forget nothing. They both have an elephant's memory.

■ MARIO VARGAS LLOSA: Rachel Tal's father—Who is Rachel Tal's father? Surely not Benjamin Tal, the geologist, the discoverer of mystical sapphires in the desert, in the Holy Land.

Is not Fisher the novelist who has created Rachel Tal so that she might teach children to read, eventually to read the book of books: the novel.

The "communicating vessels" of Cortázar and Fisher. "Hopscotch is a novel that takes place, as you may recall, in two settings, Paris and Buenos Aires, between which it is possible to establish a certain chronology….At the beginning of the book, there is an author's note suggesting two different possible readings: one (let's call it the traditional one) begins with the first chapter and proceeds in the usual order; the other skips from chapter to chapter. The third [section of the book] (expendable chapters) is not made up of episodes created by Cortázar or narrated by his narrators. It consists of texts and quotations from other sources…without a direct plot relationship to the story…They are pieces of a collage that, in its communicating vessel relationship with the novelistic episodes, is intended to add a new dimension—a dimension we might call mystic or literary, an extra rhetorical level, to the story of Hopscotch."

Cortázar's vessel is holding Fisher, or is it that all vessels are held inside of one All-Seeing, All-Embracing vessel—whose walls we can only sense in our greatest moments of feelings? Or are all these vessels, shattered, interpenetrated, each searching for its former primeval structure?

When asked at the opening dinner why His Highness had gifted the animal, the Maharaja smiled and answered, "The Director of the Institute, Rachel Tal, reminded me in a letter of certain ancient links between my house and the people of Israel, the Abendana family. Even of a long-dead martyr Sarmad. Rachel Tal's father, and especially her mother Ariel Fisher have informed her of India, of the Rajputs and our heritage in Moghul times. Even her grandmother Dosha studied Moghul art at Radcliffe. Amazing, what Rachel knows. It is not the habit of my family to forget a kindness even one centuries past. We never come out of our ancestral childhood."

As an aside, he leaned across the Mayor and stared directly at Yehoshua and Rachel. "We are both desert people. You from the Sinai, I from Rajasthan. Only our minds in future generations will irrigate our parched soil. Besides, how often does a Jew ask a Hindu descended from a Muslim for an elephant?"

But the evening paper, the Beersheva Star, was less ecstatic. "Indian Metsiah! New immigrant children who don't know where to start a Hebrew sentence, from the right or from the left, get a present: an Indian elephant!"

The article went on about the current economic crisis, shortage of classrooms, overcrowding of classes and now an elephant to compete with the dyslexic children for space in Beit Lotty.

■ HAROLD BLOOM (Genius): reminded me in a letter—Rachel Tal reminds the Maharaja of Jodhpur in a letter of the history of the people of Israel. How does she remind herself? Through memory and interpretation. "What Jewish writing has to interpret finally, and however indirectly, is the Hebrew bible, since that always has been the function of Jewish writing or rather its burden: how to open the Bible to one's own suffering."

What does Rachel remember? What she teaches: the alphabet. Where should she begin with the unlettered Maharaja, with the letter Bet—her house and her father's house. In the beginning. Did not G-d look into the Torah and create the world? Still quite a tall order for such a young woman. But she is her father's child. The child is always the teacher. Tell her, Rivka. Her father knows the secrets of the sephirot, and of sapphires he found in Yerucham, of the blue of the Abolais and Abendana family ring. The blue of Venice, of even more ancient linkages.

She has interpreted the text of Sarmad to join her Abendana diamond past through Sarmad to the House of Jodhpur.

She is both Kafka and Freud to the Maharaja. "But what about [Kafka and Freud] is Jewish? I think that finally their Jewishness consists in their obsession with interpretation…all Jewish writing tends to be outrageously interpretive…the power sought over the text is then always the same: he seeks the blessing, so that his name will not be scattered, so that more life will be granted him into a time without boundaries…Kafka makes himself uninterpretable, Freud by insisting that everything is meaningful, and can be interpreted, sets the other polarity of Jewish writing."

Rachel zoharically quoting but the first Holy Letter equates the Sinai desert and Rajasthan. "I set before you a blessing and a curse: therefore choose life."

A springtime Passover, an ever green emerald rebirth, watered by knowledge.

■ VERMEER: Beginning—In the beginning, from the very beginning, Maraika would ask me questions. What did she look like? What was I thinking? Where had my people come from? Was she so different than me? Was it true what her brother said of me? That my grandmother was from Portugal. She would not even in Delft mention the word Jew. None of these questions could I answer. For all had one answer: the light above her head shimmering. The light I could see in the darkness in my obscure camera. The soft light just above her eyelids. What could I do but stand amazed under the dark sheets of my camera. My arms and hands and lips reaching for that ever so soft spot—a light just above her eye-lids, the point of light that I could see only through the pinhole of my camera. My cousin Diego Duarte's gift to me, through his postman Huygens—G-d's gift really—for the entire universe in the beginning just a point of light. It can be felt by all of us only in the darkness, or seen, never directly only through His reflection. Eternal.

■ HERSHEL TSCHORTKOWER: Six hundred children—Not simple at all. Rachel and her six hundred children. Like my Shamas Anshel Moses Rothschild. "In a bigger city you will have a greater opportunity to succeed in business and help others. Go and may G-d bless you and your children for all generations," I told him. "*These are the generations of Noah, a just righteous man of his generation.*"

Why does the Bible speak of Noah as a just, righteous man when it is about to describe his offspring?

Rashi tells us: the good deeds the righteous do live after them. And what of Edmund de Rothschild—the Ha-Nadiv Ha-Yadua (the well-known benefactor). "*Without me,*" he told Weitzman, "*the Zionists could have done nothing but without the Zionists, my work would have been dead.*"

The vineyards from parched soil. Wine from dead earth. Vegetables from swamp lands. The first kindergarten in the Holy Land. What should his portion be? His child James Rothschild: recruiting Jewish soldiers in the Yishuv for the Royal Fusiliers toward the end of the Great War. Edmond de Rothschild expressed his "*great joy at seeing his heir carrying on his great work, to which he was completely devoted.*"

But what shall we say of Edmund's childless child? James and his beautiful Pinto Bride, Dorothy. They living in Uncle Ferdinand's Waddeston manor, larger than the Frankfort ghetto itself. Certainly bigger than Tchordkov.

Shall we not count the Cedar boys, German-Jewish refugees from Frankfurt with their guardians Mr. and Mrs. Hugo Steinhart, ransomed from the evil one's camp in Buchenwald. These children saved and educated in the village school near the manor or the grammar school of Aylesburg. Are these not the true children of Dorothy and James? Their good deeds?

Has not G-d blessed my Shamas Anshel Moses' children's children for all generations!

■ DAVID LLOYD GEORGE, Prime Minister of England: Jew…Christian…American—Rachel, a grandchild of a Jew saved by an aristocratic American Christian from the State Department. Rachel is now in the Holy Land. Her grandfather, a Yale man, not Welsh like the Welshman Elihu Yale nor Welsh like my wife Margaret Owen, though Elihu Yale and my dear Margaret, paler than any earthly pearl, were related, descendants of Prince Owen of Gwynedd. "*It is the small nations that have been chosen for great things.*" Yale saved a host of Christians and was he not saved by a Portuguese Jew? More than a wife and a mother, Hieronyma was. I too did vouchsafe Palestine to the Jewish people. I told Asquith: "*a country the size of Wales much of it barren and part of it waterless was a promising territory to plant about three or four million European Jews.*" The Welsh saved the English. The English saved the Jews. The Jews save us all. "*And in thy seed, Abraham shall all the nations of the earth be blessed.*" "*Bydded—so be it.*" A circle of blessing round and round through the millenia of all our lives.

"Whose brilliance is this? The educators, the Mayor's office, or our beleaguered, under-supported zoo-master, late of St. Petersburg, soon to retire to Rishon-le-Zion. To the Maharani and Maharaja of Jodphur we say Come in peace, and Leave in peace, preferably as you both came high on your horse or perched on your elephant."

And leave they did, but stay did Taj, a 2604 lb., two-year-old elephant.

The very next day, after the photo of the elephant, the Mayor, and the entire staff of Nitzan appeared on the front page of the Beersheva Star, more than six hundred children from two to seventeen years old stood in front of Nitzan.

Normally, the school opened at 7 o'clock precisely and remained open until 8 o'clock to fit the regular public school schedule.

Any student in the Beersheva system—Jew, Muslim, Christian, atheist, Jerusalem-Syndromed American coming down from a religious ecstatic experience—all were given a diagnostic examination. Fees were moderate though difficult for the average Beersheva resident because industry hadn't developed as quickly as in the north. But somehow, no one who applied was turned away.

■ HARRY BINGHAM IV: Jew…Christian…American….examination—She was extraordinary, standing on the line outside with child as pregnant as my wife Rose. French Jews, Jewish refugees from all parts of Europe were on lines stretching around the block of the American consulate in Marseilles.

Official documents and papers in their shaking hands. If they didn't have guarantees from saviors in America, we were told to firmly deny them entrance papers.

If they miraculously had guarantees— and but one in a hundred had— we were told to scrutinize the papers and in all cases assume the papers were false, or the people were impostors or something was awry. Evasion and delay. Washington was quite clear:

"*This government does not repeat not contenance any activities by American citizens desiring to evade the laws of the governments with which this country maintains friendly relations.*"

There she was, a woman in her early 30s, very pregnant, with large brown eyes, shy and direct, not more than five feet tall, like my Mother.

The State Department: Jew or Christian, check her paper. Conduct an examination. To me, she was my pregnant mother. I could see her son coming. She would hold his hand. He: I. When I was eight on 8 June 1911. Father pulling away by boat on the Yale Peruvian Expedition, Machu Picchu or bust! All Mother or I could do was to wave. Should I swim to Father. Hiram III. Me, wee IV. Or should I stay and protect Mother?

I could hear the woman's voice. Lotty was her first name. I remember her question always: "Why do you think it will be a boy?" I peered down at her. "Oh, my father Hiram Bingham III and my mother Alfreda had so many sons, after me," of course a girl would be a great blessing too.

I didn't say "One Yale man is coming," but that's what I thought.

Then to calm her, but more to calm my own nerves, day after day, each one of these Jews, thousands, deathly quiet, waiting all night on lines, we had to move from the center of Marseilles to the outskirts. "So what will your son be in America?" I asked her. I can't remember her last name but Lotty Joanna I do remember.

She replied with a gracious smile, the smile my grandmother had in the photographs of her from Hawaii. "I'd like him to be you."

I suppose they did escape. The papers his American brother had arranged were airtight. I added they were important political figures —nice touch. But had they not had me that day, had they seen another officer, I wouldn't vouch for them escaping from Vichy France, much less arriving in America.

But what of all the other thousands and thousands, hundreds of thousands, that were bullied, denied papers, tricked, cajoled and eventually slaughtered. All those who couldn't "be me." Even I, could I be me? When I was Hiram Bingham IV? But Lord, I tried. How I did try.

Tuesday.

Dearest,

I feel certain that I am going
mad again: I feel we cant go
through another of those terrible times.
And I shant recover this time. I begin
to hear voices, & cant concentrate.
So I am doing what seems the best
thing to do. You have given me
the greatest possible happiness. You
have been in every way all that anyone
could be. I dont think two
people could have been happier till
this terrible disease came. I cant
fight it any longer, I know that I am
spoiling your life, that without me you
could work. And you will I know.
You see I cant even write this properly. I
cant read. What I want to say is that
I owe all the happiness of my life to you.
You have been entirely patient with me &
incredibly good. I want to say that—
everybody knows it. If anybody could

■ WILLIAM FAULKNER: Past—"The past isn't dead, it isn't even past." At the University of Virginia, on April 27, 1957, at an undergraduate course in American fiction, an undergraduate stood up, with a moustache just like mine, and just about the same height but more slender. An unlit pipe was cupped in his right hand and a blue and white tie that I favored, with a checked tweed jacket to boot. I thought time was spinning backward, I forty years before.

"Question, Mr. Faulkner," he asked. "In The Sound and the Fury, can you tell me exactly why some of that is written in italics? What does that denote?" A. "Yes, sir. I had to use some method to indicate this idiot in Sound and Fury had no sense of time. That what happened to him ten years ago was just yesterday. The way I wanted to do it was to use different colored inks, but that would have cost too much, the publisher couldn't undertake it."

I the teacher, and the young man the student. Who is the teacher here, Rachel? Or is it her father Benjamin? He discovering the sapphire source that explained the riddle of Tal's blue ring that Tal received from his mother's family, the Abendana-Abolais-Duartes, and backward still into the past.

Or is Rachel the student of her grandmother Dosha who studied with Tal and taught her beau and husband to write his heart's desire: a novel?

Was her lesson plan all about Tal's lost Rachel or about Dosha the teacher explaining with a lover's persistence and a courtesan's charm that Fisher can write and should write and will write, with italics, with different color inks, that the publisher will undertake to bring to light, books of just yesterday's painted words of the past that isn't dead, that isn't even past.

■ F. SCOTT FITZGERALD: Rachel could often hear echoes of the past—Her father's child. Her grandfather's student. For what was Fisher dreaming of: what I, he and every other novelist dreams of: to write for "the youth of his own generation, the critics of the next, and the schoolmasters ever afterward."

"I was a national figure in a way." "Just like my Tom Buchanan, one of the chosen who reach such an acute limited excellence at twenty-one that everything afterward savours of anti-climax." But I was also my own Gatsby: "Trying to repeat the past." "Can't repeat the past I cried incredulously." Why of course I would. Myself: a pendulum swinging wildly between Nick and Tom. Touching upon Gatsby, always dreaming of Daisy, really Ginerva King, my 16-year-old Chicago debutante, beautiful, unattainable, St. Barbara of the Tower. I silent, still, sober and observing—in a corner of the ballroom of our lives: a writer, Nick Carraway.

Rachel can hear the echoes of the past. Fisher's attained his Barbara, my ever-fugitive as a moonbeam Daisy. I too. "I am half feminine at least my mind is....Even my feminine characters are feminine Scott Fitzgeralds."

"So we beat on, boats against the current, borne back ceaselessly into the past."

Rachel could often hear the echoes of past arguments between father and mother over the heads of the child:

"It's the school's fault. No one taught me how to read. You just learn. There's nothing wrong with our son."

The Russian Jews would say in Russian: "Everyone reads, no problem. Here everything is a problem. Right to left. Hebrew makes no sense."

If the father was Iranian, it was always: "In Isphahan, my Rabbi put the book in my hand and even if five of us shared one book, we all read."

On and on: "Wait till next year, Yigal will improve. We just came to Israel." "Deborah may be slow now but next year, next year we will have money. Why should we pay double taxes for special education?"

It was always the fathers who would complain that the children were stunned by Hebrew. Not only the changes in script but the direction in which the sentences were written.

The children's faces were different but their hands were the same, fingernails bitten, and calloused index fingers. They all had a dazed look from lack of sleep.

■ VIRGINIA WOOLF: Rachel could often hear the past—Her past. Her grandfather Raphael Fisher's writing a trilogy, inspired by her grandmother's white on white paintings, though one could see the shimmering blue with just a hint of a green overglaze like Ming colors dancing on the surface of a blue-white vase. A painting by her grandmother now hanging in her tiny kitchen. How can you keep it there? her father Benjamin always thought. But he knew that Rachel knew far better than he where the painting was destined to live.

Rachel could hear the past just as Fisher could see the future or her grandmother could do both—hear and see, write and paint pictures.

"The strength of these pictures but sight was always then so much mixed with sound that picture is not the right word. The strength anyhow of these impressions [of my childhood] makes me again digress. I can reach a state where I seem to be watching things happen as if I were there...Is it not possible, I often wonder, that things we have felt with great intensity have an existence independent of our minds; are in fact still in existence. And if so, will it not be possible, in time, that some device will be invented by which we can tap them?...Instead of remembering here a scene and there a sound, I shall fit a plug into the wall; and listen to the past. I shall turn up August 1890. I feel that strong emotion must leave its trace; and it is only a question of discovering how we can get ourselves again attached to it, so that we shall be able to live our lives from the start."

■ JAMES JOYCE: Echoes of the past—Arthur Powers, my Irish friend, though Nora and all saints tried to save me from him, Arthur Power could not hear the music of Proust's echoes of his past. "Proust," he said grandly, "lacks the necessary restraint that every artist should have and, as a pampered and over-delicate man himself, he luxuriated in his hobby and could not decide when to stop."

"It was not experimentation," I corrected him, Jesuit to Jesuit. "His innovations were necessary to express modern life as he saw it. As life changes, the style it expresses it must change also....A living style should be like a river which takes the colour and texture from the different regions through which it flows. Proust's style conveys that almost imperceptible but relentless erosion of time, which is the motive of his work."

With me Monsieur was brief. At a literary dinner party he asked me: "Do you like truffles?"

"Yes," I replied. "I am very fond of truffles." Rather brief, would you not agree?

Rachel, too, hears the echoes of the past. A fine sketch of her grandmother Dosha she is, swimming in her grandfather Fisher's Talmudic river.

◆ SIMHA PADAWER, DOSHA'S GRAND-
FATHER: Do not know what is going
on—In Slonim, Reb. Weinberg each
year before Yom Kippur's end would
tell the following story:

"Once at the close of Yom Kippur
the moon was nowhere to be seen. By
means of his holy spirit, the Baal Shem
Tov saw that if Israel were to fail this
duty on the close of Yom Kippur, they
would lose by it, G-d forbid. He
became very sad at this thought, and
tried by exercise his powers of concentration to make the moon come out,
and asked many times whether the
moon had come out yet. But the sky
was clouded over and there was no
hope that the moon would come out
that night. However, the Hasidim of
the Baal Shem Tov, may their merit
shield us, did not know what was
going on. Because it was their custom
to have a holiday at the close of Yom
Kippur, having left the House of Prayer
in peace at the end of the service (for
the service of their master, the Baal
Shem Tov, was actually like the service
of the High Priest) it so happened that
the Hasidim were very happy that
night as well, and danced with a holy
enthusiasm. At first they danced by
themselves; at last in the greatness of
their holy enthusiasm they pressed
into the room of the Baal Shem Tov
and danced and rejoiced before him.
When their enthusiasm became over-
powering, they dared to beg the Baal
Shem Tov to dance with them. So they
took him into the middle, and he too
danced with them. They were still
dancing when suddenly someone
called: 'The moon is out!' At once they
ran out to bless the new moon.

"The Baal Shem Tov said: 'What I
could not do by the exercise of my
powers of concentration, the Hasidim
did with their joy.'"

The truth is here too. Even the parents do not know what is going on and
how serious their problem really is.
Blessed be G-d that my grandchild's
grandchild, Rachel, has opened the
hearts of the children to dance about
her in great joy, bringing, please G-d,
the great redemption.

Rachel told her assistant Batya that
only students with doctor's or teacher's
notes would be allowed into the inner
courtyard for a diagnostic examination.

After a half hour, Batya returned
laughing and said, "Why is this
morning different from other mornings? On all other mornings the parents claim their children are shy
and have a minor reading problem.
On this morning, all children claim
their parents do not know what is
going on and how serious their
reading problem really is."

Faced with a crowd of people,
Rachel announced over the loud
speaker system, "For the next two
weeks, only those students with a
signed slip from a teacher will be
admitted for testing."

Then, with a familiar Tal touch,
she added, "And all students who
absolutely must see an elephant can
take the Number 2 bus from *Kikar
Ha Malhut* to Tel Aviv where mother, father and baby elephants can be
seen. They are African, however,
not Indian as here in Beit Lotty."

The children continued to come,
swelling the waiting lines all the
way down to Balfour Street.

Rachel had her assistants Edo and
Enam construct a circular track in
the inner school courtyard which
all the rooms faced. During classes,
the children could see the elephant
slowly circle the track, its right leg
just an inch away from the wall.

■ JULIUS MEYER: See—I went into Hanscom Park that spring morning in
1909 to see son. He had come all the way from Oklahoma. He would not
meet me in my home at Mrs. Adler's or even at my brother Moritz's cigar
store. "Only a place that was green," he wrote me gravely. I thought of
Hanscom Park and wrote him back: "Before the sun is highest, I'll smoke a
pipe with you and we can talk of old times, your father, Standing Bear,
before Oklahoma."

As soon as I entered the park, I could see. He was as tall as his father,
the same determined jaw. I walked to him and handed him a cigar I had
gotten in Moritz's. His eyes met mine as we both lit up. I reached into my
pocket and counted out twenty silver dollars
and handed them to Lone Eagle. I could see
him stiffen but I said: "Oklahoma is not
Nebraska. Your father saved my life," and I
pushed the coins into his pocket and he did
not refuse.

It was strange but he did not say much. I
spoke to him of my friend Spotted Tail, of his
murder and how Spotted Tail's son killed his
father's murderer. Indian kills Indian. Not a
White Man's problem. It was I who did the talking. I spoke to him of Spotted Tail, of his murder and how Spotted Tail's son killed his father's
murderer. Indian kills Indian. Not a White Man's
problem. "Why have you come," I asked him in
Pawnee. "To see you." "To talk?" "No. To see. To
look at you. To see you as my father has told
me of you. Now that I have seen you, I will
leave." "Don't leave. Your father saved my life. I
spent my nights and days of my youth with the
Pawnee. I can save you. I have heard the boarding school the whites built for your people was
burned five years ago. Now the Pawnee children are in the White Man's school. You have
nothing in Oklahoma. Bring your family here to
Omaha. We will save you." "It is too late, Box-
Ka-Re-Sha-Hash-Ta-Ka. I must save myself."

Out he walked, as straight as his father.
When he reached the park's edge, he turned
and waved. I returned the signal and shouted in
Pawnee. "May the sun ever rise on your
teepee."

And then, I saw the eyes of death. A
Southerner, by the look of him, maybe a Texan,
walking toward me slowly. His breath stank of
liquor. "What are you? An Injun or White, old
man?" he asked. "What are you, a man?" I countered for one should never show fear, Chief
Standing Bear always taught me. "I'll show you,
you half breed. Who was that young Injun? Give
your own some of that money," he snarled. "You're not my own now, before
or ever," I shouted. I reached for my revolver which I always hid inside my
coat but the Southerner leaped on my screaming, "I'll show you, you
damned old Injun. The best Injun is a dead Injun, especially one who kills
himself." Before I knew it, I was pinned against the park bench, my pistol in
his hand. In the blast of white light, I saw Standing Bear's face. Stern, all knowing, but unable to save me yet one last time.

215

倪迂作畫如
天駿騰空
白雲出岫
無半点塵
俗氣余以
暇日寫此

◆ SARAH PADAWER, DOSHA'S GRANDMOTHER: Told Rachel—This Maharaja is telling my granddaughter's granddaughter about his elephant. Like I would have a cat in Slonim or my *unmensch* daughter-in-law would have that poodle which had a hairdresser every month that costs more than any new dress I would buy for Jerusha. "Don't spoil my Dosha. I have to live with her," her mother would scold me. And I knew that she meant she had to live with my granddaughter after I died. But if she had said those words, G-d forbid, I don't know what I would have told her.

Was she the mother anyway? Who told more to Jerusha, I and my dear Simha, or her in between her rallies and marches and phone calls that never ended, her phone that never stopped ringing and the second phone that only she could use. Simha would tell me what we had to do was give love to Jerusha's mother because she was starving for love. Just like he was a mother and a father to me after my parents died, so Simha was a mother and father to our Jerusha and even to her mother if she would have let him. But she didn't. Simha always said G-d alone knows if we can't be a mother and father to her here and now we can be a mother and father in the next world.

Simha would laugh: "Even at the *Tish*—the table of Maimonides where G-d willing I'll be studying Torah and Talmud with you too dear Sarah. Still we'll have the time for our dear Jerusha and her mother. Whether she wants us or not, we'll be their teachers."

"You're not Dosha's teacher," my daughter-in-law once shouted. "She has her own memes."

"What's a meme?" I asked her.

Looking puffed up like the biggest professor in the world, she said, "Mrs. Padawer, a meme is a pattern of behavior that is considered to be passed from one individual to another by non-genetic means, especially, imitation. School lessons, not old wives tales, Mrs. Padawer."

So what should I tell Mrs. Know-It-All? How can I explain my Father's coming to me in my dreams in the forest of Belorusse. How can I speak of the feelings Simha has that his Rebbe, Rabbi Weinberg, never leaves his side. How can I speak of an almost whisper that I can hear of past times and the certainty that I will always be with my Jerusha and she with her grandchild and that the Rachel that I can see is teaching others not her children. Being a parent is a nothing. Drying a child's eyes is everything. It's so simple—either you can't understand or you forget it. G-d and all of us are forever and everywhere. We are all, thank G-d, each other's teachers.

The Maharaja of Jodphur had told Rachel that in his palace the elephant would skirt a wall to his right, and always move in a counter-clockwise path.

"Always?" asked Rachel.

"Well, I suppose if there were an earthquake, but if there is one just drop me or my descendants a line and we'll replace the animal. Remember, the House of Jodphur never forgets its friends."

Rachel had Edo and Enam paint a thin white line on the wall next to where the elephant would start his walk. Students could mount a staircase and ride on the elephant counter-clockwise around the circle. But only half way. On the other side, a thick red line extended down the side of the wall. After reaching that line, the elephant would be led slowly along the wall back to the white line where another student could mount him, each student never more than once a week. Edo and Enam both remembered each and every rider. Even the time when the delegation came from Argentina, the same group that paid for the modernization and extension of the Beit Lotty original structure. They could only visit on Saturday, but Rachel was firm. The elephant deserved a day off. If they wanted to see Taj, then Sunday or Friday it had to be. And, G-d be praised, Friday afternoon the Argentines turned up.

■ SHITAO: Paints a thin white line—Who is the teacher here Rachel or Edo and Enam? Rachel is the teacher but Edo the master—for he is the painter of the white line on the wall.

Which painter is Edo emulating? Ni Tsan, as he paints the thin white line? Simplicity itself. A slender tree perched on the front of the wall. One can imagine bamboo and rock jutting out at the view. A splendid background for this elephant from the land beyond the middle kingdom. But surely Edo is not hoping to copy Ni Zan for "*The paintings by Master Ni are like waves on the sandy beach, or streams between stones which roll and flow and issue by their own force. Their air of supreme refinement and purity is so cold that it overawes man. Painters of later times have imitated only the dry and thinnest parts, and consequently their copies have no far-reaching spirit.*"

Does Edo paint in the style of my cousin prince, Chu Ta? That is it. For Edo draws as both a painter and calligrapher: Fish and Rocks. "*He begins with the overhanging rock and chrysanthemums in big swinging strokes and accompanied by a poem which refers to the overhanging and the color as related to clouds in the sky.*"

Who is Edo not copying? Me. He knows that I know to copy the ancients is folly. One must "*show the soul instead of just the appearance of the object…one should look between likeness and unlikeness.*"

In the end, it is all one: Painting and Calligraphy. Feeling and Seeing. Writing and Reading.

■ BADA SHANREN: Rachel had Edo and Enam paint a thin white line—Why does the Chan Master, Rachel, for that is what she is, need two: Edo and Enam to paint a thin white line. Would not one of them suffice?

One can never paint. Only two: the ancient one and the painter of today. My eyes saw the scroll but Ni Zan moved my brush: "*Ni Zan painted like a celestial steed bounding the void or white clouds emerging from a ridge, showing not a speck of vulgarity. I drew this painting—landscape after Ni Zan in my spare time.*"

Mater Rachel is teaching her pupils. In her spare time she is teaching Edo and Enam.

■ HIERONYMA DE PAIVA: You're a big boy. I want you to ride on a big elephant—Over and over Elihu would ask me: "Hieronyma, sing me the song again." I would lift him above me— even in the heat of Indies—lift his shoulders up with him still inside me, sweat streaming down his temples: "You're a big boy Elihu. I want you to ride on a big elephant."

As a two-year-old he would cry—when his father left him with his mother in America to return to Cromwell's England. Elihu would laugh as a man of twenty when he came to the Fort to make his fortune—his eyes would dart suspiciously deep in their sockets, as a man of forty cuckholding his wife plump Mrs. Hynmers. Over and over we would play the elephant game. Even in the Fort itself where Virtue, his massive but cuddly elephant, and Victory, his never docile but mind-reading elephant gift to me, could not enter. Gossip enough it was we kept "our pets" in the stables by the garden house by the river.

And laugh we did when Charles was born. How Elihu would hold the boy aloft in out-stretched arms repeating the first part of a nighttime and daytime dream chanting: "You're a big boy."

But one does not forget the wedding of one's youth. Never did Jacques's face disappear from my eyes, not in India, not even when I returned to be near Elihu in London. For Elihu was my link with diamond India and India my last fraying, slender connection to Jacques. Never did I forget the ghost of the face of our big boy Charles. I knew my Lord Yale's answer before Mrs. Light's return. My Lord could not come to my quarters because London was not India. His relations: the Duke of Devonshire Lord James Cavendish, the Society for the Propagation of the Gospels, the Hoare Bank, the governors of the East India Company, were they not all about and around the streets of London?

In India it could be my elephant who perished last and his mount, Virtue, first. This time too it would be my Lord who would perish first. I didn't need Mrs. Light to tell me Elihu's response. If I go to him, it will not be India. If he comes to me, it will be our India. Yet again. Even at our age, ever spring. Even. For we both knew of that one clear moment when he was a big boy riding on the whitest, brightest elephant in the world.

● Maraika Abolais, Vermeer's painting model: Body—In the beginning Johannes would scamper back and forth next to me in the darkness of his camera, "my obscura," he would call it. In the beginning I was afraid to ask what I looked like under the camera cover and then one day he let me look at him— broad around the middle, silent, frozen, but fuzzy and shimmering, a soft circle around his head. "You melt. You do," I said to myself more than to him. "Around the edges. Do I too?" "Yes," he said breathing heavily. And he lifted the curtain and touched the soft edges of my body and I too smoothed with my tongue all of the planes of him—reaching the light that hovered in the darkness just above his eyes— carressing him all over with my hands and heart.

"Let's start the lesson, Alexander," said Rachel. "I'm going to put a piece of paper in front of you. You are going to write in Hebrew: "Alexander is the name of a big boy."

Rachel took a blue ball point pen out of her pocket and laid it in the middle of the page.

Alexander's features froze. His body turned to the right, then to the left. He picked up the pen, totally confused, hoping for a hint.

Rachel tried to open his fist to remove the pen, but he wouldn't unclench his fingers. Tears were running down his face. "I'll never get this. I hate you!" he screamed.

Rachel lifted his hand and kissed it. Alexander dropped the pen on the floor.

"Alexander, you're a big boy. I want you to ride on a big elephant. Come with me."

"Really? Now?"

Taj was eating Indian peanuts from a big bucket held by Edo when Rachel shouted: "A big customer wants to ride Taj!" She walked over to Taj. His right flank was almost brushing against the torqued wall in front of his tusk, obscuring the white line.

■ ELIHU YALE: You're a big boy. I want you to ride on a big elephant.—Land locked. Far from the water in London. And dying too. In comes Mrs. Light herself, half dead, with a message from my heart's heart Hieronyma. "It is the first day of Spring, 1721, by your count Lord Yale. What doth Lord Yale require of me? To come to your quarters in the still of night. Shall I bring the ghost of our son—'fashionable, virtuous, ever elegant, loved by all.'" I am reading this horrible letter, and damn her soul, Mrs. Light is whispering the message, Hieronyma has committed the message to Mrs. Light's memory—and the old harpy is bowing while chanting: "ever elegant, loved by all."

I came to your quarters in the garden house, even in the Fort itself. I left our Bonnie Charles's grave in Capetown to come to your quarters in Queen's Square in London. All I have I left in the East, my child, my fortune, my buried fevered Golconda explorer, Jacques, my husband who died in my arms, and you Lord Yale, surrounded by your treasures, your plate, your silver snuff boxes, your firearms, your mathematical instruments. Your unsold Chardin Rough, the gems you withheld from Rachel Levy Duarte, your worthless Devonshire relatives, your wicked wife, Elihu, you're still and ever a big boy. I want you to ride on a big elephant. Directly to me. To lie by my side forever."

■ MOSES CORDOVERO (1522-1570): White— The teacher is the engraver and the student the engraving. Direct light and reflected light is the beginning and the Queen the infinite, the child the spark and all are shining colors.

"In the beginning of the word of the king the concentrated spark engraved engraving in the supernal luster so that emerged from within the concealed of the concealed, the beginning of the infinite, a vaporous mass fixed in a ring; not white....blue or green, or any color at all. When the measure extended, it produced colors shining within. Within the spark there gushed a spring from which the colors were formed below. The concealed of the concealed, the mystery of the Infinite, broke and did not break through its aura. It was not known at all, until from the force of its penetration, one high and hidden point shown, the supernal concealed one. Beyond this point nothing is known at all. Therefore, it is called Reishit, the first command of all."

Photograph of Virginia Woolf.

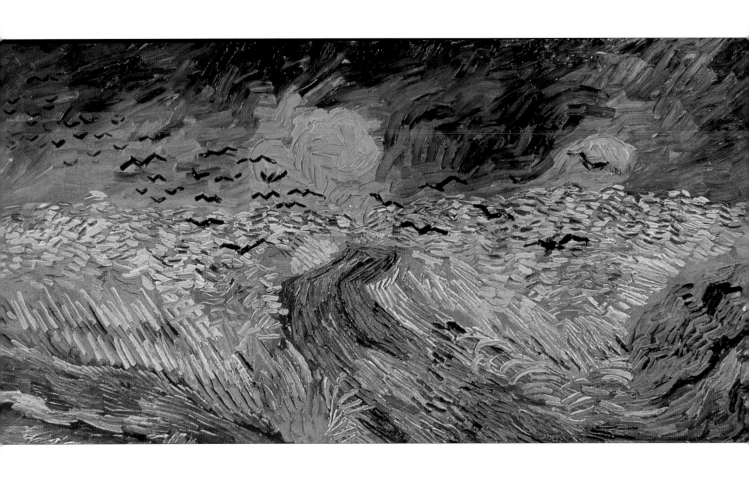

■ VAN GOGH: Where do we start…From the white…where do we end—Alexander, a pupil, is asking his teacher. She, his only teacher. Thus may not he be Alexander the Great. Himself taught only by Aristotle. Rachel is asking Alexander where do we end? For is not the finest teacher one who learns from the pupil? We, all students, searching for the right teacher who will echo what we already know. We start from the white. For there we are tending. All of us: A children's story being read by G-d. Our ends begin our story yet again. From heaven it seems white. Down Jacob's blue ladder until we are reborn in the soft green earth. *I tried to express the terrible passions of humanity by means of red and green.* Transported and transmuted via Cain's blood red, my night café. Slowly we are transported…grace of: a teacher. A child. A lover. A Bible. A novel even. All into a celestial blue. A blue that we all can reach but an arm's stretch away. Even on our death bed we can touch it—Overall: an encasing *background of the richest intense blue.* For what have I been all my life but a simple illustrator of a child's book—an arbitrary colorist. *I exaggerate the fairness of the hair, I come even to orange tones, chromes, and pale lemon yellow. Beyond the head, instead of painting the banal wall of the mean room, I paint infinity, I make a plain background of the richest intense blue that I can contrive, and by the simple combination of the bright head against the rich blue background, I get a mysterious effect, like a star in the depth of an azure sky.* Green, blue, and then, again and again, all of us fashioned into the brightest eternal stars of white in the heaven of G-d's mind.

■ BLACK ELK: Body—*"It does not matter where the body of Crazy Horse lies, for it is grass; but where his spirit is, it will be good to be."*

Vincent Van Gogh, *Wheat Fields Under Stormy Skies.*

"Where do we start?" asked Alexander.

"From the white," Rachel answered and Edo echoed immediately.

"Where do we end, Edo?"

"At the red," he trumpeted.

"At the red we stop." Rachel helped Alexander mount the ladder and sit on Taj. "Where do we start? From the white," said Edo as he led Alexander around the circle.

Alexander giggled. He felt taller than Rachel, taller than his mother and even taller than his father. He could see into the classroom on the second floor. One of the students waved at him. Suddenly, he felt the elephant stop. "Where do we stop? The red." The elephant's body had reached the end of the semicircle.

Alexander hurried down the ladder and Rachel took his hand and led him back to the classroom. She sat him down at his desk and placed another pen directly in the middle of the page. "Write your name in Hebrew. Write: 'Alexander is a big boy.'"

Alexander looked at the pen, uncertain how to begin. Where do we start? Where do we end? Suddenly Alexander saw where Rachel had put her index finger: on the white space on the right side of the page. And where do we end, Rachel kept repeating, touching the long red line down the left-hand side of the page.

■ ELIHU YALE: Elephant—Damn Hieronyma. Double damn Mrs. Light, waiting for my reply with pen and paper before me. "Ink is cheap. Paper is cheap," Chardin would tell me. "Only diamonds are dear," Paiva's relatives would write by way of Salvador to Hieronyma and then to me. What did my Portuguese know of elephants when she came as a bride still on her honeymoon holding her soon to be dead husband's rose cut diamond earrings in her hands? Diamonds she knew—they all knew—the Sephardim, the Huguenots—they had diamonds in their blood. But I knew one thing all of them did not know. The sound of an elephant approaching. The love of an elephant for water. My pet: Virtue, two thousand pounds, almost white *"rumbling raising its head, flapping its ears, spinning around, urinating,"* exiled beyond measure as my birthday gift of an elephant—Victory—the elephant I gave to Hieronyma for her royal, personal pleasure when first she came to the garden house. Wily Mather wrote me on 14th February 1718: *"There are those in these parts of Western India who have the satisfaction to know something of what you have done and gained in the eastern and they take delight in the story."*

I could not believe my eyes. The British East India Company called me crooked. Pitt swindled me. Stephens and Evance fair bankrupted me. To the English, I was Welsh. To the Welsh, I was Indian. To the Hindu, I was Muslim. To all the Fort, I was a Huguenot, or worse, a Jew. To my wicked wife, I was an adulterer. To London, a Nabob to be fleeced. To Mrs. Nicks, I was a lover of Hieronyma and to Hieronyma, I was a shadow of her lost Portuguese jewel Jacques De Paiva. And each and every one had to be paid, supported, maintained, flattered, catered to, frightened, terrified, cajoled, shouted and whispered to. All forgot me a week after payday—except Hieronyma. How our elephants would compliment each other when I on mine, would saunter down the path whistling while she calmly waiting upon her mammoth toy, Victory.

And now my lady bids me come to her lodging. Elihu, you're a big boy. I want you to ride on a big elephant. What can I do but weep? I am a man of 73. I whisper to Mrs. Light: "Tell your mistress. Surely my lady remembers that my white elephant Virtue perished in India the month before I left. As did my lady's Mount Victory a week before I sailed from the Fort. If I could approach my lady, I would. G-d I would. Dear G-d I would. But I can't. Had she ever witnessed such excitement. In London, in her natal Antwerp, even in the Portugal of her dreams. What was I to her? A port of refuge, a curse upon her brother, a poisoned pen letter to the house of Levy Duarte that neither rescued nor abandoned her. What was I to any of them? My Welsh neighbor peering through my window while I counted my Indies wages. Or the pious Chardins who roared with laughter at the Catholic French kings, and would not hesitate to grovel before the Moghul lords. Nor the Americans who reviled my church and its bishops—who railed against my mad grandmother—Puritans they claimed to be but jailers they were—only releasing her when Governor Eaton died in New Haven. Now they would build a pyramid of learning in New Haven and call it, for a pretty price, Yale College they tell me: *"And it would be better for me than a name of sons and daughters."*

■ MAGGID OF DUBNO: Mother—When a child is born, a mother looks at the child and says, "Someday this child will be someone special."

When that child grows up and has a child, the mother of that child looks at the child and says, "This child will be someone very special." And that child grows up too and has a child. Each mother, child after child, looks at the child with the same eyes. How I have prayed to G-d to see this final child.

■ ISAAC LURIA: Start—Rachel is the light lit by generations before her. The holy Zohar teaches: "*The blue in the tzitzit represents justice; the white represents mercy. When is man ready to start to read the Shema, and to receive the Kingdom of Heaven? When he can distinguish between blue and whtie, between justice and mercy.*"

■ BOB BERMAN, Astronomer: Blue....white—Why does the potential world-conquering Alexander begin his name with blue? For like each and everyone of us, from the white-capped Arctic to the green-blue Caribbean have as "*the most common element in our bodies hydrogen—comprising (two-thirds of each bit of water). The bulk of all of us dates from 380,000 years after the big bang. We started with a blue star…our common origins transcend even the most exalted individual's family tree. Each act is a confirmation that the unknown blue sun's death did not pass quite without consequence. We are made of stardust.*"

Why does Alexander's teacher speak of white? "*Because of the non-hydrogen body stuff spent billions of years in the interiors of distinct stars before finding its way here. The elements, heavier than iron, which were neither created in the big bang nor forged inside the stars came from a super nova explosion. Since only massive stars can explode and since massive stars are always white.*" Rachel can say with certainty that we all start with white.

■ LAURENCE STERNE: The two of them crossed …talking talking—"*Pray, sir, in all the reading which you have ever read did you ever read such a book—…don't answer me rashly—because many I know, quote the book, who have not read it and many have read it who understand it not.*"

Much in Master Fisher's book conceived by Dosha, though the work is of his hands, the two of them crisscrossing though the Americas, the mind of Europe, talking, talking through the pictures they have seen. Talking, talking through moonless nights ever lit by Indian gems, Fisher and Tristram:

"*Accounts to reconcile*
Anecdotes to pick up:
Inscriptions to make out:
Stories to weave in:
Traditions to sift:
Personages to call upon:
Panegyricks to paste up at
This door."

Until the day. "*When Death himself knocked at the door—ye bad him come again; and in so gay a tone of careless indifference, did ye do it, that he doubted of his commission…then by heaven! I will lead him a dance he little thinks of…*"

Tristram and Fisher, Dosha and my Eliza, round and round, a pasquinade forever.

Alexander finally understood. Shaking, he began to scrawl his name in big blue letters. His name alone filled an entire line from right to left.

Rachel jumped up and hugged him. "What a big name for a big boy who's made such a good, big start. Let's go home and get some cookies from Mama."

The two of them crossed Ben Gurion Park opposite the school, along the unused railroad tracks, talking of Alexander's older sisters, the other school children, his teacher Dov Noy and how surprised he'd be to see Alexander write, and how they'd go to India, Rachel and he, and buy another elephant just for Alexander and his sisters if they would stop teasing him. Suddenly, Rachel heard Alexander's mother's voice:

"I'm over here. Come in for tea cookies, please."

Seeing his mother, Alexander leapt into her arms. "Mama, I can write my Hebrew name."

"What a big boy you are," said his mother. "How did you learn?"

Looking at Rachel, Alexander shouted out to his mother: "First you start at the white."

■ VIRGINIA WOOLF: Mother—"*The mind is certainly a very mysterious organ, I reflected…about which nothing whatever is known, though we depend upon it so completely. Why do I feel that there are sentences and oppositions in the mind, as there are strains from obvious causes on the body. What does one mean by 'the unity of the mind' I pondered, for clearly the mind has so great a power of concentrating at any point at any moment that it seems to have no single state of being. It can separate itself from the people in the street, for example, and think of itself as apart from them, at an upper window looking down on them or it can think with other people spontaneously…It can think back through its fathers or through its mothers.*"

Rachel thinking back through her mother's father and through her mother's mother too—far back, even through Julius Meyer and the plains of America, and forward too, far far forward. Toward the greatest ever expanding unity.

■ SITTING BULL, THE HUNKPAPA: Children— "*When I was a boy, the Sioux owned the world. The sun rose and set on their land; they sent ten thousand men to battle. Where are the warriors today? Who slew them? Where are our lands? Who owns them? What white man can say I ever stole his land or a penny of his money? Yet they say I am a thief. What white woman, however lonely, was ever captive or insulted by me? Yet they say I am a bad Indian. What white man has ever seen me drunk? Who has ever come to me hungry and left me unfed? Who has ever seen me beat my wives or abuse my children? What law have I broken? Is it wrong for me to love my own? Is it wicked for me because my skin is red? Because I am Sioux? Because I was born where my father lived? Because I would die for my people and my country?*"

Now a new boy is growing tall and strong. He is different from me and from my children's children. "*If the Great Spirit had desired me to be a white man He would have made me so in the first place…Each man is good in the sight of the Great Spirit. It is not necessary for eagles to be crows. Let us all put our minds together and see what kind of life we can make for our children.*"

■ VERMEER: White—Blue is a color I can remember when I was three years old. We had visited my grandmother's house in the Hague. The kitchen faced the garden by the river. I was thirsty. I came into the kitchen in the middle of the night. But it wasn't the middle of the night. It was morning. Grandmother was very old. She had lifted a pitcher of milk and was pouring it into a flat silver tray to soak the bread for egg bread. Before I could ask for milk, she had ladled out a beakerfull for me. Her right hand was extended and I came over to the window to reach for the beaker. I took the cold metal beaker in my hands when, suddenly, her face turned blue. I burst out crying and dropped the beaker on the floor. The milk, running over my feet and onto the floor, was blue. "It's blue, you're blue," I cried. Grandmother gathered me into her apron and whispered, "It's the light of The Hague. Everything looks blue in the morning here, my little darling." She gave me another cup of milk and heated it. I sat in my room with her and drank it, and it turned back to white.

Jan Vermeer, *The Kitchen Maid.*

NOTES

Page 1

Virginia Woolf: Malcolm Bradbury, ed., *The Atlas of Literature* (London: De Agostini Editions, 1996), p. 181.

Jacques (Jacob) de Paiva: See Benjamin Zucker, *Blue* (New York: Overlook Press, 2000), p. 231. De Paiva, a Sephardic Jewish diamond merchant, traveled to Fort St. George (Madras) in 1684 with his wife Hieronyma de Paiva. He took ill at the Golconda diamond mines and died in 1687. His Sephardic widow Hieronyma subsequently lived with Elihu Yale and bore a child, Charles Almanza, with Yale.

Joseph Salvador: The brother of Francis Salvador (Jacob Salvador) who operated a diamond polishing plant in Amsterdam. His older brother, Abraham Salvador, married Rachel Duarte, a daughter of Manuel Levy Duarte (1631–1714), an Amsterdam merchant-jeweler who was part of the diamond syndicate that funded Hieronyma de Paiva's purchases of rough diamonds in India. Hieronyma, after the death of her husband Jacques de Paiva, purchased diamonds with another Salvador brother, Isaac Salvador (alias Salvador Rodrigues). See: Edgar Samuel, *Manuel Levy Duarte, 1631-1714: An Amsterdam Merchant Jeweler and His Trade With London* (Jewish Historical Society of England, Transaction xxv11, p. 21).

Van Gogh: Bernard Denvir, *Vincent: A Complete Portrait* (Philadelphia: Running Press, 1994), p. 51, 52, 82.

Richard Mühlberger, *The Unseen Van Gogh* (Cobb, California: First Glance Books, 1998), p. 24.

Crazy Horse (1841–1877): Tashunca-uite. Military leader of the Oglala Sioux. He fought under Chief Red Cloud in the Fetterman massacre 1866, and against the American forts in Wyoming 1867 and 1868. Attacked by General Crook in 1876, after he was ordered by the War Department to return to the Indian reservations and refused, Crazy Horse inflicted heavy losses on Crook. On June 25, 1876 Crazy Horse, under the leadership of Sitting Bull (a Hunkpapa Sioux) routed and killed General Custer. Crazy Horse continued to fight the United States Army. (Although Sitting Bull retreated to Canada). In 1877, Crazy Horse surrendered—the last of the important chiefs to do so."

In Sept. 5, 1877, Crazy Horse was arrested at Fort Robinson. When it was clear to him that he was being led to the guard house, he fought back and with his arms held by a fellow Indian, was killed by a soldier's bayonet.

Crazy Horse, more than any other Indian Chief, rejected any accommodation with non-Native American people: "…you are taking my land from me: you are killing off our game. So it is hard for us to live. Now you tell us to work for a living…we do not interfere with you, and again you say, why do you not become civilized? We do not want your civilization! We would live as our fathers did, and their fathers before them." Howard R. Lamar, ed., *The New Encyclopedia of the West* (New Haven: Yale University Press, 1998), p. 270.

Lee Miller, ed., *From the Heart* (New York: Alfred A. Knopf, 1995), p. 351.

James S. Cassidy, Jr., *Through Indian Eyes* (New York: Reader's Digest, 1995), p. 318.

Chief Joseph: Lee Miller, editor and narrator, *From the Heart: Voices of the American Indian* (New York: Alfred A. Knopf, 1995), p. XIII.

Page 3

Laurence Sterne: David Thompson, *Wild Excursions* (New York: McGraw Hill, 1972), pp. 7, 9.

Photo of Virginia Woolf: "It's more like Virginia in its way than anything else of her," said Leonard Woolf to Richard Shone. "The featureless but slightly modeled face, though in part a result of Bell's increasing avoidance of detail in her work, also suggests Woolf's impatience with being scrutinized and her elusive mobility of expression." Richard Shone, *The Art of Bloomsbury* (Princeton, N.J.: Princeton University Press, 1999), p. 99.

Simha Padawer: Talmud Yoma, 73.

George Orwell: David Thompson, *Wild Excursions: The Life and Fictions of Laurence Sterne* (New York, McGraw Hill, 1972), p. 135. Quoting George Orwell to F.J. Warburg May 16, 1949. Sonia Orwell and Ian Angus, eds., *Collected Essays, Journals and Letters*, pp. 562-563.

Virginia Woolf: Virginia Woolf, *The Waves* (London: Hogarth Press, 1931), p. 202.

Laurence Sterne: *Tristram Shandy* (New York: W.W. Norton, 1980), Book II, Chapter 12.

Page 5

Elihu Yale: Sir John Chardin and his brother Daniel were Huguenot diamond traders, partners of Elihu Yale in Fort St. George (Madras) in the late 17th century. See Benjamin Zucker, *Green* (New York: Overlook Press, 2002), p. 233.

Hieronyma de Paiva: Jacques de Paiva's widow, eventually became Elihu Yale's business associate and lover. See Hiram Bingham, *Elihu Yale: The American Nabob of Queen Square* (New York: Dodd Mead and Co., 1939), pp. 198, 238 and Edgar Samuel, *Manuel Levy Duarte 1631-1714: An Amsterdam Merchant Jeweler and His Trade With London* (London: Jewish Historical Society of England) pp. XXVII, 22.

Shitao (1642–1707): Shitao, a noted Chinese painter, was a descendant (like Bada Shanren, his distant cousin) of a Ming prince. Zehng Xie (1693–1765) described Shitao's painting: "Shitao excelled in ten thousand sorts of paintings; his orchids and bamboo were just an afterthought…Shitao's methods of painting have a thousand transformations and ten thousand changes; he could be extraordinarily strange and hoarily ancient, and then delicately elegant and proper. Compared to Bada Shanren, he certainly went further; there was nothing he couldn't do. Yet Bada's reputation fills the world, while

Shitao's is restricted to Yangzhou. Why? Bada only used a short-hand method, whereas Shitao's methods are intricate and luxuriant. Only that one name, which makes him easy to remember, but Shitao's names are endless….It's just confusing." See my remarkable friend and teacher Jonathan Hay's extraordinary study *Shitao: Painting and Modernity in Early Qing China* (Cambridge, England: Cambridge University Press, 2001), p. 2.

Tao-Chi: James Cahill, *Fantastics and Eccentrics in Chinese Painting* (New York: Asian Society, 1967), p. 82.

James Cahill, *Chinese Painting* (New York: Rizzoli, 1977), p. 176.

Bada Shanren (1626–1705): He was born into a branch of the Ming family. After the Ming dynasty fell in 1644, he fled into a Buddhist monastery. Like his father and grandfather, Bada Shanren was a painter and calligrapher. After 30 years he left monastery and entered the world. Both inside and outside the monastery, Bada Shanren had fits of madness—either feigned or genuine—and long periods of dumbness. His attempt at a happy marriage was unsuccessful. "I was looking for a harmonious marriage, but unfortunately I met Lady Dong, so I am still without a home."

Although he never met his distant cousin, the painter Shitao, the two collaborated on several scroll paintings and works of calligraphy (posted to each other through friends). Both artists dealt with personal loss and immense political and historical upheaval and displacement in a haunting and most profound manner.

Maggid: A guide who tells you a mystical truth in your sleep.

Tecumseh: John Gugdem, *Tecumseh* (New York: Henry Holt, 1997), p. 310, 311.

Page 7
Meshugeneh: Yiddish—A crazy person.

Rabbi Meir: Psalm 90:3.

Elisha ben Abuya (2nd century C.E.): One of the great Jewish scholars of his day but later became an apostate. He was called in the Talmud *Aher* "another person." Rabbi Meir transmitted his teachings. Elisha is quoted as saying: "Learning in youth is like writing with ink on clean paper, but learning in old age is like writing with ink on blotted paper." "It is said that Elisha saw a son heed his father's injunction to go up on a ladder and took care to drive away the mother bird before taking the nestlings. The son thus fulfilled two injunctions of the bible—honoring parents, Exodus 20:12, and sparing the mother bird, Deuteronomy 22:12, Elisha saw the son descend the ladder and fall down, dead. This flagrant denial of the doctrine of reward and punishment caused Elisha's apostosy. Encyclopedia Judaica, Vol. XIV, p. 135; Vol. VI, pp. 668-669 (New York, Israel: Macmillan Company, 1971).

Van Gogh: Kodera Tsukasa, Yvette Rosenberg, eds., *The Mythology of Vincent Van Gogh* (Philadelphia: John Benjamin's North America, 1993), p. 167.

Yiddishe Kallah: Bride.

Page 9
Sitting Bull: See Benjamin Zucker, *Blue*, p. 235. Benjamin Zucker, *Green*, p. 228. Meyer was a Jewish trader who settled in Nebraska in 1866. He spoke six Indian tongues and was given a Pawnee tribal name: Curly-Headed-White Chief-Who-Speaks-With-One-Tongue. He led a party of Indians to the Paris exhibition of 1889.

Tumler: Yiddish—a person who frolics, "stirring the pot" with his personality.

Van Gogh: Bernard Denvir, *Vincent: The Complete Self-Portraits* (Philadelphia: Running Press, 1994), p. 48.

Isaac Luria: See Benjamin Zucker, *Blue*, p. 226. A noted Kabbalist in Safed who taught a devout mystical circle of people doctrines of creation, the shrinking of G-d to make room for the world, the divine sparks emanating from the presence of G-d, and the doctrine of *Tikkun*, the restoration of the world. *Encyclopedia Judaica*, Vol. XI, p. 578. Lawrence Fine, *Safed Spirituality: Rules of Mystical Piety, the Beginning of Wisdom* (New York, Paulist Press, 1984), pp. 66, 67.

Gauguin: Bradley Collins, *Van Gogh and Gauguin: Electric Arguments and Utopian Dreams* (Cambridge, Ma.: Westview Press, 2001), p. 40. Douglas W. Druik and Peter Kort Zegers, *Van Gogh and Gauguin: The Studio of the South* (Chicago: Art Institute of Chicago and Thames & Hudson, 2001), p. 25.

Coffee: Ralph S. Hattox, *Coffee and Coffeehouses* (Seattle: University of Washington Press: 1985), pp. 14-15. Abu al-Qadir al-Jaziri was an early writer on coffee who visited Mecca often in the 16th century and quotes from jurists who ruled on the permisability of drinking coffee. Hattox, p. 31.

Page 11
Isaac Luria: Leviticus 19:18.

Albert Camus: Herbert Lottman, *Albert Camus in New York* (Corte Madera, California: Gingko Press, 1997), pp. 9, 27.

Marcel Proust: Jean-Bernard Vaudin, Anne Borrel and Alain Senderens, *Dining with Proust* (New York, Random House, 1992), p. 118.

Percival Lowell: Leon Jaroff, *New York Times*, "What Lowell Really Saw When He Watched Venus." In 1911, Percival Lowell claimed Mars had intelligent life.

Page 13
Isaac Tal: S.Y. Agnon, *Days of Awe* (New York: Schoken Books, 1965). p. 121.

Gauguin: Douglas W. Druik and Peter Kort Zegers, *Van Gogh and Gauguin: The Studio of the South*, p. 111.

Mikhail Tal: Dmitry Plisetsky and Sergey Voronsky, *Russians vs. Fischer* (New York: Chess World, 1994), p. 62.

Tigran Petrosyan: Ibid, p. 69.

Paul Morphy (1837–1884): A child prodigy who learned chess at 10. He defeated Hungarian master Johann Löwenthal. Murphy was known for playing with lightening speed and willingness to sacrifice material provided he gained position to help him as well as spectacular king hunts. He left for Europe at 21 and was widely considered the greatest player in the world—other than Howard Staunton. Staunton refused to play Morphy—declaring the "best players in Europe are not chess professionals and have other more serious advocations."

Morphy returned to America and "issued a challenge to the world that he would spot anyone a pawn for a match in the world's championship. No one accepted and Morphy consequently proclaimed himself champion." Morphy had to wait for a year (until he became of legal age) to practice as a lawyer in Louisiana and played most of his chess game in 1857 and 1858. After 1861, he developed an aversion to the game. Eventually he descended into madness and died in poverty: In 1964, Bobby Fischer declared: "Morphy was perhaps the most accurate player who ever lived. He had a complete sight of the board and never blundered, in spite of the fact that he played quite rapidly, rarely taking more than five minutes to decide a move." Chris Ward, *The Genius of Paul Morphy* (London: Cadogan Chess, 1997), pp. 8-9. Frank Brady, *Bobby Fisher: Profile of a Prodigy* (New York: Dover Publications, 1985), p. 71.

Page 15
Delmore Schwartz: James Atlas, *Delmore Schwartz* (New York: Farrar, Straus & Giroux, 1977), pp. 195, 199.

Semir Zeki: Semir Zeki, *A Vision of the Brain* (Oxford: Blackwell Scientific, 1993) and Semir Zeki, *Inner Vision* (Oxford: Oxford University Press, 2000), p. 4.

Chu Ta: Sherman Lee, *The Colors of Ink* (New York: Asia Society, 1974), pp. 45, 117.
Gauguin: Druik and Zegers, Van Gogh and Gauguin, pp. 151, 268.

Vincent van Gogh: Vincent van Gogh, *The Complete Letters of Vincent Van Gogh* (Greenwich, Conn.: New York Graphic Society, 1959), p. 21. And Bruce Bernard, ed., *Vincent by Himself* (Boston: Little Brown, 1985), p. 17.

Page 17
Emily Post: Emily Post, *Etiquette* (New York: Funk & Wagnalls Co., 1922), pp. 299, 302.

Page 19
Shul Klopfer: A person whose job it was in the shtetl to knock on each household door in the morning, summoning the people to awaken and go to the synagogue to pray.

Shul: synagogue.

Tzeddakah box: A charity box in a synagogue. "Even a poor man living on charity should give charity." (Talmud, Gittin).

Mesillat Yesharim: "The Path of the Just." See Benjamin Zucker, *Blue*, p. 226. Moses Hayyim Luzzato (1707–1746) wrote this ethical guide in Padua, Italy, to teach one how to avoid sin and attain holiness. He stressed Torah Study and having faith in the sages. "To what may we compare this? To a maze, an entertainment designed by kings....Anyone walking along the paths has no way of knowing whether he is on the right path or on a false one, for they are all alike, and to the eye, there is no difference between them....The one who is standing in the tower can see all the paths and he can distinguish between the true and the false, and so he can direct the walkers as to which way to go. Whoever is willing to believe him will reach his destination, but someone who does not want to listen to him, but would rather follow his own judgement, will certainly stay lost and never reach it. The same is true in our case. A person who has not yet gained control of his yetser [inclination, natural instinct] is as if he is walking along the paths without being able to distinguish between them. Those who have mastered their yetzer are like those who have already reached the tower...and can see all the paths clearly in front of them. They [the sages] can offer advice to those who are willing to listen, and it is them we must trust." Moses Hayyim Luzzato, Mesillat Yesharim, English translation Shraga Silverstein (New York: Feldheim Publications, 1974), Chapter 3. Avraham Yaakov Finkel, *The Great Torah Commentators* (Northvale, New Jersey: Jason Aronson Press, 1996), p. 134.

Pessach: Passover.

Hassoner: Wedding.

Hometz: Unleavened bread not to be eaten on Passover.

Sedarim: Plural for Seder.

Chol Hamoed: Intermediate days of Passover.

Hershel Tschortkower: Hanoch Teller, *Courtrooms of the Mind* (New York: New York City Publishing Company, 1987), pp. 203-212. (Heard from Rabbi Hillel David) Copyright 1987 by Hanoch Teller Rechov Yahoyariv 4/7, Arzei Habira, Jerusalem 97354, Israel and Feldheim Publishers 200 Airport Executive Park, Spring Valley, NY 10977. These are marvelously told tales, full of morality and vitality.

Page 21
Rachel Beller: Abraham Tal's girlfriend. See *Blue*, p. 1; *Green*, p. 215.

Henri Peyre: Professor of French Literature at Yale in 1962.

Marcel Proust: William C. Carter, *Marcel Proust* (New Haven: Yale University Press, 2000), p. 633.
Virginia Woolf: Virginia Woolf, *A Room of One's Own* (New York: Harcourt Brace Jovanovich, 1989), p. 4

Delmore Schwartz: Elizabeth Pollet, ed. *Portrait of Delmore* (New York: Farrar, Straus & Giroux, 1966), p. 327.

Page 23
Bob Dylan: Copyright Ram's Horn Music, 1973, renewed 2001. And: Steve Matteo, *Dylan* (New York: Metro Books Friedman/Fairfax Publishers, 1988), p. 74.

Marcel Proust: Marcel Proust, *Remembrance of Things Past* (New York: Random House, 1961). C.K. Scott Moncrieff and Terence Kilmartin, pp. 402, 420, 421.

Swift Bear: George E. Hyde, *Red Cloud's Folk: A History of the Oglala Sioux Indians* (Norman, Oklahoma: University of Oklahoma Press, 1975), pp. 137, 138.

Mikhail Tal: Harold V. Ribalow and Meir Z. Ribalow, *The Great Jewish Chess Champions* (New York: Hippocrene Books, 1986), p. 88.

Page 25
Bokhara: A rug.

Isaac Luria: Laurence Fine, ed., *Safed Spirituality*, p. 67.

Herman Melville: Herman Melville, *Moby-Dick* (New York: W.W. Norton, 1967), pp. 163-171.

Delmore Schwartz: James Atlas, *Delmore Schwartz*, pp. 339, 345.

Elizabeth Pollet: Elizabeth Pollet was Delmore Schwartz's second wife. A shy woman, she was "frightened by the emotional violence he practiced." On June 10, 1949 they married. Schwartz said, "I got married the second time in a way that, when a murder is committed, crackpots turn up at the police station to confess the crime." (Ibid, p. 278). By 1964, Delmore was psychotically deranged on the subject of his ex-wife. "7.22.64. It is now seven years to the day since my wife, Elizabeth Pollet, left me suddenly at the Hotel St. George in Brooklyn.

The man for whom she left me—after many preparations over a period of two years designed to conceal the real motives of her actions—was Nelson Rockefeller. His great wealth, his status as a married man, and his political ambitions were all very much involved in her effort to conceal the real reasons for her actions." (Ibid, p. 345).

Sitting Bull the Hunkpapa: William K. Powers, *Ogalala Religion* (Lincoln: Nebraska: University of Nebraska Press, 1982), p. 61. Albert Marrin, *Tatan'ka Iyota'ke: Sitting Bull and His World* (New York: Dutton, 2000), p. 38. Also see: Robert M. Utley, *The Lance and the Shield* (New York: Ballantine Books, 1993).

Photo: Susan Strong notes perceptively in her book, *Painting for the Moghul Emperor: The Art of the Book 1550–1660* (London: Victoria and Albert Press, 2002), pp. 139, 141, "Jahanghir's artists also painted personalities of the court whose existence is otherwise unrecorded…the title of the stocky individual honored with a portrait by Manohar does not appear anywhere in his writings, however, and Fil-e Safed (White Elephant), might have disappeared from history had not his name been written by Jahanghir on the painting, in his distinctive spidery writing.

"Interestingly, the wrestler is shown with his face turned toward the viewer, rather than in the standard profile of most moghul court portraits. It is tempting to explain this in terms of ancient traditions such as those represented by the Chitrasutra [Sanskrit rules of painting], where it is explicitly stated that combatants such as wrestlers should not be depicted looking sideways, and should be shown 'tall and well-built, thick-necked, large-headed and close-cropped, overbearing and massive.'"

I'm enormously indebted and thankful to Susan Stronge, over the years, for having suggested so many avenues of research in moghul art and in the wider world of art history. Her friendship and encouragement have filled the journey with pleasure.

Page 27
Maharaja of Patiala: Gilles Néret. *Boucheron* (New York: Rizzoli, 1987), p. 121. Maharaja Bhupindar Singh ruled the state of Patiala in the Punjab from 1910-1938. He was the father of Indian cricket, chancellor of the of the Chamber of Princes from 1926 to 1931, 1933-1938, Cartier's largest customer and "for many in Europe was India." See Zucker, *Green*, p. 234.

Page 29
Samuel Clemens: Mark Twain, *The Adventures of Tom Sawyer* (Hartford: Conn.: American Publishing Co., 1876), Chapter 22.

Mark Twain: Michael Patrick Hearn, *The Annotated Huckleberry Finn* (New York: Clarkson Potter, 1981), p. 193.

Charles Dudley Warner: Justin Kaplan, *Mr. Clemens and Mark Twain* (New York: Simon & Schuster, 1966), pp. 268, 269.

L. Beebe: L. Beebe, *The Big Spender*

Page 31
Simha Padawer: Marc-Alain Oaknin, *The Burnt Book* (Princeton, N.J.: Princeton University Press, 1995), pp. 12, 13.

Charles Foley: Charles Foley, "Tales from the Nursery: How Baby Elephants Grow Up In the Wild," *Wildlife Conservation*, August 2002, p. 26.

Page 33
Havdallah: The passage from the holy time, the day of the Sabbath,

to the start of the secular week, Saturday night. Traditional Jews "bid the Sabbath farewell by lighting a candle, thereby fulfilling the verse 'Glorify the Lord with light' (Isaiah 24:15)….This is also intended to draw the light of *Shabbat* into the profane, so that the weekdays will not be entirely gray and colorless, but rather illuminated by some of the Sabbath light." Rabbi Adin Steinsaltz, The Miracle of the Seventh Day (San Francisco: Jossey-Bass, Wiley, 2003), p. 137.

Rembrandt: H. Perry Chapman, *Rembrandt's Self-Portraits* (Princeton, New Jersey: Princeton University Press, 1990), pp. 70-71.

Page 35
Jean Baptiste Tavernier: See Benjamin Zucker, *Blue*, p. 234. Tavernier was born in Paris in 1605 into a Protestant family that had fled Antwerp in the late 16th century. He traveled extensively in the Near and Far East from 1631 to 1668. Because Tavernier had been a successful goldsmith jeweler in Paris, his familiarity with gemstones enabled him to purchase gems in the East and resell them to the kings of France. The large blue diamond called the Tavernier Blue, sketched in *The Six Voyages of John Baptiste Tavernier Baron of Aubonne Through Turkey into Peris and the East Indies for the Space of Forty Years*, is the first reference to the Hope diamond.

Tavernier's book—an adventure story, a travel guide and a primer for connoisseurs, was published in French, English, German and Italian in many editions in the seventeenth and eighteenth century.

"Up to 1684, Tavernier is believed to have led an active, commercial, though somewhat refined, life but in 1685 he sold his land and barony" and voyaged yet again, at age 80, to the East in search of gemstones—diamonds, pearls, rubies and emeralds. He died in Russia and was buried near Moscow in a protestant cemetery.

Taverneir knew and probably dealt with the Chardin Brothers (John and Daniel)—also, like him, French Huguenots (See Benjamin Zucker, *Green*, p. 233). Tavernier visited Fort St. George before Elihu Yale. Tavernier's work was undoubtedly a primer and inspiration for Yale in the geography and customs of the gem world in the East. John Sinkankas, Gemology: An Annotated Bibliography (Metuchen, New Jersey: The Scarecrow Press, 1993), Volume 2, pp. 1020-1021. Valentine Ball, trans. and ed., *Travels in India by Jean Baptiste Tavernier Baron of Aubonne* (London and New York: Macmillan and Co., 1889), p. XI, XXXVI.

Simha Padawer: S.Y. Agnon, Judah Goldin, *Days of Awe*, forward by Arthur Green, page IX (New York: Schocken Paperbacks, 1995), p. IX. Nachum Alpert, *The Destruction of Slonim Jewry* (New York: Holocaust Library, 1989), p. 202. Gertsovski and Didko, *The Fire Almost Consuming.*

Shmuel Yosef Agnon: A noted Hebrew writer of novels about loss of faith and contemporary spiritual concerns. He left the world of the *shtetl* and settled in Palestine in 1907. Subsequently he wrote *A Guest for the Night, Edo and Enam* as well as a compendium of philosophical thoughts, *Days of Awe* about Rosh Hashanah and Yom Kippur. In 1966, Agnon was granted the Nobel Prize for Literature, the first granted to a Hebrew writer. Agnon said, after being presented with the prize by the king of Sweden. "*Finally I was able to recite the blessing: 'Blessed be the name of the Creator who shares his glory with Kings.'*" Encyclopedia Judaica (Jerusalem: Macmillan Company, 1971), Volume 2, pp. 367, 369, 371.

Unmench: Yiddish–not human.

Page 37
Van Gogh: Franz Erpel, *Van Gogh: The Self Portraits* (New York: New York Graphic Society, 1963), p. 33.

Moses Benjamin: See S.Y. Agnon in *Days of Awe* where he quotes from Matteh Moshe, p. 19. "Moses Benjamin was an 18th century Rabbi and Kabbalist in Baghdad. He was the first of the Baghdadi scholars known to have studied much Kabbalah and was an expert in Lurianic Kabbalah. Very little is known about his life. His wife and children died in an epidemic before 1737, and he never fulfilled his desire to immigrate to Jerusalem. Matteh Moshe is his commentary on the Torah as well as an explanation of Rabbinic verses and sayings. His *Sha'arei Yerushalayim* [the gates of Jerusalem] completed in 1731 contains Kabbalistic principles according to the Zohar and Isaac Luria. The book was stolen while en route to the publishers and the author was left with only the first draft." *Encyclopedia Judaica* ,Volume IV, p. 53.

Another Matteh Moshe printed in Cracow 1591 was written by Moses ben Abraham Premsla. Agnon, *Days of Awe*, p. 289.

Imre Emes: Rabbi Yitzchak Kasnett, *The World That Was: Poland* (Cleveland: Hebrew Academy of Cleveland, 1997), p. 115.

For notes on Imre Emes, see Benjamin Zucker's *Blue*, p. 227. The Gerer Rebbe (Mordekhai Alter, 1866–1948), known by the title of his book, Imre Emet (words of truth) was "a man of great personal warmth. He was like a father to all his Hasidim, sharing their joy and plight, taking a lively interest in all their problems. He believed that sometimes just listening can be enough. He interpreted Deuteronomy 1:17 'Moses instructed the judges' as 'Do not give anyone special consideration when rendering judgement. Listen to the great and small alike, and do not be impressed by any man, since judgement belongs to G-d. If any case is too difficult, bring it to me, and I will hear it' as follows: Moses said only 'I will hear it' he did not say he would find an answer to the case or offer a solution. This tells you that often when people have a difficult problem they only need to tell it to the Rebbe and unburden themselves to him. No answer is required. Reaching the rebbe's compassionate ear is quite enough." Avraham Yaakov Finkel, *Contemporary Sages: The Great Chassidic Masters of the Twentieth Century* (Northvale, New Jersey: Jason Aronson Press, 1994), pp. 90, 93, 94.

Page 39
Laurence Sterne: Lodwick Hartley, *Laurence Sterne* (Chapel Hill: North Carolina Press, 1968), pp. 109, 156. Laurence Sterne, *Tristram Shandy*, p. 89.

Elizabeth Sterne: Lodwick Hartley, *Laurence Sterne*, p. 216.

James Joyce: *Portrait of the Artist as a Young Man*, Chapter 5. Richard Ellman, *James Joyce* (New York: Oxford University Press, 1982), p. 37. *Ulysses*, 1922, Penelope section, Oxen of the Sun chapter.

Nora Joyce: Brenda Maddox, *Nora* (Boston: Houghton Mifflin, 1988), p. 121.

Lucia Joyce: Richard Ellmann, *James Joyce*, p. 743.

Page 41:
Max Brod: Hillel J. Kieval, *Languages of Community* (Berkeley: University of California Press, 2000), pp. 22, 218.

Franz Kafka: Johann Bauer, *Kafka and Prague* (New York: Praeger Publishers, 1971), p. 184.

Maharal of Prague: Be'er ha Golah, Chapter 1. *Encyclopedia Judaica*, Volume X, pp. 375,378, 381.

Page 43
Franz Kafka: Albert Manguel, *A History of Reading* (New York:

Viking, 1996), p. 93, quoting Pawel, *The Nightmare of Reason* (New York: Random House, 1985).

Shitao: Wang Yao-T'ing, *Looking at Chinese Painting* (Tokyo: Nigensha Publishers, 2000), p. 193. And Jonathan Hay, *Shitao: Painting and Modernity in Early Qing China*.

Elihu Yale: Bingham, *Elihu Yale*, p. 297.

Salvador Rodrigues: Jacques da Paiva's last will and testament .

"London, 3/13th February 1685/6

Mr. Antonio Rodriques Marques,

If you shall happen to read this I require noe other favour from you then that you would carefully cause my last Will to be performed in case I shall dye before my Wife, and if she shall dye before me, in such case you may be pleased to open the packet No. 1 whereby we make each other Heyres with consent of my Father in Law, and in case I shall Dye you will find alsoe in the packet No. 2, my last Resolution and Will, And I doe nominate you by these presents with all the power that can be given before any Notaries whatsoever to be my Executor and not to deliver anything to any person unless they all agree and if there be any disputes I doe say that my onely Heyre is to be my wife she giving or allowing to my Mother what is contained in my other paper No. 2 dureing her Life and after her decease to my Sister a Widoe, and in case of the death of my Wife and of me, which God forbid, I doe leave all to Mariana Gonsales upon Condition that her Father gives her in marriage to my Couzin Moses who goes with us to the Indyes, and if he shall dye all and whatsoever shall be found shall remaine one halfe of the whole for the portion of the said Mariana the other halfe to her Mother at her disposal and will for the great love which I and my wife Alsoe hath for her, thus all is disposed of untill my further order. And I hope in God that he will grant us life that I may be able to acquitt my Selfe of the Obligation which I owe to my Sr. Marques and whosoever shall Speake ill of me shall doe it unjustly, and in regard you know the rest and alsoe my Couz I pray God give us all Life and keep you—

Your affectionate and cordiall Friend,
Jaques Paiva

I carry with me what appears in folio 236 which is in a bagg Sealed up in the house of Gonsales.
1/4 in L500 Corall L126. I.5 Wine to Robin
—Insurance—   L86.
Emeralds and wine L32. 3.– watches   L50.
The Sefrt [sic] in the hands
of Gonsales and a
Silver Lamp
Valued L200.
—Empty bottles— L30.15.—
—Plate on Board—L7. 4.—
1/5 in 5000 pieces of
8 with Cooke
and Woolly   232. 4.2 All that Dorislaus
                owes belongs to
              me alone—

Francis Francia hath my booke of all my Effects, I carry two books with me of two Quires of paper, The Necklace of Pearle which my wife carrieth with her and two pendants and Jewells are worth L150: be pleased to give Almes for our Soules to the Summe of L50 for each of us Husband and Wife, and if you find that my wife dyes before me, read this paper to your Selfe Couzin Franco, and lett nothing be knowne of it, but open the Packet No. 1, and keep this private and let none know that I have money.

I believe I have nothing more to say, God be with us and grant us Life that we may doe good to all people, and if it shall be needfull to open the packet No. 2, alsoe, you may doe it with Couz Franco making use of what may be for my advantage. But I have transferred before the Magistrates my three houses to Francis Francia, declaring that I received of him tenn thousand Guilders, I did it *pro forma*, for I never received one penny of him as appears by the paper which he made me on the first of February 1685/6 before Narsis and Joseph Almansa, Fr hath a Coppy and by the paper booke of the Effects which I leave with Fr Francia under my own hand the remainder appears.

Jaques Paiva
Witnesse Benjamin Franco

[Directed on the outside:]
To Sr. Antonio Roiz Marques whome God keep many yeares.

This is truly translated by me
Antony Wright, Notary

Cecil Roth, ed., *Anglo-Jewish Letters* (London: Soncino Press, 1938), pp., 78–81.

Page 45
Pierre Lebrun: *Essays on the Wonders of Painting.* 1635.

Diego Duarte: Walter Liedtke with Michiel C. Plomp and Axel Rüger, *Vermeer and the Delft School* (New York: Metropolitan Museum, 2001), p. 9. *Vermeer: The Delft School*, National Gallery London Painting, pp. 15, 23.
"Gaspar Duarte is the son of Diego Duarte I (born Lisbon 1544 died Antwerp 1626). Diego Duarte, a Portuguese Marrano, was one of the most prominent diamond dealers." He was "dean of the Portuguese nation in Antwerp for a long time." Gaston Duarte succeeded him as a banker, jeweler and art dealer. Gaspar was a friend of Constantijn Huygens, Secretary to the Prince of the Nothern Netherlands, and a jewelry supplier to the English court. He sold Mary of England and Prince William II of Orange a diamond pendant worth 80,000 pounds, which was worn by Mary at her wedding. (See the wedding portrait of the Prince and Princess.)
Diego II inherited his father Gaspar's "Hotel on the Meir" in Antwerp and further enlarged his father's collection. Hundreds of paintings, including a "Mary Magdelene" by Andrea del Sarto, Raphael's "Vision of Ezekiel," a Titian portrait and works by Raphael were bought and sold by Diego Duarte II. Upon his death in 1690, Diego Duarte II left his sumptuous collection of paintings to his great niece Rachel Duarte. Her father, Manuel Levy Duarte, left Amsterdam, lived in Antwerp, from 1690–1696 selling the works of art on his daughter's behalf.
"The Duarte family were crypto-Jews," writes E. Samuel. "Diego Duarte I had come to Antwerp from Lisbon to escape the Portuguese Inquisition. In Antwerp as in Portugal the family had to conform to the Roman Catholic practice and keep their Judaism a secret. Subject to this, they enjoyed economic freedom and little risk of heresy proceedings."
Diego II's father Gaspar also outwardly conformed to Roman Catholicism as did Diego II. "Manuel Levy Duarte was a professing Jew and elder of the Amsterdam Portuguese synagogue." Iris Kockelbergh, Eddy Vleesschdrager and Jan Walgrave, *The Brilliant Glory of Antwerp Diamonds* (Antwerp: Ortelius, 1992), p. 49. Also see: Edgar R. Samuel, *The Disposal of Diego Duarte's Stock of Paintings, 1692–1697* (Antwerp: Jaarboek, Museum Voor Schone

Kunsten, 1976), pp. 305–324. And: *Manuel Levy Duarte 1631–1714: An Amsterdam Merchant Jeweler and His Trade with London* (London: Jewish Historical Society of England, Transactions), p. 27.
I am deeply thankful to Edgar Samuel for patiently tutoring me in the intricacies of Sephardic history and relationships in London, Amsterdam, Antwerp and India. Portuguese and Spanish Jews often have two names, e.g. Manuel Mendes de Valle Levy who traded under the alias Immanuel Levy Duarte. His wife Constantia Duarte also had an alias, Deborah Abolais Duarte. In addition, Sephardic Jews often married cousins and often in succeeding generations there were, for example, a Diego Duarte I, II, a Rachel Salom, a Rachel Levy Duarte etc., which can be bewildering. Studying the documents in Portuguese, Dutch, English and Hebrew, Edgar Samuel was able to decipher very complicated merchants' contracts, business books and art sale records and has provided an extraordinary picture of the 16th and 17th diamond and art trading world. Edgar Samuel's marvelous scholarship has brought to life this fascinating world.

See also Edgar Samuel, *From The Ends of the Earth* (London, Jewish Publication Society, 2004).

Page 47
Simha Padawer: Louis I. Newman, *Hasidic Anthology* (New York: Schocken Books, 1963), p. 487.

Sitting Bull, the Oglala: Born in 1841 south of the forks of the Platte River, in his youth he studied about Napoleon. In 1866 Sitting Bull led attacks the Bozeman Trail.
"In 1870 the Oglala Sitting Bull went to Washington as the right-hand man to Red Cloud, who insisted he was going only to tell the Great Father about the thieving Whites who starved his people." At Omaha they stopped and were feasted and had their pictures taken with Julius Meyer.
"Nothing came of the Black Hills sale either. The Southern Sioux Sitting Bull (the Good) sat quietly with the Oglala delegation at Washington and kept out of the squabbling of Red Cloud and Spotted Tail, both between themselves and the Whites."
After the humiliating defeat of Custer (in June 1876) the sale of the Black Hills was forced upon the Indians who were told "there would be no rations for the women and children until it was done."
Sitting Bull the Good refused to sign and stormed out of the Black Hills negotiations only to return, starving, to the Red Cloud Agency. When General Crook prevailed, he proposed Sitting Bull the Good carry a lance and a white flag to Crazy Horse to induce him and other hostiles to surrender, a band of Crow pounced upon the unarmed Oglala Sitting Bull and killed him.
Good Sitting Bull saved the Whites at Red Cloud Agency from massacre twice, and was given a gold-mounted and inscribed presentation rifle by President Grant in May 1875—only to have this presentation rifle used as evidence of the treacherous nature of the Hunkpapa Sitting Bull because he was in the Custer fight in June 1876, little more than a year later. The Oglala Sitting Bull [was] entirely lost in the personality of the other Sitting Bull newspapermen."
Mari Sandoz eloquently sums up the importance of the two Sitting Bulls: "History is the memory of the race, and like the individuals memory, it plays odd tricks. Not the least of these was the almost total disappearance, within eighty years, of one of the nation's real friends, and the transfer of his achievements and rewards to another, where they served as the final evidence of a treacherous nature."
Mari Sandoz, *Hostiles and Friendlies* (Lincoln, Nebraska: University of Nebraska Press, 1992), pp. 87, 89- 90, 100, 103, 106.

Sitting Bull, the Hunkpapa: Mari Sandiz, *Hostiles and Friendlies*, pp. 91-92. Leader of the Hunkpapa subtribe of the Teton Sioux

(Dakota). "His followers attributed his war success to the strength of his visions, and Sitting Bull himself believed that his power came from a complete accord with the mystical force of the universe.

"In 1876 a great number of Sioux, Cheyenne and Arapaho had gathered with Sitting Bull in the vicinity of the Rosebud and Little Big Horn rivers to discuss the White threat. After much fasting, Sitting Bull experienced a vision of dead soldiers falling like rain into the Indian camp. Soon after, warriors led by Crazy Horse defeated General Crook's command in the battle of the Rosebud (June 17), and on June 25 Lieutenant Colonel George A. Custer and five troops of the 7th calvary were annihilated at the Little Big Horn when they tried to attack the great encampment.

"During the battles, Sitting Bull took no active part in the fighting, having surrendered that pleasure when he assumed the head Chieftency....

"Sitting Bull was from his youth an uncompromising enemy of Euro-Americans...An ethnocentrist, he felt that contact with non-Indians could only pervert and weaken the Teton Culture, for he had observed treachery and brutality displayed by the Euro-Americans, who had pressed in on the Sioux country...

"[After Custer's defeat] Sitting Bull had retreated into Canada, but faced with starvation, returned to the United States and surrendered at Fort Buford on July 19, 1881.

"During 1885 Sitting Bull traveled with Buffalo Bill's Wild West Show. In 1890 the government feared a resurgence of Indian power in the Ghost Dance movement and moved to arrest Sitting Bull. After a fight on Dec. 15, 1890 Sitting Bull was killed." Howard Lamar, editor, The New Encyclopedia of the American West (New Haven: Yale University Press, 1998), pp. 1055-1056.

I am indebted to my marvelous friend Thomas Powers for sending me Mari Sandoz's account and for guiding me through all things Indian (and lots else).

Page 49

Red Cloud (1821–1909): The Oglala Chief Red Cloud—*Makhpiya-luta*—was the "most photographed nineteenth century Native American." This is because after the U.S. Army constructed forts on the Bozeman Trail (to protect White Men who cut across Indian lands to the western gold fields) Red Cloud was the leader in the "Fetterman massacre." Dec. 21, 1866. This began what came to be known as Red Cloud's war. Red Cloud only accepted a peace treaty with America after every fort along the Bozeman Trail was, abandoned by the Americas and subsequently burnt by Red Cloud and his fellow Sioux (1868).

Red Cloud traveled with Spotted Trail to Washington in 1870 to discuss the road development of the Black Hills (sacred to the Lakota). Unable to sway President Grant, Red Cloud went to New York and spoke at the Cooper Institute:

"I have tried to get from my Great Father what is right and just....I represent the whole Sioux nation. They will be grieved by what I represent. I am no Spotted Tail who will say one thing one day and be bought for a fish the next. Look at me! I am poor, naked, but I am a chief of a nation. We do not ask for riches; we do not want much, but we want our children properly trained, brought up....Riches here do no good. We can not take them away with us out of this world. You [White Men] belong in the East, and I belong in the West."

Red Cloud's life was marked by an attempt to deal with the ever-increasing American pressure on the Indians. In 1876, he signed a treaty ceding control over the Black Hills. Later from 1881–1889, he had extensive friendships with various friendly Whites—demonstrating his "ability to wear different faces for different audiences in order to promote good relations. Unlike the resistance of such Lakota leaders as Crazy Horse and Sitting Bull, Red Cloud's activism promoted a possible reconciliation between the two nations." See Frank H. Goodyear's *Red Cloud: Photographs of a Lakota Chief* (University of Nebraska,

2003), pp. 11, 14, 152. Goodyear examines various photographs of Chief Red Cloud (among which are several with Julius Meyer, see pp. 26, 29) and artfully distills the "different faces of Red Cloud."

Abraham b. Modechai: Zohar V, pp. 255, 267. The Zohar, see Benjamin Zucker, *Green*, p. 226.

Hayyim Vital: Born in Safed, 1543. Died in Damascus, 1620. When Isaac Luria (see Benjamin Zucker, *Blue*, p. 226), the renowned mystic, arrived in Safed in 1570, Vital became his closest disciple. Vital had studied the Kabbalah with Rabbi Moses Cordovero (1522–1570). "After Luria, called the Ari, died in the epidemic that ravaged Safed, Vital was considered his successor and spiritual heir. Hayyim Vital wrote 'Even if a person rises early for the purpose of studying and engrossed himself in the Torah, nevertheless his higher soul does not return to him until he prays and responds: Blessed is G-d, the Blessed One, for all eternity. At that point, the soul returns to the body.'"

Yanuka: child mystical genius.

Spotted Tail: George E. Hyde, *Red Cloud's Folk: History of the Oglala Sioux Indians*, pp. 173-175. A leader of the Brulé Sioux "During his captivity at Fort Kearney (1854–1856) Spotted Tail learned to know the Whites and appreciate their power as no other Sioux Chief ever had and in later times only the most outrageous injustice could drive him into hostility, for he realized the futility of struggling against a government whose resources were so vast.

"A rivalry between Red Cloud, who had defeated an American army, and Spotted Tail was intense. In 1870, an Indian delegation headed by Red Cloud, but joined by Spotted Tail, was summoned in Washington for a 'peace conference.' Spotted Tail and his fellow Brulé were given horses, enabling them 'to dash about Washington mounted and in glory while Red Cloud and his men were compelled to ride in carriages, which they despised as shiny black wagons.'

"Spotted Tail was Crazy Horse's uncle. In 1877, he agreed to induce Crazy Horse to surrender. 'Spotted Tail appears to have been the only Sioux chief who was big enough to consider the interests of the people outside the narrow limits of his own band." George E. Hyde, *Red Cloud's Folk: History of the Oglala Sioux Indians*, pp. 175, 289-290.

Page 51

Jerry Fodor: Jerry Fodor, *Times Literary Supplement*, in a review of Charles Traubs' *Unshadowed Thought*, July 6, 2001.

Mu Xin: I am grateful to my "renaissance friends" Alexandra Munroe and Robert Rosenkranz for sharing with me the extraordinary achievement of Mu Xin.

Mu Xin was born in 1927. He received a classical education in Shanghai, mastering the "*elegant pursuits*" of Chinese calligraphy, poetry and music. During the Japanese occupation of China, he had access to the enormous secluded library of Moa Dun (1896–1981), a distant relative. There Mu Xin studied Western philosophy, art and literature. Mu Xin refers to Leonardo da Vinci as his early teacher.

During the Cultural Revolution, after holding a low-level functionary job, Mu Xin was imprisoned under extraordinarily harsh conditions in a people's prison located in an abandoned air raid shelter. There, risking death, he wrote an enormous philosophy tractate, a synthesis of Eastern and Western knowledge, and hid the manuscript inside his prison jacket. After being released, he painted a series of haunting and exhilarating works of art, all of which were published with sumptuous elegance in *The Art of Mu Xin: Landscape Paintings and Prison Notes*, introduction by Alexandra Munroe, essays by Richard M. Barnhart, Jonathan Hay and Wu Hung (New Haven: Yale University, 2000), pp. 6, 13, 14. The book, exhibitions, the art and writings of Mu Xin are an extraordinary example of the finest human spirit. Robert Rosencranz aptly quotes Jacob Burckhardt's definition of the Renaissance man. "When this impulse to the highest individual development was combined with a powerful and varied nature which mastered all the elements of the culture of the age, then arose the 'all-sided man' *l'uomo universale*...Mu Xin is such a man, and that is why he fascinates me."

David Lloyd George: Andrew Bonar Law (1858-1925) was the leader of the Conservative Party in 1911 and a partner in running the First World War government with Prime Minister Lloyd George. Robert Lloyd George, *David and Winston: How a Friendship Changed History* (London: John Murray Books, 2005, and Woodstock, New York: Overlook Press, 2008), p. 251.

Page 53
Li Liu Feng: James Cahill, *The Distant Mountains: Chinese Paintings of the Late Ming Dynasty 1570-1644* (New York: Weatherhill, 1982), p. 133.

Leonard Woolf: Peter Dally, *The Marriage of Heaven and Hell* (New York: St. Martin's Press, 1999), pp. 77-79.

Apostles: An honor society at Cambridge University.

John Lehmann: John Lehmann was a partner of Leonard and Virginia Woolf in Hogarth Press. Peter Dally, *The Marriage of Heaven and Hell*, p. 147.

Vanessa: Virginia Woolf's sister.

Virginia Woolf: Peter Dally, *The Marriage of Heaven and Hell*, p. 151.

Mary Cassatt: Edward Lucie-Smith, *Impressionist Women* (New York: Abbeville Publishing Group, 1993), p. 141.

Page 55
Shih T'ao: Jonathan Hay, *Shitao, Painting and Modernity in Early Qing China* (Cambridge: Cambridge University Press, 2001), p. 126.

Hayyim of Sanz: Hassidic rebbe born in Poland, 1793, died in Sanz, Poland in 1876. "His torah commentaries, published under the title Divrei Chaim (words of Hayyim) reflect his phenomenal Torah greatness, his humility and his compassionate nature. His five sons all became famous *Tzaddikim* (righteous men or rabbis) the most prominent of whom was Rabbi Yehezkel of Shiniava [after whom the author's father, Charles Zucker, may his memory be a blessing, was named]. His seven daughters all married Hassidic leaders. Commented Hayyim of Sanz on Genesis 24:1: 'Abraham was now old, advanced in years, and G-d had blessed Abraham in all things. Abraham was now old. The Talmud remarks that until Abraham appeared on the scene, old age did not exist. This is difficult to understand, for the Torah records that long before Abraham there were people who lived for hundreds of years. In the spiritual realm, days that are wasted on idle pursuits do not count. Until the advent of Abraham, people lived lives of emptiness and futility since they did not spend their days on self-improvement, their years did not count. And even though they lived for many centuries, in a spiritual sense, they did not reach old age. Abraham was the first to proclaim G-d's existence, making people aware of spiritual values, and giving meaning to their lives. Now their days and years counted. Thus it may be said that Abraham introduced the concept of old age to the world.'"

Avraham Yaakov Finkel, *The Great Chasidic Masters* (Northvale, New Jersey: Jason Aronson Press, 1992), p. 140.

Julius Meyer: M.L. Marks, *Jews Among The Indians* (Chicago: Benison Books, 1992), p. 52.

Page 57
Hillel Seidman: Hillel Seidman, *Warsaw Ghetto Diary* (New York: Targum Press, 1957) as quoted in Nehemia Polen's extraordinary book, *The Holy Fire* (Northvale, N.J.: Jason Aronson Inc., 1999), p. 148.

Hoshanot: prayers recited on Sukot asking for G-d's salvation.

Shah Jahan: *The Moonlight Garden* discussed.

Michelangelo: I am indebted to David Mee for introducing me to the remarkable Semir Zeki. In *Neural Concept Formation and Art* (London: Journal of Consciousness Studies, NO. 3, 2002), Semir Zeki noted and analyzed the fact that "three-fifths of Michelangelo's sculptures are unfinished." Dr. Zeki theorizes that Michelangelo "felt he could not represent in a single work the inseparable concept of love and beauty that had formed in his brain." Zeki links ambiguity, and essential laws of the brain, to present to the reader an explanation of what great art is. Michelangelo's sonnets are taken from J.A. Symonds, *The Sonnets of Michelangelo* (London: Vision Press, 1950) but are modernized by, Dr. Zeki.

Shao Changheng: Joseph Chang and Quianshen Bai, *In Pursuit of Heavenly Harmony: Paintings and Calligraphy by Bada Shanren from the Estate of Wang Fangyu and Sum Wai* (Washington, D.C.: Freer Gallery of Art, 2003), p. 3.

Page 59
Virginia Woolf: Jane Lidderdale and Mary Nicholson, *Dear Miss Weaver: Harriet Shaw Weaver* (New York: Viking Press, 1970), p. 148.

Leonard Woolf: Ibid, p. 148.

Harriet Weaver: Ibid, pp. 148-149.

Samuel Beckett: Ibid, p. 455.

Emil Fisher: See Benjamin Zucker, *Green* (New York: Overlook Press, 2002), p. 129.

Page 61
Shah Jahan: Pratpadityal Pal, Janice Leoshko, Joseph M. Dye II, Stephen Markel, *Romance of the Taj Mahal* (Los Angeles: Los Angeles County Museum, 1989), p. 53.

Chuang Tse: H.A. Giles, trans., *Chuan Tse*, Chapter 2.

Li Po: David Hinton, *The Selected Poems of Li Po* (New York: New Directions, 1996), p. XII.

Rabbi Noson of Breslov: See Benjamin Zucker, *Blue* (Woodstock, New York: Overlook Press, 2000), pp. 13, 23, 227. I was introduced to Rabbi Jonathan Omer-Man by my friend Rachel Cowan who has done so much to spread the moral essence of Judaism. Of the many versions and translations of this tale, the one by Rabbi Omer-Man to me has best captured the extraordinary mystical levels of Rabbi Nachman's ever-vibrant story. Rabbi Noson wrote down the extraordinary tales told orally by the Hassidic mater, Rabbi Nachman of Breslov, a 19th century Polish Hassidic rebbe. See Benjamin Zucker, *Green*, p. 227.

Page 63
Nabokov: Brian Boyd and Robert Michael Pyle, *Nabokov's Butterflies* (Boston: Beacon Press, 2000), pp. 27, 711.

Bob Dylan: First Quote: "Sad-Eyed Lady of the Lowlands," copyright 1966 Dwarf Music, renewed 1994. Second Quote: "Stuck Inside of Mobile with the Memphis Blues Again." Copyright 1966 Dwarf Music, renewed 1994.

The Kotzker Rebbe: Zalman Meshullam Schachter-Shalomi, *Spiritual Intimacy: A Study of Counseling In Hasidism* (Northvale, New Jersey: Jason Aronson Press, 1996), p. 186. See Benjamin Zucker, *Green*, p. 225.

Page 65
Constantijn Huygens (1596–1687): A Dutch diplomat, secretary to Prince Henry, scholar and paint expert. He purchased a camera obscura in London in 1622. In 1669, with a friend of Diego Duarte, Pieter van Berkhout, Huygens visited Vermeer. Vermeer's extended circle of friends included: Leewenhoek, the Delft microbiologist who was sponsored by van Berkout for membership in the Royal society in London, and who eventually was the executor or Vermeer's will; Huygens, father and son, and Diego Duarte as well as scientists, art connoisseurs, merchants and poets. Anthony Bailey, *Vermeer: A View of Delft* (New York: Henry Holt, 2001), pp. 150-151, 201.

Rukkers: a musical instrument.

Page 67
R. Ahre Dokshitzer: Hassid of 3rd Lubovitcher rebbe, the Zemach Tzedek, 1789-1866. Menachem Mendel's scholarship was unflagging. "I generally study for eighteen hours a day, which includes five hours of writing. In the past thirty years, I have spent a total of thirty-two thousand hours of studying the works of Rabbi Scheur Zalman (the first Lubovitcher Rebbe). *Chassidic Rebbes* by Rabbi Tzvi Rabinovicz (N.Y.: Feldheim, 1989), p. 145.

Julio Cortázar: Julio Cortázar, *Hopscotch* (New York: Pantheon Books, 1966), p. 526.

Joseph B. Soloveitchik: Each year between Rosh Hashanah and Yom Kippur, Rabbit Joseph B. Soloveitchil ZT'l (may the memory of the righteous be for a blessing) would deliver a two to three hour discourse on repentance (*Al Hateshuvah*). Rabbi Soloveitchik was one of the greatest Halakhic (Talmudic) minds of the 20th century. His discourses have been elegantly organized topically by Dr. Arnold Lustiger. See Rabbi Joseph B. Soloveitchik on "The Days of Awe," summarized and annotated by Arnold Lustiger, *Before Hashem You Shall Be Purified* (Edison, New Jersey: Ohr Publishing, 1998), pp. 29-34.

Page 69
Cynthia Moss: Milbry Park, Mary Tiegreen, *Women of Discovery* (New York: Clarkson Potter, 2001), p. 151.

Nigel Nicolson: Nigel Nicolson, *Virginia Woolf* (New York: Penguin Putnam Inc., 2000), p. 1.

Virginia Woolf: Irene Coates, *Who's Afraid of Leonard Woolf?* (New York: Soho Press, 1998), p. 215.

Sitting Bull, the Oglala: Mari Sandoz, *Hostiles and Friendlies*, p. 89.

Page 71
Azariah Rossi: 1511–1578. The "greatest Jewish scientific scholar of the Renaissance." In 1571, when Rossi was living in Ferrara, the city was struck by and earthquake. He attributed his deliverance, and the city's deliverance, to Divine Intervention. In his book, *Me'or Einayim* (The Enlightenment of the Eyes) he presents a classical, medieval, Jewish and non-Jewish, compendium of explanations of earthquakes and other phenomena. He quotes extensively from the Church Fathers: Augustine, Clement of Alexandria and Justin Martyr as well as biblical, Talmudic and later Jewish sources—Philo of Alexandria, etc. *Encyclopedia Judaica*, Vol. XIV, pp. 316-317.

Hiram Bingham IV: Alfred Bingham, *The Tiffany Fortune*, pp. 201, 202. Woodbridge Bingham was the only one of the seven Bingham children not to attend Yale.

Page 73
Proust: *Remembrance of Things Past.*

Page 75
Van Gogh: Fritz Erpel, *Van Gogh: The Self-Portraits*, p. 26.

Isaac Luria: Zohar II, 109 9. Edmond Jabes, *Skipping.*

Gauguin: Druik and Zegers, *Van Gogh and Gauguin.*, p. 29

Franz Kafka: Kathi Diamant, *Kafka's Last Love: The Mystery of Dora Diamant* (New York: Basic Books, 2003), pp. 10, 15.

Page 77
Emily Post: Emily Post, *Etiquette*, pp. 24-25.

Julio Cortázar: Julio Cortázar, *Hopscotch* (New York: Pantheon Books, 1966), p. 203.

Buffalo Bill: R.L. Wilson with Greg Martin, *Buffalo Bill's Wild West: An American Legend* (New York: Random House, 1988), p. 125.

Page 79
Gerda Mayer: Anthony Grenville, *Continental Britons: Jewish Refugees from Nazi Europe* (London: The Jewish Museum, 2001), p. 61.

Sitting Bull: Albert Marrin, *Tatan'ka Iyota'ke, Sitting Bull*, p. 48.

F. Scott Fitzgerald: F. Scott Fitzgerald, Edmund Wilson, ed., *The Crack-Up* (New York: New Directions, 1962), p. 69, 70.

Franz Kafka: Kathi Diamant, *Kafka's Last Love: The Mystery of Dora Diamant* (New York: Basic Books, 2003), pp. 15, 18.

Page 81
Rabbi Nahum of Chernobyl (1730–1797): Fischel Lachower and Isaiah Tishby, *The Wisdom of the Zohar* (London: The Littman Library of Jewish Civilization, 1994), pp. 87- 88. Rabbi Menachem Nahum Twersky of Chernobyl was a student of the founder of Hassidism The Baal Shem Tov. Rabbi Nahum explained the sentence in Exodus 33:11: "G-d would speak to Moses face to face, just as a person speaks to a close friend." "In Kabbalistic terminology, the face-to-face spiritual encounter of G-d and Israel is called the 'clinging of the female to the male.' The people of Israel aroused themselves to a great desire for the Creator, and G-d in turn awakened within Himself a deep yearning for Israel. The giving of the Torah represents, as it were, the culmination of this great mutual love in the Kiddushin, marriage, between G-d and the people of Israel, as expressed in the phrase *vekidashtem*, 'sanctify them' (Exodus 19:10). This spiritual love finds its counterpart in the phys-

ical love between man and wife and in their union, which generates new life." Avraham Yakov Finkel, *The Great Chasidic Masters*, p. 45.

Lulu Cody: Robert A. Carter, *Buffalo Bill Cody* (New York: John Wiley & Sons, Inc., 2000), p. 406.

Page 83
Isaac Tal: Fishel Lachower and Isaiah Tishby, *The Wisdom of the Zohar,* pp. 336, 337.

Rachel Tal: Ibid, p. 340.

Chief Sitting Bull: Albert Marrin, *Sitting Bull*, pp. 41, 97.

Winkte: Half man, half woman "The Winkte were skilled at tanning and clothing decoration. They were also persuasive love talkers. That is, they delivered the proposals of the young men too shy to speak for themselves. Although they did not fight, they joined war parties to care for the wounded." Albert Marrin, *Tatan'ka Iyota'Ke, Sitting Bull*, p. 41.

Page 85
A.B. Yehoshua: Bernard Horn, *Facing the Fires: Conversations with A.B. Yeshuaa* (Syracuse: Syracuse University Press, 1997), pp. 150, 155.

Lewis Carroll: Martin Gardner and John Teniel, illustrator, *The Annotated Alice* (New York: Clarkson Potter, 1960), pp. 93, 95, 97.

Page 87
Photo of Vita Sackville West: "During her short affair with Virginia… we have Vita, exceedingly bold at one moment, and exceedingly shy at the next, falling in love with Virginia, ten years older than herself and scared of her." Nigel Nicolson, *Virginia Woolf* (English Edition), p. 70.

Vita Sackville West: Married to Nigel Nicolson; both had homosexual affairs. She had an affair with Virginia Woolf. On May 23, 1930, Vita took Virginia to see Sissinghurst for the first time. Victoria Glendinning, *Vita* (New York: Alfred A. Knopf, 1983), p. 229.

Chang Wei: Michael Beurdeley, *The Chinese Collector Through the Century: From the Han to the 20th Century* (Rutland, Vt.: Charles E. Tuttle Company, 1966), p. 75.

Page 89
Bada Shanren: Jonathan Hay, *Shitao* (Cambridge: Cambridge University Press, 2001), pp. 128, 138, 140, 331, 332. The letter from Shitao to Bada Shanren, circa 1698-1699, is in The Art Museum, Princeton University. Jonathan Hay, *Shitao*, p. 128.

Emile Fisher: Marseilles to Lisbon transport ship the Serpa Pinto docked on State Island, March 30, 1941, 640 passengers questioned in Bermuda en route for 3 days. Sheila Eisenberg, *A Hero of Our Own* (New York: Random House, 2001), p. 83.

Vodka and Orange Soda: Jay Tolson, *Pilgrim in the Ruins: A Life of Walker Percy* (New York: Simon & Schuster, 1992), p. 158.

Page 91
Fat mouth: fool.

Blind Lemon Jefferson: Born blind in 1897 in Wirtham, Texas, south of Dallas, Jefferson wandered through Texas signing and wrestling (he was an enormous man). His was a complicated musical style "Mississippi blues men accused him of 'breaking time' and playing music that wasn't danceable." In 1925 his blues, the first unaccom-panied Soutern folk music, were recorded by Paramount Records. He later became a highly successful recording artist but continued as a rambler. In 1929–30, returning home after playing at a house party, Jefferson froze to death alone in the snow." Laurence Cohn, ed., Nothing but the Blues (New York: Abbeville Press, 1993), pp. 55–57.

"There is no evidence that Jefferson was 'schooled' in Tennessee, the line is traditional and is found in many blues stanzas." Jeff Todd Titon, *Early Down Home Blues* (Chapel Hill, N.C.: University of North Carolina Press, 1994), p. 112.

The Yud: Niflaoth ha-Yehudi, A.J. Kleinman, Warsaw, 1925. Louis I. Newman, *Hassidic Anthology*, p. 79.

Page 93
Alfred Bingham: Bingham, *The Tiffany Fortune* (Chestnut Hill: Mass.: Abeel and Leet, 1996), pp. 169, 213, 396.

Common Sense: A progressive magazine, founded in 1932 by Alfred Bingham.

Page 95
Sitting Bull the Good: M.L. Marks, *Jews Among the Indians* pp. 50, 51. Mari Sandoz, *Hostiles and Friendlies*, p. 99 and photograph caption opposite p. 106. As well as a personal communication from the remarkable publisher (Steerforth Press), essayist, novelist (*The Confirmation*) and good friend, Thomas Powers who wrote me of *Green*: "On page 112 that's Sitting Bull the Oglala, not Sitting Bull the Hunkpapa, who fought Custer. Otherwise the book is dazzling and flawless. Your friend, Tom."

Billups Phinizy: Patrick H. Samway, S.J., *Walker Percy: A Life* (New York: Farrar, Straus & Giroux, 1997), p. 120.

Van Gogh: Douglas W. Druick and Peter Kort Zegers, *Van Gogh and Gauguin: The Studio of the South*, p. 107.

Dora Diamant: Jerome Mintz, *Legends of Hasidim* (Chicago: University of Chicago, 1968), p. 300. Rabbi Tzvi Rabinowicz, *Chassidic Rebbes from the Baal Shem Tov to Modern Times* (Southfield, Michigan: Targum Press, 1989), p. 253.

Page 97
Joseph Salvador: Abraham Salvador's brother, a printer in Amsterdam, c. 1660.

Page 99
Caitlin Thomas: Paul Ferris, *Caitlin: The Life of Caitlin Thomas* (London: Random House, 1995), pp. 58, 60, 64-65.

Leonard Woolf: Richard Shone, *The Art of Bloomsbury*, p. 70.

Paul Gauguin: "Misery" was considered by Gauguin his best painting done in Arles. See Druik and Zegers, *Van Gogh and Gauguin*, pp. 193-194.

Page 101
Illui: a genius.

Havrusa: a study partner.

Simha Padawer: See Alberto Manguel, *A History of Reading*, pp. 89, 90. And: Talmud Bavli, *The Art Scroll Stories*, The Schotenstein Edition (Brooklyn: New York, Mesorah Publications, 1998) Yoma Yom Hakippurim, p. 73b.

Page 103
Virginia Wolf: *The Common Reader*, 1925, Knowing Greek. Between the Acts, 1941.

Duncan Grant: George Spater and Ian Parsons, *Marriage of True Minds* (New York: Harcourt Brace Jovanovich, 1977), p. 19.

Simha Padawer: Deuteronomy 33.

Jeremy Kalmanofsky, the remarkable Rabbi of Ansche Chesed in *Judaism* (a quarterly) (New York: The American Jewish Congress, Spring 2002), p. 177, movingly explains the essence of "Amen." He quotes R. Bahye of Saragossa, the 13th century Bible commentator and Kabbalist. "The one who blesses testifies that the blessed Holy One is the source of blessing. But the one who responds Amen authenticates the document, and he is the critical one. For no testimony is valid with only one witness…And the one who responds Amen is the second witness….with him the testimony is valid.*"

Rabbi Kalmanofsky argues that "one who blesses when alone has the effect of one who testifies when all alone: his statement is factually accurate but meaningless in the human community. Now, one cannot over-apply this Aggadic point; if you find yourself all alone, you still can eat and say the appropriate blessing. However, the strength of his rhetoric drives home that for R. Bahye, responding Amen is the way that a society can officially endorse an act of worship, give it status and heft. For one human being all alone cannot make true a blessing. We need partners."

Diamond Jim Brady: 1856-1917. Multimillionaire railroad tycoon. He ate, gambled and lived to excess. The owner of Charles Rector restaurant in New York described Diamond Jim as "his best 25 customers." Diamond Jim gifted his girlfriend, actress and singer Lillian Russet with a bike of mother-of-pearl and spokes studded with sapphires and rubies. Diamond Jim had a well-balanced and diversified portfolio—$10 million in stocks and railroad bonds—and personal jewelry (which he wore during the day and night) of $2 million.

Page 105
Elizabeth Otis: Jay Tolson, *Pilgrim in the Ruins*, pp. 282-283.

Shelby Foote: Ibid, pp. 84, 224.

Stanley Kauffmann: Walker Percy, *The Moviegoer* (New York: Alfred A. Knopf, 2000), p. 89.

Page 107
Mittevoch und Donnerstik: Wednesday and Monday.

Tsuris: troubles.

Tseddakah: Charity.

Sefer: A book in Hebrew.

Page 109
Louis Cartier: James Cuno, *Harvard's Art Museum: 100 Years of Collecting* (Cambridge: Harvard University, 1996). Note by: Stuart Cary Welch, p. 136.

Su Dong Po: Michael Sullivan, *The Three Perfections* (New York: George Braziller, 1999), p. 46.
Livy: Samuel Clemens' wife.

Clara: Samuel Clemens' daughter.

Søren Kierkegaard: William Hubben, *Dostoevsky, Kierkegaard, Nietzsche and Kafka* (New York: Simon & Schuster, 1997), p. 9, 42.

Isaac Luria: Isaiah Tishby, *The Wisdom of the Zohar* (London: Littman Library of Jewish Knowledge, 1994), pp. 930- 931.

Cartier: See Cartier note above.

Page 111
Annie Oakley: "Annie Oakley had brought fifty pounds of her favorite English Schultze gunpowder with her [to the Wild West Show at the Universal Exposition in Paris in 1889] but she was told she could not land it because France had a monopoly on gunpowder. Annie was very disappointed. She didn't have time to experiment with a new brand. Frank, her husband, would have to figure out new loads and proper packing. A mistake not only could throw Annie's shooting off, it could be dangerous, especially when instructions were written in French.

"The way Annie Oakley saw it, there was only one thing to do: smuggle the powder in. She rounded up five hot-water bottles and four lady riders, whom she enlisted as co-conspirators. They pored the Schultze powder into the hot-water bottles, and then each woman put on a dress with a bustle, hiding the bottles within. Annie had never worn a bustle before, but on this occasion, she said, "I was glad to." She led the procession down the gang plank and safely onto French soil. 'We sure did attract some attention when we went down the gang plank,' Annie said. 'For although the bustle originated in France, it was going out about that time.' Out-of-style as the bustle was, the scheme worked. Pragmatic and resolute as always, Annie just winked at the law and explained: 'I was advertised very strongly and much was expected of me.' She needed that Schultze powder to shoot well, and that was all that mattered. 'It not only meant success for myself,' she said, 'but for the Wild West company.'" Shirl Kasper, *Annie Oakley* (Norman, Oklahoma : University of Oklahoma Press, 1992), p. 105.

Abraham Joshua Heschel: Abraham Joshua Heschel of Apt in Sifran Shel Zaddikim (Hasidic Sayings), ed. Eleazar Dob ben Aaron. Lublin, 1928, as quoted by S.Y. Agnon, *Days of Awe*, p. 196. See Benjamin Zucker, *Blue*, p. 229.

Louis Orswell: Marjorie B. Cohn, *Lois Orswell, David Smith and Modern Art* (Cambridge, Mass.: Harvard University Museum, 2002), p. 16, 18, 23.

With thanks for the many blessings I've received from Lee Grove who recited lines of Dickenson from memory at Yale, talked of the novel at Harvard, kept Cambridge alive and full of wonder for me (and Barbara), and walked me through Lois Orswell's treasures at the Fogg.

Lois Orswell's gift of over 340 objects of art donated because "she had a beau who was a Harvard man. You know me: passionate and obstinate" (Lois Orswell, p. 14). Both the study by Marjorie B. Cohn and the collection itself illuminate both art and the art of collecting. Orswell observed: "I do think private collections are the most fascinating things to study. It is like paintings you give yourself away completely in your brush stroke when you paint and one can study the collector through his collection as well as enjoy the art of myself."

Page 113
Søren Kierkegaard: Søren Kierkegaard, *Fear and Trembling* (New York: Penguin Books, 1985), pp. 47, 48.

John Flattau: I have attended a fabulous tutorial with John Flattau beginning at Horace Mann School, continuing at Harvard Law School, Greenwich Village coffee seminar ('65 to the present) as well as selected seminars abroad (Provence, London, Paris, Halong Bay, Vietnam, etc.). *Recent Memories* sumptuously published by Leica Gallery (Jay Deutsch) of Flattau's photographs as well as *Bridges* (Lustrum Press) are essential texts to begin to appreciate Flattau's extraordinary world. John Flattau, *Recent Memories* (New York: Ianda Leica Gallery, 2000) cover and p. 1.

Page 115

Van Gogh: Douglas W. Druick and Peter Kort Zegers, *Van Gogh and Gaugain: The Studio of the South*, p. 151.

Yasuari Kawabata: Yasuari Kawabata, *The Master of Go* (New York, Alfred Knopf, 1972), p. 3.

Shah Jahan: Elizabeth B. Moynihan, ed., *The Moonlight Garden: New Discoveries at the Taj Mahal* (Washington, D.C.: Arthur M. Sackler Gallery, 2000), pp. 51-52 (in the chapter "Botanical Symbolism Function at the Mahtab Bagh"). See also James L. Wescoat Jr's elegant chapter: "Waterworks and Landscape Design in the Mahtab Bagh," pp. 59-75. Also, Koran 18:4-5. Inscription written on Southeastern Arch, Taj Mahal.

Chitarman: A powerful mogul miniature portrait. "Few illustrations by Chitarman have been identified but he was clearly a skilled portraitist," wrote Milo Beach in *The Grand Moghul Imperial Painting in India 1600–1660*, "His illustrations are often effective in ways unknown to more Orthodox painters." (Williamstown, Mass: Clark Art Institute, 1978), p. 111.

Page 117

Denbighshire: The Yale ancestral estate in Wales.

Elihu Yale: Elihu Yale as a diamond merchant. In the 17th century rough diamond (uncut) were found exclusively in India (other than small amounts of diamond mined in Borneo).

The Indian diamonds were panned in the rivers near Golconda Fort (see *The Six Voyages of John Baptista Tavernier*). Rough diamonds would enter Fort St. George and be shipped onward to London. Edgar Samuel, in his marvelous study *At the End of the Earth* (London: The Jewish Historical Society of England, 2004), has noted several transactions involving Elihu Yale. In 1686 Antonio Rodrigues Marques, a Portuguese Sephardic Jew residing in London shipping 1,000 English pounds worth of Spanish pieces of eight to India. He organized a syndicate of investors, some of whom wished to be offered the rough, uncut diamonds to cut and polish and sell into the wholesale London market or to the Amsterdam market.

The 1,000 English pounds were shipped on Athias and Manuel Levy Duarte's account. They were Amsterdam traders whose families had fled The Inquisition in Portugal. Marques charged only nominal handling charges and asked for the right also to purchase diamonds once they reached London.

Because Elihu Yale was governor of Fort St. George (Madras), the money was consigned to him for delivery to Jacques de Paiva, Athias and Levy's buying agent in India. De Paiva was also a Portuguese Jewish diamond merchant. He was married to Hieronyma de Paiva, also from a Portuguese émigré family. According to Samuel, Hieronyma probably was born in Antwerp. De Paiva had received the right to travel to Madras with his wife and purchase and sell diamond rough from the British East India Company. His special expertise in cleaving diamonds (hitting the diamond at a cleaving plane) as well as his selling experience of cut diamonds made him an ideal buyer for the entire Madras syndicate.

Unfortunately, in 1687 Jacques de Paiva fell sick at the Golconda mines and tragically died quite young in Madras. His widow Hieronyma de Paiva became Elihu Yale's mistress in 1688. Salvador Rodrigues a Portuguese Jew who was a brother of Abraham Salvador, the son-in-law of Manuel Levy Duarte, became a 1/2 partner with Hieronyma de Paiva who continued her husband's business. The rough diamonds Salvador bought at Golconda were then traded with Hieronyma de Paiva.

Yale was also partners with Sir Chardin, a French Huguenot who settled in London after many years living in Persia. Yale's other partners included John's brother Daniel Chardin as well as various other partners, Catherine Nicks, and "Diamond Pitt" who eventually bought and sold the most valuable 17th century diamond, the Regent.

Elihu Yale's diamond activities revolved, as did all diamond merchants of his time, around the late 17th century advances in cutting thick table-cut diamonds or heavy rose cuts as well as newly polished stones into a more modern "brilliant cut" diamond. This created a much more scintillating diamond and led to a vastly greater European demand for diamonds.

On a macroeconomic plane, Elihu Yale's trading with Muslim as well as Hindu merchants, his trade with China as well as Siam and his maritime links between India and England make him into a truly modern global, political and economic figure.

Elihu Yale was relieved of his presiding of Fort St. George owing to charges of corruption and self-dealing by the East India Company in 1693. Elihu Yale returned to England in 1700 having cleared his name with the East India Company. He had settled his debt in 1697 to Athias and Levy 11 years after he received their share of the Antonio Rodrigues Marques diamond syndicate.

Yale brought back a staggering 150,000 British pounds treasure merchandise, jewels and works of art, in all two tons of merchandise. He married two daughters into British aristocratic families: Devonshire and North. After his death, 10,000 of his works of art were sold at auction in the largest series of auctions held up to that time in England.

But he is known to us because of his gift, almost an afterthought of about 1,162 British pounds of books, paintings and cloth so that the University College of Connecticut's name might be changed to Yale University.

Hiram Bingham notes: "As Cotton Mather prophesized in his letter to Elihu Yale, his gift obtained for him 'a commemoration and perpetuation of his valuable name' much better than an Egyptian pyramid."

Haham: A Sephardic rabbi.

Page 119

Harry Bober: Professor of Art, Institute of Fine Arts, NYU. Malcolm Lowry note in "Blossoming Plum" scroll by Liu Shiru in James Cuno, *Harvard's Art Museums, 100 Years of Collecting*, p. 60.

Professor Bober (1916-1988) served as an inspiration to decades of students from 1960 through the 1980s. He taught connoisseurship, bringing objects of medieval art to class and often loaned them for weeks to a student for a term paper. He encouraged my collecting of antique rings predicting it would lead to books, fiction and non-fiction about jewelry.

Liu Shiru: Translated by Hans Frankel in Maggie Beckford, ed., *Bones of Jade, Soul of Ice: The Flowering Plum in Chinese Art*, exhibition catalog Yale University Art Gallery (New Haven, 1985) p. 261, no. 23 on p. 60 James Cuno, *Harvard's Art Museum's 100 Years of Collecting*, p. 60.

Shitao: Jonathan Hay, *Shitao: Painting and Modernity in Early Qing China*, p. 328. T.C. Lai, *Understanding Chinese Painting* (New York: Schocken Books, 1985), p. 237.

Groucho Marx: Groucho and Zeppo Marx in *Animal Crackers*, Stefan Kaufer, *Groucho* (New York: Random House, 2000), pp. 134-135.

S.Y. Agnon: S.Y. Agnon, *Days of Awe*, pp. 226, 227.

Page 121
Sarah Padawer: See Benjamin Zucker, *Green* (Woodstock: Overlook, 2002), p. 51.

Page 123
James Joyce: *Finnegans Wake*, p. 30. Genesis 3:6. *Ulysses*, p. 34-40. Cited in Ira B. Nadel, *Joyce and the Jews* (Iowa City: University of Iowa Press, 1989), pp. V, 112.

Ben-Edar: The Celtic name for the Hill of Howth.

Lydia: Mary Cassatt's sister, who suffered from Bright's disease, a degenerative sickness of the kidneys. She was Cassatt's favorite model.

F. Scott Fitzgerald: *The Great Gatsby* (New York: Scribner Classics, 1996), p. 45.

Page 125
Simha Padawer: M. Ben Ezra. R. Alcalay, *Words of the Wise* (Jerusalem: Massada Press, 1973), pp. 35, 475.

Berahot: Blessing.

Shah Abbas II: 1642–1666.

Rembrandt: Leonard J. Slatkes, *Rembrandt and Persia* (New York: Abaras Books, 1983), pp. 126-127. Gary Schwartz, *Rembrandt: His Life, His Paintings* (New York: Penguin Books, 1991), p. 214.

Assadullah Souren Melikian-Chirvani: I am deeply grateful for having had the great joy to attend lectures by Dr. Assadullah Souren Melikian-Chirvani where he has opened the minds of this generation to the philosophical underpinning of Moghul Painting and treasured objects. See Dr. Melikian's "Mir Sayyid 'Ali: Painter of the Past and Pioneer of the Future" in Asok Kumar Das, ed., *Moghal Masters Further Studies* (India: Marg Publications, 1998), pp. 30–51 and Marianna Shreve Simpson, with introduction by Stuart Cary Welch, *Arab and Persian Painting in the Fogg Art Museum* (Cambridge, Mass., Fogg Art Musuem, 1980), pp. 13, 58–60.

Page 127
Blake: See Joseph Viscomi, *Blake and the Idea of the Book* (Princeton, N.J.: Princeton University Press, 1993), p. 21. for a discussion of "error" in Blake's *Jerusalem*. "To suppose that text was transferred because it was 'unlikely that Blake could have written the whole of 100 plates of Jerusalem alone, not to mention the other books, backwards [Todd, Techniques '34]' without making a mistake is to respond impressionistically to the task. The task seems difficult when the autographic effect of pens and brushes on composition is dismissed and the mode of production is misunderstood. Jerusalem's one hundred plates, for example, were not produced in one sitting but over a fourteen to seventeen year period, which means that the work was far less intense and taxing than might be supposed."

Aryeh Judah Leib ben Ephraim Ha-Kohen (1658–1720), Moravian Rabbi: "Aryeh was the younger son of Ephraim b. Jacob Ha-Kohen, Rabbi of Ofen. He studied under his father together with his nephew Zevi Hirsch Ashkenazi (the Haham Zevi). His eldest brother Hezekiah died in the plague which broke out in Ofen in 1678 and Aryeh was taken ill; according to his own statement (introduction to the responsa Sha'ar Efrayim) his father prayed that he be taken instead of his son. Aryeh Leib recovered, but his father succumbed to the plague. Before he died, he ordered his son to publish his books. After the death of his mother in 1684, Aryeh Judah decided to emigrate to Eretz Israel with his family and they were joined by Aron, son of his deceased brother Hezekiah. They arrived in Jerusalem in 1685. There he began to arrange his father's book for publication although he found the preparatory work difficult; 'it involved much trouble because of the confusing handwriting and the loss of many pages.' About a year later, he returned to Prague and published it under the title Sha'ar Efrayim (Sulzbach, 1688). It comprises 150 responsa on the four parts of the Shulhan Aruch. The end of the work contains Kunteres Aharon, 'Last Pamphlet,' consisting of Aryeh's explanatory notes on the Talmud and the Tur, Hoshen Mishpat. Aryeh later returned to Erez Israel, where he died in Safed. His son Jedidiah, pupil and later son-in-law of Abraham Yizhaki (the Sephardi rabbi of Jerusalem) also wrote responsa, only one of which was published." Encyclopedia Judaica, III, p. 667. See Benjamin Zucker, *Blue*, p. 239. The author is a lineal descendant of Aryeh Judah Leib.

Rabbi Isaiah Hurwitz: A noted Kabbalist born in Prague ca. 1565. Rabbi Hurwitz moved to the land of Israel in 1621 and served as Rabbi in Jerusalem. In 1625, he was imprisoned by the Pasha and ransomed. He died in Tiberia in 1630. From Jerusalem, he wrote many letters to his children still living in Israel.

Page 131
Mu Xin: Alexandra Monroe, *The Art of Mu Xin: Landscape Paintings and Prison Notes*, p. 13.

Bada Shanren: Joseph Chang and Qianshen Bai, *In Pursuit of Heavenly Harmony: Paintings and Calligraphy by Bada Shanren from the Estate of Wang Fangyu and Sum Wai*, pp. 4, 6. I thank Joseph Chang for his illuminating for me many of the characteristics of Bada Shanren and Shitao.

Page 133
Simha Padawer: The idea that certain Talmudic problems can be only resolved by the wisdom of the Messiah after He arrives, is at once charming, mystical and profound. See Louis Jacob, *TEYKU: The Unsolved Problem in the Babylonian Talmud* (East Brunswick: New Jersey: Cornwall Books, 1981), p. 94.

R. Levi Yitzhak of Berditchev: Louis Jacob, *TEYKU*, pp. 311, 312.

Vita Sackville-West: Ursula Buchan, ed., *A Bouquet of Garden Writing* (Boston: David R. Godine, 1987), p. 63. Louise DeSalvo and Mitchell Leaska, eds., *The Letters of Vita Sackville-West to Virginia Woolf* (San Francisco: Cleis Press, 2001), p. 201.

Virginia Woolf: Louise DeSalvo and Mitchell Leaska, *The Letters of Vita Sackville West to Virginia Woolf*, pp. 201- 202.

Page 135
M.K. Heeramaneck: Susan Stronge writes that the work of art as "drawing from the end of Akbar's reign depicts a fantastic creature that appears in a number of other media. The half-lion, half-elephant known as Gaja-simha had such a prodigious strength that it could hold in its talons seven elephants while simultaneously fighting off the attack of a simurgh, the mythological bird of the Persian national epic, the Shah Nama or 'Book of Kings.' It was used on ivory in layers on wood, by carpet weavers, and is found on architecture as well as in painting, but its significance in the moghul context remains an enigma." Susan Stronge, *Paintings for the Mughal Emperor: The Art of the Book, 1560–1660* (London: Victoria and Albert Museum, 2002), pp. 106, 182,

She goes on to note that the drawing was "bought from Mr. M.K. Heeramanneck with two Kangra paintings for a total cost of 50 pounds in 1914."

Page 137
Saida-ye Gilani: See A.S. Melikian-Chirvanis brilliant Mogul detective work in Bulletin of the Asia Institute 1999, volume 13.

Ferdinand de Rothschild: Derek Wilson, *Rothschild: The Wealth and Power of a Dynasty* (New York: Charles Scribner's Sons, 1988), p. 228. Michael Hall, *Waddesdon Manor: The Heritage of a Rothschild House* (New York: Harry N. Abrams, Inc., 2002) pp. 73, 74, 99.

David Linsay: Derek Wilson, *Rothschild*, pp. 227, 228.

Page 139
Zelda Fitzgerald: Eleanor Lanahan, *Zelda: An Illustrated Life* (New York: Harry N. Abrams, DATE), p. 3.

F. Scott Fitzgerald: Ibid, p. 22.

J.P. Morgan: Ron Chernow, *The House of Morgan* (New York: Atlantic Monthly Press, 1990), p. 256-257.

Page 141
Herman Melville: Alfred Kazin, *God and the American Writer* (New York: Alfred A. Knopf, 1997), pp. 99-100.

Samuel Clemens: Mark Twain, *Adventures of Huckleberry Finn*, Chapter 12. Mark Twain, *Following the Equator vol. 1, Pudd'n Head Wilson's New Calendar*, Chap. 36.

Rabbi No'am Elimelech of Lizensk (1717–1786): Avraham Yaakov Finkel, *The Great Chasidic Masters*, pp. 18-19.

Abraham Sachatzov: *Siah Sifre Kodesh* by Rabbi Abraham of Sachatzov is quoted by S.Y. Agnon in "Hebrew Authors and Holy Writing" in *Essays on Jewish Booklore* (New York: Ktav Publishing, 1976), pp. 167-178.Said the Sachatzov Rabbi (1839-1910), a Hassidic Rebbe who was also a great Talmudist, in his introduction to *Eglei Tal, How To Study*, "I always wrote down the Torah thoughts I developed but it never occurred to me to have them published....But in my old age, I am suffering from coughing and I am unable to teach my students which is a source of great anguish to me. Therefore, I intend to have my novellae published in order to enable my students to learn the proper methods of Torah study…if you find pleasure in learning Torah, the words of the Torah are absorbed in your blood. And when you enjoy learning Torah, you become attached to it." Avraham Yaakov Finkel, The Great Chasidic Masters (Northvale, NJ: Jason Aronson Press, 1992), p.184.

Page 143
Gauguin: Douglas W. Druik and Peter Kort Zegers. *Van Gogh and Gauguin in Arles*, p. 155.

Page 145
Bada Shanren: Jonathan Hay, *Shitao: Painting and Modernity in Early Qing China*. James Cahill, *Fantastics and Eccentrics in Chinese Painting* (New York: The Asia Society, 1967), p. 76.

Shitao: Jonathan Hay, *Shitao: Painting and Modernity in Early Qing China*, pp. 126-127.

Page 147
Van Gogh: Druick and Zegers, *Van Gogh and Gauguin in Arles*, p. 183.

Herman Melville: "The waif is a pennoned pole…inserted upright into the floating body of a dead whale, both to mark its place on the sea and also as token of prior possession."

Rachel Abendana Tal: S.Y. Agnon, *The Days of Awe* (New York: Schocken Books, 1965), p. 211, quotes the Mahzor Vitry, no. 351. The *Mahzor Vitry* is "a compendium of prayers and synagogal usages by Simha ben Samuel Vitry (12th century), ed. S. Hurwitz, Berlin 1889–1893. The earliest manuscript version was owned in the 20th century originally by David Solomon Sasson. Victor Klagsbald, perhaps the greatest connoisseur of Jewish art today has studied the manuscript thoroughly and confirmed this description of the three cantorial chantings of Kol Nidre. Over the years Victor has been an unending source to me of inspiration and knowledge about Jewish art in particular and art and philosophy in general.

Page 149
Van Gogh: *Van Gogh and Gauguin: The Studio of the South*, p. 183.

Louis Cartier: K. Natwar, *Singh, The Magnificent Maharaja* (New Delhi: HarperCollins, 1998), p. 31.

Princess Labanoff: Gilberte Gautier, *Cartier: The Legend* (London: Arlington Books, 1983), p. 112.

Page 151
Rachel Tal: Hanan S. Ayalati, *Yiddish Proverbs* (New York: Schocken Books, 1963), pp. 34, 50.

Reb. Yechiel: Moshe Mykoff, ed., *Rabbi Nacham of Brelsov* (Jerusalem: Breslov Research Institute, 1987), p. 252.

Tk'way Thunderhorse: Evan T. Pritchard has written a remarkable history of New York through Lenape eyes. *Native New Yorkers: The Legacy of the Algonquin People of New York* (San Francisco: Council Oak Books, 2002), pp. 80, 202, 204, 206.

Page 153
Rachel Tal: Mishley 20:27.

Virginia Woolf: Virginia Woolf, *A Room of One's Own*, pp. 94, 99.

Page 159
Tuviah Gutwirth: Avraham Yaakov Finkel, *The Great Chassidic Masters*, p. 110.

Gustave Eiffel: Meg Greene, *The Eiffel Tower* (San Diego, Calif.: Lucent Books, 2001), pp. 43, 45, 56.

Red Shirt: L. G. Moses, *Wild West Shows and the Image of American Indians* (Albuquerque: University of New Mexico Press, 1996), pp. 82-83.

Page 157
Wallace Stevens: Thomas C. Grey, *The Wallace Stevens Case: Law and the Practice of Poetry* (Cambridge, Mass.: Harvard University Press, 1991), p. 87. Joan Richardson, *Wallace Stevens, The Early Years, 1879-1923* (New York: William Morrow, 1986), pp. 295, 381.

Søren Kierkegaard: *Fear and Trembling*, p. 45. Jonathan Rée and Jane Chamberlain, *Kierkegaard: A Critical Reader* (Oxford: Blackwell Publisher's Ltd., 1998), p. 115.

Franz Kafka: Richard Winston and Claire Winston, eds., *Franz Kafka: Letters to Friends, Family and Editors* (London: John Calder, 1978), p. 16.

Israel Friedman: Avraham Yaakov Finkel, *The Great Chassidic Masters*, pp. 145-146. Also see Benjamin Zucker, *Blue*, p. 5.

Page 159
Julius Meyer: M.L. Marks, *Jews Among the Indians*, pp. 56-57.

Max Meyer: Ibid, pp. 50, 57.

Page 161
Bob Dylan: "Ballad of a Thin Man" copyright Warner Brothers, Inc.; renewed 1991 Special Rider Music. "The Times They Are A-Changin" copyright 1963, 1964 by Warner Brothers; renewed 1991, 1992 by Special Rider Music. "Just Like a Woman" copyright 1996 Dwarf Music.

Page 163
Isaac Tal: Asarah Batanim. See *Encyclopedia Judaica*, Volume II, pp. 66-68 and Dr. Israel W. Slotki, *Moses Maimonides: His Life and Times* (London: Jewish Religious Education and Publications, 1964), p. 33, for notes on Abendana. Fernando (Abraham) and Manuel, Manuel Pereira Continho as well as Francisco Nunez Pereira and David Abendana. Isaac Sardo Abendana, Isaac Abendana and the Ibn Danan family of Fez.

Yichus: ancestry.

Mari Sandoz: "I grew up near the Sioux reservation at Pine Ridge, South Dakota, in the free lands region of Northwest Nebraska. I was the eldest of six children. Our father, a cripple, was less interested in routine physical labor than in his Indian friends, and in providing good homes for the landless of the world, including experimenting in fruit and crops adapted in the new country...I lived in a storyteller region. All the old traders, the old French trappers, all the old characters who had been around the Black Hills...the Indians were wonderful storytellers. There was an old Indian woman who told of Sand Creek and the Washita and Fort Robinson and of buffalo hunts and of fights with the snakes and the crows. But not much of wars with the whites for these were still touchy and unhappy affairs. Many a night, I sat in the woodbox and listened. As long as I kept still, I did not have to go to bed..."

"Father came from an upper-middle class professional family. He didn't believe in fiction. That was for the hired girl and the hired man. So I had to borrow books and smuggle them into the house in the sloppy front of our low-belted dresses." (*Hostiles and Friendlies*, pp. XV, XVII)

Mari Sandoz passed the rural teacher's examination and was allowed at twenty-one to enroll at the University of Nebraska. She wrote short stories and "a bad novel that, fortunately, no one would publish." Finally, in 1935, *Old Jules*, an account of Indian and Western life, was published. Her fiction and nonfiction are considered to be among the most sensitive and accurate portrayals of Western life in the late 19th and early 20th centuries.

Mari Sandoz, *Hostiles and Friendlies*, p. IV.

Page 165
Kalim: Annemarie Schimmel, *A Two-Colored Brocade* (Chapel Hill: The University of North Carolina Press: 1992), p. 139.

Page 167
Gauguin: Druick and Zegers, *Van Gogh and Gauguin: The Studio of the South*, pp. 206, 207, 209.

Laurence Sterne: Ian Campbell Ross, *Laurence Sterne: A Life*, pp. 57, 209-211.

Page 169
Virginia Woolf: Virginia Woolf, *A Room of One's Own* (New York: Harcourt Brace Jovanovich, 1989), p. 10.

Candia: Crete.

Simha Padawer: S.Y. Agnon, *Days of Awe*, p. 263.

Page 171
Li Tianfu: 1635–1699. A retired grand secretary in Anhui. He was host of Shitao in the summer of 1692, a richly creative period in the life of Shitao.

Shitao: Jonathan Hay, *Shitao: Painting and Modernity in Early Qing China*, pp. 115-116.

Bada Shanren: Yang Xin, Richard M. Barnhart, Nie Chongzheng, James Cahill, Lang Shaojun, Wu Hung, *Three Thousand Years of Chinese Painting* (New Haven: Yale University Press, 1997), p. 253-257. Badashanren's verse was written in 1682.

Page 173
Gauguin: Druik and Zegers, *Van Gogh and Gauguin*, p. 224.

Virginia Woolf: Virginia Woolf, *A Room of One's Own*, pp. 101-102.

Mu Xin: *The Art of Mu Xin: Landscape Paintings and Prison*, p. 143.

Page 175
Harold Nicolson: Tony Lord, *Gardening at Sissinghurst* (London: Francis Lincoln Limited, 1995), p. 128-129.

Virginia Woolf: Mitchell Leaska, *The Hidden Life of Virginia Woolf* (New York: Farrar, Straus & Giroux, 1998), p. 414. Louise DeSalvo, Mitchell Leaska, eds., *The Letters of Vita Sackville-West to Virginia Woolf*, p. 363.

Page 177
Gabbay: Treasurer.

Manuel Levy Duarte: See the tombstone of Rachel Abolais (died 1656). Her husband, Imanuel Abolais, died in 1632. Rachel Abolais Duarte was named after her grandmother Rachel Abolais. David Henriques de Castro, *Selected Gravestones from the Portuguese Jewish Cemetary at Orderkerk aan de Amstel* (Orderkerk aan de Amstel: 1999), p. 54.

Page 179
Chief Red Cloud: Chief Red Cloud, July 16, 1870. Ulrich W. Hiesinger, *Indian Lives* (New York: Prestel-Verlag, 1994), pp. 75–85.

Page 181
Konya: A city in Turkey where they have whirling dervishes.

Abu Sa'id ibn Abi-l Khair: "The first to draw up a simple monastic rule for his Sufi community." Anniemarie Schimmel in her extraordinary *Mystical Dimensions of Islam* writes: "Yet the great masters have always acknowledged that hunger is only a means to spiritual progress, not a goal in itself. Just as Abu Sa'id ibn Abi-I-Khair after years of incredible ascetic hardships eventually enjoyed food—and good food! Many of the later mystics would agree that the saying that 'soul-dog is better when its mouth is shut by throwing a morsel into it' is correct. Dara Shikoh was the son of Shah Jahan, Dara Shikoh was killed by his brother Aurangzeb who seized the moghul throne in India. Anniemarie Schimmel, *Mystical Dimensions of Islam*, pp. 88, 116.

Antoon Geels, *Kabbalah Om Judisk Mysticism* (Kabbalah and Jewish Mysticism) (Stockholm: Jewish Museum, 2002), p. 9, 10. This book and exhibition, like many others, owes its existence to the wisdom and enthusiasm of Bill and Lisa Gross. The Gross family collection, built up lovingly over decades, illustrates the story of the Jewish people, both in its internal philosophy and inherent beauty as well as in its relationship to the secular and religious world at large. The Judaica collection and Bill and Lisa are wonderful cultural ambassadors. I thank them for all their warm encouragement over the years.

Hiram Bingham III: In Hugh Thompson's artful *The White Rock* (Woodstock, New York: Overlook Press, 2002), pp. 77, 78, Thompson observes: "Almost as soon as Bingham saw Machu Picchu, he began the ceaseless stream of hypotheses that have flowed ever since about its origins." Bingham thought one of the buildings "contained riches in which mummies could be kept and venerated (having been reared as a boy on tales of Egyptology, Bingham was obsessed by the idea of mummies). The place was a blank canvas on which explorers could superimpose their pet theories." Alfred Bingham, *The Tiffany Fortune and Other Chronicle of a Connecticut Family* (Chestnut Hill, MA: Abeel and Leet Publishers, 1996) p. 169. Alfred Bingham writes, "On the dock to see him off stood Alfreda, holding her little boy Harry [Hiram Bingham IV] by one hand and waving frantically with the other."

Alfred Bingham: In Alfred Bingham's *Portrait of an Explorer: Hiram Bingham, Discoverer of Machu Picchu* (Ames, Iowa: Iowa State University Press, 1989), p. 351, Alfred Bingham quotes Professor Georg F. Eaton's observation that "the meagerness of the artifacts found with the [women's] bones suggests that persons buried were not of the 'chosen women' but rather of minor retainers and servants." See also Bruce Fellman, "Rediscovering Machu Picchu," Yale Alumni Journal, Dec. 2002, pp. 40, 45.

Page 183
Shtum: One who is silent.

Maggid of Dubno: *Encyclopedia Judaica*, Vol. VI, p. 652. Benno Heinemann, *The Maggid of Dubno and his Parables* (New York: Feldheim Publishers, 1978), p. 193-194. Rabbi Nossun Scherman, *The Complete Art Scroll Machsor Rosh Hashanah* (Brooklyn: Mensorah Publications, 1988), p. 435. For the Gaon (genius) of Vilna, an extraordinary Talmudic scholar, see Benjamin Zucker, *Blue*, p. 230 and *Green*, p. 228.

Page 185
Virginia Woolf painting: Virginia Woolf painted in 1911–1912 by her sister Vanessa Bell. "The portrait soon followed the Post-Impressionist Exhibition, which strongly influenced Vanessa's art and indirectly Virginia's writing."

Virginia Woolf: "Roger Fry was the most civilized man I ever met," claimed Virginia Woolf. Jan Marsh, *Bloomsbury Women* (New York: Henry Holt and Company, 1955), p. 47.

Virginia Woolf: Nigel Nicolson, *Virginia Woolf*, p. 37.

Page 187
Gauguin: Bengt Danielsson, *Gauguin in the South Seas*, p. 25, 27. Douglas W. Druik and Peter Kort Zegers, *Montfried's Sunflower Seeds; Van Gogh & Gauguin: The Studio of the South*, p. 350.

Julius Meyer: Bengt Danielsson, *Gauguin in the South Seas*, p. 26.

P. Jenot: Stephen F. Eisenman, *Gauguin's Skirt* (London: Thames & Hudson, 1997), p. 27.

Jeremy Kalmanofsky: Jeremy Kalmanofsky, *Amen and Amen:*

Blessing of a Heretic (New York: The American Jewish Congress, Issue No. 202, Volume 51, No. 2, Spring 2002), p. 177.

Sarah Padawer: Daniel C. Matt, *The Zohar* (The Pritzker Edition) (Stanford, Calif.: Stanford University Press, 2001), XXIII.

Page 189
Bada Shanren: Joseph Chang and Qianshen Bai, *In Pursuit of Heavenly Harmony*, p. 5.

Page 191
Gauguin: Druik and Zegers, *Van Gogh & Gauguin*, 61, 352.

"Bonjour Monsieur Gauguin": This panel hung in the dining room of La Burette above "Caribbean Woman." It is a parody of the painting "Bonjour Monsieur Courbet" by Gustave Courbet (1819–1877) which Van Gogh and Gauguin had seen together in Montpelier. In it the artist is shown meeting his wealthy patron. Gauguin painted himself a lonely pilgrim, not awaited by his patron, but by a sombre peasant woman. The dejected mood agreed with reality: Gauguin's benefactor Theo van Gogh had criticized his recent work and sales were bad." John Leighton, Van Gogh and Gauguin, notes to the show in the Van Gogh Museum, 2002.

Rachel Abendana: Rabbi Yisroel Simcha Schorr and Rabbi Chaim Malnowitz, eds., *The Talmud*, Schottenstein Edition (New York: Me'sorah Publications, Ltd., 1998), p. 2a.

Rachel Zucker: Rachel Zucker, *Annunciation* (New York: Center for Book Arts, 2002).

Page 193
Lord Sandwich: Lord Sandwich was eaten by cannibals.

Virginia Woolf: Peter Stansky, *On or About December 1910: Early Bloomsbury and Its Intimate World* (Cambridge, MA: Harvard University Press, 1992), pp. 2-3.

Leonard Woolf: Peter Stansky, *On or About December 1910*, p. 13.

Page 195
Talmud Yerushalmi Yoma: Micah 7:8. Ester 2:19. Ester 6:11. Ester 8:15. Jacob Neusner, *The Yerushalmi: An Introduction* (Northvale, N.J.: Jason Aronson, 1993), p. 93. See Shulamis Frieman, *Who's Who in the Talmud*, for the life of Rabbi Hiyya, pp. 110-112.

Rabbi Hiyyah ben Joseph: Jacob Neusner, *The Yerushalmi: The Talmud of the Land of Israel: An Introduction* (Northvale, New Jersey: Jason Aronson Press, 1993), p. 45.

Bob Dylan: Bob Dylan, New Morning, copyright 1970, renewed by Big Sky Music.

Rabbi Kalonymus Kalman Shapira of Piasetzno, the Rebbe of the Warsaw ghetto: He was a descendant of many noted Hassidic masters, including the Maggid of Koznitz and the Seer of Lublin. Rabbi Shapira continued to teach and write from the beginning of the Holocaust through the destruction of the Warsaw ghetto. He was killed in 1943 but his writing, which he hid in a jar in the earth beneath the ghetto, miraculously survived.

"On the first day of *Chol Hamo'ed* [the intermediate days of *Sukkot* 1939] the Piasetzner Rebbe's only son was killed in a bombing raid on Warsaw and was laid to rest in a funeral attended by thousands. Six days later it was *Simhat Torah*. That year, the *hakafot* [seven joyous circular processions around the Torah reading platform] bore a different character. Only a limited number of people took part in the service. The *hakafot* were held in great haste. With death lurking in every corner, people rushed home with downcast and gloomy faces. Only a handful of young students who were loyally devoted to the Rebbe sensed that the Rebbe's soul still held a spark of excitement that would burst forth at any moment. A student graphically described what happened afterward in the Rebbe's *bet midrash* [house of study and prayer]. 'There were fewer than ten of us, crushed in spirit and despondent. Suddenly, the Rebbe walked up to the *amud*[reader's stand]and intoned the [Karlin-Stolin] *niggun of Eishet Chayil* [an accomplished woman who can find a tribute to the Jewish people and the Torah], his voice vibrating with ecstasy and deep emotion.

"He continued singing this enchanting melody for more than an hour, with an unquenchable thirst and yearning for nearness to G-d. He stood there, unaware of any bystander, oblivious to the world, tears flowing freely down his cheeks, his magnificent voice enrapturing our hearts. Nobody would have believed that the Rebbe was deeply mourning the tragic death of his only son. Imperceptively, our mood began to change. Insensible to the outside world, our fears and sadness vanished. What war? What troubles? Everything was forgotten. Forgotten were the…devils prancing through the streets, the bombings, shelling, and the dead bodies. We were swept away into a different world. The feverish excitement of the Rebbe's singing slowly reaching a crescendo had us completely spellbound. It seemed as though everything were lifted to a higher sphere together with the fire bursting from his heart. Each of us felt palpably how the "perfect dove," the Jewish people, symbolized by the *eishet chayil* [the accomplished wife] was united with her beloved [G-d] on this day, under such distressing circumstances. We could hear G-d's voice piercing the dense mist and the somber clouds. No 'concealment of G-d's face' here. The radiance of the *Shechina* [the Divine Presence] was shining upon us."

"'These moments of pure bliss,' the student—a lone survivor—said in conclusion, "will remain forever engraved in my heart. I'll never forget them." Avraham Yaakov Finkel, *Contemporary Sages: The Great Chasidic Masters of the Twentieth Century*, pp. 74, 77, 78.

Page 197
Elihu Yale: The *Yale Journal of Criticism* (New Haven, Conn.: Spring 1994) published an excellent essay by Gaur Viswanathan, studying Elihu Yale as a colonialist and British imperialist. Elihu Yale was an Anglican and yet he supported the creation of a dissenter's university. Viswanathan quotes Cotton Mather's letter to Elihu Yale: "The people for whom we bespeak your favors are such sound, generous Christian and Protestants that their not observing some disputable rite (which no act of parliament has imposed on these plantations) ought by no means to exclude them from the respects of all that are indeed such, and from the good will which we all owe to the rest of the reformed churches, all of which have their little varieties."

Viswanathan goes on to hypothesize that the death of Elihu Yale's son David (and the birth of his illegitimate son Charles, born of his union with a Portuguese Jewish woman, Hieronyma de Paiva) may have "brought out the deepest insecurity in the British male colonizer. His apparent power and authority in the military and political sphere was undermined by his inability to ensure the continuity of his biological line. The compulsive urge to name towns, streets, buildings and other sites after themselves or their deceased children marks a persistent tendency by European colonizers to bestow their paternity on the colonial landscape as a gesture of ultimate conquest." Viswanathan, p. 7.

Seen in this light, Cotton Mather's words to Yale: "If what is forming at New Haven might wear the name of YALE COLLEGE, it would be better than a name of sons and daughters. And your munificence might easily obtain for you such a commemoration and perpetuation of your valuable name, as would indeed be much better than an Egyptian pyramid."

Hiram Bingham, the biographer of Yale, opinioned that "if the governor had been the Elihu Yale of his early married life…as he was before his son died and his wife went back to England, it is not likely that he would have forced measures though against the opposition of proactively all the members of his council."

"The naming of Yale College," Viswanathan observes, can be seen "as a conquest of death itself (even sons and daughters can not extend a man's life the way institutions can)."

Sarah Padawer: Daniel C. Matt, *The Zohar* (The Pritzger Edition) (Stanford, Calif.: Stanford University Press, 2004), p. XXIII.

Page 199
Elihu Yale: Hiram Bingham, *Elihu Yale: The American Nabob of Queen Square*, pp. 307, 325.

Mrs. Light: See Hieronyma da Paiva's last will and testament. Note, p. 110.

Van Gogh: *Van Gogh & Gauguin*, p. 97, 188.

Rachel: The prostitute Van Gogh gave his ear to was named Rachel.

Weijving: Endless philosophical discussions.
Virginia Woolf: Virginia Woolf, *The Waves*, 1931.

Page 201
Isaac Tal: Irving Howe and Eliezer Greenberg, *A Treasury of Yiddish Stories*, "Chaim Grade: My Quarrel with Hersh Rasseyner" (New York: Viking Press, 1954, and Schocken Paperback,1973), pp. 594, 595, 596, 599, 603, 606.

Page 203
Shah Tahmasp (1525–1576): Ruler of Persia.

Humayum: Bamber Gascoine, *The Great Moguls* (New York: Dorset Press, 1971), p. 54. Susan Stronge, *Painting for the Moghul Emperor: The Art of the Book 1560–1660*, p. 12.

John Godfrey Saxe: Pratapaditya Pal, *Elephants and Ivories in South Asia* (Los Angeles: Los Angeles County Museum of Art, 1981), p. 8.

Rachel Abendana Tal: Irving Howe and Eliezer Greenberg, *A Treasury of Yiddish Stories*, pp. 604-606.

James Joyce: James Joyce, *Finnegans Wake* (London: Faber and Faber, 1968). James Joyce, *Ulysses* (New York: Random House, 1961), p. 405. Philip F. Herring, *Joyce's Ulysses Notesheets in the British Museum* (Charlottesville: University Press of Virginia, 1972), p. 1.

Page 205
David Birnbaum: Through six decades, David Birnbaum has been the closest of friends to me. Encouraging, whimsical and knowledgeable about virtually everything, he has made so much of writing fiction and non-fiction a pleasure. All matters Chinese sprang from David's sojourn in the East. Little matters such as earning a good living during the writing of these novels have been helped immeasurably through his advice and friendship. Who could believe that David could be so smart and so much fun?

Laurence Sterne: Lawrence Sterne, *Tristram Shandy*, p. 268.

Page 207
Emily Post: Emily Post, *Etiquette*, p. 269.

Mu Xin: *The Art of Mu Xin*, p. 137.

Mikhail Tal: The oldest foreign reference to the practice of chess in India is by Al-'adli (circa 840 A.D.). The Indian Elephant is the ancestor of our present-day castle or rook. H.J.R. Murray, *A History of Chess* (Oxford: Oxford University Press, 1913), p. 57. Dmitry Plisetsky and Sergey Voronkov, *Russians Versus Fischer* (New York: Chess World Ltd., 1994), pp. 64, 65.

Page 209
Julio Cortázar: Julio Cortázar, *Hopscotch*, p. 214.

Harold Bloom: *Yosef Hayim Yerushalmi*, forward by Harold Bloom (New York: Schocken Books, 1989), p. XXIII.

Bet: Second letter of the alphabet. Also means house in Hebrew.

Sarmad: See Benjamin Zucker, *Blue*, p. 231 and *Green*, p. 227.

Mario Vargas Llosa: Mario Vargas Llosa, *Lettters to a Young Novelist* (New York: Farrar, Straus & Giroux, 2002), pp. 125, 126.

Page 211
Shamas: A person who collects charity at a synagogue.

Hershel Tschortkower: Hanoch Teller's remarkable telling of the Rothschild beginnings in *Courtrooms of the Mind* (Spring Valley, New York: Feldheim Publishing, 1987), p. 203-211. Michael Hall, *Waddeston Manor: The Heritage of a Rothschild House* (New York: Harry N. Abrams, Inc., 2002), pp. 244-246. *Encyclopedia Judaica*, volume 14, pp. 342-345.

David Lloyd George: *David and Winston: How a Friendship Changed History* (London: John Murray, 2005), elegantly written by my friend Robert Lloyd George, gives a fascinating portrayal of how a Welsh outsider (his great grandfather Prime Minister Lloyd George) was a decisive force in saving Britain in the First World War as well as an adviser to Churchill in World War II. Prime Minister Lloyd George's understanding and sympathy for the creation of Israel: "when Dr. Weizmann was talking of Palestine, he kept bringing up place names which were more familiar to me than those of the Western front." See Barbara W. Tuchman, *The Bible and the Sword* (New York: Ballantine Books, 1984), p. 325. Such warmth toward the aspirations of the Jews was undoubtedly traceable to Lloyd George's early biblical training. See *David and Winston*, pp. 172-181. Robert Lloyd George also notes that in addition to supporting the Balfour Declaration, Lloyd George wrote: "We made an equal pledge that we would not turn the Arabs off his land or invade his political and social rights."

Hiram (Harry) Bingham IV: I would like to thank the entire Bingham family for sharing with me so much of their extraordinary devotion to ideals generation after generation. John and Katherine Bingham kindly read the manuscript and suggested changes consonant with Harry Bingham's personality. David Bingham and Doug Bingham were my classmates at Yale and continue to be friends and were so helpful with *White*. Nathan Zucker, my uncle, tirelessly and miraculously obtained at least sixty American visas in 1940 for our family, which combined with the exit permissions through Harry Bingham enabled my extended family to start anew in the United States.

Eric Saul: Extraordinarily knowledgeable about the righteous during the Second World War, Eric Saul continues to be indefatigable in shedding light on the heroes of conscience during the Holocaust. The individuals he studies give me hope for a humane future.

Page 213
William Faulkner: Quoted by Judith Hauptman in *Rereading the Rabbis*. "Fully acknowledging that Judaism as described in both the bible and the Talmud was patriarchal, Hauptman demonstrates that the Rabbis of the Talmud made significant changes in key areas of Jewish law to benefit women." *Rereading the Rabbis* (New York: HarperCollins, 1998), p. 1. Frederick L. Gwynn and Joseph L. Blotner, *Faulkner in the University* (New York: Vintage Books, 1965), p. 94.

Virginia Woolf: Virginia Woolf, *Moments of Being* (New York: Harcourt Brace Jovanovich, 2000), p. 67.

James Joyce: Arthur Power, *Conversations with James Joyce* (Dublin: Lilliput Press, Ltd., 1999), pp. 90-92.

F.Scott Fitzgerald: I: He. I rejoice in the fact that my marvelous Mother, Lotty Johanna Gutwirth Zucker, raced to the hospital on Rue Tsarovitch (by fire truck as all civilian cars were forbidden to move in those war-time nights) in Nice, on the French Riviera, to give birth to me, Benjamin Zucker, at the very instant F. Scott Fitzgerald passed away in California on Dec., 21, 1940. Fitzgerald quote, "I write..." Matthew J. Bruccoli, F. Scott Fitzgerald's *The Great Gatsby: A Literary Reference* (New York: Carroll & Graf Publishers, 2002), back cover.
F. Scott Fitzgerald, *The Great Gatsby* (New York: Scribner Classics, 1996), pp. 20, 152.
Harold Bloom, ed., *F. Scott Fitzgerald's The Great Gatsby* (New York: Chelsea House Publishers, 1986), p. 61.
Dinitia Smith, "Love Notes Drenched in Moonlight," *The New York Times*, Arts Section, p. E1, Sept. 8, 2003.
"Ginerva King, a celebrated debutante who Fitzgerald met in 1915 when she was a 16-year-old at the Westover School and he was a 19-year-old at Princeton..." According to James L. West III, Fitzgerald "lost her but his ideal of her remained throughout his life."

Page 215
Simha Padawer: S.Y. Agnon, *Days of Awe*, pp. 274- 275.

Page 217
Ni Tsan: Chinese painter, 1301–1371. Sherman E. Lee, *A History of Far Eastern Art* (New Jersey: Prentice Hall, Inc., 1964), p. 412. Yang Xin, Richard M. Barnhart, Nie Chongzheng, James Cahill, Lang Shaojun, Wu Hung, *Three Thousand Years of Chinese Painting*, p. 258.

Bada Shanren: Ni Tsan, 1306–1374, was one of the four great masters of the Yuan Dynasty (1279–1368). His work is marked by great simplicity, and served as an aesthetic and moral model for Bada Shanren. Joseph Chang and Qianshen Bai, *In Pursuit of Heavenly Harmony*, p. 140.

Tish: table.

Page 219
Virginia Woolf photograph: This colored photograph was taken much against Woolf's will by Gisele Freund. Virginia Woolf wrote to Vita: "I'm in a rage. That devil woman Giselle [sic] Freund calmly tells me she's showing these d—d photographs and I made a condition she shouldn't. I loathe being hoisted around on top of a stick for anyone to stare at."

Elihu Yale: "Ever elegant, loved by all." These words are on the gravestone of Charles Almanzo, the son of Hieronyma da Paiva and Elihu Yale.

Hieronyma Da Paiva: Lyall Watson wrote: "All elephants greet each other, but when the encounter involves members that are directly related, the reunion is effusive. Cynthia Moss, who followed one family in Amboseli for thirteen years, described it as thrilling. 'The two subgroups of the family will run together, rumbling, trumpeting and screaming, raise their heads, click their tusks together, entwine their trunks, flap their ears, spin around and back into each other, urinate and defecate and generally show great excitement. A greeting such as this will sometimes last for as long as ten minutes.'" Lyall Watson, *Elephantoms* (New York: W.W. Norton, 2002), p. 69.

Elihu Yale: Mrs. Light—I am again indebted to Edgar Samuel for his unflagging assistance. Hiram Bingham, in his biography *Elihu Yale: The American Nabob of Queen's Square*, p. 312, states that Hieronyma da Paiva was buried in Capetown next to the child she bore to Elihu Yale, Charles Almanza. Bingham describes the tombstones:

"His epitaph, copied by the Dutch naturalist governor Luten of Ceylon, was in Latin and set forth that it was erected by his mother, 'Jeronima de Paiba' who for the love she bore him 'left India that she might be buried with him.' It describes him as her only child and the only son of 'Lord Yale, once the governor of Madras but not of Hieronima.' It calls Charles 'fashionable, virtuous, even elegant, loved by all.'"

Other than the tombstone inscription, Bingham makes no mention of where Hieronyma spent the rest of her life. As a novelist and devoté of Barbara Bessin Zucker, I could not imagine after such a tumultuous courtship Hieronyma and Elihu would be separated from each after Elihu left Madras for India. Edgar Samuel, whose tastes run to history, not fiction, disagreed. He posited that it was all too consonant with the spirit of the 17th century English life in the Indies to take a mistress and abandon her upon returning to England. It is a measure of Edgar's fidelity to researching the period that he responded to my repeated "novelist's dreams about Elihu and Hieronima" and serendipitously found Hieronima da Paiva's last will and testament:

"PRO ProbII/582 (Buckingham 722)

26th June 1723

Memorandum that Jeronima de Paiba of the Parish of St Mary Woolnoth London Widow being indisposed in her health did on or about Wednesday the last day of May last send for Mrs Jane East with whom the said Jeronima was intimately acquainted to come to her at her lodgings at Mr Thrumballs in Stocks Market and the said Jane East, being come to her she the said Jeronima told the said Mrs East that she was in worse condition as to her health than she had ever been in her life and that she was not a Woman for this world and that she feared she should never see her the said Mrs. East any more and she then told the said Mrs East that she had sent for her to declare to her who should be her heir in case she dyed and she the said Jeronima de Paiba did then declare that she did make her Will and that she gave all she had in the world to her Nephew Mr Abraham Gonsales and made him her sole heir which said words or very same in effect she the said Jeronima did then utter and declare in the presence and hearing of the said Mrs Jane East, John Higton her Footman Susann Gomes and Mary de Fonseca her servants whom she desired to take notice that such was her Will and that she should not rest in her grave if Abraham Gonsales her Nephew should not have all and she the said Jeronima was at all and singular the premises of sound mind memori and understanding and discoursed very rationally and well and she the said Jeronima departed this life on Saturday last. Jane East, John Higton *Signum* Susanne Gomes et Maria Fonseca *Jurati fisese veritate*". Public Record Office, London, England.

Edgar Samuel stated, "There is no record of her burial in the Portuguese Jewish cemetery."

Indeed, Hieronyma and Elihu Yale were in London for perhaps all of the period after Yale returned from India in 1700—or for part of it. Grist indeed for a novel, or a film. (I can be reached through Overlook Press.)

Page 221
Van Gogh: Meyer Schapiro, *Van Gogh* (New York: Harry N. Abrams, Inc., 1983), p. 21, 22, 26.

Page 223
Cordovero: Pinchas Giller, *Reading the Zohar* (New York: Oxford University Press, 2001), pp. 69-70.

Isaac Luria: Zohar IV 175a.

Sitting Bull the Hunkpapa: Kent Nerburn, ed., *The Wisdom of the Native Americans* (Novato, Calif: New World Library, 1999), pp. 51-52.

Virginia Woolf: Virginia Woolf, *A Room of One's Own*, p. 101.

Laurence Sterne: Laurence Sterne, *Tristram Shandy*, Book II. Chapter ii. 70; I. xxx. 32; Book I. Chapter xix. 32.

Bob Berman: Bob Berman, Secrets of the Night Sky (New York: William Morrow and Company, Inc., 1995), p. 40; *Woodstock Times*, January 29, 2004, p. 5. "What We're Made Of?" by Bob Berman.

ACKNOWLEDGMENTS

Peter Mayer's encouragement and enthusiasm has enabled me to complete this trilogy. It's been a great pleasure to work with him.

All at The Overlook Press have helped me enormously: Tracy Carns, George Davidson and *Jamais deux san trois*—never two without three —Bernie Schleifer for yet a third time has been a true miracle to me.

Tasha Blaine's advice and wisdom on every aspect of each variation of this manuscript has made this novel what it is.

The skillful and honest molding of George Blecher and literary discussions I've had with Rachel Zucker and Josh Goren have crystallized my thinking about how a novel should be structured.

Mary Flower enabled me to gather the rights that fill these pages. Alison Jasonides' remarkable eye and unfailing sense of beauty has made this novel as beautiful as it is.

To understand the world of art and jewelry, I am greatly indebted for many discussions over the years with Jan Mitchell, Alastair B. Martin, Ralph Esmerian, Dr. Assaudullah Souren Melikian Chirvani, Semir Zeki, Derek J. Content, Jesse Wolfgang, Richard Camber, Jack Ogden, Milo Beach, Stuart Cary Welch, Amy and Bob Poster, Mary McWilliams, Jonathan Hay, Michael Gill, Susan Stronge, Diana and Peter Scarisbrick, Gary Vikan, Jock Reynolds, Martin Norton (whose wisdom I still hear each day), Nicholas Norton, Jonathan Norton and Francis Norton.

This novel was fundamentally conceived in college. A coterie of friends—Lee Grove, Bill and Libbie Reilly, Robert and Nancy Gray, William and Lucy Hamilton, Tom and Candice Powers, Derek and Nicole Limbocker, Richard and Franny Zorn and William and Priscilla Rope—enable those Yale days to remain "forever young."

Coffee was the fuel that made me believe this trilogy would be completed. David Birnbaum's extraordinary whimsy and friendship and Milton Moses Ginsberg's creative example have sustained me.

Abbie Bingham Endicott and William Endicott, John and Katherine Bingham, Robert "Kim" Bingham, Dave Bingham, Doug Bingham and many others of the Bingham family were untiring in their gracious help. Eric Saul, continues to illuminate the dark days of the Second World War for me. So many thanks to Al Moldovan, Dan Friedenberg, Al and Harry Kleinhaus, Jim Traub, Buffy Easton, Laurel Beizer, Ricky Borger, Bill and Lisa Gross, Itchie Heschel, Michael and Elizabeth Varet, Eden Collingsworth.

White is a book based on other books. My friends at Gotham Book Mart as well as at The Golden Notebook and The Reader's Quarry (Woodstock, New York) are wonderful.

My inspiration for *Blue*, *Green* and *White* flows from the teachings of Elie Wiesel and Jay Margolis.

My whole family before the beginning until this day have been so understanding and supportive throughout the writing. Above all, Barbara's immense charm, wonderful laugh and ever youthful love has made writing this book a passionate joy.

ART SOURCES

Overlook Press would like to thank the following for their kind permission to reproduce their photographs and illustrations.

Every effort has been made to trace the copyright holders. Overlook Press apologizes for any unintentional omissions, and would be please, if any such case should arise, to add an appropriate acknowledgment in future editions.

Cover: Gem Indian diamond, 3.22 carats. Photo: Peter Schaaf.

Frontispiece (opposite title page): Side view of pear-shaped diamond. Gem Indian diamond, 3.22 carats. Photo: Peter Schaaf.

Page vi
Van Gogh, *Self-Portrait dedicated to Paul Gauguin.* 1889. Fogg Art Museum, Harvard University Art Museum, collection of Maurice Wertheim, class of 1906.

Page viii
Mu Xin, *Pure Mind Amid Colored Clouds*, 1977-79. Ink and gouache on paper. Collection of the Rosenkranz Foundation. Photograph courtesy of the Yale University Art Gallery.

Page 2
Vanessa Bell (1879-1961). *Virginia Woolf*, 1912. National Portrait Gallery, London.

Page 4
Shitao (Tao-Chi, 1642-1707), *Thirty-six Peaks of Mount Huang Recollected.* Hanging scroll; ink on paper. The Metropolitan Museum of Art, gift of Douglas Dillon, 1976. (1976.1.1) Photograph © 1980 The Metropolitan Museum of Art.

Page 6
Jeweler, Mechlin, Belgium, 17th century. Private collection.

Page 8
Paul Gauguin (1848-1903), *Self-Portrait*, c. 1876-77. Oil on canvas. Courtesy of the Fogg Art Museum, Harvard University Art Museums, Gift of Helen W. Ellsworth in memory of Duncan S. Ellsworth '22, nephew of Arhibald A. Hutchinson, benefactor of the Hutchinson. Photo: Katya Kallsen. © 2004 President and Fellows of Harvard College.

Page 10
Julius Meyer (1851-1909), "Box-Ka-Re-Sha-Hash-Ta-Ka." Indian trader and translator. Calling card. Private Collection.

Page 12
Paul Gauguin, *Breton Girls Dancing*, Pont Aven. Collection of Mr. And Mrs. Paul Mellon, Image © Board of Trustees, National Gallery of Art, Washington 1888, oil on canvas.

Page 14
Shitao, *Fish and Rocks.* Chinese, c. 1624-1705, Qing Dynasty. Handscroll, ink on paper. © The Cleveland Museum of Art, John L. Severance Fund, 1953.247.

Page 16
Talmud Yoma (The Day). Gutman Gutwirth's study copy of the Talmud.

Page 18
Rothschild Ewer, Frankfurt, 1773-1806. (Private Collection, ZFC/GFC)

Page 20
Photograph of Virginia Woolf playing croquet with her sister Vanessa. St. Ives, 1894. Courtesy of the Houghton Library, Harvard University.

Page 22
Vincent Van Gogh (1853-1890), The Loyer's House, Vincent's boarding house on Hackford Road, London, 1873-74. Gouache, pencil. © Van Gogh Art Museum, Amsterdam (Vincent Van Gogh Foundation).

Page 24
Portrait of Jahangir's Court Wrestler, Fil-e Safid (White Elephant), c. 1610. Gouache and gilt on paper. Victoria & Albert Museum, London/Art Resource, NY.

Page 26
The Emperor Don Pedro II Diamond. A vivid green transmitter diamond. Photograph courtesy of Tom Moses, GIA. Private Collection.

Page 28
Franz Kafka standing in front of the Opoltz House, 1920-21. Courtesy of Klaus Wagenbach.

Page 30
Payag, *The Battle of Samugarh.* Gray-black ink, opaque watercolor, gold and metallic silver paint over white wash on off-white paper. Gift of Stuart Cary Welch, Jr. © President and Fellows of Harvard College (1999.298).

Page 32
Rembrandt van Rijn, *Self-Portrait on a Stone Sill.* Etching. The British Museum, London.

Page 34
Diamond-cutting machine in 17th century Amsterdam. Print: Jan Luycken. From "Picture of Human Occupations." "The rough diamond, how dark, receives in polishing all its brightness. The one that falls clear of water and big of body is called a gem."

Page 36
Vincent Van Gogh (1853-1890), *Self-Portrait*, Paris, 1887. Oil on pasteboard, 19 x 14 cm. © Van Gogh Museum, Amsterdam (Vincent Van Gogh Foundation).

Page 38
Berenice Abbott, Nora Barnacle (James Joyce's wife).

Page 40
Giuseppe Arcimboldo, *Vertumnus (Emperor Rudolf II)*, 1590. Oil on wood. Skoklosters, Slott, Sweden. Credit: Erich Lessing/Art Resource, NY.

Page 42
Bada Shanren (1626-1705), *Lotus and Ducks* with Colophon by We Changshuo. Hanging scroll. China, c. 1696, ink on paper. Freer Gallery of Art, Smithsonian Institution, Washington DC: Bequest from the collection of Wang Fangyu and Sum Wai, donated in their memory by Mr. Shao F. Wang, F. 1998.45.

Page 44
Lucas Vosterman the Edler (1595-1675), *Portrait of Gaspar Duarte* (d. 1653). Municipal Print Room, Antwerp.

Page 46
Edward Hopper, *Rooms by the Sea*. Yale University Gallery. Bequest of Stephen Carlton Clark, B.A. 1903.

Page 48
Bada Shanren (1626-1705), *Flower, Buddha's Hand Citron, Hibiscus* and *Lotus Pod*. Album leaf (one of a set of four). China, c. 1692, ink on paper. Freer Gallery of Art, Smithsonian Institution, Washington, DC: Bequest from the collection of Wang Fangyu and Sum Wai, donated in their memory by Mr. Saho F. Wang, F1998.56.1.

Page 50
Dara Shikoh riding the imperial elephant, Mahabir Deb. Tinted brush drawing with gold details, c. 1645. Given by Mr. R.S. Greenshields. Victoria & Albert Museum, London/Art Resource, NY.

Page 52
Mary Stevenson Cassatt, *In The Loge*, 1878. Oil on canvas, 81.28 x 66.04 cm (32 x 26 in.). Museum of Fine Arts, Boston. The Hayden Collection, Charles Henry Hayden Fund, 10.35.

Page 54
Sita Ram, The Taj Mahal by Moonlight. 700.1983. Sackler Museum of Art, Harvard Art Museums, Cambridge, Ma. Courtesy Stuart Cary Welch.

Page 56
Roman Vishniac, *Isaac Street, Kazimierz, Cracow*, 1938. Gelatin silver print. © Mara Vishniac Kohn. Courtesy of The International Center of Photography, NY.

Page 58
Vanessa Bell (1879-1961), *Leonard Woolf*, 1940. National Portrait Gallery, London.

Page 60
Shah Jahan as an old man. Private Collection.

Page 62
Balchand, *Royal Lovers: Prince Shah Shuja and his wife*. Arthur M. Sackler Museum, Harvard Art Museums. Courtesy of Stuart Cary Welch.

Page 64
Jan Vermeer, *Young Woman Seated at a Virginal*. Oil on canvas. The National Gallery, London.

Page 66
Mississippi John Hurt at the Newport Folk Festival, Summer 1964. Photo: Gerrie Blake. © Mimmosa Record Productions.

Page 68
Marriage contract (Ketubah). Sinigalia, Italy. 19th century. Private Collection, RCZ/GFC.

Page 70
Sitting Bull and Buffalo Bill, Montreal, QC, 1885. McCord Museum of Canadian History, Montreal.

Page 72
Anonymous, *Antwerp in the Province of Brabant,* 1518-1540. Detail: Portuguese cargos in the Antwerp harbor. National Maritime Museum, Antwerp.

Page 74
Table-cut diamond ring, Antwerp, c. 1620. Photograph: Peter Schaaf. Private Collection.

Page 76
Annie Oakley holding an 1890 marlin, 9.375 x 6.25, c. 1890. Buffalo Bill Historical Center, Cody, Wyoming; Vincent Mercaldo Collection.

Page 78
Zelda Fitzgerald at Saulies-de-Bearn, 1926, painting F. Scott Fitzgerald. From: Eleanor Lanahan, ed., *Zelda: An Illustrated Life* (Harry Abrams, New York, 199).

Page 80
Je Viens, Lithograph, 1889. Buffalo Bill Historical Center, Cody, Wyoming; 1.69.442.

Page 82
Gian Lorenzo Bernini. *Kneeling Angel*. Fogg Art Museum, Photograph courtesy of Harvard University Art Museum, Cambridge, Ma.

Page 84
Bill of lading of corals sent to Elihu Yale for delivery to Daniel Chardin and Salvador Rodrigues, 1686. Beinecke Library, Yale.

Page 86
Julius Meyer with a group of Omaha Indians, under the leadership of Yellow Smoke, that visited Paris and other European cities/ Roland Bonaparte, Paris. 1889. Courtesy of the Nebraska State Historical Society.

Page 88
Walker Percy. Photograph by Lyn Harris.

Page 90
Blind Lemon Jefferson, from Paramount Records, 1926.

Page 92
Devil's Tower, New Mexico. © David Muench, photographer.

Page 94
Vincent Van Gogh (1853-1890), *The Yellow House (The Street)*, 1888. Oil on canvas. © Van Gogh Museum, Amsterdam (Vincent Van Gogh Foundation). Vincent Van Gogh.

Page 96
Roman Vishniac, *In the old Jewish cemetery of Lublin*, 1938. Gelatin silver print. © Mara Vishniac Kohn, courtesy the International Center of Photography.

Page 98
Paul Gauguin, *Human Miseries. The Wine Harvest*, 1888. Ordrupgaard, Copenhagen.

Page 100
A representation (cut-stone inlaid in marble) of a lotus flower on the side of the Taj Mahal, 1999. Courtesy of the Freer Gallery of Art, Smithsonian Institution, Washington DC. Photographer: Neil Greentree.

Page 102
Duncan Grant, *Portrait of Virginia Woolf*. Oil on pressboard. Signed and dated (lower left): D. Grant 1911. The Metropolitan Museum of

Art, Purchase, Lila Acheson Wallace Gift 1990. (1990.236). Photograph © 1991 The Metropolitan Museum of Art.

Page 104
Vermeer. Details from *Girl Reading a Letter at an Open Window* (1659). Staatliche Kunstsammlungen Gemaldegalerie, Dresden.

Page 106
Roman Vishniac, *Rabbi Baruch Rabinowitz in discussion with his students*, c. 1938. Gelatin silver print. Copyright Mara Vishniac Kohn, courtesy the International Center of Photography.

Page 108
Attributed to Mir Sayyid Ali (c. 16th century). *Nighttime in a Palace*, c. 1539-1543. Opaque watercolor, gold and silver on paper. Courtesy of the Arthur M. Sackler Museum, Harvard University Art Museums, Gift of John Goelet, formerly in the collection of Louis J. Cartier. Photo: Katya Kallsen. © President and Fellows of Harvard College.

Page 110
Paul Cezanne (1839-1906), *Study of Trees (Arbres, Winding Road)*, c. 1904. Oil on canvas. Courtesy of the Fogg Art Museum, Harvard University Art Museum, The Lois Orswell Collection. Photo: Katya Kallsen. © 2004 President and Fellows of Harvard College.

Page 112
John Flattau: *Face in Mirror*. Courtesy of John Flattau.

Page 114
The Taj Mahal at sunset. Courtesy of the Freer Gallery of Art, Smithsonian Institution, Washington, DC. Photographer: Neil Greentree.

Page 116
John Flattau, *Everything is Cumulous*. Photograph courtesy of John Flattau.

Page 118
Liu Shiru (c. 1517-after 1601), *Branch of Blossoming Plum*, c. 1550-1599. Hanging scroll, ink on silk, with signature reading "Xuehu." Courtesy of the Arthur M. Sackler Museum, Harvard Art Museums, Edward B. Bruce Collection of Chinese Paintings, Gift of Galen L. Stone. Photo: Photographic Services. © President and Fellows of Harvard College.

Page 120
Julius Meyer with Indian Chiefs Red Cloud, Sitting Bull, Spotted Tail, Swift Bear, 1875. Courtesy the Smithsonian Institution, Washington, DC. Photographer: Frank Currier.

Page 122
Photograph of the Calderwood Courtyard, Fogg Art Museum, Harvard University Art Museums.

Page 124
Rembrandt, *Shah Jahan*, c. 1654-56, Dutch. Pen and brown ink and brush and brown wash. © The Cleveland Museum of Art, 2004. Leonard C. Hanna, Jr. Fund, 1978.38.

Page 126
William Blake (1757-1827), "What do I see...", plate 92 from "Jerusalem" (Bentley Copy E), 1804-20 (relief etching with pen and watercolor on paper). Yale Center for British Art, Paul Mellon Collection, USA. Photograph courtesy of The Bridgeman Art Library.

Page 128
"How I see myself," photographer unknown. Private collection.

Page 130
Birthplace of Franz Kafka, July 3, 1883. Photograph courtesy of Klaus Wagenbach.

Page 132
The White Garden, Sissinghurst Garden. Photograph courtesy of The National Trust, England.

Page 134
The *Simurgh* attacks a *Gaja-Simb*a carrying off seven elephants. Tinted brush drawing, c. 1600-1620. Purchased from M.K. Heeramaneck, 1914. Victoria & Albert Museum, London/Art Resource, NY.

Page 136
Sculptural relief of a lotus flower on the side of the Taj Mahal, 1999. Courtesy of the Freer Gallery of Art, Smithsonian Institution, Washington, DC. Photographer: Neil Greentree.

Page 138
John Flattau. *The Luxembourg Garden, Her Chair*. Photograph courtesy of John Flattau.

Page 140
Samuel Clemens (Mark Twain), 1907. Courtesy of The Mark Twain House, Hartford, CT.

Page 142
Paul Gauguin, *Self-Portrait with portrait of Bernard, Les Miserables, Pont-Aven*, 1888. Oil on canvas. © Van Gogh Museum, Amsterdam (Vincent Van Gogh Foundation).

Page 144
Bichitr, Central Asiatic Merchants Receiving Noble Customers. Photograph courtesy of Arthur M. Sackler Art Museum, Harvard University Art Museums (647.1983).

Page 146
Vincent Van Gogh, *Eugene Boch, The Belgian Painter*, 1888. Oil on canvas, Musée d'Orsay, Paris. Photo: Herve Lewandowski. Credit: Reunion des Musees Nationaux/Art Resource, NY.

Page 148
Elihu Yale's strong box. Courtesy of Hotspur Gallery, London.

Page 150
Vincent Van Gogh, *The Lover (Lieutenant Millet)*, c. September 25, 1888 (F473, JH 1588). Oil on canvas, Collection Kröller-Müller Museum, Otterlo, The Netherlands.

Page 152
Photograph of a Jewish wedding ring. Venice, late 16th c. Private Collection (RCZ), New York. Courtesy of Peter Schaaf.

Page 154
Anonymous, 19th century. The construction of the Eiffel Tower as seen from one of the towers of the Trocadero (December 26, 1888-January 20, 1889). Musee D'Orsay, Paris. Photo: R.J. Ojeda. Credit: Reunion Musees Nationaux/Art Resource, NY.

Page 156
Venetian diamond exchange, c. 1720. ZFC Collection. Photograph courtesy of Peter Schaaf.

Page 158
Julius Meyer's Indian Wigwam store, Omaha, Nebraska, c. 1875. © American Jewish Historical Society, Newton Centre, Massachusetts and New York, NY.